Ali Harris is a magazine journalist and has written for publications such as *Red, ELLE, Stylist, Cosmopolitan* and *Company* and was deputy features editor at *Glamour* before leaving to write books and have babies. She lives in Cambridge with her husband and their two children. Follow Ali on twitter @AliHarrisWriter and on facebook at www.facebook.com/AliHarrisWriter

By the same author:

Miracle on Regent Street
The First Last Kiss
A Vintage Christmas (ebook-only)

written

in the
stars

ALI HARRIS

**SIMON &
SCHUSTER**

London · New York · Sydney · Toronto · New Delhi

A CBS COMPANY

First published in Great Britain by Simon & Schuster UK Ltd, 2014
A CBS COMPANY

Copyright © Ali Harris 2014

7 9 10 8 6

Simon & Schuster UK Ltd
1st Floor
222 Gray's Inn Road
London WC1X 8HB

www.simonandschuster.co.uk

Simon & Schuster Australia, Sydney
Simon & Schuster India, New Delhi

A CIP catalogue record for this book
is available from the British Library

Paperback B ISBN: 978-1-47112-552-2
eBook ISBN: 978-1-47112-554-6

'Shipping Good' reprinted by permission of Lemn Sissay.

Typeset by M Rules
Printed and bound by CPI Group (UK) Ltd, Croydon, CR0 4YY

To my two little stars Barnaby and Cecily,
I love you to the moon and back

The clock clicks in a child's hand
As she skips to the tics and tocs
Under the park tunnels run from the dark
While sun circles the clocks

Flowers grow for those that know
To bloom is to know your roots
To give the earth all it's worth
Tend to the new shoots

And a horse on course its hooves
Drum beneath the earth
Where dreadnought's sleeping seamen
Are weeping for the berth

While the marshes sigh at night
When sky dives into The Thames
Greenwich and I will sleep again
And wake again as friends

It is the thudding in my ear
Upon the pillow that sounds
Like a black mare churning
Dreams from the ground

As she charges towards
The Meridian Line
Leaps Sheperds Gate
And dives into time

Where an Ancient mariner
His guest no longer cross
Sings songs of his wrongs
To a circling albatross

(What you bring home and take away
Are the goods that become
The story of Royal Greenwich
And all she has done)

A coffee cup lifts to the face
In its reflection a woman sees the sea
Where a small girl in a boat smiles
She whispers *this must be me*

And the girl cranes her neck
She sails the swirls in the cup
And smiles for a minute and frowns
And holds the flowers up

Here lies the beginning of time
Where the river cradles the land
Here lies the roundabout
About the sun and the sand

And the star rises on observatory hill
and watches them watching him
And the water spills on a quiet wharf
Where the silver mermaids swim

And a woman collects the crests
and takes them home to spin
She makes Sails for the high road
For our dreams to begin

'Shipping Good', Lemn Sissay

Prologue

30 April 2014

'I didn't intend to be a runaway bride. Honestly, I didn't. I didn't wake up that morning thinking: What can I do to cause as much shock and distress as possible to the people I love most in the world? The person I love most in the world . . .' I trail off momentarily, unable to continue my well-practised speech. I look around at all the expectant faces shining as brightly as the tulips. Is it really worth dragging all this up again? Today of all days, when everyone just wants to celebrate this momentous occasion?

There are a couple of awkward coughs, a few whispers and I feel a rising panic in my chest, like I'm about to be sick, or worse, pass out. Oh God, please not that. Not again. Just then I feel a squeeze of encouragement to my left hand and I suddenly feel buoyed by warmth and support, anchored by familiarity and self-belief. I turn and look at him and he smiles and nods and I know that he's telling me to trust my instincts.

'The truth is, I'm not sure I was thinking much at all that day,' I continue. 'I knew I was nervous, but that was all. I was just focused on dealing with each "Got To" stage as it came. You know, got to get up, got to get ready, got to get in the car, got to walk down the aisle. And well . . .' I pause and smile wryly. 'We all know how *that* turned out.'

Laughter floats like petals through the air.

'There were many times that I questioned myself,' I go on. 'Leaving my husband at the altar was the hardest decision I've ever made. Many people said it was the worst.' I smile at my best friend, Milly, who nods and holds her hand up in a gesture of agreement. 'But no matter how much I doubted myself, I knew that wasn't true.' I close my eyes momentarily, remembering a long-ago mistake. I will never forget, but now at last I *have* moved on. Even though it was heartbreakingly hard, I always *knew* it was the right choice.

I look around at everyone again and then back at the man standing next to me. It feels like he's always been there; like this was all meant to be . . .

One Year Earlier

April

Dear Bea

I've never believed that 'April is the cruellest month'. For me April has always signified new beginnings. It is truly Mother Nature's New Year. Suddenly we witness beautiful displays of colourful flowers exploding like fireworks in our gardens. The grass glitters with golden daffodils, grape hyacinths burst through the earth like rockets, anemones dancing next to them like purple rain showers. Hellebores and tulips bop enthusiastically in the breeze like bridesmaids on a hen night.

Amongst all these new shoots there are many decisions to make - and even the most experienced gardener can find it overwhelming. Sometimes I'm sure it feels like all you can see is bare soil. And in my experience, dear daughter, spring has often been the time that I've felt an urge to bare my soul. To speak up.

Pause and take a moment to reflect on how I'm feeling underneath the surface.

Contrary to popular opinion, I find raking over old ground a very therapeutic – and necessary – exercise. As an experienced gardener I say, cut any dead growth otherwise new shoots will be at risk of being damaged. Don't be too hard with the pruning though, or you may accidentally cut off this year's flowers. And remember, don't let the grass grow under your feet or it will yellow, weaken and die.

Do all this and your garden is sure to bloom as much as you will.

Love, Dad x

Chapter 1

30 April 2013

Bea Bishop is about to take the plun—

'This is no time to be doing a Facebook status update, Bea!' my younger brother Caleb chastises, sounding more like a parent than a sibling as he snatches my phone off me.

'Hey!' I look at him in annoyance, half-expecting to see standing next to me outside the church the curly-haired kid who used to chase me round the beach like a puppy. Instead, there's this charming, sensible, responsible twenty-eight-year-old man in a morning suit – a *dad* no less. I still can't believe Cal has two children. Where did the years go?

I try to grab my phone but he holds it above his head teasingly and then puts it in his pocket. Infuriated, I turn to Loni who is standing on my right but she just puts her hands up as if to say, 'Off-duty.' Then she peers down her cleavage and rearranges her neckline so she's showing more skin.

'Ready to strut your stuff, sis?' Cal says lightly. Then he leans in and winks. 'Because Loni certainly is . . .'

I look at them both, wanting to tell them that, without Dad here, I'll never be ready. But instead I smile, take a deep breath and turn to face the heavy, walnut church doors. Harder than it sounds in this ridiculously tight lace fishtailed frock. I know it's the wrong dress for my body shape – made for someone tall and graceful, not petite and a bit tomboyish. It was thrust upon me because I couldn't make up my mind what I wanted and because my future mother-in-law, Marion, told me I'd look 'uncharacteristically elegant' in it. I should've hit the eject button right then. Instinct now tells me it's probably better to look as much like you as possible on your wedding day. A scrubbed-up version of yourself, obviously, but still like you.

Instead, the hairpiece my wayward curls are coiled tightly around is as heavy as lead, as is the enormous Hudson family tiara that is clinging to the top of my skyscraper bridal hairstyle like King Kong on the Empire State Building. Marion told me at my final dress fitting that I had to wear it because – and these were her exact words: 'Unfortunately, Bea, you're the closest thing to a daughter I'll ever have.' Emphasis on unfortunately!

'Bea!' Cal says impatiently, reminding me where I am and what I'm meant to be doing, 'I said, are you ready . . .'

'. . . for your prison sentence?' Loni intercepts, nudging me playfully as her giant purple and pink fascinator bobs on top of her crazy corkscrew hair which bounces down her back in swirly silvery curls.

Cal shoots her a warning glare. She holds her hands up innocently as if to say, 'What? Joke!' and then takes a swig from a little bottle she's clearly swiped from the hotel minibar. 'Just a little snifter for Loni to ease the pre-wedding wobbles,' she says with a wink. My mum often refers to herself in the third person.

Apparently it's what happens if you are mad – I mean, a tiny bit famous. She writes books about relationships. Her first one was *Why Be Married When You Can Be Happy?* It was a surprise hit and stayed in the bestseller charts for twenty-three weeks. Over twenty years, and countless books later, people still see her as the go-to guru for marriage break-up guidance. Not so helpful on your wedding day, it turns out.

Loni is not the biggest fan of the institution of marriage. She's a free spirit, a single soul, and has been ever since my dad walked out when I was seven and Cal was five. She's always said marriage is an unnatural state. And as a result, so have I.

I blink, the familiar panic rising as I remind myself of what I'm about to do.

'Are you OK?' Milly whispers. I turn around and look at her and, as I do, I see a glimpse of Holkham Hall in the distance, the elegant Palladian-style mansion with its stunning grounds that this church sits within and where our wedding reception will take place. The venue is the one decision I managed to make for this wedding. It had to be here, in Holkham. Close to where I grew up, opposite my favourite beach, and where, even as a little girl, I told my mum and dad I'd one day get married. Marion wasn't happy. She'd wanted somewhere bigger, grander, nearer London than Norfolk. But for once, I stood firm. I didn't care if they wanted to invite a hundred people I'd never met (which they practically have) but it *had* to be here.

I focus back on Milly. She is the picture of poise and calm in her shimmering gold bridesmaid dress that glides over her Bond-girl body. Milly is a striking mix of her Persian mother and Indian father and is always the most beautiful person in any room. Her dark burnished shoulder-length hair is always perfect. A thick, blunt fringe frames her chocolate eyes, which are usually so serious, thanks to her stressful job as a hedge fund manager. They are now swimming with concern. I'm pretty sure most best friends don't go to the lengths Milly does to look out for me. She has done ever since she found me on my first day wandering the school grounds like a lost sheep, unable to find my Year Seven French class. She says it was like I had no idea what direction I was meant to be going in.

I still haven't.

I can't do this, a voice in my head whispers.

I glance at Milly with an agonised, rabbit-caught-in-the-head-lights expression, trying desperately to bat the doubt away – or for her to do it for me.

'You can do this, Bea!' Milly says instantly, reading my mind. She clasps my hand. 'You're marrying Adam, remember? The love of your life.'

'Mills,' I blurt out suddenly, overcome by panic. 'I need to ask you something.'

'Really? Now?' she says, smoothing back an escaped curl into my tight bridal chignon. 'OK,' she sighs. 'Fire away.'

'How did you know Jay was The One?' Milly's eyes flick to me and then to Cal. She smiles brightly back at me but I can see the alarm behind it. *Watch out, people, this bride's about to blow!*

'How did you know?' I press, looking down at Milly's left finger and the two rings that have been firmly planted on it for three years. Jay is Adam's best man and her husband. She met him the same night I met Adam, but Milly and Jay's relationship moved much quicker than ours. Ad and I have been playing catch-up ever since.

'I – I . . .' Her eyes dart nervously from me, to Cal and then to Loni. 'I mean, I can't explain *how* I knew, Bea, I just did.'

I swear my heart plummets down to my stupidly high wedding shoes because the truth is I don't 'know'. I'm not sure, or certain, and I don't know *why* that is. Why, when Adam is so wonderful, don't I *know*? What is wrong with him, or rather, me?

'Come on, sis!' Cal says as if reading my mind. 'This is you and Adam we're talking about. You're made for each other. You're crazy and he's utterly crazy about you.'

'Ba da doom tish,' I reply with a weak smile.

I snatch the miniature from Loni and try to take a swig but the combined weight of my hairpiece and tiara has rendered my head incapable of movement.

'Ready?' Cal says gently like I'm one of his two-year-old twins. *I DON'T KNOW!* I think. 'Yes, ready!' I squeak instead.

Cal goes to open the doors of St Withburga's Church and I start to hyperventilate a little. The thick lace of my dress is making me itch. I resist an urge to claw at my thighs.

'Take this, will you, bro?' I say, thrusting my beautiful bright bouquet of yellow primulas (*I can't live without you*), blousy honeysuckle ranunculuses (*radiant charm*) and forsythia (*anticipation of an exciting moment*). Milly ordered them for me when I called her in a panic because I'd forgotten. She was still at work but went to her local flower shop in Greenwich just before it closed and asked specifically for the yellow wedding flowers I wanted. My handful of sunshine. They kindly made up the bouquets and buttonholes at the last minute and presented them in a vintage wooden crate that had the shop's name – 'Cosmos Flowers' – painted on the side along with a smattering of stars. She and Jay arrived with it at the crack of dawn this morning. Cosmos are my birth flower and, when I saw the name painted on the crate filled with my favourite flowers, it felt like a sign that I was doing the right thing. But now . . .?

Oh God, I feel sick.

'You OK, Bea?' Milly repeats as she steadies me.

'I think my dress is bringing me out in a rash,' I groan as she tries to locate the itch. 'Maybe I'm allergic to it?'

Milly grasps my chin and makes me look at her. 'You have nothing to worry about. All you have to do is walk down that aisle. I'll be right behind you, OK?' She lifts up my train and Cal nods in agreement and squeezes my hand.

I take a deep breath and tell myself that most brides feel this amount of fear, doubt and overwhelming anxiety. It's perfectly normal. But once you get that ring on your finger, all your misgivings fall away. Yep, I'm positive that's what happens.

'Adam *is* the right guy, Bea,' Cal says as if reading my mind. 'He always has been. It just took a while for you to realise it. Now, remember, all you have to do is take it one step at a time . . .'

I nod, marvelling at how my little brother got so grown-up. And how I got so scared.

'Let's do this thing!' I squeak and give a little mini air punch for good measure.

Cal heaves open the church door and looks at me. I notice his porcelain-blue eyes so like Loni's are glistening with emotion as Mendelssohn's Wedding March floods through the open doors and the guests' heads execute a perfect Mexican wave as they turn to gawp at me. I take Cal's arm and smile nervously behind my veil.

'You look beautiful, sis,' Cal whispers through his smile as we begin to walk slowly down the aisle. 'Now,' he adds with a grin, 'whatever you do, don't wee at the end like you did at Auntie Cath's wedding.'

'I was *three*,' I hiss but I laugh anyway.

As we carry on down the aisle I find myself desperately looking for Dad. No one knows this – not even Cal – but he's the real reason I was so determined to get married in this church so near my childhood home. I've never let go of my dream that it would be here on this special day that we would finally be reunited. I've spent months telling myself that even if the invitation I insisted on sending to Cley-next-the-Sea, his last known local address before he disappeared, didn't reach him, or if he didn't see the wedding notice Adam put in his favourite national paper, then maybe, through some cosmic connection, he might just sense that his daughter was getting married today. He'd instinctively know that I'd never wanted to get married without him. He'd recall how I told him when I was a little girl that I'd get married in this church one day. He would sense that, even at the age of thirty, I still missed him every day. And that's why I can't help but hope, even though I haven't seen or heard from him for twenty-three years, that maybe, just maybe, he'll be here to watch his daughter walk down the aisle. I know it's ridiculous. I know I should just let go, move on, but I've never lost hope that my dad will one day come back into my life. Today feels like his last chance, the final milestone before I say goodbye to being his daughter, Bea Bishop, and begin a new life as Mrs Bea Hudson.

My eyes dart desperately over the guests seated either side of me. Caleb squeezes my arm and I know he's realised who I'm looking for. He tries to understand but Cal has never seemed to feel Dad's absence as much as I do. My little brother's always just ... got on with his life – in an understated but rather incredible way. Not only is Cal a brilliant dad to his two-year-old twin girls, a loving partner of their mum, Lucy, his girlfriend of almost ten years (commitment problems clearly *don't* run in the family ...) but he's a great support to me. And he lives close to Loni (which means I have the freedom to live where I choose) and on top of all that, he saves lives every single day in his work as a paramedic. In other words, my kid brother, who used to run around wearing Superhero costumes, is now basically a real-life one. Dad would be so proud. It always amazes me that two siblings with the same roots can grow to be so different.

A memory reverberates in my mind as I see an image of Dad, arms outstretched to me.

Come here, my little climber . . .

I feel a sharp jolt of pain as I recall Dad's nickname for me, given because I was so clingy. I close my eyes for a moment and replay the memory of running into the garden and entwining myself around his legs, looking up at him as he laughed and pulled me into his arms.

I continue to scan the congregation, stumbling as my eyes fill with tears and my heart with disappointment when I realise that of course Dad isn't here. It was stupid to hold on to such a far-fetched dream.

It doesn't matter, I tell myself sternly. *I don't need him any more. I've got Adam now . . .*

Everything will be fine if I can just make it to him, but the end of the aisle seems so far away that it is almost in soft focus. Everything goes blurry.

I gasp and briefly put my hand to my forehead whilst trying to keep walking towards Adam. But it's like I've stood up too quickly and someone's turned the lights out. The itchy dress is unbearable, I feel like I'm being suffocated and my head is ridiculously heavy. A hundred people are looking at me and taking photos, and I realise I'm holding my breath like I'm about to dive into the sea.

I keep taking steps forward. I think I'm still walking down the aisle but it feels more like I'm being pulled back, pulled under.

Drowning.

And then I see him and feel a wave of relief crashing over me. Because there waiting at the end of the aisle for me is Adam. My tall, strong, so-sure-of-himself Adam. He's standing with his back

to me, next to Jay. I stare at his broad, solid silhouette, his perfectly pressed suit and the slightly unruly curl of his dark hair on
his crisp white collar. It must be the only thing in his life a little
out of place. Unless you count me. He turns then and I stare into
his calm wide-set grey eyes that are sheltered by thick, dark,
arched eyebrows. He is the calm to my storm, I realise.

I raise my hand and wave at him. He smiles, a gentle beam
that starts at the corners of his mouth and then rises like the
dawn until it reaches his eyes and burns brightly like the midday
sun, bathing mine in light. He nods deliberately, then gestures
for me to come to him. Then he turns back to face the priest. So
certain of his every move.

I look to my left and it is then that my world collapses like a
house of cards. He's here. Not my dad, like I'd hoped, but
another man. A man I've spent the last eight years trying to
forget. I feel bile rise in my throat as the memories rush at me
like a tsunami, flattening every wall I have made, everything I
have built to protect me from the past. I can't believe he is here
after all this time.

Kieran Blake. My first real love.

He's staring at me intently. His face is instantly recognisable,
even after all this time. He's lost the wild, straggly, indie-boy hair
he used to have that was streaked blond from years of travelling.
It is now shaved in a dark buzz cut, making his forest-green eyes
even more dazzling. I try to look back at Adam, but I can't. I can't
drag my eyes away from Kieran. He lifts his hand then, swipes
it over his head, and it is then that I see the glint of silver on his
finger and I'm lost again in the past, taken back to a place, a
moment, a time I've tried so hard not to return to.

*I promise I'll come back. Once I've sorted myself out. Wait for me,
please? I'll wear this ring till then and you wear yours . . .*

I look down at my right hand, at the finger where my

platinum promise ring used to be until I gave up waiting for him and took it off.

'Kieran Blake,' I murmur, and Cal shoots me a look.

'What did you say?' Cal whispers, his eyes scanning the congregation until he spots him. He looks at me with horror. 'Did you invite *him*?' I shake my head and, as I do, I stagger sideways. It's as if my feet don't want me to go on any more.

I try to move forwards. Why now when I want to be so sure of every step towards my future, do I feel this overwhelming pull to my past? It feels like I'm being torn in two different directions. I push through the doubt and force my vertiginous heels to clip onwards across the cold, tiled floor.

'Hey, Bea,' Cal says. 'Watch ou—'

His warning comes too late. I feel my feet slip and the ground disappears. I hear the wedding guests take a collective gasp as I cry out and am thrust backwards. Cal tries to grab my arm, but he can't hold me and I crash to the ground.

As I do, I feel my life flash before my eyes, exactly like they say it does when you're about to die.

Oh God, am I *dying*? No, surely not. I don't want my epitaph to be a *Daily Mail* headline: 'Tragic size 12 bride dies on wedding day' (the tragedy clearly being that I was a size 12, not that I died). I'm struggling to stay focused, present, as the searing pain in my head shoots through my body. I'm clinging on to my life. Except . . .

I blink again, feeling my eyes roll backwards into the impending blackness. It's not my life I'm clinging to; it's my *lives*. The one I had before and the one I was heading to up till now. I can make out Adam and Kieran next to me or have I just imagined them? I'm not sure what is happening or where I am, but I feel like I can see the ghostly white shapes of my future and my past grappling with each other in some ethereal fight. One is on my shoulder, like an angel, desperately pulling me forward. The other is dragging me back. Two loves, two possible lives – but which one is mine? Which path am 1 meant to take? I can't decide. I drop my head back against the tiles and begin to see stars. Then there's just black.

Chapter 2

I'm sitting on a chair in the small, cold chapel to the side of the nave, rubbing my head as Cal examines me. It was Adam's deep soothing voice that pulled me back out of the darkness. I don't know how long I was out for, or what he was saying, I just know that since I woke up I've felt different. Like I've lost my anchor and I'm drifting out to sea. Loni, Cal and Adam are flanking me as I clutch my head in my hands. Adam's parents George and Marion are looking on, as are Milly and Jay. They think I'm just in pain – and they're right: but not because of the bump to my head.

I feel like I'm having an out-of-body experience. The world has rewound and I'm back there, back then, with Kieran on Cromer Pier.

It's all my fault: my thought applies to both then and now.

Cal pulls my eyelids back and studies my pupils. I feel like I'm about to be interrogated except I'm the one with all the questions. *Am I losing my mind?* I want to ask him. You did see Kieran, didn't you? It *was* him, wasn't it? He's here. He's come back. Seven years later than he promised, but he's back.

I don't get any answers from Cal's drawn eyebrows and frowned concentration.

'I was worried there for a moment, sis,' he mutters.

'That I wasn't going to make it or make it down the aisle?' I manage to say.

A muscle strains in his cheek and he shakes his head, then he looks at everyone. 'No concussion,' Cal says, smiling as he steps back from me. 'Or brain damage. If we're lucky it might even have knocked some sense into her!' There's a ripple of relieved laughter from the semicircle of family and friends.

Someone hands Cal an ice pack and he presses it to my forehead. 'Ow!'

'Here, let me,' Adam says and Cal steps obediently away. Adam has that effect on people. They listen to him. *I* listen to him.

'Shall we go ahead now then?' our priest says brightly, clapping his hands and then glancing at his watch.

'Can you just give us a moment, please?' I reply shakily, and he looks at me for a beat too long before he ushers everyone out of the chapel. Cal is the last to go, giving me one long lingering look before leaving Adam and me alone.

I look up at at Adam, he kisses my forehead then replaces the ice pack. The contrast of the warmth of his lips and the cold of the ice feels symbolic somehow. His grey eyes are cloudy with concern and I feel the urge to cup his perfectly carved jaw and mould the imprint of his generous lips to mine so I always remember my final kiss with the man who has made me happier than I ever thought possible. The man who has brought calm and security to my life when before there was only noise and chaos. The man I thought could save me from my past, even if I couldn't bring myself to be truly honest with him about it. I think of Kieran, waiting out there, and feel sick at what I'm about to do.

'How you doing, huh?' he says, crouching down and removing

the ice pack. 'Ready to get back out there and face the bridal music? That was quite a stunt you pulled there, you know! Definitely one to tell the kids about one day . . .' He grins and laughter lines appear around his eyes like cracks of glass cutting into my heart. He's so perfect.

Too perfect for me.

I have to tell him. I have to do this. I have no choice any more. Besides, I don't deserve him.

I look at the ice pack, at the melting opaque cubes swimming before my eyes and blending with my tears so they seem like a river that my perfect future is being carried away in.

'Come on,' he says gently, cupping my elbow with his palm.

I shake my head. I can't look at him. I feel like I'm an executioner, about to drop the guillotine. 'Adam,' I whisper, pushing his name out past the lump in my throat. 'Y-you know I love you. I hope you've never doubted that—'

'Of course, that's why we're getting married!' He smiles, leans in and kisses me softly. I close my eyes and put my fingers to my lips. 'Come on,' he says, getting up and holding his hand out to me. 'Let's do this. Just promise me, no more acrobatics down the aisle, OK? You almost made Dad stop checking his emails!' He grins, but I don't mirror it. His hand is still stretched out waiting for me to take it in mine.

'Adam,' I say quietly, trying desperately to control the tremble in my voice.

'Bea, I know you're nervous but there's nothing to be frightened of. We'll get married and then everything will go back to normal. Nothing has to change, not really.' His voice is soft, soothing, melodic. He's doing that thing where he metaphorically talks me off the ledge. 'Remember when we got engaged? You were so scared of taking the next step that I decided the only way to stop you hyperventilating with fear when I proposed was to slip the ring in a little bouquet of lavender, jasmine and orange blossom to calm you down, relax you and ease the shock . . .' A smile forms on my face at the memory. I loved the gesture, it was so thoughtful and showed how well he understood me. I see Kieran's face again and am hit by a wave of anxiety. I don't deserve Adam's kindness. If he knew . . .

I have to just get this over and done with. Throw myself off the edge of the cliff. I have to finish this.

'I can't do this. I can't marry you, Adam,' I blurt out abruptly like I'm ripping off a plaster. I close my eyes. It still hurts. 'I – I'm so sorry . . .'

He dismisses my statement with a stroke of my hair. 'You don't mean that. You've just had a bit of a shock. You'll be fine as soon as we get back out there . . .'

I want to believe Adam but it feels like Cal's right, finally some sense has been knocked into me with my fall and I can't pretend any more. Kieran's come back and everything has changed. Adam doesn't deserve this, but he also doesn't deserve me. I can't keep burying my past, pretending that my life began when I met Adam. No, it ended the night of the tragedy. And all because of me.

I lift my head, my eyes on the ice pack. The ice is still melting. All of it is melting away. 'No, Ad. I'm sorry, I can't. I just can't . . .' My voice is uncharacteristically firm. There is no wavering, my decision has been made.

Adam stares at me for what feels like an eternity, his face passing through stages of disbelief, denial, shock and hurt before he steps away from me.

'You really mean it.' His voice is low, a whisper. I bury my face in my hands, feeling like I've just plunged a knife into him and then me.

Adam walks over to the cold stone wall and leans against it like he can't hold himself up. 'Why?' he says quietly. His broad shoulders seem to have shrunk. His left hand is against the wall, his fingers splayed as if to give him much-needed support but also to remind me of the glaring absence of a ring on his wedding finger. His other hand is raised to his forehead, as if it were he who had experienced a severe blow to the head. Which I suppose he has. 'The least you can do is tell me why?'

'I – I don't know ... I just can't ... I can't explain ... I'm sorry ...' I'm trying and failing to find the words I need to say: that I love him and need him and miss him already but that I don't know who I am. I got lost a long time ago. I gaze up at Adam desperately, tears pouring down my face, wishing that things could be different but knowing that in that one split second before I fell, everything changed. Because Kieran came back.

Chapter 3

The cold tiles are like ice against my bare shoulders as I come to. Did I faint or am I dead? I open my eyes and blink to try and disperse the black fog in front of them. I can see I'm all dressed in white, like an angel, oh God, I was kidding about the dead bit. It all comes back to me, then. Well, nearly all. I have a vague recollection I should be looking for someone but I can't remember who. I feel different, but I don't know why.

Adam comes into focus, his grey eyes full of concern. He's stroking my temples with his thumbs then touching my forehead with the palm of his hand. Marion suddenly pushes in front of him and snaps her fingers in my face several times, making me blink rapidly like I'm having a convulsion. Not particularly helpful when a hundred people are wondering if I've just had some kind of prenuptial seizure. Then she holds her hand up.

'How many fingers, dear?' she barks, her perfectly painted lips opening like a chasm. 'Can you tell? One? Four? Five?'

'Hopefully not two,' I say weakly, 'because that would be rude.'

There's a swell of laughter at this.

'She's all right, everybody,' Cal diagnoses. 'She just wanted to show how head-over-heels in love with Adam she is!' He and Adam bend over me, arms poised to help me up.

'Wait there a second, son,' George calls. 'I'm still filming. This'll get millions of hits on YouTube!'

'George!' Marion admonishes.

'I'm fine, really I am!' I say, batting Cal and Adam away and struggling into a sitting position.

And even though to all intents and purposes I am – there isn't a scratch or a bruise on my body – I do feel strange. Woozy. Present in the moment, but like I'm missing something big: a part of me that was there before but isn't now. I squint at my outstretched fingers and count them in case Marion has a point. It's then that I notice an absence of wedding ring. That must be it, I conclude. That's the missing piece!

I tilt my head back and look up at Adam. His eyes are dark clouds, his brow crumpled with anxiety.

'Can we just get on with it now, Ad?' I plead. 'I just want to get married.'

'Oh thank God,' he laughs in relief.

'Were you worried I wasn't going to make it – or make it down the aisle?' I say teasingly. I close my eyes as this moment resonates in my brain like it has happened before, but differently. I feel like there is something I should remember too, something big, but there's a black spot, like a fingerprint, where that memory should be.

I shake my head, smile and turn to the guests on either side who are all looking at me with almost sick anticipation, like onlookers at a car crash.

'It's all right,' I call out weakly. 'I'm OK! Serves me right for trying to wear high heels!' There is a ripple of laughter. 'It's good luck for something to go wrong on your wedding day, right?' I add. 'And now that I've gone arse over . . .' Marion glares at me and I hurriedly change my sentence '. . . apex, it stands to reason that everything else is going to go *perfectly!* So let's do this thing! Let's have a wedding!'

This receives a round of applause and as I take my bouquet from Milly and thrust it in the air, I hurriedly get into position. For some reason I feel like I have to marry Adam as soon as possible – before it's too late.

I take Cal and Loni's arms and then the three of us begin to walk, with me leading us quickly – but carefully – towards Adam. I glance over my shoulder; I know I'm ready for my future now but I can't quite shake the feeling that my past is hovering in the shadows somewhere, watching every single step I take.

Chapter 4

Adam won't look at me. Everything I say seems so wretchedly, pathetically clichéd. I stand in the chapel waiting for him to speak. It feels like forever before he does.

'I know you're scared, but this doesn't make any sense.' He turns as if with renewed belief that he can change my mind. 'We're meant to be together, Bea, you know we are! Hey, do you remember the night when we first met?' he says hurriedly, running his hand through his head of thick hair and holding it there. 'We were sitting outside the Greenwich Tavern, it was about 10 p.m., the sky had turned this amazing colour of purple and we were telling each other about our exes and how we'd never be crazy enough to fall in love again ...'

'When "Crazy" by Cee Lo Green started playing through the speakers ...' I finish softly. I close my eyes, taken back to that moment again. It had felt like a sign: a split second when time had tipped, changing the course of our lives. We'd looked at each other, Adam and I, and we'd known that we were crazy enough to do *just* that. Fall in love. I shake my head. Adam's still talking, still reliving the happy moment for me, but I put my hand up.

I want to tell him what I can't seem to articulate: that I'm not worthy of him. I couldn't live with myself if I were to go through with this, that I'm hurting him now to save him future heartbreak and disappointment when he finds out the truth about me.

'I'm so sorry, Adam.' I stifle a cry with my hand, drop my bouquet on the floor and then I stagger past him blindly into the nave where the hushed guests are still waiting. They know something is wrong; they're staring at me like I'm some sort of alien. I pause for a moment in the centre of the aisle. Maybe I am crazy? Maybe I always have been. And with that thought I bow my head and begin to run, ripping off my veil as I push through the doors and head down the path towards the white vintage Rolls-Royce that has just magically appeared in front of the church.

The driver looks over his shoulder inquisitively as I get in. He clearly was not expecting me so soon.

I glance out of the window and see that Adam is standing in the arch of the church doorway. His left hand is lifted above his eyebrows, shading his eyes from the sun. He looks like a movie star in his morning suit. I imagine for a moment that I'm next to him, holding his hand, and that we are both wearing wedding rings. The image is so clear in my mind that when I close my eyes it's like I am stepping into it. Adam and I are laughing as we kiss surrounded by a horseshoe of our friends and family. They throw rose petals over us until all I can see is a white floral mist. I open my eyes and the image of us is gone as quickly as it came.

'Please, just go,' I beg, and the driver shrugs, starts up the engine and pulls away.

Chapter 5

'You may now kiss the bride!' An eruption of cheers and applause explodes through the church. Adam and I laugh into each other's lips as we kiss before turning to walk hand-in-hand back down the aisle. I feel at once like I'm walking on air but I also still have this horrible sense of déjà vu. I have an urge to run down the aisle as fast as I can, but I force myself to walk nice and slowly; to savour this moment.

I glance round and see Loni walking down the aisle behind us, waving like a celebrity and leaning against Cal who is standing tall despite her weight, the twins entwined around his legs and Lucy's arm wrapped round his waist. Then I look back at Adam, my handsome, strong, kind, easy-going husband, and I dismiss any further thoughts of my absent dad. I feel like the missing piece in our family has been replaced by something better. *Someone* better. I nestle my head in Adam's shoulder, beaming as we continue up the aisle. Adam is shaking hands with everyone he passes and I find I'm recognising more and more people now. There's the gang from Eagle Recruitment, the temp agency I've been signed to for seven years. I spot Tim towering over all the others and ignoring us completely as he tries to make eyes at the female guests. Nick, my boss and good friend, is smiling sardonically and looking like he'd prefer to be anywhere but here. Glenda's here too, my lovely Welsh 'work mum'. She waves at me delightedly and throws up her hat and yells, 'We love you, Bea!' and Jeeves – another colleague – shouts 'Hear, hear!' and waves a pink handkerchief.

I squeeze Adam's hand and he smiles at me and then we are outside in the fresh air, holding hands, rings glinting in the sunshine as the guests flood out of the doors like champagne fizzing out of a bottle and surround us in a crescent. They throw rose petals over us as we kiss in front of a hundred flashing cameras. I laugh shyly into Adam's shoulder as everyone claps and cheers, but when I look up again at the crowd the only person I see is Kieran Blake.

I stare at him in horror, the black smudge in my memory dissipating as I suddenly remember spotting him standing nonchalantly in the congregation as if he hadn't disappeared for eight years.

Eight years. Not one, like he promised.

He had stared at me imploringly as I froze in the aisle, those green eyes telling me everything I once dreamed he would come back and say.

I still love you. No one will ever know you like I do. No one has our connection. No one ever will.

I'd tried to look away, to carry on walking towards Adam, but I'd felt myself pulled back to Kieran with every step. The moment I'd waited so long for had finally come, but at entirely the wrong time. And then I'd fallen and when I came to – I had forgotten it had happened. Blotted out the memory. Like I've been trying to do for years: erase the memory of everything that happened that summer.

I wish I could black him out again now. He's not welcome

here, not now, not today. Not when I've finally got myself together. But he doesn't go. Instead, he's throwing petals like they're flowers on a grave instead of confetti.

I waited for you, I try to tell him with my eyes. I waited but you didn't come. And now it's too late. I've made my decision.

I turn to look at Adam who lifts me up in his arms and kisses me, and as I wrap my arms around his neck and kiss him fervently back I'm so very thankful that we are married.

Bea Bishop is gone; my new life as Mrs Bea Hudson has begun.

'Are you happy?' Adam murmurs and I nod, but the truth is the main emotion I'm feeling is relief. I'm so lucky to have Adam: the only man who has never left me. The One that *didn't* run away.

'It's all about us now, you, me, our future.' I glance back to where Kieran was standing seconds before and at the space next to Loni where my dad should have been. 'I don't need anyone other than you, Adam,' I add ardently. 'Not any more.'

He kisses me again and I try to melt into the moment. But out of the corner of my eye I can see the silhouette of a figure walking away from the church, towards Holkham Hall, and – if I know Kieran – towards the stretch of beach beyond. I cling on to Adam like he's the shore. And I tell myself that I *am* sure. About him.

For the first time in my life I am certain I have made the right decision.

Chapter 6

My car whips quickly through the Holkham estate, past the lake and down the oak-lined Lady Anne's Drive, and I realise with grim irony that my driver is whistling what appears to be the Wedding March.

Maybe it's in his contract to do this when he drives a newly married couple away. And judging by the nervous glances he's throwing me in his rear-view mirror he hasn't worked out what tune to replace it with when ferrying a runaway bride. I think about making some suggestions: Paul Simon's '50 Ways To Leave Your Lover' would work, as would 'Another One Bites The Dust'.

As we pull up alongside The Victoria, the boutique hotel where I stayed last night and where Adam and I were meant to spend our first night as a married couple, I lean forward and tell the driver to pull over in the beach car park across the road ahead.

Holkham Bay is just visible through the trees. I need space to breathe, and there isn't a better place than this unspoilt, expansive stretch of beach that, despite its enormity, I once knew like the back of my hand. I haven't been back here for eight years.

Not since Kieran left after that summer . . . I shake my head to try and dislodge him from my mind.

I think of Loni's shambolic home, and the garden I still think of as Dad's. I blink and swallow. Another unwelcome memory. I feel like I'm being haunted by the men who have left me, which seems ironic given my recent actions. I think of Adam standing in the church doorway, watching me drive away.

'You going to be all right, love?' the chauffeur says, glancing at me as he turns the ignition off and I open the car door. 'You're not exactly dressed for a beach amble . . .'

I glance down at my wedding dress. He's right. But it's too late now. I slip off my shoes and pick them up

'I'll be fine.' I smile weakly.

'Do you want me to wait here?' he says gently.

'It's all right. I'll be fine,' I repeat. But my chin wobbles disobediently.

He looks at me for a moment and in that one glance I can tell that he is a father himself.

'Reckon I'll just wait here a while anyway, love. Might as well enjoy the glorious view.' He smiles kindly at me and I feel tears swell, threatening to fall.

I walk away from the car and turn left through the pine trees and along a well-trodden track that I've taken many times with Loni and Cal. And Kieran, I think, but I push away those unwelcome memories again along with my tears.

I step off the boardwalk and onto the beach, inhaling the sea air. As I stand there time seems to collapse and it's like I can picture my twenty-two-year-old self, roaming the endless dunes, sobbing as I tried to accept that Kieran had really gone.

I hitch up my dress now. The tide is in so there's not much beach. I run across the sand, feeling the wind pierce my cheeks. Then I clamber up the dunes and gaze out at the glistening

North Sea stretching out calmly and languorously before me. The sun's golden rays are bouncing off the sand and throwing glitter over the ocean. I feel betrayed by the view. Where are the thrashing waves and pelting rain that would be a better backdrop to this moment?

Have some respect, Mother Nature! I feel like yelling. *At least give me a clap of thunder! An angry wave? A cloud? I'll take some drizzle! Anything!*

But the bright spring sunshine just beams back teasingly and I notice how the sea lavender has created a misty purple halo around the angelic-looking bay. I remember how as a kid I used to bring my nature books down here with Dad so we could identify each type of bramble and scrubland plant by name. It was blissful, carefree. Then, as a teenager, I used to run along the coastline for miles, fuelled by fresh air and an urgent need to fill my head with something other than noise. And then there were the endless days and nights of that summer I spent here with Kieran and his twin brother, Elliot. Swimming, drinking, laughing, loving, living.

For the first time in my life I was happy. I thought nothing could ever go wrong. How naïve I was.

I sit down and absent-mindedly draw a ring in the sand with my finger and then brush it away with my palm.

'I thought I'd find you here.'

When I hear his voice I stiffen and my heart stops. I feel the oxygen flood from my body and my chest heave and swell with panic. It's like I'm hyperventilating – thank God I'm already sitting down or I'd probably faint again. I glance over my shoulder and seeing him now has the same impact as it did at the church. He unbalances me; I'm instantly on terra *un*-firma. Unanchored. Untethered. I can already feel myself slipping helplessly back to my past.

'Hi,' Kieran says simply and his smile sends filtered sunshine into his mossy green eyes. The sun is shining directly behind him, circling him with an aura of light that makes him seem ethereal, angelic almost. He looks the same, despite the years that have passed. He looks like his brother.

I gaze down at the sand, feeling my heart rise and dip like the boats on the distant horizon. I can't let him see that he has unearthed me.

'What are you doing here?' I say evenly, trying to turn away from him. But once again the tight fishtail dress has rendered me incapable of movement. I'm like a mermaid thrashing helplessly at the water's edge. When I look at him I feel like I'm both blinded by the beautiful summer we spent together and tainted by what tore us apart.

'I know I shouldn't be here,' he says ruefully, 'but I wanted to check you were OK. After all, I'm not averse to running away from things myself . . .' He looks down and kicks his foot in the sand. He's not dressed for a wedding, I notice. He's wearing a T-shirt and jeans, leather bracelets adorn his wrist, a necklace with the letter E hangs around his neck.

I remember us being on this same beach vowing to wear our promise rings as the waves crashed behind us and our hearts pounded against each other's chests and the tears fell from our eyes.

One year, he'd whispered into my mouth as I kissed him again and again, desperately clinging to him like a mollusc to a rock. *One year and I'll be back for you.*

Do you promise?

I do.

I blink and see the same silver ring on his finger, even now after all this time. The ring I saw when I was walking down the aisle. I'd worn mine on my right hand for a whole year until I moved to London, where eventually, reluctantly, at Milly's persuasion, I buried it in a suitcase of memories. A month later I met Adam. I should be wearing *his* ring now. Would I be wearing it if Kieran hadn't come back?

I think of Adam standing in the church doorway, and imagine myself back there.

What have I done?

Chapter 7

Bea Bishop has changed her name to Bea Hudson.
Relationship status: 'Married'.

I look around at our guests covertly as I change my Facebook profile, my wedding ring glinting as I tap expertly away on my phone. I know straight after the wedding ceremony and during the formal wedding photos on the lawn is not a particularly appropriate moment to do this, but the guests are happily talking and laughing, milling around in front of the marquee like brightly coloured ballroom dancers, and in this moment, I have an overwhelming urge to let everyone I've ever met hear how perfect it all is and how happy I am. Maybe because now I remember how close I came to ending this day very differently. When I saw Kieran in the congregation I wanted to run out the church and far away but then I'd fallen and forgotten and I'm *so glad*. I'm safe now. I have Adam. I glance around to check that Kieran hasn't returned, trying to quieten the pounding of my heart that seems intent on giving me away. Why was he there? What could he possibly hope to achieve by turning up after all this time – and at my wedding? When he was the one who left and didn't come back? I want to know, but equally, I'm frustrated that I'm thinking about him. I'm married. When I made my vows I resolved to put him out of my mind, to focus on the here and now – but he remains stubbornly in my head.

I walk across the lawn towards Adam, who is standing in front of the lake surrounded by a group of guests. My body is here but my brain is drowning in memories. I stop and hold on to a tree before I faint again. I'm trying to calm my breathing, to prevent the panic attack that I can feel rising up through my body. I look at the clear, tranquil water of the lake glimmering in the spring sunshine and try to remind myself that nothing has changed.

Kieran's gone and no one knows my secret. And hopefully no one ever will.

'There she is! Come here, my beautiful, perfect wife!' Adam calls, and waves.

I pause, take a deep, calming breath and then I let go of the tree and with a smile on my face I walk slowly towards my husband, my wedding dress threatening to trip me up with every single step.

I'm standing on the lawn sipping tea from a china cup in what I hope is an elegant, ladylike way, a string quartet playing behind me as I hold court with some distant family of Adam's.

'Yes I *am* very lucky, yes of course I know what a catch he is! Why did it take me so long to say yes? Er . . . well, you know a girl has to be a hundred per cent sure these days, ha ha!' I can tell from their expressions this is the wrong answer. 'No, seriously, the truth is it was just very hard to find a gap in Adam's diary.' They nod sagely at this. They understand how busy and important he is, his whole family does. 'And,' I continue, 'I didn't want a long engagement so I kept him hanging on until I knew we could marry as quickly as possible.' I pause. 'Couldn't risk any other girl getting her hands on him!'

They laugh along with me and I smile brightly before making my excuses and walking away. They're happy that I've given them a funny but believable reason for my indecision that is far preferable to the truth: that I just wasn't sure before.

I'm gagging for a glass of champagne and a proper chat with someone who actually *knows* me. To be honest I'm still feeling embarrassed and shaken by what happened during the ceremony. Not just about falling over, but what – no, *who* – precipitated it.

Despite the vast swarm of guests I'm surrounded by I suddenly feel incredibly alone. There is only one person I can talk to about what happened in the church.

'Milly,' I hiss as a goddess in gold glides past me, holding two glasses of champagne aloft. 'You, me, in the Portaloo now!'

'You saw *who*?' Milly gasps and looks down at me in horror.

I'm slumped on the toilet, skirts held aloft by Milly, white lace knickers down by my ankles, and clinging on to my champagne flute as I self-consciously try to empty my bladder (and my conscience) before my best mate.

'Kieran Blake.' I whisper his name quietly in case anyone else has come in.

'Former breaker of your heart?' Milly hisses.

I nod.

'The guy who swept you off your feet for a single summer and then nearly destroyed your life, leaving me and Loni to pick up the pieces? The one who watched his own brother *die* because of his own stupid recklessness and left you to carry the guilt?' I close my eyes. 'He was here? And that's why you fell when you came down the aisle?'

I nod again.

She narrows her eyes. 'So, how did you feel?'

I look at her and then down at my feet guiltily. 'Like I was drowning.'

'Did you talk to him?' She pauses briefly. 'Well, did you?'

I shake my head.

'Good. You know that him being here doesn't change anything, don't you?' she says urgently. 'Except to prove what a selfish bastard he still is.' She looks at me, as if waiting for me to echo her character assassination of him. But I can't. What happened to Elliot wasn't his fault.

'Milly, you don't know him, that isn't fair—'

She rolls her eyes as if she has heard this a million times before. Milly tends to make snap judgements. It's partly to do with her job as a hedge fund manager that she operates entirely on gut instinct. And so far it has seen her become a partner at one of the biggest investment companies in the City, marry her perfect man and make brilliant decisions in all other aspects of her life including: The flat she bought eight years ago (a two-bedroom dump opposite Greenwich Park acquired in an auction without seeing – now worth nearly a million pounds). Her clothes – the woman has never got it wrong, ever. Her hairstyle – a chic, sharp bob that she had cut aged thirteen after seeing *Pulp Fiction* – and has never ever changed because she nailed her look right then (I mean, who manages that as a teenager?). So when she says she never liked Kieran and that she always knew he couldn't be trusted even before he left me, I should listen. She was my saviour after that summer. She visited me throughout the year that I barely left Loni's house, and when he didn't come back when he said he would, she and Loni intervened and moved me up to London to live with her.

I didn't really have a choice in the matter and that suited me. As far as I was concerned I didn't deserve one any more.

'You know how I feel about Kieran Blake,' Milly says now. 'He tried to ruin your life once and he didn't succeed. I can't believe he's come back today of all days to do it again. Well, I hope he realises he's too late . . .'

I don't reply.

'Bea?' Milly says, grasping my arms and looking into my eyes. 'This doesn't change anything, does it? Him being here? I mean, you *know* that you and Adam are perfect for each other, don't you?'

I think of how I felt after my fall, and when I said my vows, and I know she's right. Kieran coming back hasn't changed anything.

'I do,' I say for the second time today. And then again, more emphatically, 'I do.'

Chapter 8

'I've waited for this moment for eight long years, Bea. Do you know, wherever I've been in the world, at any particular moment, when I close my eyes I've always been taken back to this beach, gazing at this view. With you . . .'

I stare at Kieran and then shake my head, fighting a compulsion to laugh manically at his words even as a desperate sob rises up through my body. I want to throw my arms around him and tell him to fuck off at the same time. Clearly I'm having some sort of breakdown. And not just of the marriage kind.

Instead I say nothing. I just lift some sand in my palm and watch as the grains slip through my fingers like time itself. I glance up at Kieran. He's looking at me dreamily, like he too has one foot in the past and one in the present. He crouches down and tries to put his arm around me.

'Kieran—' I protest sharply, pulling away. 'Don't. Just, don't. Have you forgotten—'

'I've *never* forgotten you, Bea!' Kieran says fiercely. 'You should know that. How could I forget what we went through together?' He reaches out his hand. I look at the ring on his finger and then at him and pull my arm away from his touch.

'I was going to say have you forgotten about my *wedding*. You know, the one you just crashed? Funnily enough I don't feel like reminiscing with you right now.' I turn away from him, my pulse throbbing, heart pounding, hands shaking. I don't want to look at him or be drawn into this conversation. But even though I have my back to him his image is still imprinted on my eyes. I can feel his presence in every one of my pores. It's like he is insidiously making his way under my skin again and I'm unable to resist him.

I can't help it. I glance over my shoulder and study him defiantly, without restraint. He has undoubtedly grown into a strong, fit, capable, magnetic man. But then I blink and it is as if the sand-timer has suddenly been flipped and the years dissipate before my eyes like a sandcastle swallowed up by the incoming tide. His gym-honed body shrinks and becomes the lean surfing machine it was when he was in his early twenties, his cropped hair grows long over his eyes, the sunken lines around his mouth and forehead fade into nothingness. I know he is imagining me too as I was then: with longer, looser hair, less make-up, fewer frown lines. And without the wedding dress.

'Why are you here, Kieran?' I ask warily. Wearily. 'Why now?'

He waits for a moment before he answers. 'It just felt like the right time, I guess.'

I force a laugh. 'Oh really? Right for who?'

Kieran looks at me sorrowfully. 'You're angry at me.'

'No, I'm angry at me.' I exhale. 'This is not the time, Kieran. Eight years ago was the time.' I go to stand up but find I can't in this stupid tight dress. I flail around for a moment like an upturned beetle before giving up.

'Here, let me help you,' Kieran smiles.

'No, thank you.' I slump back on the sand and fold my arms.

Kieran sighs and turns his back to me. 'Bea, I know you don't want to hear this right now but I need you to understand something. No matter how far I travelled and how long I stayed away, you've always been with me. You, Elliot, that summer' – he looks down – 'that night. In many ways I feel like I never left. A big part of me has always been here, with you.' He steps towards me as if taking my silence as acquiescence. Acceptance. 'I've missed you so much, Bea . . . you're the only one who understands me, who knows where I come from, who I am. You're the only one who could ever understand what it's like to lose someone you love . . .' His voice cracks. 'I still miss him, you know. Every day.'

I close my eyes and instantly see an image of Elliot jumping gleefully off Cromer Pier. I hear his cry as he slipped and caught his head on the side. I see his lifeless body as Kieran dragged him out of the sea.

He reaches out and offers me his hand and this time I find myself taking it. As I do I notice the tattoo of a star sign just visible on his wrist. Gemini. The twins. I run my finger over it for a second and he clutches my hand and then smiles sadly, his lips flicking up and then down in a quick movement like a cat's tail. Instead of getting up I pull him down so he's next to me.

We sit in silence watching as a flock of Brent geese arc across the sky. It's then that I allow the memories to come flooding back of that halcyon summer when we met. He was twenty-five, I was twenty-two. He and his twin brother Elliot had been to Norfolk many times before but had never stayed long enough to settle down. They were ex-foster kids whose foster parents had split up and then moved abroad, neither of them willing to go on looking after them. He told me that when they were in care, he and Elliot became wilder and wilder until their lives effectively evolved into an extended childhood game of chicken. When they turned eighteen and left the care home, they worked their way along the coast, finding jobs at campsites, in bars and restaurants, each encouraging the other to go for the next prohibited thrill.

The very first time we slept together, Kieran told me he didn't answer to anyone. He made his own decisions and always followed his heart and his instinct, wherever they took him. I remember exactly how he'd looked at me when he said that. 'And now I know why they brought me here,' he'd added, lowering his head and resting it on my chest as we fell asleep under the stars, entwined round each other's bodies. We didn't untangle ourselves for another four months. It was blissful. My summer of love. Until . . .

I remember with a jolt what he'd said to me the day he left after Elliot's funeral, on this very beach: *I can't do this. I'm sorry.* I feel a sudden wave of remorse as I remember how Adam looked when I told him the very same thing earlier today.

'What am I doing?' I didn't mean to but I realise I've said this aloud. Using his arm as a hoist I pull myself up to my feet before trying to run down the dunes, my feet sinking into the sand, grains flying up around me and into my eyes as I stagger awkwardly across the beach. Kieran's empty words from all those years ago are still echoing in my head. *I just need some time. You'll wait for me though, won't you? I need to know you'll wait . . .*

'Bea!' Kieran calls. 'WAIT!'

'WAIT?' I swing around, fuelled by fury, fear and guilt. 'What do you think I did for an entire year, Kieran? I waited for you, I waited and waited but you never came. And I understand why, I do. You blamed me for Elliot's death. I know you said you didn't but when you didn't come back I knew. I bet you couldn't bear to even think about me, let alone look at me . . .'

'What? Bea, no! You know I told you it wasn't your fault!'

'I don't want to hear it!' I cry, putting my hands over my ears. 'It's too late, OK? IT'S TOO LATE!'

He lurches forward but I start to run across the beach, hands still clasping my ears as if trying to drown out the crescendo of noise that is the deafening roar of my long-buried guilt.

A young man died because of me, and I'll never ever forgive myself. I don't deserve to be happy. Kieran has reminded me of that. Thank goodness I realised in time.

Chapter 9

Adam expertly finishes telling an anecdote of one of our first dates that has everyone roaring with laughter and then ahhh-ing with pleasure. Then he takes my hand and strokes my ring finger with his thumb as he turns to me and raises his champagne glass to signify the end of his speech.

'So will you join me in raising a glass to my beautiful and perfect wife, the woman I love with all my heart – the new Mrs Hudson. Thank you for *finally* agreeing to marry me,' he says jokily and there's a ripple of laughter and an outburst of applause as we kiss.

Once we've sat down, I allow myself a moment as the applause continues to take in the opulent and lavishly decorated marquee: the gold chairs complete with gigantic satin bows, the enormous crystal-encrusted chandeliers suspended from the draped ceiling, creating a stardust effect on the shiny floor. The round tables are covered in pristine white tablecloths. In the middle of each table is a jaw-droppingly gigantic floral centrepiece in a mirrored vase; lilies standing tall and gypsophila cascading like a fountain, the vase flanked by two tall white tapered candles in antique silver holders. Ornate silver-pronged candelabras sit on a fake mantelpiece behind the head table, alongside a large display of white freesias that spell out 'Adam and Bea'. I know it is meant to be a touching detail but the effect is slightly funereal. Each guest has a blue Tiffany box at their place setting; the female guests' contain a bracelet with one specially chosen silver charm. The men have cufflinks. It is an astonishingly extravagant detail, embarrassingly so, actually – and yet I know the blue boxes are mere drops in the vast oceanic expense of the day.

Loni winks at me. 'So much for your low-key wedding!' she whispers. 'The Hudsons could have fed a small country with the amount they've spent on this wedding!'

Cal leans across Loni and waves an empty bottle. 'Shis,' he slurs. 'Thish ish good shtuff. Thish wine is about eighty quid a pop!' Cal's hospital shifts mean his body clock is all over the place – and what with that and the twins' still-erratic sleeping patterns, he's a total lightweight these days.

He blows a kiss to Lucy, his childhood sweetheart, who is sitting with their girls, Nico and Neve, at a table far further back than I requested. They appear to have been relegated in favour of Adam's dad's business contacts, even though I'd specifically asked for them to be seated in front of the top table. But I don't have time to think about it any more as just then Jay stands up, adjusts his glasses, draws out his iPad and pulls down a screen. He grins and Adam groans audibly and our guests start laughing as a picture of Adam aged three appears on it. He's beaming brightly and is dressed in a suit and is sitting in the boardroom at Hudson & Grey.

'My little boy!' Marion exclaims.

'Ahhh, my baby,' George adds, wiping a pretend tear away before delivering his punchline. 'It was the proudest day of my life when . . . the company was born!'

Everyone laughs and I squeeze Adam's hand. I know his dad's obsession with his advertising agency has always been a sore point. It's no surprise to me that Adam ended up following in his father's footsteps. It felt like his career path was pre-determined. George's first love is his career, and so joining the company was Adam's only chance to get some attention. He shares his dad's talent and vision too – if not his passion. I know there are other things he would love to do. He told me on our very first date when I asked him. 'Study art, paint, be a designer . . . but they're all pipe dreams, not reality. I'm lucky to work with such inspiring people, and closely with my dad, even if sometimes it can be tricky . . .'

'I always knew Adam was destined for greatness.' Jay points at the screen. 'Even at this young age he was asking the secretaries to stay late and play with him.'

'He's his father's son!' George guffaws.

'Adam has always known exactly what he wants out of life,' Jay continues. 'Unlike the rest of us who seemed to veer precariously through our twenties from one job to another, one relationship to another, Adam has always known his goal: to follow in his father's footsteps. Not just in business but in a long and happy marriage, too . . .' I see Marion pat her coiffed hair proudly as George jokily pulls a pained face and downs his glass of red.

'Obviously Adam has never been short of girlfriends . . .' Jay continues. 'We met at uni and I knew instantly that if ever a ginge like me was to succeed with the ladies, I needed to stick with a guy like Ad . . .'

'Ain't that the truth!' one of Adam's schoolfriends calls out.

'But I was there the night that Adam met Bea,' Jay laughs, 'and I can assure you that no one has ever turned his head quite like her. And he's never looked away from her since.'

'Ahhh,' our guests sigh appreciatively.

I glance at the table next to us and see Eliza Grey's delicate features tighten. She is Adam's beautiful, blonde childhood sweetheart and she's here because she's Robert Grey, George's business partner's, daughter. I'd rather she wasn't here to be honest, and I made that clear to Marion when she was doing the guest list, but she just told me to stop being so silly and sensitive. 'Adam and Eliza have a long history. She's a lovely girl, the least you can do is offer her an olive branch for stealing her future husband!' Marion had laughed, but it was a tight, forced sound.

I'd acquiesced only because I felt sorry for Eliza, which is ridiculous really. I mean she's stunning and successful, but I know from Jay that she's constantly living in hope that she can rewind her life and get Adam back.

I re-tune into the speech. 'But even though Adam was sure from day one that Bea was The One it took Bea a while to be convinced.' Jay pauses and looks around the room. 'A long while.' Another pause as he looks at me and winks. 'A really, *really* long while.' He looks over at Adam. 'How many times did you propose again, mate? Six? Seven times?'

'OK, *mate*, thanks for that!' Adam grins and throws a cork at him. It's true. He did propose to me many times. I just kept putting him off. We were too young, I said. I wasn't ready. Why spoil something perfect? All the usual excuses – except the real one. I didn't deserve him.

'If you must know, Jay,' I call, 'playing hard to get was my ultimate game-plan!' This is not strictly true but I can't bear anyone to think that I wasn't sure about marrying Adam. 'And it worked!' I force out a laugh as I lift up my left hand and the whole crowd laughs along with me.

Everyone except Eliza. And Marion.

*

'Smile!'

Adam puts his hand over mine and we lean in to each other and beam at the photographer as we cut into the gigantic, white, five-tier cake. Each layer has been monogrammed with intricate pearl and fleur-de-lis decoration as well as an iced version of the family crest that Marion had designed especially for this wedding. It has been on all the invites, the order of service, the napkins, the tablecloths. I raise a piece of cake to Adam's mouth and he takes a bite before covering my mouth in sweet, icing-covered kisses as everyone applauds.

Then the band starts to play and he runs his fingers through his black hair as he backs away from me towards the middle of the dance floor. Jay and some of the guys gather behind him and begin to click their fingers and step in time. I recognise the song instantly. It's 'The Best Is Yet To Come' by Frank Sinatra. Adam winks at me as he dances across the room with suave, sliding moves like a latter-day Dean Martin. I laugh as Milly comes and links my arm and then leads me slowly towards him and I bashfully swing my dress to the music before he lifts me up and twirls me around. He mouths the words of the song whilst lowering me to the floor. He leans me back, kisses me lightly on the lips and then swings me commandingly across the dance floor. I throw my head back and look up at the canopy of fairy lights twinkling like stars and it is then that I know with every ounce of certainty I have that as long as I am with Adam I will see that sunshine place Sinatra is singing about. And it will be far, far away from the shadows.

And Kieran.

At midnight and on the verge of a new day and the dawn of our new life, Adam and I wave joyfully at our guests who have all spilled out onto the drive and I throw my bouquet into the waiting crowd. It's caught by Loni, who screeches like it has burned her.

'It's a sign, Loni!' I shout. 'You'll be next!'

'Only in some strange parallel world, my darling!' she calls back. 'I've done my time!' I push away thoughts of my dad and watch as she throws it again. This time Cal's girlfriend Lucy catches it. She immediately jumps up and down and waves it in front of Cal.

Still laughing, Adam and I get in the car and settle back in the seat. Then we both turn around and wave as our car pulls away from Holkham Hall and down Lady Anne's Drive. Everyone cheers and Milly, Jay and Cal run behind the car, waving wildly at us before they disappear into the darkness.

'Our future starts now . . .' Adam murmurs as he turns and looks at me.

I smile, lean my head on his shoulder and close my eyes. It does. It really does.

Chapter 10

As I pelt across the beach, I know I'm no longer just running from Adam, our wedding and the safe, secure life I've cultivated for myself since I met him seven years ago. I'm also running from my life before it. The one where my dad left me, I took risks, fell in love, made mistakes, horrible, tragic mistakes that I will never forgive myself for. Mistakes that left me paralysed.

Walking down that aisle today I realised that I'd been treading water since that summer. Not making decisions. Not following my dreams. Trying not to get pulled back to that dark, dangerous place while Adam desperately tried to keep me afloat. I think of how he has always been so good at lifting my spirits. He has this incredible capacity to remember things in detail, and whenever I'd feel myself sinking, he'd take me in his arms and start murmuring, 'Do you remember when . . .' before describing a moment in our lives so vividly that I'd be transported to that 'happy place'. But the shadows – and my secret – came back. Even Adam wasn't strong enough to stop that happening.

I can see the wedding car ahead and I scramble determinedly towards my Cinderella carriage that, by rights, should have turned back into a pumpkin but which is still, thankfully, waiting patiently in the beach car park to take me home.

I jump in and slam the car door, trying my hardest to shut the world out with it.

'Where to, miss?' the driver says.

'Home, I want to go home.'

The only problem is, if home is not with Adam, where on earth is it now?

May

Dear Bea

I always think of May as the swollen, overdue belly of spring; flowers bursting along well-pruned borders like flesh against elastic. Baby-blue clematis climbing walls and fences. Sometimes it's hard to keep yourself firmly rooted in the here and now, but May is the time to do it. After all, you've survived the uncertainty of early spring, which means, in theory, only bright summer days lie ahead. Try to embrace the freshness of feeling, not just in the air, but in the surfeit of colour and life that is blossoming before your eyes. It is sometimes easy to forget that even the strongest perennial and the hardiest twining climbers don't last forever. The short-lived bridal-wreath shrub that flowers in May is a reminder of that.

So, Bea, don't rest on your laurels expecting the weather to always be fine. Hoe old ground to stop weeds from germinating, and keep feeding and watering to encourage more growth. Night frosts are not uncommon this month, so cover vulnerable plants to

protect them if temperatures drop. And always
remember that a surplus of sunny days is just around
the corner.

   Love, Dad x

Chapter 11

Bea Bishop changed her relationship status to: 'It's Complicated'.

I wake up and become aware that everything hurts; my head, my throat, my ears, my skin, my heart. I sit up and try to prise my swollen eyes open, desperately pulling off clumps of thick, dried mascara so I can tentatively blink into the sunlight of a new day, a new month, a new *life*, all without Adam. I'm back here, back at home, where it all began.

Oh God.

Oh God. Oh God. Oh God. It's all coming back to me now: running away from Kieran at the beach, arriving at Loni's and collapsing into her arms as she half dragged, half carried me crying into the kitchen; and then she, Cal and Lucy trying to extract the truth from me. It had reminded me so much of that fateful night eight years ago when they brought me, a shivering wreck, home from the pier. I was in shock, not just at what I'd seen, but what I'd done.

'Did he do something to you?' Loni had demanded last night,

just like she'd asked back then, meaning Kieran. The vehemence
in her voice surprised me. Even though she's naturally on the
offensive when it comes to the men in my life, wanting to protect me, she has always loved Adam. She once told me she trusted
him with my heart.

'And that's a big deal, for me,' she'd added.

'Has Adam *cheated* on you?' she'd asked last night, unable to
hide her disbelief. 'Is that why you left him?' I'd shaken my head;
I couldn't speak for sobs.

'Have *you* cheated on him?' Cal had asked, and both Lucy and
Loni had admonished him.

'What? It's a fair question,' he said, eyeing me suspiciously. I
looked away. We hadn't talked about Kieran since we both saw
him in the congregation.

'No! There's nothing, no one . . . I just . . . I just couldn't. I
c-can't . . .' I'd broken down again then and they'd been unable
to get any more out of me. I'd spent two hours crying in bed
with my head buried in my hands, during which time they
served me tea and sympathy whilst whispering worriedly to each
other. The phone had rung every two minutes and they'd taken
turns to answer until they'd eventually taken it off the hook.
When I'd calmed down a little, I'd picked up my phone and
checked for messages but there was no reception in Loni's house,
so I put it in my bedside drawer. I realised I didn't actually want
to hear from Adam's family or our wedding guests, anyway. I
couldn't even begin to imagine what terrible things they were
saying about me.

I stare at the drawer and suddenly open it, grab my phone
and, clutching it tightly like it's a portal to another life, I try to
get out of bed. I don't want to stay in this room a moment longer
than I have to. My cosy little childhood attic room should be a
comfort, a blanket of warmth and security. But after the year I

spent here, barely getting out of bed, it has become simply a painful reminder of a time I'd rather forget. Oh, it's nice enough with its Velux windows looking down on the rambling garden below, my bed tucked cosily under the eaves, sloping walls painted primrose yellow and covered in a patchwork of Monet garden prints: *Water Lilies, Nymphéas, Reflections of Weeping Willows, Roseway at Giverny.* The prints – better than any sleeping tablets – had been Loni's idea that year; most things that worked were. I would only have to stare at them, allow my vision to go hazy, and no matter how much I'd been crying, no matter how low, how desperate, how guilty and hurt, how confused, heartbroken and paralysed with regret I felt, those pictures would carry me to a calm and safe place where I could lose myself in sleep. Until I met Adam.

Adam.

I swallow back fresh tears, wriggle out of my dress and find a pair of newly laundered fuchsia-pink silk pyjamas of Loni's that she has laid out for me. They are rather big, but I slip them on anyway, roll over the waistband several times and, wrapping my arms around my body, I shuffle towards the door. I run my fingers along my bookshelves as I pass. They are still groaning with the books of my childhood, as well as my garden diaries, the ones I started writing after Dad left, noting down every change, every growth and death, every bud and weed, so he could see how well I was following in his footsteps. The garden was our bond and I thought as long as I kept that I wouldn't lose him. Not completely anyway. I pick up one of the diaries now and gaze at the cover with its flower doodles and my name and age scrawled in bright, bold bubble letters. I quickly flick through the pages. He'd only been gone two years and I clearly still harboured a belief that he would come back because there are so many references to him.

Four years later, in the notebook marked 'Beatrice Bishop aged thirteen', there is barely a reference to him. Just intricate diagrams and notes, tips ripped out of gardening magazines and paragraphs copied from my treasured Royal Horticultural Society books and encyclopedias. I continued writing the diaries until I met Kieran. And then I left them all here when I moved in with Milly – as well as the reference books bought for my degree course in Garden Design that I was in the middle of studying for at UEA. Books on small gardens, landscaping, garden colour palettes, planting, and designing roof terraces and urban spaces – the module I was studying just before I dropped out. I didn't need any reminder of my past life.

Feeling I might suffocate if I stay in there much longer, I walk out of my bedroom and head downstairs.

The noise and chatter in the kitchen stops abruptly when I appear in the doorway. Loni, Cal, Lucy and the kids are momentarily frozen; quite a feat, particularly for Neve and Nico who seem unable to stay still – even when asleep. Loni moves first, her round, beautifully fleshy and expressive face morphing expertly from shock into delight as she steps forward, and with the sleeves of her bright kaftan fanning out, she opens her arms wide to me like an ebullient butterfly.

'Bea, darling! It's such a JOY to see you up and about.' Her arms close around me and I shut my eyes. She smells reassuringly familiar, a scent of patchouli and sweet orange wafts under my nose. Her hair is tied into a messy mermaid's plait and hangs over her shoulder like wisteria, her plump face is free of make-up and glowing with vitality. Under her kaftan she's wearing a pair of bright silk patterned trousers. On her feet are gladiator sandals and gigantic bead earrings dangle noisily from her ears. 'We were just saying, weren't we, Cal, that you have absolutely nothing to be ashamed or embarrassed about. No need to hibernate in your room!' This line is delivered in a high-pitched, sing-song voice. She knows better than anyone how capable I am of hiding myself away. 'What you did was very brave, Bea, very brave indeed. It's much better to make a decision like that now rather than six months into the marriage. You can walk with your head held high, darling. After all, if there's one thing that Buddhism has taught me it's that the secret of life is to have no fear. There's this saying—'

'Never fear what will become of you, depend on no one. Only the moment you reject all help are you freed!' Cal and Lucy chorus. I don't join in. It is Loni's motto. One she delivered for months after Dad left. My motto is: Not the bloody Buddha quotes again.

'Well, I'm definitely free now . . .' I blink up at the ceiling, trying to stop the tears.

'Oh Bea . . .' Lucy instantly darts around the table and gives me a cuddle.

I wriggle out of her embrace and go and stand in front of the Aga. I don't deserve comfort.

'H-have you heard from anyone? Milly maybe?' I ask. I want to see her but at the same time I'm petrified of what she is going to say. I know that she more than anyone won't hold back. I don't think she saw Kieran at the wedding – if she had she'd probably have disowned me – but she's been waiting for Adam and me to get married for years. I can't bear the thought of letting her down, and though I want to believe she'll support me, I know that Adam is as much her friend as I am. I can't rely on her support. And besides, I don't deserve it.

Loni shakes her head. Even though I can't face Milly, I can't help feeling hurt that she hasn't come round, or at least phoned. She'd know her's is the first place I'd run to. 'Marion?' This comes out as a mousy squeak, displaying more fear than I'd intended. Cal shrugs and nods. I groan. I can't bear to think about what

Adam's family and friends think of me. I'm sure I heard the phone ringing in my dreams last night. Part of me wants to know. The other just wants to get back in bed and pull the duvet over my head. Maybe it's a blessing that Loni's house is in the middle of nowhere and has such shockingly bad Wifi and no phone signal so I don't have to find out. I pick up my phone again nonetheless. I need to know what everyone is saying. Or maybe even tell them how terrible I'm feeling. Surely that's the right thing to do in this situation?

I open up Facebook. I see my profile says 'In a relationship with Adam Hudson' and I wonder if I should change it. I start manically tapping out a status update in the vain but optimistic hope that I will get one magical, fated spark of a signal.

Bea Bishop has made a terrible mistake.

My thumb hovers over the post button but even as I'm writing, I know that what I'm saying isn't true. I delete the message and tap out a different status.

Bea Bishop is so so sad.

This *is* true but I frown as I stare at it. It looks too self-indulgent written in black and white like that. I delete it, biting the inside of my lip, rolling the flesh between my molars, enjoying the sharp pain. I close my eyes for a moment and think. Then I write another update.

Bea Bishop is so so sorry.

This one feels right because I *am* sorry. Terribly, awfully sorry and this seems like the best way to apologise without having to deal with seeing anyone. Cowardly, maybe, but why change the personality trait of a lifetime?

I hit post but nothing happens. I hold the phone out, swearing under my breath as I fail to get a signal. I try kneeling up on the window seat and holding the phone up to the ceiling, standing on one leg over by the back door and crouching by Loni's Welsh dresser. But there's nothing. Cal wanders over and crouches down next to me.

'Hey ...' he says, gently prising the phone from my hand and rubbing my back. 'Do you think that's such a good idea?' His face is pulled into a frown and suddenly I see how tired he looks. His shock of curls has always made him look childishly cherubic – both at school and at home he seemed to get away with anything, which used to drive me mad – but recently his responsibilities seem to be drawn on his face like marks on a map. The frown line between his eyes is Loni. He's constantly worrying about her being on her own. The group of lines stretching out from the east and west of his eyes are all Neve and Nico, a combination of laughter and exhaustion that they've brought since they were born two years ago. And the faint lines across his forehead are his job; they tell of each emergency he deals with and how he does it with humour, patience, urgency and passion.

'What else am I meant to do, Cal?' I ask desperately. 'I need to let everyone know how sorry I am. I need to apologise for this mess ... I need to ... I – I need to ...' I start crying again and Cal rubs my shoulder.

'Just give it some time, sis. Sort your head out in private. And more importantly, let Adam sort out his.'

I look at the screen. My unsent status is blinking accusingly at me. I'm torn because although part of me is desperate to make contact with the outside world, to pour my heart out with apologies, I also know that Cal's right.

Why is it that every decision I try to make is always the wrong one?

Suddenly I'm aware of a doorbell piercing the silence. In a panic, I look at Loni.

She comes over, strokes my hair and kisses my forehead. 'Let Loni deal with it.'

As she walks out of the kitchen, I pick up my phone and rush back upstairs. I run down the corridor that is painted a lurid purple and covered with photo montages of Cal and me. Dozens of them are packed into various clip frames. In every single one we are outside, on beaches, in pine forests, in the garden. Our skin is nut-brown, our noses covered with freckles, the sunlight shining through the lens in a warm filtered glow that comes from happy memories. There are a lot of Cal standing, hands on hips, dimpled chin stuck out, proudly wearing one of his Superhero costumes. I remember the Christmas after Dad left. Cal was five and he dressed up as Superman every day of the school holiday. It became a standing joke – not so funny when you realised his reason for it. Outfit aside, I think it's what he's been pretending to be ever since.

I pause at the end of the corridor in front of a display of recent family shots. There are more of Lucy, Cal and their kids than of Adam and me, mainly because – as Cal and Loni have never failed to remind me – we hardly ever come, *came*, past tense, home.

I can hear a faint murmuring of voices downstairs, but I can't even make out who it is. I stare at the one photo of Adam and me and I remember it was taken six months ago. We're sitting in the garden leaning into each other, my arms threaded around Adam's neck, his lips resting on my cheek and eyes smiling into the camera. We'd just got engaged, and he'd insisted we drive to Norfolk and tell Loni and Cal in person. We were so happy. We look so perfect together. No one could ever have guessed that just six months later, on our wedding day, it would all have fallen to pieces.

The front door slams shut and footsteps sound on the stairs. I dart behind my door and lean against it. Just then my phone begins to vibrate and buzz with message after message, one voicemail after another. It must be a weird Wifi hotspot. I stare blindly as they keep coming and then, without listening to a single one of them, I switch the phone off and slump down to the floor.

Chapter 12

'*Come ON, mon grand* hunk of *jambon*, stop being ze slowcoach!'
I grab the sleeve of Adam's jacket and attempt to drag him down
the platform at St Pancras. I glance at the clock and see we have
just a few minutes to board our train. He's being as cool, calm
and collected as ever. Nothing ruffles Adam. He glides through
life as if everyone and everything will just wait for him. Which,
to be honest, they kind of do.

'ALLEZ ALLEZ ALLEZ!' I grab his hand and try to run down
the platform. But he merely strides alongside me, every step of
his matching several of mine. He is smiling wryly, eyes on his
phone.

I pull him harder, but he's too busy tapping away at his phone
to respond. If that's a work email I'll kill him. It'll be like an
Agatha Christie novel: *Death on the Eurostar.*

'Don't worry, Bea. We've got plenty of time.' I automatically
relax and slow down. If he says so, it must be true. Adam never

panics. He expects everything to work out his way. It's not his fault. He had everything bestowed on him as a kid and so is unpractised in the art of disappointment. I am so lucky that he didn't take no for an answer with me. I told him so last night as we were lying in each other's arms, limbs entwined, breath mingling, hearts pounding against each other.

'Didn't you ever tire of waiting?' I asked, curling my fingers through the criss-cross of dark hair on his chest, marvelling at how perfect my engagement ring and my wedding ring looked on my finger.

He'd leaned up on his elbow and gazed at me as he shook his head; a sexy, teasing smile had danced across his lips. 'I didn't mind *when* you came to your senses,' he'd replied, 'I just knew that you would . . . eventually.'

'Oh, the arrogance of the man! Always so sure of yourself, huh?' I'd teased.

'No,' he'd corrected me as he laid a meaningful kiss on my lips. 'I've always been sure of *us*.'

Adam picks up his stride and so do I, and I realise that he's right.

Adam and I were meant to be. Who cares that my dad wasn't at the wedding and that Kieran was? Adam is my destiny. He has been from the moment I met him. I'd just lost faith in my ability to make the right decision. That wasn't Adam's fault, or a sign of a bad relationship, it was just another consequence of what had happened after Elliot died.

Thankfully, it's all about the future now. Mine and Adam's.

Adam leads me into the first-class carriage, puts our luggage up on the rack and then sits opposite me and smiles as two glasses of champagne appear, brought by a member of staff who has clearly been tipped off that there is a honeymoon couple aboard. She congratulates us as she places them on our table, I thank her and am about to lift my glass in a toast with Adam but he's too occupied with pulling his buzzing phone out of his pocket and staring at it with a harassed expression.

'Just give me a second to reply to this email. Some client meltdown that no one else can deal with.' He bends his head, his brows locked in concentration. I stare at him for a moment, taking the opportunity to marvel at the fact that the man I'm looking at is actually my *husband*. It is a strange sensation to look at someone you have been with for seven years and yet feel like it's the first time you've really *seen* them. I look at him as a stranger might, taking in his sleek black hair, serious grey eyes, carved jawline with an added shadow that tells me he's on holiday, but yet doesn't lessen his air of authority. Then I glance down and take in my going away outfit that Milly chose for me. A cream dress with capped sleeves, nude heels and navy blazer. I think how my dark hair is blow-dried and tied loosely at the nape of my neck, softly curled tendrils float around my face. I'm wearing diamond earrings Adam bought me for my thirtieth and a simple gold watch on one wrist and a gold bangle on the other.

From the admiring glances we got when we stepped onto the train, I know we *look* right together. I tug at my skirt and wipe my hands on my blazer.

The only problem is, when I'm dressed like this I just don't *feel* like me.

Adam smiles at me apologetically as his phone starts ringing. 'Dad?' he says as I hear a series of demands fired down the phone. 'Yeah, but I'm off on honeymoon, remember? Yes, of course I'm committed. Yes, I know that there's no such thing as a holiday when you have your own business. Of course I want the responsibility … yes, I appreciate how lucky I am … I just … Fine. OK. I'll deal with it …'

Adam rubs his forehead as the call is ended. I stretch my hand across the table to his and he takes it. 'You OK?'

He nods. 'Sorry about that . . .'

'You need to be stronger with your dad.'

'Easier said than done. No one says no to George Hudson,' he says wearily.

'And as of yesterday, no one says no to you, remember?' I say, waving my left hand at him. His eyes crinkle into a smile and I know he's back. Adam takes his champagne glass, leans across the little table and links his arm through mine so that we are glass to glass, lip to lip, eye to eye.

'Here's to our future, Mrs Hudson,' he murmurs. 'Thank you for making me the happiest man on the planet.' We clink glasses and kiss softly and then I settle back, my fingers curled through Adam's, squeezing them tightly like I'm scared to let him go. My engagement ring and my wedding ring glitter in the light of the sunshine streaming through the carriage window as we speed out of the city and make our way towards Paris. I can't help but think, if life is two sides of a coin, I've most definitely landed heads up.

Chapter 13

Bea Bishop: Cal Bishop is trying (and failing) to amuse me at Wells-next-the-Sea.

Cal has brought me to the arcades at this cute little seaside town not far from Loni's place in Holt and one of our favourite childhood haunts. I know why he's brought me here and I find myself imagining the Facebook update I'd post if I hadn't sworn off social media. We used to come here all the time as kids. Then, when we got older, we'd hang out in French's, the fish and chip shop, and play the slot machines after going for runs together on the beach. Running was something Loni encouraged us to do when we were both under pressure studying for our exams and I was having a particularly bad bout of anxiety and self-doubt – I was doing my A levels, Cal his GCSEs. There was something about running side by side – usually in total silence – that made me feel connected to my little brother in a way I sometimes struggled to. He was always so sorted, so together, but when we ran it made me realise that sometimes he too needed to de-stress, clear his head and take time to work out where his life was going.

Today he looks tired, of course, with the strain of worrying about his pathetic big sister alongside everything else, but at the age of twenty-eight my little brother *usually* has the assured air of someone much older. I smile as Cal bounds over with a bag of two-pence coins and a gigantic grin and I feel grateful that he's trying so hard to cheer me up. He makes for the slot machines and waves me over like I'm one of his two-year-old twins. 'Come on, sis!' Cal says as he hands me the bag of copper coins. 'It's OK to take a gamble for once in your life!'

'Like I tried to on marriage?' I say wryly.

Cal's smile fades. 'Adam wasn't a risk, Bea. You know he was the most stable thing you've ever had in your life.' He rubs his hand over his forehead and across the crown of his springy hair.

'I know.'

'So why leave him then?' he says in exasperation. 'It doesn't make any sense!' He pauses and glances down at the bag of coins. Then he takes one out and flips it. 'Except, of course, because of Kieran Blake . . .' He slams the coin onto his hand and looks up at me confrontationally. 'Heads or tails? Kieran or Adam . . . was that it?'

'It wasn't like that, Cal. You have to believe me when I say that! I had no idea he'd be there. None at all!' He stares at me and I crumble. 'OK! I admit seeing him threw me but you know I'd been having doubts long before that. I just . . . I just . . . don't think I'm cut out for marriage. You must understand that?' I look at Cal pointedly. He's been with Lucy for nearly ten years, they have two kids together and they've never got married. We always joke that Dad's leaving didn't make us commitment phobes, just marriage phobes. That seems even truer now.

'I suppose so,' he concedes. 'But I didn't leave Lucy standing at the end of the aisle like an idiot.'

'Well, maybe you haven't spent most of your life hoping that Dad would be there to give you away on your wedding day!'

'Oh sis,' Cal slides his arm around me and rests his head on mine. 'When will you accept that he's never coming back?'

I bite my lip. I feed two-pence pieces into the machine and watch as each drops onto the shelf and disappears. 'Don't you ever feel like there's something missing? A big part of you that means you'll never feel complete until you find it?'

Cal shakes his head. 'No, I don't. I have everything I need in Loni, you, Lucy and the kids. Why should I spare a second thinking about some stranger who walked out on us without a backward glance?'

'But Loni was the one who *told* him to leave!'

'But *he* was the weak, pathetic man who accepted it and never came back! He didn't exactly fight for us, did he?' Cal slams the side of the machine with his hand, making me jump. 'Come on, Bea, is this really what yesterday was all about? Our dad who left over twenty years ago?'

My eyes are brimming with tears as I persist with my line of questioning. 'But surely you've wondered if we're like him?'

'I bloody well hope not,' Cal says vehemently.

Cal and I have always had an opposing stance on the decisions our parents made. I have always – not exactly *blamed* Loni – but certainly accepted her admission that she was totally responsible for Dad leaving. Apparently, he made it clear that he wanted her to be a traditional wife and mother. He couldn't handle her desire for a career and a life outside the home. She soon realised they wanted very different things out of life. So she told him to leave.

'Maybe I've always been more like Dad than you, maybe I was destined to leave my family too ...'

'Don't be ridic—' Cal begins but I carry on.

'. . . but I did it before anyone could get really hurt. Adam will get over yesterday. He'll move on,' I say dully, feeling a shard of pain even as I say the words. 'I guarantee he'll have a new girl-friend before the year is out. But if we'd got married, had kids, well . . . history often repeats itself, doesn't it? I've just accepted my destiny a bit earlier than Dad did . . .'

'You'd never have left your family, Bea,' Cal says quietly. 'I know you.'

'Then you know why I think I'm better off alone,' I say. 'People like me always are.'

Cal grasps my arms and stares into my eyes. 'You know what I think? I think you're a better person than you think you are. I think you're capable of loving and being loved. I think you *can* feel secure in a relationship and not scared. Because *that's* what I think really happened yesterday. You got scared that history would repeat itself – not that *you* would leave, like you believe, but that Adam would leave you, just like Kieran and Dad did . . .' He stops as he sees my expression crumple. 'I'm right, aren't I?' he murmurs. 'That's what it was all about! Oh Bea, Adam's a good man, a great one, he loves you, he'd do anything for you! All you had to do was take a leap of faith . . . why couldn't you, eh?'

I don't reply. I don't know what to say.

Cal is watching me play whack-a-mole, intermittently shouting encouragement. 'That one's for Dad leaving us! That one is for Adam's mum taking over your entire wedding!' I give it several hits. 'Now do a whack for every time Loni has embarrassed you!'

I give him a sideways glance. 'I'll need a new arm!'

'So what now?' he asks as I continue thumping moles on the head with a toy hammer. I must look ridiculous but it is cathartic.

I haven't told Cal but the only person I'm imagining bashing on the head is me.

'I don't KNOW.' SMACK.

I hate the fact that I don't know. I feel the self-flagellation descend quickly like mist over the sea.

THWACK.

That one was for me. I could do with a bloody good push in the right direction. Like those two-pence coins.

WHACK! I pause, my mallet in mid-air. 'Go back to the flat to get my STUFF?' I say, hitting the target with a certainty I do not feel. Then I spot another mole and bring the mallet down with an almighty thud. 'HA! Got you!'

Cal eyes me warily. 'I'd offer you our sofa but number one, you're scaring me. In fact, I'm starting to think Adam got off lightly . . .' I turn to him and raise the mallet menacingly and he laughs and holds up his hands in truce. 'And number two, the twins still aren't sleeping, so I'm currently on the sofa myself! Have been for weeks, in fact!' I look at him sympathetically. I want to ask him more but just then my phone starts buzzing in my pocket and I pull it out and look at it nervously.

'It's Milly,' I say. 'I'd better take this. I can't avoid everyone forever.'

I hand Cal the hammer and go outside. I stand by the ice-cream counter, and stare out at the boats moored in the harbour, their masts piercing the sky like great white needles, brightly coloured bunting flapping beside them. Every sense is being invaded by memories, the salty brine of the sea air mixed with the smell of fish and chips from French's (the irony that I should be in France on my honeymoon right now is not lost on me), the sweet familiar smell of ice cream and candy floss. I can almost see Kieran's bright yellow VW camper van speeding down the street, me in his passenger seat, bare, nut-brown feet resting on the dashboard, my head thrown back in laughter as Kieran sings at the top of his voice. I focus instead on the view beyond the boats of the salt marshes and the beach with the brightly coloured huts I used to dream about owning with Kieran. It's as if the day he crashed my wedding, he also broke down my walls. I can't get him out of my head now, even though I'd managed to for the seven years I spent with Adam.

Except did I? Did I really forget him, or was he the reason I was never willing to fully commit to Adam?

I just don't know any more.

I put the phone to my ear reluctantly and try to muster up the strength to talk to my best friend.

'Hi Milly,' I say.

'At sodding last! Where are you? How are you? When are you coming back? Are you OK? Hang on.' I hear a muffled sound as she puts her hand over the receiver. 'I'm OK, thanks, Loni, I'm not actually a big fan of rosehip tea . . . or nettles.'

The line clears again. 'I'm at your mum's . . .' She lowers her voice. 'Please come back soon and save me, she wants me to chant with her. But I'd do it, I'm not leaving here until I've seen you, and you know how stubborn and strong-willed I am.'

'I do.'

'Unusual choice of words, Bea,' she says lightly. 'Shame you didn't use them yesterday, eh?'

'Don't, Milly, please, I—'

'I know, I know, I'm sorry,' she interrupts. 'I promised myself I wouldn't be judgemental. Or start shouting at you. I just want to know if you're OK. And,' she adds, 'I know I said I'd wait here as long as it takes to see you, but it is possible Loni may break me. She's been reading passages of her new book to me for the past half an hour.'

'Sorry,' I say sympathetically. 'But I just don't think I can face anyone right now. I can't bear thinking about how I've let everyone down.'

'You haven't let anyone down. Except Adam,' Milly says pointedly.

'How is he?' I say quietly. I can't say his name. I don't deserve to.

'He's heartbroken. He feels like his life has been torn in two.' She pauses. 'And how are you?'

I consider her words. 'The same.'

'Then why?' she demands. 'I mean, I just don't get it. You love him, he loves you, so why leave?' She makes me sound like an investor pulling out of a sure-fire interest earner. I don't answer. 'Jay and I were with Adam most of the night,' she continues. 'He's completely blaming himself.'

'It's not his fault!' I exclaim. 'I told him that!'

'And so did we.' She pauses. 'Obviously we told him what a horrible, selfish person you are . . .'

'You're right, I am.'

'Oh Bea,' she sighs. 'I'm joking! But *why* didn't you talk to me if you were having second thoughts? You know I can always help when you're being pathetic and indecisive . . . it's what I do.'

This is true, but still, her words prickle. She does always help, if helping is steamrollering me into life choices I'm not always ready to make.

'I – I tried . . . before I started walking up the aisle. But then I decided to just ignore my doubts and go for it . . .'

'And that was the right decision! So what changed your mind? *Kieran did.*

I don't reply.

'Seriously, Bea, what happened?' Milly presses. 'Maybe Cal got it wrong and you *were* concussed.'

I don't tell her that actually I was thinking straight for the first time in years. I don't say anything, in fact. The silence hangs between us; invisible but tangible all the same, like the missing sails on the boats opposite me. I want to open up to her, but I know she'll judge me.

'Well, if you don't want to tell me . . .' Milly says huffily, breaking the silence.

I look up and blink and raindrops begin to fall from the sky, landing like teardrops on my face. I step back into the amusement arcade. The noise of the games is ringing in my ears.

'It's not that I don't want to, it's just . . . I – I don't know . . .' This isn't true. I do know. I know damn well what happened.

There's a lengthy pause before she speaks again. 'Look,' she says. 'As long as you know that I'm here for you. If you need me.'

'Thank you, Milly.'

Another silence in which I sense that she is giving me one final chance to come clean. Maybe if we were out together, or I'd drunk some alcohol, I would. But I'm not brave enough right now. I can't tell her, I just can't.

'OK,' she sighs resignedly at last. 'I know you're not ready to talk but I also know you can't stay at Loni's forever. Obviously you won't be going back to your and Adam's place but you always have a space with Jay and me at the flat if you need it. We've got plenty of room. You and me back together in Greenwich again – and in the same flat. It'd be just like the old days!' she adds faux brightly.

'Thanks, Milly,' I reply, subdued by her generosity.

The old days. Her words echo in my head long after we end our call.

An hour later, after I've finally convinced Cal that it's OK to leave me and he's gone to work, I head down to the beach. I can't face going back to Loni's in case I've had any more visitors. It has stopped raining and I have an urge to go for a run. I'm not dressed for it but I don't care. I pound along the sand towards the nature reserve, the sharp sea breeze blowing against my face, my calf muscles burning, my heart pumping, and I feel the mists part like the clouds above and my path ahead suddenly begins to appear more clearly than it has for years.

The old days.

I run for miles until I get to Holkham Hall. I weave my way up the drive through the oak trees and reach the lake. I stand there panting and holding my waist as I stare at the scene in front of me. Another wedding reception is taking place in the grounds today. Same marquee, different couple. I watch them as they thread easily through their guests; every so often they pause to kiss, or whisper to each other. Even when they are apart having separate conversations they seem together, their movements mirrored, eye contact frequently made. They look so happy.

That could have been me, I think, feeling like I'm witnessing the alternative reality of yesterday. I would have been clutching a champagne glass, chatting to our guests like this, basking in the glory of the most important day of my life.

But now I feel like I've crossed a line and instead of being on the path that was leading me to the future I am ... where? Where will my new trajectory, my new *life,* take me? Am I always going to be suspended in time, unable to make any real decisions, any actual steps forward until I deal with the past? I may have run from Kieran yesterday but now I feel like my life has actually been on pause since the day he left. Maybe even before ...

I watch an older man with charcoal-grey hair and a broad smile, and dressed in a morning suit, approach the couple. He shakes hands with the groom and kisses him on both cheeks and then, beaming with pride, he throws his arms around the bride, who must be his daughter.

My breath catches in my throat as I suddenly remember the

last time my dad hugged me. I'd been in the garden, sitting under the willow tree. He'd embraced me, pressing his face against mine as he placed a book in my hands. Then he'd kissed my head several times before he quickly and quietly got up, turned round and walked across the lawn, into a white mist of magnolia trees, before disappearing out of the side gate, changing my life forever.

Chapter 14

Bea Hudson has just been carried over the threshold . . .
27 likes, 3 comments.

'Here we are,' Adam says as he picks me up, swings open the door of our hotel room and carries me in.

'You're meant to carry me over the threshold of our *home*,' I laugh, 'not our honeymoon hotel!'

'Oh sorry, my mistake!' He goes to drop me and I squeal and cling on to him as he strides across the room and throws me onto the bed. I giggle as he lowers his body to mine then I close my eyes contentedly, relishing the warmth I feel as he covers me.

'So we did it then, Mrs Hudson,' he says, stroking back my hair and kissing me softly on my lips, my cheeks and my eyelids.

'Not yet, we haven't.' I smile cheekily and tug at the buckle on his belt.

'You could at *least* wine and dine me first!' he says with mock offence.

'I'm only hungry for one thing.' I undo his belt and whip off his trousers and sit astride him again, feeling the hard swell of him between my legs. I take off my blazer and pull my dress over my head and lean down, brushing my lips over his softly and then biting his plump bottom lip gently. His dark stubble grazes my chin and I kiss his neck, working my hands down his body, pinging open his shirt buttons as I go. I lean against his chest so we're skin against skin. Our kisses deepen, becoming more and more urgent as we allow ourselves to get lost in the welcome warmth of each other's mouths. Nothing has ever felt as good as this.

'Mmm,' Adam murmurs as he flips me over onto my back. 'If this is what marriage is going to be like, I'm glad I've signed up to it for the rest of my life . . .'

'So am I,' I smile. 'So am I.'

I roll up on one elbow and nuzzle Adam's neck. His arms are stretched languorously over his head.

'*Wow*,' I breathe, looking around the room.

Adam opens one eye, his lips curl up on one side and a line appears on his cheek like a comma, punctuating his smile. 'That was pretty incredible, huh!'

'I was talking about the room!' He tries to grab me and I giggle as I bound out of bed and begin exploring our suite, opening doors and exclaiming as I take it all in. It isn't a big, plush, soulless room in a staid, overpriced suite overlooking the Eiffel Tower as I expected Adam to choose. Instead we're in a quirky boutique room that is a rainbow of vivid, wondrous colour. 'Ooh look at this beautiful wallpaper! It feels like we're in a garden!' I can't disguise my delight at the trees that shimmer with pink blossom, the green leaves and flashes of bright blue sky.

The bathroom is small but perfectly formed with a roll-top bath and rose-pink and lime-green tiles. I gaze through the net curtains and out of the window that overlooks the little cobbled streets of Montmartre. 'It's perfect,' I sigh. I peer out of the bathroom and spot Adam leaning over the bedside table to look at his phone. I put my hands on my hips and tap my foot but he doesn't notice so instead I leap across the room and onto the bed and confiscate his phone.

He smiles apologetically then prods me gently. 'You thought I'd get it wrong, didn't you? You were imagining some expensive faceless suite on the Champs-Elysées. A suite most women would probably kill to stay in, might I add . . .' His prod turns into a tickle.

'But I'm not most women,' I reply through my giggles, wriggling away from him and then switching his phone off and putting it on my bedside table.

'No, you are definitely not. And that's exactly why I married you . . .' Adam says as he rolls towards me. He always says the right thing. He has always accepted me for exactly who I am.

Maybe now I've left Bea Bishop and my secret behind, I will too.

Next morning, after a gorgeous breakfast, we're excitedly exploring the glorious and glamorous Champs-Elysées. It's all very impressive but I can't help wishing I could kick off my pumps and go and lie in the grass.

'We're nearly here,' Adam says now and I stop behind him, taking a moment to enjoy watching him studying the map. His head is bowed over it, blue-black hair flopping over his forehead. He glances up and grins at me as I take a photo. He looks so much younger and less stressed than usual. I glance at the sign behind him. We're standing on the corner of a pretty, maple-tree-lined street called the avenue Franklin D. Roosevelt in the 8th arrondissement. Adam takes me by the shoulders and turns me around to face the ornate stone façade of the Grand Palais; the historic exhibition site that was built in the architectural style of the Beaux-Arts.

'Inside is the science museum, the Palais de la Découverte,' he informs me in a perfect French accent.

'Great! Are we going in?' My heart sinks a little at the thought. I can't think of anything worse than looking around a fusty old museum right now.

'We're not going in there!' he laughs. 'Come on, this way.' Adam grabs my hand and starts pulling me away. I hear his phone buzz in his pocket but he pulls it out and switches it off. The gesture sends a warm glow through me.

'What's that?' I ask Adam, pointing at a large sculpture next to the museum. He'll know, because he always does.

'It's of a guy called Alfred de Musset,' Adam says.

'Bless you,' I say as if he's just sneezed and he laughs again.

'Why, what do you think of it?' Adam asks. I panic a little. I hate being asked my opinion on anything, I never feel like I know the answer, I'm constantly battling my inner instinct to shout, 'I don't know!' It's why I don't like museums. They're one of the many places you're meant to be confident of your opinions. And it's been a long time since I trusted my judgement.

'I don't know . . .' I pause and try to gather my thoughts, forcing myself to take control, to be more like Adam. More like a Hudson. 'I suppose, well, I – I guess I kind of like how he looks all whimsical and sort of . . .' I pause. 'In repose. As if he's trying to make a decision.' I feel myself grow in confidence as I speak and I tilt my head thoughtfully. 'It looks as if he's looking back and forward all at once.' Suddenly I feel that I can relate to this strange piece of apparently unremarkable art. 'He's a dreamer,' I finish assuredly.

'He certainly is,' Adam agrees and I feel a swell of pride at being right.

'Maybe I've missed my calling as an art critic. Because that sculpture just kind of spoke to me, you know?' Adam leans in towards me and raises an eyebrow.

'That's funny because he's *meant* to be daydreaming about his former lover.'

'Oh,' I say, trying to stop my face reddening. Suddenly I'm not so keen on it after all. 'Alfred de Mussct, you say? Alfred de *Muppet* more like. I mean, what an idiot, getting hung up on his ex like that!' Adam chuckles and I take his hand. 'So where *are* we going?' I change the subject swiftly.

Adam smiles and points at some old rickety stone steps. I peer and see that the steps curve down and round to somewhere just out of sight.

'What's down here?' I ask as Adam takes my hand and we begin to slowly descend the steps.

He glances sideways at me and winks. 'You'll see . . .'

He leads the way down the higgledy steps, looking back at me to make sure I don't stumble as I carefully follow. Ahead of him is a stone entrance: it's like a giant has smashed his outstretched hand straight through a wall to make his way through. I can see a flash of green beyond, and, utterly intrigued, am led into a beautiful hidden garden, filtered by rich, golden sunlight. When Adam speaks again he's smiling broadly.

'Welcome to the Jardin de la Vallée Suisse, a secret garden in the heart of Paris that I found especially for you.'

My heart soars. He knows me so well.

'Adam, this is perfect!' I throw myself into his arms and he lifts me off the ground. Then he leads me over to a bench and begins unpacking a picnic lunch. I stop him as he pulls out a bottle of champagne and starts to open it. I just want to soak up this perfect moment.

'Shh,' I say. 'Listen.' Along with the birdsong, I hear the rustle of leaves, like soft-soled feet dancing across a stage, the gentle inhale of each flower as it bends to the sun, the exhale of the trees as the breeze sighs through the branches.

'It's beautiful.' I sink back on the bench, allowing the view to wash over me. The scent of maples and lilac fills my nose, as does the summery, Mediterranean scent of lemon trees. Evergreens wall the garden, like elegant, emerald-clad ladies waiting for a dance at a ball.

I glance at Adam; both of us laugh as he pops the cork on the champagne and pours it into the two glasses he is holding. He begins to retell the moment he proposed to me in Kew Gardens and, as he does, I close my eyes and I feel like I'm back in that blissful moment, that the scent under my nose now is that of an English summer – lavender and jasmine, roses, not a Paris spring, and as he takes my hand now I feel like we're actually back in that moment where he convinced me of the happy future I'd never believed I deserved. I hear him telling me again that he'll look after me always, that he'll make me happier than I've ever thought possible, and as the sun warms my face and his words my heart, I remember how ardently I believed him. I believed that I had a chance to make the right choice and so, despite the fear that had encased my being for so long that I wasn't destined or deserving of a happy ending, I said yes.

As we lock eyes now and I'm pulled back into this moment, I tell myself again that I've done the right thing. I know Adam loves me and he's not going to leave me. He won't. I gaze around, taking in every inch of the beautiful hidden garden. Suddenly Adam is kissing my neck and as I turn and meet his lips with mine I feel myself letting go of the past and swirling towards a happy, sunny, floral oblivion – my future safe and secure in his hands.

Chapter 15

Bea Bishop has changed her relationship status to 'Single'.

The luxury apartment of 5, Canary Wharf Place feels alien when I walk in. It's a giant shiny spaceship of a building that doesn't resemble a home in any way, let alone mine for the past five years. I walk robotically through the communal entrance and towards the lifts, observing the shiny lockers and the modern paintings like I'm seeing them for the first time. Heart pounding, I glance at Demetri, the security guard, whom I catch staring at me, before quickly looking back at his computer screen without acknowledging me. Perhaps he doesn't recognise me wearing the grubby old T-shirt and gardening jeans I pulled on this morning. Or with my new short hair. I chopped it off in Loni's bathroom the night after my non-wedding. Loni stood behind me as I wept in front of the mirror and I could see she was fighting back tears too. I'd been growing my hair ever since I met Adam and the act of cutting it had felt like leaving him for a second time.

'Shhh, shhh,' Loni had said soothingly, as she'd brushed the tatty tendrils before gently tidying the ends with some proper hairdressing scissors so they fell in soft waves around my jaw. 'You've always been too beautiful to be hidden behind all that hair. This is much more you. You look like my girl again . . .'

And I do *feel* more like me. I haven't missed my wardrobe of suits, my rails of colour co-ordinated blouses and skirts, the high heels and the expensive jewellery that Adam loved to buy me. I glance down at my bare ring finger. OK, that's a lie. I have missed my engagement ring. I keep finding myself circling it with the thumb and forefinger of my right hand just to feel some pressure there. The air around it seems lighter too, colder, like that one finger has been relegated to a social Siberia by the other fingers.

Which is where I feel I've been for the past two weeks, too. I've barely spoken to anyone except Loni, Cal and Milly. She's persisted with me where all my other friends have gradually stopped ringing, texting or even sending me messages on Facebook.

'You have to take your life off pause and work out what to do next,' Milly said last night on the two-week anniversary of my non-wedding.

'I know, I know,' I'd said, staring blankly at some terrible early evening game show and pulling at a stray thread in my pyjamas as Loni delivered soup and sandwiches to my bed.

'And that means going back to the flat, collecting your stuff and moving in with me.'

'But I can't!' I'd protested, nearly spilling my soup in my horror.

'Of course you can!'

'I can't face Adam . . .'

'You don't have to. He's gone away for a while. So you need to get on a train tomorrow, go pick your stuff up and I will meet you a couple of hours later and bring you back to mine where you will stay indefinitely. That isn't a request, by the way. It's an order.'

'But-but . . . I can't just leave! What about——'

'I've already arranged it with Loni. You have to go back to work and sort yourself out. You can't take sick leave forever . . . you'll get the sack!'

'I'm a temp, Milly,' I'd reminded her. 'I *can't* be sacked. And besides, Nick has been very understanding. He said I could take as long as I need . . .'

'Of course he did, but what does he know? What you *actually* need is to get back on your feet again. And that is not going to happen hiding away at Loni's. You need a call to action, and as your best friend I'm making that call!'

The way she presented it I seemed to have no choice. So now I find myself facing up to the moment I have been dreading for weeks, setting foot back in my old life, my old flat.

The lift doors open and I am spat out onto the eighth floor. I'm in a vast, air-conditioned grey corridor with six doors, three on each side. They are steely grey with round studs and I realise now that they resemble prison doors. I put my key in the lock and open the door tentatively.

The flat itself feels cold and unfamiliar despite it being a bright, summery afternoon. It's hard to believe that it was only just over two weeks ago that I'd excitedly packed for my wedding day and honeymoon and waved goodbye to this place thinking I would come back as a different person – a *wife*. I gaze at the simple décor and expensive, functional furniture – all chosen by Adam long before I moved in. I can't see one thing that belongs to me. Not a candle, or a cushion, or a book. There are photos of Adam and me all over the place, but they look like those fake photos you get when you buy frames. Models posing, laughing, showing you what a perfect life you could lead.

As I carefully place my rucksack on the shiny, galvanised-zinc island unit, I acknowledge that this place has never felt like my home. From the moment I moved in I felt like a lodger in a life that didn't belong to me. Not through any fault of Adam's. He made me feel welcome and told me I could make any changes I liked. But everything had been done so perfectly, every corner and shelf filled, that I saw nowhere, no *way* that I could make an impression. Besides which, I remember feeling like every surface of the shiny, silver, space age-style kitchen was reflecting someone else back at me: someone prettier, more accomplished, more sure of herself. Someone like Adam's ex, Eliza Grey, with whom he originally moved into this flat.

I tried not to be paranoid, but the flat had her name all over it. Grey: fifty sodding shades of the stuff. In the lounge, the kitchen, the bathroom – even our bedroom was painted in various fashionable Farrow & Ball hues.

Looking around, I realise that there's only one place I've made an impact on here. One space I made a mark on in a way that Eliza never could.

I run up the architect-designed floating staircase, push open a heavy, fire exit door and step out onto the roof terrace.

And as I do I suddenly feel at home. I look down at what I'm wearing, the comfortable gardening clothes I left at Loni's when I moved to London, and I realise that I didn't leave the old me behind when I met Adam – not completely. I just kept her up here all this time.

I turn around slowly, taking in the glorious space that I lovingly designed, planted, tended, *curated* over the past five years until it became this beautiful haven. Every detail, every decision up here has been made by me – and with Adam and me in mind. There's the hardwood IPE decking I chose because I knew it would take on a silvery-grey tint and look both more natural and in keeping with the flat's interior. I'd thought about fake grass but I didn't want it to be twee or a pastiche of a garden, but a modern, fresh space that was a blend of both of us: as well as a mix of both the country and the city. I walk around it now, noticing with pride how I cleverly divided the overwhelmingly large space into four smaller, more intimate 'rooms'. At the front there's the 'lounge' with an outdoor corner sofa and a 'kitchen' with a built-in stone island unit complete with herb garden planters, and then the 'bedroom' and 'garden room' behind them. Gazing around, I remember how I made the internal screens from bamboo trees and espaliered fruit trees, adding pretty mood lighting designed to subtly give each space a moderately different atmosphere at night. In the 'garden room' I planted climbing roses and curled fairy lights around a pergola and the branches of some potted silver birch trees, giving the sense of a secret garden. In the 'bedroom', a modernist rocking hammock sits next to the outer steel boundary. A runway of soft, subtle uplights leads the way to it down the centre of the space. No tall planters or trees are on the boundary edge – just a border of lavender and echinacea to bring a calming, sleepy scent. I wanted us to be able to lie there with a glass of wine in our hands enjoying an uninterrupted view of the city.

I sigh with a mixture of satisfaction and sadness. This is where I made my mark; right here is my home.

Correction. *Was* my home.

Suddenly I feel overwhelmed by a longing to see Adam. I might have left him but I haven't stopped loving him. Not for a minute.

I head through the fire exit door, turning to say one last goodbye to my roof garden just as a gust of wind brushes through the branches of the trees, the scent of the May flowers – the early blooming roses and peonies – tickling my nose before being carried away. I will miss it. But not as much as I will miss the times I spent up here with Adam. I feel like the wind is already blowing my old memories away, carrying my old life with it.

I hurry down the staircase and back into the flat. The sooner I pack up my stuff and get out of here the better. But I find myself hunting for clues as to where Adam has gone. I pick up my rucksack from the island unit and go into the bedroom. The room is pristine, bed made perfectly, grey walls shining like brushed concrete, the wall of built-in wardrobes shut tight. The dressing table cleared of my make-up and toiletries and all packed into a box. Adam must have done it. With a lump in my throat, I open the wardrobe and start throwing my clothes and shoes into my bag. In a matter of minutes it's like I was never here at all.

I exit the room, not wanting to stay in there a moment longer than I have to. I had checked the pillow for a note, the mirror for a Post-it, but I found nothing. I did have a sneaky peek in his bedside drawer and notice with a sinking heart that his passport was gone. Milly told me just that he felt he had to get away for a bit. It's hard to imagine my strong, stoical Adam admitting that to anyone.

With my bulging rucksack on my back I head back out into the lounge and over to the desk. Maybe there's a hotel address left on a piece of paper by the phone, flight details, that sort of thing? But the cleaner has been, the computer is switched off and everything is spick and span. He hasn't left a single clue to where he's gone. I can't blame him for not wanting to be found after what I've done.

I double lock the front door and am just posting the keys through the letterbox when I hear the landline ring. The answerphone kicks in, and Adam's voice fills my ears. I close my eyes as I listen to him, partly to savour the memory of his voice, partly in shame.

'Hi,' he says in a deep, sad, resonant tone. 'This is Adam Hudson, I'm not here right now . . .'

I open my eyes. The recording used to say, 'This is Adam *and Bea. We're* not here right now . . .'

Looks like I have been erased already. Wiped out of his life with one press of a button.

'. . . but please leave your name and number,' Adam continues, 'and *I'll* get back to you as soon as *I* can.'

I'm about to leave when the beep cuts off. I recognise the shrill, clipped voice immediately.

'Adam. It's your mother, darling.' I press my ear closer to the door. 'I can't get hold of you on your mobile. Why have you not turned up for work this past week? Your father is fuming! The company needs you back immediately and George has threatened to *withdraw* the generous promotion to MD he offered you if you don't show up soon. I know you're upset about *her* but business goes on. Hopefully you're on your way to the New York office as planned. If so I'll let Eliza know and she can meet you at the airport and look after you. She's already offered to do *anything* she can. That girl has been a godsend to me the past couple of weeks, I don't know why you—'

The beep sounds, cutting her off mid-sentence, and I lean back against the door, trying to piece together what I've just heard.

Has Adam gone away to New York with Eliza? I turn around and lean my cheek against the hallway wall and close my eyes. I know this is all my doing, but it doesn't seem to matter to my heart that I left Adam or that I'm meant to not care. It still hurts.

I run down the corridor towards the lift and dart into it. Once I'm back on the ground floor I find myself running across the shiny floors, staring at my phone to see if Adam has updated his Facebook status to say something like: 'In New York With the

Girl I Should Have Proposed to'. I slip in my haste to get outside, not caring that Demetri must think that I've totally lost it. I feel a hand on my shoulder and as I look up I'm relieved to see Milly. Obediently, I allow her to lead me away from the building.

'Come on, Bea, let's get you back to mine,' Milly says, putting her arm round me. Suddenly I have a flashback to her saying the same thing seven years ago when she led me away from Loni's. I feel like I've gone back in time. And that's when it occurs to me.

'Maybe *that's* what I'm meant to do . . .' I mutter to myself.

'What?' Milly says, looking at me worriedly. Clearly talking to oneself is a sign of Another Breakdown. Something Milly, Cal and Loni have spent the past seven years anxiously looking out for.

'Go back!' I exclaim. 'I'm going to go back through my Facebook timeline, see all the things I did, the places I went to and paths I chose. But this time I'm going to do them all differently! Live an alternative life!'

'Ri-ght. How, exactly?' Milly says slowly like she's talking to a complete nut-job.

'Instead of relying on Adam I'm going to find a proper career, find my dad and also find . . .' I stop. I daren't tell Milly about Kieran. She'll go mad.

'Find what?' she presses, her dark, arched eyebrows pulled tightly together.

'Myself, of course!' She looks at me searchingly before holding out her arm to me again, but instead, I stride confidently ahead of her.

I'm taking the lead and making my own decisions now.

Chapter 16

Bea Hudson doesn't want to come home!
22 likes, 4 comments.

It's our last night in Paris and we have stumbled across a lovely little bistro in the heart of Montmartre to celebrate the end of our honeymoon.

'What a perfect week,' Adam says in satisfaction as he finishes the last of his gratin of crayfish tails and sits back in his chair. His face is illuminated in the candlelight, his dark stubble enhancing his prominent cheekbones, his eyes the colour of rain-soaked Paris streets. He looks so happy. I love that I've made him that way.

I nod. 'I wish it didn't have to end.' He leans forward and takes my hand.

'It doesn't have to, you know . . .' He smiles at me, the corners of his mouth turned up teasingly. He looks so sexy in his crisp white shirt, the top few buttons undone, hair artfully ruffled. Paris suits him, holidays suit him. He rubs his chin and his wedding ring glimmers. He stares at me and I see my husband, the

Adam I know and love, looking as he always does, handsome, together, strong – but also, more unusually, completely relaxed. I wish I could freeze time and keep him like this.

'Of course it does, Ad, holidays can't go on forever, no matter how much we want them to. Ugh,' I sigh, 'I'm *dreading* going back to temping. I don't know why but I don't think I can face flitting from one place to another any more . . . I want to be more . . .'

'Permanent?' Adam grins. 'I knew it, marriage has changed you already!'

'I was *going* to say fulfilled, inspired, challenged . . .'

'So do something else,' he says with a teasing smile. 'Jack in your job and do something you really love.'

'Ad, you know I'm not qualified for anything.'

'You've always wanted to be a garden designer – and you have real talent,' Adam says, leaning forward, his eyes sparkling with encouragement. 'Just look what you did with our roof terrace. Everyone always says how amazing it is and that you could be a professional.'

'Oh, I couldn't,' I protest bashfully.

'Why not?'

'I never finished my degree, for a start.'

'So go back to university! You don't have to be a temp for the rest of your life, Bea, you know I'd support you every step of the way.'

He always makes everything seem so easy.

'Look,' he says, taking my hands. 'I know not finishing your degree really knocked your confidence. I know you're scared of . . . you know . . .' He trails off. He's never sure how to refer to my 'blips'. I see him scrabbling around for an appropriate phrase. 'what happened to you . . .'

'My breakdowns,' I state firmly. He twizzles his wine glass, clearly discomfited by my choice of words. As hard as he tries,

Adam doesn't know how to refer to my 'lost' years. He says it upsets him to think of me so unhappy, so unable to cope with the stress and pressure of my A levels and then my degree. It's why he's always tried to make my life so easy, make decisions for me.

'But that won't happen again,' he says. 'You know I'll support you in anything you want to do.'

'I know, Ad. I just don't want to think about it right now, OK? I don't want to think about going back to London, or going back to work. I don't want to think about any big decisions I may have to make. I don't want to think abut anything other than being here now with you.' I close my eyes and take a deep, satisfied, yogic breath through my nose. Loni would be impressed. I open my eyes and see Adam has pulled something out from under the table. 'What's that?' I ask, peering at the sheet of paper he's holding up.

'It's our wedding in the "Celebrating" section of the *Tribunal*,' he says proudly. 'Mum faxed it to me. I thought if he saw it your dad might get in touch. I've even told the journalist at the paper to give out my details if a Len Bishop contacts them . . .'

I reach across the table and take his hand. 'It's so thoughtful of you, Adam, but I've decided the wedding was his last chance. I'm not interested in him now. I want it to be all about the future now – our future.'

Adam squeezes my hand and I smile at him.

'OK, well, as long as you're sure,' he says slowly. 'I just hate the idea of you always feeling there's something missing.' His jaw muscle flickers in frustration as he rubs his hand through his hair. It's so typical of Adam to try and fix everything. I think he feels guilty that he has never had to deal with big life problems himself, so he feels duty bound to solve everyone else's. Sometimes I wonder if that's what attracted him to me in the first place – he wanted to fix me.

'It *was* perfect because you were there, standing at the end of the aisle, looking so handsome in your morning suit and waiting for me so patiently . . .'

'*Very* patiently,' Adam points out with a sly wink.

'Even when I wiped out walking down the aisle! But it was worth the wait, right?'

He laughs into my lips before kissing me.

'Here's to our future, Mrs Hudson,' he says as we pull apart. 'I know it's going to be such a happy one.'

'Me too,' I say. And for the first time in my life I believe it.

Chapter 17

Bea Bishop feels like she's gone back in time ...

I tentatively lift the blackout blind, blinking as a bright shard of early morning sunshine pierces my eyes. I peer out of the spare-bedroom window – a room that used to be mine when Milly and I lived together – at the view of Greenwich Park, waiting until I hear the front door slam and I know that Milly and Jay have gone to work. I look at the pom-poms of blossom, the bright coats of spring leaves, and spot the Royal Observatory, just visible over the tops of the trees, up on the hill. I feel like I can almost see the famous Shepherd Gate twenty-four-hour clock. Part of me believes that the Observatory's time ball dropped the moment I ran away from my wedding, and since then I'm sure the hands have been slowly going into reverse, sending my life the same way.

Sighing, I lift my laptop from the floor, hop onto the bed and click open Facebook, typing Adam's name into the search box. My heart constricts as his face appears on my screen. It's a picture from *Campaign* when he first joined Hudson & Grey as Account Director five years ago. He's wearing a charcoal-grey suit and a crisp white shirt with the top button open and is looking directly into the camera. I lean my chin on my hand, staring at his dark hair that's been carefully styled. He's clean-shaven and looks every inch the successful businessman that 512 of his Facebook friends, family and colleagues know and love. But I know this isn't Adam. This serious 'suit' isn't the guy I woke up to every day for seven years who was tender and loving, who could make me roar with laughter, who would do naked karaoke for me on demand, who can't drink red wine because it brings him out in a rash, who makes amazing fish finger sandwiches. The guy who, when we met, acted like I was the most important thing in his life. The guy who always made me feel like, even if I didn't know where I was going, he could carry me to wherever I wanted to be.

I go into my message folder and open up a new message. I have an urge to write to Adam, to try and explain my actions better than I did at the church. He deserves that. I hate the thought that I have hurt him and I need to give him some clarity so that he is able to move on. I start typing, the words flowing as freely as my emotions.

Dear Adam
I don't expect you to reply to this message – I wouldn't be surprised if you immediately deleted it after what I've done. I just hope you can find it within yourself to read it because I want you to know, again, how sorry I am. That word seems so empty, doesn't it? Sorry. You can be sorry for bumping into someone, sorry for missing a phone call – but how can it possibly be enough to convey how I feel about destroying our relationship, our future?

From the moment we met, you made me happier than I ever

thought possible. Happier than I deserved. But that has always been the problem. I don't believe I deserve you. You are an amazing, loving, kind, thoughtful man. You are so together, so capable and you have always made me feel so safe, Adam, so loved. I loved being loved by you – and being looked after. You made me feel that nothing else mattered as long as I was with you. For seven wonderful years you made sure I never had to worry about a thing. But walking down that aisle I realised that it isn't right to piggy-back along someone else's well-plotted path. We get one life, Ad, one chance to get it right, and I've hidden behind you for too long. You made my present so perfect I haven't dealt with my past – or worked out who I want to be in the future. I know now that I need to take responsibility for who I am and who I want to be before I can give myself to anyone else.

I know I can't ask you to wait for me but I want you to know that I am better, stronger, happier than I could have been because I've been loved by you. And because of that, a piece of my heart will forever be yours.

Bea xx

I am sobbing as I press send. I don't know if I've done the right thing and I stare longingly at his picture for a moment more. I can't help but wonder what he's thinking. I wish he was on here more often, but his profile and status have stayed stubbornly the same ever since he changed his relationship status to 'Engaged' and wrote a status update that said, 'Bea Bishop finally said yes!' No macho pretence or crude jokes about putting a ring on it. The comments underneath are all so happy; from the people who love Adam. Who loved *us* together.

And then I click on my timeline. I scroll back, back, back, watching my life flash before my eyes, until finally I reach it.

17 September 2006

My very first update. I remember it because it was the week after
I'd moved in here. Milly had assured me that the social networking website was going to be the biggest thing to happen to
our generation. Obviously it took me ages to decide what the hell
to put as my very first status. After nearly an hour of ruminat-
ing, I'd typed:

Bea Bishop is ON.

Once I'd posted it, Milly had cracked up laughing because she
said it sounded like I was talking about my period. I tried to
delete it, but I couldn't work out how and Milly wouldn't do it
for me – she said it was too funny to change.

I met Adam that same night.

I look at my page with that first update and think of how the
date and the memory of meeting Adam and my being back in
this flat are all now inextricably entwined.

I start going through my status updates from then on. There
must be a clue here somewhere, some reason why Adam and I
weren't meant to be.

I look at the one the morning after I met him:

Bea Bishop has just had the best night ever – with *Milly Singh*.

There are three comments underneath:

**Milly Singh: I didn't fancy yours much. Tall, dark, handsome,
clever . . . *yeuch*.**
**Bea Bishop: And that's why we're best friends – we've always
had entirely different taste in men! Cute and quirky and cool**

**works for you. Speaking of which, when are you seeing Jay
again?**
Milly Singh: Now! ;-)

I still find it amazing that I'd even gone out that night at all. I
hadn't wanted to but despite my protestations Milly had dragged
me out to the Greenwich Tavern. The pub was opposite
Greenwich Park and had a cute little outdoor area where the walls
had been whitewashed and painted with brightly coloured tulips.

'It's not far, Bea. You have to get back out there sometime.
You're almost twenty-three years old. You can't hide away from
the world forever. It's not healthy . . .'

She'd promised me she wouldn't leave me, but had abandoned
me to go and get drinks from the bar. I'd sat there alone, trying
to keep my panic attack at bay, breathing through the dark
tunnel that I was trapped in, trying to tell myself that it was OK.
I could do this. I was in a pub, no big deal. But still the waves of
fear and nausea had come. I didn't deserve to be out, I told
myself. Not after what happened. What right did I have to be
building a new life now?

Despite my introspection, I noticed Adam immediately – it was
hard not to. It was a balmy September evening and he was wearing a short-sleeved white shirt that emphasised his coal-black hair.
He smoothed back the curls that were threatening to fall into his
eyes and I couldn't help but gaze at the tanned sinews of his arms,
momentarily blinded by his watch that glittered in the evening
sun. He looked up at me then and silver sparkles lit up his eyes as
he smiled a sweet, lopsided smile that belied his heroic good looks
and seemed to give me an insight into his soul. I looked away
immediately, heart pounding, pretending to busy myself by
searching through my bag. When I looked up he was standing by
my table. I found I could barely breathe. Let alone speak.

'Hi,' he said simply.

I didn't answer.

'Can I get you a—'

'I'm not interested,' I replied curtly, finding my voice at last.

He seemed taken aback before a wide, unapologetic smile had appeared on his face, a smile that turned into a laugh which somehow made me laugh too. But then I caught myself, clasped my hands together on the table primly and looked away.

At that moment Milly came back out from the bar, talking and laughing easily with a short male companion. He had messy ginger hair, dark rimmed glasses, was wearing a hoodie and jeans and they looked like the odd couple, what with her in her designer work suit and sleek dark hair.

'Bea! You have to hear this! I've just been saved by this *man* . . .' She purred the word and Jay blushed profusely '. . . from a fate worse than chat-up death . . . oh, *hello!*' She looked startled when she spotted Adam hovering over our table. She looked at me and then at him and then gave me this horribly obvious thumbs-up. Then she leaned forward and whispered, 'Bea Bishop is ON!' before introducing me to Jay.

'Bea meet Jay, Jay meet Bea. And who, may I ask, are you?' she said, turning to Adam.

'I can answer that,' Jay replied, putting his hands in his pockets and grinning. 'This is Adam, my annoyingly good-looking, successful best mate who overshadows everything I do, and who I resent horribly but who I need in my life because his insane good looks have been proven to have the power to redress the Curse of the Ginge.' Milly and I looked at each other and laughed and Jay continued self-effacingly, 'When I started hanging around with him, girls actually talked to *me*! It may have been to get close to him but I've never let him out of my sight since. Clever, eh?'

'I talked to you without seeing him,' Milly said.

Adam sat down on the bench next to me, nudging me. Milly and Jay struck up an intimate conversation that ruled out any involvement from Adam and I. It was like they had crossed over into a parallel universe where no one else existed but them. Working in the City and being as beautiful as she is, Milly has never been shy with men. But I'd never seen her so relaxed, so at ease with anyone like she was with Jay that night.

'Well, this is awkward,' Adam said. My skin prickled as his leg brushed mine.

'Mmm,' I replied. I took a sip of wine, turned my back on him and started searching through my bag again.

'Can I help at all?' Adam said. I looked at him quizzically. 'I mean, with what you're looking for,' he elaborated with a smile, and I remember I felt like I had just seen my future. A different future, far better than the one I'd been imagining for myself.

Because in that moment I'd been struck by this overwhelmingly intense feeling that, despite all my fears, all my promises to myself to never fall for anyone again, to not follow my heart, to shut myself off from hurt, to live a life where I took no risks, a life which required no decisions, I realised there was another, better, safer, happier option right here. I just needed the courage to cross the line, take the leap . . .

'It's fine,' I smiled shyly. 'I've just found it.' I held up a pen. But I wasn't talking about that.

He started talking to me then, easily and lightly, and I loved listening. He was honest, funny, not trying to impress me, just allowing me to get to know the real him. Slowly, gradually, I found myself opening up to him, not about my breakdown – or what had happened with Kieran – I didn't want to completely freak him out – just about how in the past year the direction I thought my life was going in had suddenly changed and brought me to London. A place I never thought I'd live.

'I love that you've been brave enough to do that,' he said admiringly when I'd finished talking. 'I've always known exactly what I'm doing, where I'm going next. What A levels to do, which uni to go to, who I'm – who I *was* going to date – it's like everything's been meticulously planned and plotted before I have a chance to form an opinion.' He looked downcast, wistful.

'Well, personally, I'd welcome such certainty in my life,' I said. 'I'd love to know exactly what was going to happen next.'

We gazed at each other and I felt like we were clutching the tail of the same comet. One that you only see once in a lifetime. Then, as if suddenly acutely aware of the poignancy of the moment, we downed our drinks and looked over at Milly and Jay who were deep in conversation, their heads close together, like acorns dangling from a branch. We turned to each other to comment on the fact that it was closing time and when we looked back a moment later we found them attached at the mouth and practically horizontal.

It hadn't surprised me. Once Milly knows what she wants she's always just gone for it. University, men, jobs, property. It takes her a split second to make an enormous life decision – but in that moment she's always assessed every single possibility, worked out what would be her best investment. It's why she's so incredible at her job. Whereas I've always held back until I'm absolutely sure.

Adam and I said an awkward goodbye with Adam asking if he could see me again to which I replied with an evasive 'Maybe' because I couldn't even decide on that. Even though I'd loved talking to him and had felt more myself in that couple of hours than I had for months. Even though I instinctively liked Adam and was attracted to him – perhaps more than I'd ever been to anyone before – something was holding me back. I just couldn't let go of my fears of what might happen if I made that jump.

My stomach rumbles and I reluctantly peel myself away from the computer and pad downstairs, the noise of my feet against stripped floorboards sounding in my head like the ticking and tocking of a clock. I make my way into the kitchen, open the fridge door and peer inside: there's a neat line of champagne bottles – but a lack of anything in the way of actual food. Nothing has changed. It was the same when we lived together. Milly was always too busy at work to food shop, and I had no real interest in eating. I pull out a curious combination of snacks: a tub of guacamole, some olives and some blue cheese. I find some crackers in her cupboard and piling everything up I grab a knife and plate out of the drawer and take it all upstairs.

I throw myself down on the bed, dip a cracker in the guacamole and take a bite as I scroll down to my next post. It was a week after our first date. Adam had taken me out for a picnic in the rose garden in Greenwich Park.

Bea Bishop has just had the best date ever.

I close my eyes as I allow myself to get lost in the memory of us playing Frisbee. Adam was showing off. I was positive he was jumping so high in order to show me flashes of tanned, toned stomach as his T-shirt rose with each stretch. I, however, was reminded of just why I'd opted out of any sport other than running. I remember how I'd thrown the Frisbee only for it to land in one of the trees.

'I'll get it,' he said, but I pushed him back.

'No way!' I said. 'I threw it and I am more than capable of climbing up there myself.'

'OK, if you insist.' Adam raised his eyebrows, a small smile curling at the corner of his lips as he made a queen's chair with his hands for me to stand on.

'Nearly got it!' I said as I put my foot on the next branch up. 'Just a teensy ... bit ... further.'

'Take your time,' Adam called from below. 'The view is great from here!'

I glanced down, wobbling precariously as I realised that the floaty skirt Milly had made me wear was revealing more than I'd intended.

'Cheeky!' I exclaimed, and laughed when he replied, 'Just what I was thinking!' I pulled the skirt around my thighs with one hand and then with one last stretch I grabbed the Frisbee, wobbling before falling backwards into his arms. I'd been breathless with anticipation as he'd bent his forehead to mine.

'I'm really bad at throwing,' I murmured.

'Maybe, but you're an incredible catch.'

He lowered me to the ground then, leaned me against the trunk of the tree and almost painfully slowly he moved his lips towards mine and kissed me softly. I remember how the branches of the tree had swept the floor, creating our own little secret cave; slants of summer sunshine were trickling through the branches making me feel like I was glowing on the outside as well as in. I decided it was a kiss happiness was made of. Funny how things change. I quickly scroll through to a later status update.

Bea Bishop is co-habiting!

I fast forward in my head to the moment I agreed to move in with Adam after we'd been seeing each other for two years. In the preceding months Adam had gone into overdrive, sending me emails every day of amazing apartments in beautiful spots in the city. He told me he'd buy our dream flat, anywhere I liked. He bombarded me with ridiculous ad-land-style images of how perfect living together could be: couples curled up barefoot on sofas laughing at something the other had said. He made me laugh by sending me silly poems, or links on YouTube to songs. 'You Gotta Move' by the Rolling Stones, 'Something in the Way She Moves' by the Beatles – and then, the moment I said yes was the night when, having learned all the lyrics to Lisa Stansfield's 'Live Together', he drunkenly sang it down the phone to me complete with 'oh yeahs' and a hilariously high-pitched 'sweet harmony'. How could a girl say no? In the end Adam didn't want to wait to find somewhere new, and I wasn't comfortable with him buying a place for the two of us when I couldn't contribute anything financially to the deposit or mortgage. For some reason moving in to his flat and paying bills felt less like I was a kept woman. It also felt less of a commitment. The only thing tied up in the place was me – and I could remove myself at any time.

I scroll through yet more status updates. All of them so happy, so full of love and fun. It's hard to believe I have ever been anything other than happy with Adam. But as I read on, I remember the feeling of dread that crept up on me as our relationship grew more serious. I knew Adam wanted to get married but I was petrified of being asked the question because I just didn't know the answer. I'd avoided big decisions for years by either not making them, or letting Loni, Cal or Milly make them for me. But this one would be solely on my shoulders and the truth was, I couldn't handle it. My view of marriage had been so coloured by my dad leaving – and by my own actions – that I couldn't contemplate saying yes to Adam. But equally I was worried that if I said no I'd lose him. So I tiptoed around talk of commitment. I made awkward, spiky jokes about marriage, laughing at bridezilla friends, constantly spouting terrible statistics about marriage and generally making it clear that I had no intention of ever getting married in the hope that it would put him off the idea of proposing. After all, that's hard enough for guys, but when there's a ninety-nine per cent chance they'll be turned down? No one would be mad enough to try it, right?

Wrong.

Adam's first proposal, six months after I moved in with him, was up on our roof terrace, the place I had poured hours of my time into creating, my home from home. He'd got down on one knee and asked me softly if I'd do him the honour of being his wife. I'd laughed and kissed him and told him that we were happy as we were, why ruin it? I'd given examples of Loni and Dad, friends of Adam's who had seemed to change drastically as soon as they'd got married, moaning at each other and nagging about petty things. I wanted things to be different for us, I said.

I didn't tell him the truth behind my rebuttal. That I couldn't handle the responsibility that comes with making a leap of faith like that. I couldn't risk what we had for the sake of an ill-judged adrenalin-fuelled risk. And most of all, I couldn't say yes to him when he didn't know everything there was to know about me.

I'm so absorbed by the thought of my painful secret that I don't hear Milly coming in.

'Oh Bea,' Milly says, before I can hide my laptop. I feel her hand on my shoulder. 'Not *again*.' She must have got back from work early. I glance down guiltily at the pyjamas I'm still wearing. Shit, I promised her I would get dressed today. Where has the time gone?

I can't have been sitting here for – oops – six hours? I look at my watch. It's 7.30 p.m. The last time I went downstairs was to make myself lunch.

I glance back at the laptop screen and quickly shut down Adam's profile.

'Remember what I said?' she chastises.

I nod sorrowfully. 'One week of moping,' she'd said when she brought me back to her flat ten days ago. 'I will allow one week of crying, obsessively looking at Facebook, checking your phone and beating yourself up for being so scared of being happy that you messed up your marriage before it began ...' I'd flinched. That had hurt. 'One week,' she'd continued briskly, flinging open the front door. 'Then the rules are that you pick yourself up, brush yourself down and get the hell on with getting on with your life.' She'd led me down to the vast basement kitchen, like I was a puppy on a lead, opened the fridge and extricated a bottle of wine. Grabbing two glasses from the sink she unscrewed the cap and poured a generous amount into each. She handed me one – taking my rucksack off my back first like I was a child who'd just got back from nursery school – and then helped me up onto the bar stool in front of the island unit and swung herself up onto the seat next to me. 'Then, you go back to work, you go out, you get drunk, you book a holiday, you have unsuitable sex with strangers – but at their place, *obviously* – if I don't know then I don't have to deal with lying to Adam. You have to pull yourself together, Bea. Start working out what you're going to do instead of obsessing about what's already happened. You're not going to find any answers on your Facebook timeline. Or Adam's,' she added pointedly. 'I know you've looked. I checked your internet history.'

'That's snooping!'

'No,' she'd said, with a brisk shake of her head. 'That's caring.'

'Oh Bea, this is crazy,' Milly says in exasperation now. 'You can't obsess about what-might-have-beens when you're the one that ran away from it all.' I gaze sorrowfully at the screen just as a red icon appears in my message box. Milly looks at me as I scrabble to open it.

'It's from Adam!' she gasps. 'But he swore he wasn't going to get in contact unless ...'

'... I contacted him first?' I murmur, opening up the message. 'I did, earlier.' My heart is pounding as I start quickly scrolling through the sentences, the black words crawling like ants in front of my eyes as I try to formulate them into meaning.

Dear Bea

Thanks for getting in touch. I understand why you left and if it helps you come to terms with it, I want you to know that in the last couple of weeks I've realised that you have done me a favour. I have a lot of stuff to work out too – and I couldn't do that when we were together. You've given me the push to reevaluate my life and work out what I want. You think I'm so great at making decisions? So in control? So why then, do I feel like everything in my life so far has been determined by my parents? Everything, that is, except you (and I couldn't even get that right). I still believe that we had ... have ... something special, but I'm beginning to realise that maybe it was a case of right person, wrong time. Perhaps our paths are destined to cross again one day, when we're older, wiser and more certain of what we want. Perhaps they won't. But promise me one thing, Bea. That you'll stop blaming yourself for everything; don't worry about the future, or focus too much on the past. Your choices don't change the world, just your universe. I hope you now feel free to shine like the star you are.

   Love always,
Adam x

'Wow,' Milly whistles, wiping her eyes as she finishes reading his message. 'Are you OK?'

I flop back on the bed and stare at the red time ball that is sitting on top of the octagon tower like a planet around which all of time revolves. It is one of the world's earliest time signals used by ships on the Thames and Londoners since 1833 and is still operating today. Each day at 12.55 the time ball rises halfway up its mast, at 12.58 it rises to the top. At 13.00 exactly the time ball drops, providing the signal to anyone who can see it.

I nod. Strangely I am. Adam is OK. His note has me even more certain that I made the right choice – for both of us. It doesn't mean it's not painful, but at least we're now free to move on.

'Doesn't it make you want to call him straight back and tell him you've made a terrible mistake?' she says desperately. 'You've assessed your assets, you want to go back on your merger, pop him back in your portfolio, hang on to his holdings . . .' When Milly's emotions are riding high she always talks trader.

I smile and grasp her hand. 'I'm not like you, Milly. You've always known where your life is going. I know Adam was the best thing that ever happened to me but I've made the right choice. I don't deserve him.'

'Oh Bea, that's just not true!' Milly wails. 'I wish I could help you see how wonderful you are! One thing is for sure though,' she says, 'you won't see it locked away in this room. Or on sodding Facebook . . .' she adds, flipping the laptop shut again. I notice she has slipped something on top of it.

'What's this?' I ask, furrowing my brow.

'I managed to get my hands on a ticket for the Chelsea Flower Show. It's this week, remember?' I nod slowly. I'd watched some of it on the TV last night, but I found it hard to focus on. 'Go Bea, get some space and fresh air,' Milly says encouragingly, patting my hand. 'Gardens always make you happy.'

I nod again. She's right, they do. I'm just not convinced that even they can work miracles right now. 'I need to find myself a place to live, not waste time moping around a load of gardens . . .'

'You know you can stay here as long as you like.'

'Oh Milly, I can't keep running back to you every time something in my life goes wrong.'

'Yes you can, it's what best friends are for,' Milly says emphatically, slipping her arm around me.

I lean my head against her shoulder and look out of the window. I don't know what I'd do without her.

Chapter 18

Bea Hudson: What do you call a temp that's just got back from honeymoon? A perm! I'm MARRIED – woohoo! (Have I mentioned that before?!)
37 likes, 7 comments.

I send my status update as I'm walking along the river from the DLR to Eagle Recruitment. The bright May sunshine is making the journey surprisingly joyful instead of the walk-the-plank trudge I imagined. Canary Wharf is looking beautiful – maybe not the kind of beauty that stirs my soul, like in Norfolk, but it has its own particular kind of majesty.

And right now there's nowhere I'd rather be than here. My future – my new life as Mrs Bea Hudson – is stretched gloriously out before me.

I'm really looking forward to seeing all my friends at Eagle's. I may not have ever worked there full-time, only popping in briefly here and there to pick up my pay slips and be briefed on my next temp positions, or covering for people's holidays and sick leave, like I am this week, but they've always made me feel like a real member of their team. I feel it's fitting that something monumental should happen here, too. I mean I've finally made my romantic life permanent, I'm married, I'm a *wife* now; this is no time to be weaving unrealistic dreams that something better might come along. That's why I've decided to take the recruitment job Nick's been offering me for so long. Which means I'll be helping *other* temps get placements. Helping them make decisions about *their* careers. Strange how suddenly it doesn't sound so ridiculous after all.

Just then my phone beeps and I look down, expecting it to be an alert on my Facebook app, but smile when I see it's a text from Adam.

Good luck today! I love you. Ad xx

I love that he's made such a sweet, thoughtful gesture when I know he doesn't really want me to commit to Eagle's. In fact, he tried to convince me again last night to have one last stab at garden design. He says it's because he can see that, no matter how positive I am about it, and how much I love the people, it doesn't make me happy.

'This job isn't you, it's the easy option,' he'd said yesterday afternoon, when I was laying out my 'Accepting a Job' outfit that I, *not* Milly, had chosen. I'd perched on tiptoe in my bare feet, holding a blouse and tailored City shorts in front of the mirror. It was an outfit that said, 'Chic, serious and certain.' He was right. It wasn't me at all.

'Maybe it's the me I want to be now,' I replied, surprised that he wasn't being as supportive as I'd hoped. 'I've thought it all through, Ad, and I'm sick of being stuck, not ever moving forward. I just want to get on with life now, and the quickest way for me to do that is at a company that knows me. And while I agree it may be the easy option, it isn't a *bad* option. I love the people at Eagle's, I'm comfortable there; I know the office and the job inside out. So instant promotion and a pay rise, as well as all the benefits if I should ever, you know . . . need time off.' I raised my eyebrow in what I thought was an endearingly enigmatic way. We'd talked about our desire to have a family on honeymoon. 'I could be a manager in a matter of months, Ad! I feel like I'm starting a whole new life now   and I just want to make you and your parents proud . . .'

'You already make me proud, Bea!' Adam replied.

I'd pulled my long hair into a chic up-do and turned my face to study it at every angle. 'But I'm a Hudson now, which means I have to be more ambitious, more driven, more determined to get to the top in my chosen career.'

'And you're telling me recruitment really is it?' Adam had said doubtfully.

I nodded and beamed brightly. Then I let go of my hair, slipped a pair of flip-flops on my feet and went up to the roof terrace where I spent the next two hours re-potting my sweet peas.

As I reach the riverside building where Eagle Recruitment's office is, it occurs to me that I'm no longer scared of the decisions that have paralysed me for so long. Adam, this job – they are my *choices* now. For the first time in eight years, I feel in control. I'm steering my life instead of endlessly drifting along waiting for things to change.

I take a deep breath to slow my heart rate, glance down and see my engagement ring and wedding ring sitting reassuringly on my finger. I roll my thumb over the curve of them and with a big smile on my face I step inside.

'She's HERE! BEA'S BACK, everyone!' Glenda sing-songs excitedly as I walk into the open-plan office and stand there laughing as they all gather around me. 'How's married life, petal?' She beams at me proudly and then opens her arms as if I'm her daughter.

'Wonderful, thanks, G.' I look over her shoulder at my window boxes as she envelops me in an enthusiastic hug and I feel a flush of pleasure. I love how safe I feel here.

James Purves – one of the senior consultants – steps forward and bows. I extricate myself from Glenda's embrace and take his proffered hand.

'Many congratulations, Miss Bishop!' he says, pumping my arm like I've just won a polo match.

'Thanks, Jeeves,' I grin, 'but it's Mrs Hudson now!'

'Oh-honch,' he snorts. 'Methinks the lady doth hath a twinkle in her eye!' James Purves – or Jeeves as we call him – is only in his late thirties but could be from another decade entirely.

Tim is standing by his desk, lifting hand weights and gazing at each bicep as he does so, but he lowers them to the floor in order to jubilantly emulate my wedding day fall. He picks himself up off the floor and cracks up laughing. Tim is the office 'joker'. A twenty-eight-year-old ex-City kid with an ego bigger than his biceps, he joined the company just over a year ago as Senior Recruitment Consultant. From what I know of him his life seems to work in the following order: gym, diet, women, work. But behind all his bravado he's just trying to make his mark in the world. He had to start his career again after he was made redundant in the credit crunch and due to bad financial decisions lost everything he'd worked for and had to move back home with his parents. Eagle's was his thirteenth interview and by then he had lost hope of ever finding work again. Luckily Nick, my old friend and boss, recognised his experience and desperation, plus the fact that his personality made him perfect for the world of recruitment. And Nick was right. We may tease Tim but I have a lot of respect for how he has been brave enough to start from scratch. And he says he's happier than he ever was in the City. I glance at him gazing at himself in the reflection of his computer. He's still incorrigibly vain though.

'Ah, thanks, Tim,' I say. 'Which reminds me, is it true you can't do an actual press-up, only the girly ones where you kneel on the floor?' I wink at Glenda and we watch as Tim immediately does a burpee squat and begins banging out push-ups, on clenched fists, while singing 'Don't Stop Me Now' by Queen. That should keep him busy for a while.

'Oh Bea!' Glenda says emphatically, cupping my cheeks with her soft, plump hands, hazel eyes shining with delight. 'What a wonderful wedding it was – and you made such a glorious bride. That husband of yours is *gorgeous*. He's just so naturally athletic, isn't he?' she adds loudly as she glances over at Tim. 'I mean,' Glenda goes on, raising her voice a little more, 'I bet Adam doesn't have to work out much to maintain a body like his, am I right?' Tim is now doing one-armed push-ups by the side of his desk, the other arm pointing at the ceiling, and we burst out laughing as he jumps up.

'What? What?' he says defensively, smoothing back a rogue piece of gelled hair. 'Nor do I! I'm naturally fit but it properly pumps me up between work calls!'

Laughing, I glance around, looking for Nick. And then I spot him, stepping out of his office, his hands thrust deep into his pockets like a schoolboy. He nods at me and grins. His thick brown hair is sticking up on end and his tie is skew-whiff. I wave at him and he gestures for me to come over to his office. I do my best to sashay across the floor in my high heels like a pro.

'So, you're back! I knew you couldn't keep away!' Nick smiles, gesturing to the seat on the other side of the desk. He switches on his posh coffee machine.

'One of the perks of being Manager,' he'd told me when it arrived six months ago.

He pops the brown capsule into the machine and a brown cappuccino cup under the spout. Everything in Eagle Recruitment is brown – except for the window boxes I planted. Nick has always said I bring colour to this place. The dreary interior has been a bone of contention for everyone who works here and when Glenda had asked – again – during a recent staff meeting why we couldn't redecorate, Nick had replied wearily, 'Brown is the colour of the bird of prey we're named after. Instead of moaning about it, try using it to inspire you to soar to ever rising heights!' I'd sniggered at this and he'd raised his eyebrow warningly at me, eyes twinkling. We get on so well because we joined Eagles on the same day, when he was still a young, hungry ex-film student who who needed to temp until he got his big break. He was desperate to write screenplays. He spent every spare moment jotting down ideas, watching and rewatching his favourite sci-fi films, taking writing classes. We used to go out for drinks after work and he would tell me his plans to move to LA when he was twenty-five. He told me it's what he was saving up for. But then, after two years, he was offered a permanent position with a good base salary. One that with his savings would enable him to get on the property ladder. He was torn, but always says maturity and common sense prevailed. He didn't want to live at home with his parents forever. He felt like he was living in the past: unable to move on, get a girlfriend or be taken seriously until he was independent. So he took the job, bought the flat, got promoted. As the years have passed he says the need for money and security has outweighed his desire to follow his dream. And so here he is. And here I am: I'm the only person here who has stuck around long enough to witness him rise (reluctantly) through the ranks to Manager of

Eagle Recruitment – and therefore the only person who knows how big his dreams had once been. The Nick I had first met had no ambition to work his way up. We'd bonded over the fact that both of us had chosen the path of least resistance. We were both happy living life in the middle lane. And both of us had kept our promise for a while, but then somewhere along the line we both *crossed* the line. Suddenly we had responsibilities on different sides of the fence. Me to another person, Nick to a team of people. We'd done what we said we wouldn't do. Settled.

'Face it, Bish. It's a misrepresentation of your job role to even call you a temp,' he says now. 'I don't know why you don't just bite the bullet and make this permanent. You can't live in limbo forever . . . just think, you could be like me!' he adds, stretching his arms out with an ironic smile on his face.

'I know, Nick. That's why I'm here.' He looks at me in surprise. I take a sip of scalding coffee and put down the cup quickly, crossing my legs and clasping my hands over my bare knees. 'I've thought a lot about my future whilst I've been on honeymoon and I've decided I would be honoured to accept your rolling offer of a permanent position.' I scroll through my brain, trying to memorise the speech I'd prepared. 'I've realised that Eagle's is the place I always feel free. Free to be myself, free to fly to career highs, free to . . .'

'Spout total bullshit?' he interrupts. 'Or should that be bird shit?' He grins, crossing his feet on his desk as he leans back in his chair. 'That's all very noble of you, Bea, but we're mates. You don't need to insult me with motivational speeches that are as bad as mine. It's enough that you're telling me that you've given up on anything better coming along and so have settled for this. It makes me feel less alone. Less of a total loser. And you know that goes no further than these four walls.' He removes his feet from his desk and gazes at me. 'I have to keep up the pretence of being a hot-shot manager somehow!'

'Then maybe you should get rid of that Chewbacca pencil behind your ear,' I point out, trying to suppress a smile.

Nick does so with a flourish, looking at the pencil before setting it down on the desk in front of him beside a mug that says 'I may not be the best, but I am the boss'.

'Welcome to the world of settling, Bish! May you be as ambivalent about this job as I am!'

I take his hand and grin at him, trying to ignore the thud that is the sound of my heart sinking to my feet.

As I sit down at my desk I click on my Facebook page, pulling a croissant out of its packet and taking a giant bite as I rap out my latest status update.

Bea Hudson is now PERMANENT.

I feel a little glow of warmth and security at being back. Yes, the office is damp due to the proximity of the river and draughty due to the lack of double glazing – a heady combo – and OK, the 'view' is of a rain-soaked alleyway, but with my window boxes and the lovely employees at Eagle's, this job is the closest thing I've had to feeling at home in my career. I open up hotmail and spot an email in there from Loni.

Darling Bea!
Hope you're settled back in and over the shock of being a WIFE. I can barely type that word, let alone think it! I mean, my daughter, a WIFE! I'd love to see you and Adam when you have a spare weekend. Cal and I miss you terribly. You're

welcome here whenever you like. The door is always open, even if the house is often full.

I love you.

L xx

I feel a wave of guilt. Not counting the wedding it has been weeks since Ad and I went back for a visit. *Months,* my turncoat memory points out. I swallow the lump of discomfort lodged in my throat; torn as ever between my two lives. The problem is when I go back home (no matter how long I'm away, or how old I get, it will *always* be home) I feel like I can hear things: not just the creaky croakiness of Loni's rambling cottage, but echoes of my past. It feels like every nook and cranny, every crack, every corner, every picture, every blade of grass in the beautiful garden is dragging me back to another time.

I shake my head. *I have moved on,* I tell myself. *I'm starting a Whole New Life. Marriage, career, maybe even babies soon!* I pause for a moment, distracted by the glow of the Facebook icon at the top of my home page.

It's probably Milly wanting to find out how my first day back is going, or Adam . . .

My mouth drops open as I begin to read, my eyes skimming across the screen, like stones over water.

Dear Bea

I hope you don't mind me sending you a message but I just had to get in touch. I haven't been able to stop thinking about you since I saw you . . . although if I'm truly honest I have never stopped thinking about you.

I know me turning up at your wedding must have been a shock for you. But I couldn't keep away any longer. I know it's been too long but I hadn't felt ready to see you; I knew it

would have brought back too many memories of that
summer, of Elliot. And part of me was always worried it'd be
too late. But when I was back in Norfolk and I heard about
the wedding it just felt like . . . fate. I had to see you, Bea. You
looked so beautiful, and yes, so incredibly happy.

I'm glad, really I am.

After the ceremony I went down to the beach. I just felt the
need to be there, you know? Take a step back into the past. I
wish you all the happiness in the world, Bea. I really do.

Kieran x

I gaze at the message, feeling the walls of the office closing
in on me. I feel like I'm drowning.

I look back at my computer screen and see the icon telling me
I have a friendship request. I open it and look at Kieran's picture,
at the face that I once loved so much until it all went so tragically
wrong. He's in a bar wearing some sort of uniform, grinning languidly and surrounded by people like he always was. People who
knew the twins used to say that Kieran and Elliot didn't go to the
party, the party came to them. They both had this charisma and
confidence, partly from always looking out for each other, and
partly because they felt free not to care what other people thought
of them. Elliot didn't seem to care about anything, in fact. He had
a harder edge than Kieran, an impenetrable wall, a bitterness that
made him mean sometimes. He could turn in an instant, especially
on me. I always knew he struggled to accept how serious Kieran
and I got so quickly. But he was also hilarious, the life and soul, a
joker always playing for laughs. Kieran walked the line better than
his twin. He was the oldest by two minutes, and those a hundred
and twenty seconds seem to have given him a maturity, a stability,
a sense of responsibility lacking in Elliot. But he could be restless,
too. From the moment I met him he made me feel that way too.

But not any more, I think angrily. Why is he dragging the past up now when I've pulled myself up and moved on? *I have moved on*, I think defiantly as I grip my desk.

I shut down Facebook, then I dutifully pick up the phone, ready to do some work.

Chapter 19

Bea Bishop is trying to get back on her feet again.

I glance around, suddenly overwhelmed by the bustling, excited people flooding past me and into the show and have to stop myself running back to Milly's flat and getting back under the duvet. I can do this, I tell myself. I've come to the Chelsea Flower Show every year since I moved to London. I may have given up on the dream of being a garden designer myself, but it has never stopped me appreciating the work and talent and vision, precision and dedication that go into making these prize-winning gardens. It's this time of year that I miss my dad the most. I know he would get it. If he hadn't left us I'm sure coming here would have been our annual father–daughter outing. A bonding moment no one could have taken away from us.

I pat my pocket and pull out the diary he left for me. It was on my first night back at Milly's that I found a suitcase in the small loft space hidden above the bathroom door. I remember leaving it there when I moved in with Adam because I wanted to take as little stuff as possible. Have a fresh start. Leave my past behind. Opening it had been like unlocking a giant box of memories. In there, underneath the plaid shirts, battered old jeans and the Monet garden prints from my teenage bedroom, was Dad's diary.

It was the one item in that suitcase I wasn't expecting, the one I thought I'd lost forever. I hadn't meant to put it there, you see. It was meant to come with me. Even though I knew every month off by heart as I'd read it so many times as a child. This diary had been every birthday and Christmas card I'd missed from Dad, it was my GCSE and A level congratulations when he wasn't there to give them. It was my shoulder to cry on when I needed support and guidance, my secret confidant and counsel when I had no one else to turn to. This diary was there through it all, including stuff I was too cowardly to tell Loni, Cal or Milly about . . .

This diary became another version of my dad. A dad who didn't walk out without a backwards glance, but instead stayed and taught me all about gardens, and life, in his own unique way. Whenever I opened it, I knew I could instantly be by his side, or he by mine. This diary was the reason I'd never lost hope that one day he would come back. It was why I couldn't properly forgive Loni for pushing him out, and it was why I had a connection to him that Cal just couldn't comprehend. This diary was everything to me. And when I lost it, I lost my dad all over again.

It was the day after my seventh birthday. I'd had the best day I could remember for a long time. I got a new bike and a wild-flower-spotting book and we'd gone to Holkham beach for a long walk; me and Dad dithering behind Loni and Cal who had raced ahead, as always. We were meandering slowly, pausing to study each plant and find it in my new book. I was savouring the moments with him as Dad had not been around much recently. Even when he still had his job as a History of Art lecturer he often went off on resource trips, or to some course, or just to find space and solitude to paint and study. But for the past year he'd not taught and even though he seemed to be at home more, it was like he was with us less and less. I can't explain it, but he just wasn't present. It was like he was always in another world. I'd learned when I was very young that the only way I could have his full attention was in the garden, but now he spent most of his time in the caravan at the bottom of the garden and when I went in to see him he would cover up whatever it was he was writing. When I told Loni she just brushed away my concerns. 'He just wants space to work, that's all, darling.' Then she'd instigated an epically riotous game of hide and seek. But as I lay in my hiding place under their bed, I knew there was something more serious going on. Dad *never* needed space from me. He said he was never happier than when he was with me and that I reminded him of everything that was good in the world. That's when I saw the small suitcase hidden under the headboard. I dragged myself towards it and unzipped it slowly, feeling my heart rate quicken out of fear that someone would discover me. I lifted the lid and peered inside. It was packed to the brim, pyjamas, socks, pants, Dad's washbag and a clear wallet that was full of family photographs.

I jumped as I heard Cal's squeals of delight and then anger at being found. As I heard him and Loni thundering towards the bedroom I zipped the case shut quickly and pushed it back under the bed and then hid behind a curtain with my arm deliberately sticking out so they wouldn't have to look anywhere else to find me. I pretended I no longer wanted to play after that and the game petered out. Cal went off to play Superheroes, Loni was doing some studying whilst making my birthday tea and I decided to make a card for Dad.

After tea, Dad led me into the garden; he said he had a special present to give me. It was, he said, a secret; a special little gift from him to me. He didn't want Cal to feel left out but he knew I was the only person who'd appreciate it. I unwrapped the gift, gasping when I saw the beautiful, palm-sized book with its soft blue lambskin cover and the gold-embossed letters that said 'Bea's Guide to Gardening and Life'. The pages were gilt-edged and featherweight and on the first page Dad had written a message accompanied by a pen-and-ink drawing of our horseshoe garden. And there, kneeling under the willow tree at the end of the garden, just in front of the gate that led back into the spinney, was a little girl, lost in thought, surrounded by a collection of garden tools.

'It's me!' I exclaimed and he nodded and kissed the top of my head. He told me to promise to read it on my own, after he'd gone. I'd thought he meant from the garden. A few days later I realised that he'd actually meant for good.

I flick to the front of my book now as I reread the words that were his final goodbye. Then I slip the book back in my pocket. I've always believed that the diary was his way of telling me that he would be back soon. Now I've found it again I've been slowly making my way through the pages, feeling a renewed sense of connection to him and an urgent need to rediscover the girl I used to be, and to know my dad as the man he is now.

I need to find him, I'd thought as I'd sat in the bathroom that day, slowly making my way through the pages, feeling my loss, longing and disappointment resurface. My wedding day had been my final deadline for him – and for me. If he didn't come, I'd told myself, I would give up. Part of me wonders if the reason I ran away that day was because I'd rather give up my own chance of happiness than give up on him. Do I think *he* deserves a second chance more than *I* do?

As I hand over my ticket and walk through the bull ring gate of the Royal Hospital, I feel like I'm walking in his shadow and that every step is taking me to Dad.

I spend a happy couple of hours looking at all the different categories of gardens on display. So many of them stop me in my tracks and I feel myself soaking up ideas for the future; floating trees, a grass-free lawn, ideas for small spaces on small budgets.

But there's one particular garden that has the biggest impact on me. It's simply called 'Time'. The garden has been split into four quarters: 'Day', 'Night', 'Past' and 'Future'. Down the centre is a line of *Heucherella* hybrid perennials, their glossy bronze leaves signifying the Greenwich meridian line. 'Night' features a suspended ceiling of star jasmine over a pond of water lilies: like a starlit sky reflected in water. 'Day' is a giant yellow burst of sunshine, with beautiful orange, yellow and white wildflowers. On the other side of the timeline, 'Past' is a formal, classic, Victorian-style garden with flowers cleverly planted in reclaimed vintage containers, such as a Victorian roll-top bath. 'Future' is an urban office terrace and features an iPad/herb bar. In the middle of the garden, holding all four quadrants together, is a large round hedge on a raised platform, the hedge acting as an oasis for hundreds of bright red cosmos – my birth flower. A weather vane is on the top just like the Royal Observatory's time ball. It is brilliant and beautiful. I stare at the garden for what feels like an eternity and then read the plaque that tells me all about the designer, James Fischer of JF Design, who is based in Greenwich. I want to Google him immediately and see what other work he's done. I feel like I have some creative connection to him somehow.

I drag myself away to explore the rest of the show feeling happier, more excited and more certain of the direction I want my life to go in than I have for weeks.

Chapter 20

The next morning I wake up early again, buzzing with newfound determination.

'You look happy. Good day yesterday, was it?' Milly says airily over breakfast. I know she's pretending not to appear too interested as she's learned I tend to shut down when she grills me.

I take another bite of toast and munch on it thoughtfully. 'It really was. Actually, going there helped me make another big decision about what I'm going to do with my life.'

'Oh?' Milly replies distractedly; she's staring at her phone, reading emails and scanning the headlines. Milly has always been incredibly driven. She says it's partly to do with her parents who are both doctors, partly to do with her Indian heritage and partly because she knew being successful was the only way to get out of Norfolk – and she'd wanted to do that from the first day I met her. She said she felt like an outsider there, like it wasn't her world.

'I'm going in today to tell Nick to take me off the books at Eagle's.' I look at Milly but she hasn't glanced up from her phone. 'I'm going to quit temping.' Again, nothing. Her silence is making me nervous. 'I know it's not the sensible thing to do,

Milly,' I add quickly before she can say it, 'I'm not a complete
idiot . . . it just feels like my only option, you know? I mean, like
you said, if I don't work out what is going to make me happy
then I've thrown everything away for nothing! And I can't do that
whilst I'm temping.'

She opens her mouth but I continue jabbering, desperate to
get my point across.

'I've thought about everything you're about to say to me,
Mills, honestly I have. And believe me, I haven't made the decision lightly. I know that it isn't the best time when I haven't got
anywhere to live and I've just walked away from a seven-year relationship but I just think it's now or never and—'

'Bea, ENOUGH!' Milly holds her hand up. 'Can I say what
I actually think? Please?'

I squeeze my eyes shut, preparing for a telling-off.

'Three words for you: Bloody Brilliant Idea!'

'Really?' I'm shocked. 'But don't you think I'm being irresponsible and completely . . . Aren't I taking a ridiculous risk?'
These are things I would have bet money on Milly saying.

'Yes, of course you are!' she replies, slipping her arm round me
and resting her head against mine. 'But if you want your life to
change so desperately it's the only option. It's something you should
have done a long time ago. Maybe then you would have seen that
Adam wasn't the problem in your life – but your lack of career, your
lack of self-worth is.' She leans over the unit and gives me a maternal kiss on the cheek, stealing a bit of toast as she does so. And with
that, she throws her bag over her shoulder and walks out.

As the door of Eagle Recruitment swings shut behind me I look
back one last time at the architecturally uninspiring building that
has been the centre of my so-called 'career' for the last seven
years. I've made lifelong friends in Nick and Glenda – and even

Jeeves and Tim. It hasn't been the perfect job by any stretch of the imagination, but it has been safe and comfortable.

I see my old colleagues gazing through the window, watching me as I walk away, and I turn quickly when I realise I'm about to cry. I swipe my fingers across my eyes and give myself a firm talking to as I walk along the river, my own bag thrown over my shoulder, my head held high.

I pull out my phone and do a quick status update, feeling a thrill at the knowledge that my life is taking a different direction. It's strange, because I don't feel scared, more invigorated, like I'm finally ready to take a risk.

Bea Bishop is so excited to be making the leap at last!!!!!

I carry on walking. Milly's is only a couple of miles from South Quays. I go over the bridge and through the shiny locale of Canary Wharf and West India Docks, past the Chinese floating restaurant and Millwall Football Club before taking the sloping, white-tiled foot tunnel under the Thames to Greenwich. I walk past the market – quiet on a weekday afternoon – and up the hill by Greenwich Park. Cal calls me on the way having seen my Facebook update. He sounds jubilant that I seem so well and so I spend ten minutes discussing all the things I could do, laughing when Cal suggests various ridiculous jobs, from Prime Minister to air traffic controller. 'Can you imagine,' he teases. 'Left – no, right? I don't know! Oh Bea, I'm happy you're happy,' he says. 'We've been so worried that you'll, well, you know—'

'I'm fine, Cal,' I interrupt. We have an unspoken pact not to talk about my illness. Cal saw me at my worst, and I sometimes wish I could turn back time and change that. 'I'm not that girl any more. Honestly. I'm starting a whole new life and I'm excited about it!'

We say goodbye just as I reach Milly's road. I open the front door, walk into the lounge and over to the big bay window that looks out over the park. From here I can see an endless stretch of green, lined with ancient sweet chestnut trees and criss-crossed with paths. In the distance the grey city peers superciliously at me and at the top of the hill and I can just make out the time ball and the black cross of the compass on top of the Royal Observatory's tower. I've felt drawn to it ever since I moved here. Like it is guiding me, helping me to make decisions, telling me what I should do, where I should be. As I look at it now, it seems to be saying 'so far, so good'.

June

Dear Bea

It's time to say goodbye to the cheerful (but often unpredictable) spring weather and welcome the glorious days of summer when, due to all the hard work you have put in during the preceding months, your well-tended garden really gathers momentum. This is the month where you must make time to stop and smell the wonderfully fragrant roses (and delphiniums, irises, honeysuckle and violas!). Rest assured that your past vigilance in pulling up old, stubborn weeds will allow beautiful new plants to develop and grow.

That said, there is lots of hard work still to be done, but it should feel like a pleasure rather than a chore on these warm summer days and evenings. Keep watering and weeding new plants, fill any gaps with summer bedding plants, remove fading blooms and remember to tie errant climbers firmly to supports or they will trail over other plants and make a mess of everything.

Take my advice and your garden is sure to grow into the perfect plot you've always dreamed of.

Love, Dad x

Chapter 21

Bea Bishop is spending these long summer days flat-hunting, career contemplating and soul-searching ...

It's a sunny Friday afternoon at the end of my first week of being unemployed. I gaze up at the forget-me-not blue sky and exhale in satisfaction. No longer cooped up in an office all day, I feel completely revitalised. It's amazing how liberating it feels to have nothing. I may have lost my fiancé, my job and my home, but I feel like I've gained something else. A chance to start again, live a different life. I know how lucky I am to have this chance – and with it the support of my family and best friend. I sometimes wonder what I've done to deserve it.

I've spent most of the time happily pottering around in Milly's garden, which she admits she's rather neglected. 'You know the only hedges I'm familiar with are financial ones!' she'd said, barely glancing up from her portfolio performance reports when I queried her about it. 'Feel free to do whatever you like out there though!'

Five blissful days pruning and dead-heading roses, tying in the clematis that had got rather out of control, forking over the borders and generally having a tidy-up. I've even planted some bedding plants that will flower for her by the beginning of September, giving a lovely second flush of bright technicolor to the garden – yellow sunflowers and fuchsia-pink zinnias. I've even popped in some cosmos. I like the idea of them flowering once I've moved on. It's like I'll be leaving behind a little piece of myself. With all this time on my hands, I can't help wondering where I'm going to end up next. I know I can't stay here forever, it's not fair on Milly and Jay. But it's strange because I just can't picture a place of my own. Instead I keep thinking, dreaming, about going home to Norfolk. I've been remembering how, before Kieran left, I was at my happiest there. I swore I'd never leave, that my heart was lost to the epic skies, the pretty villages and awe-inspiring coastline, not to mention Loni's garden. It is the place I have always felt closest to myself – and my dad.

I have a desperate urge to go back now. I keep telling myself it isn't that I want to see Kieran, but I've lost count of the amount of times I've looked at his Facebook profile, and his message. It doesn't help that Loni keeps pulling the umbilical cord, too.

'Why don't you come home for a bit?' she says every time she calls me. Which is every day at the moment. 'There's nothing keeping you in London now, is there, darling?' I haven't wanted to offend her by replying, 'Except my sanity.'

'So hop on a train and come and have some quality time with me!' she'd said last night. 'We can go for long walks on the beach, you can go for runs, meditate, you can even type up my latest manuscript for me!' I baulked at this. The last time I made the mistake of doing that for Loni she was writing *The Art of Finding Female Freedom in Your Forties and Fifties*. I'd been traumatised by the amount of sex in it. I'm not sure I've ever got over it.

'Oh *please,* darling, it would be such a joy to have you here!'

'I'll think about it, Loni,' I replied. It's strange because whilst usually I'd make up any manner of excuse to stay away, now I find myself genuinely wanting to go home. Am I just running away again – but this time from my problems here in London? Or am I running *to* something else. Some*one* else . . .

I down gardening tools and stand up, raising my arms to the sky and then bending over to ease my back. In that moment I decide to take a walk. I could do with stretching my legs, getting out, seeing some people, otherwise all I'll have talked to today is the flowers. And that isn't going to convince *anyone* that I'm not on the brink of another breakdown. I know everyone is waiting for me to tip over the edge. Milly asked me this morning if I was planning on hiding myself away here forever. 'I'm not hiding!' I tried to reassure her. She raised a dark arched eyebrow. She knows I have a history of hibernating when times are tough. 'I'm just . . . revitalising. It's not like before – I promise.' She hugged me then, holding me a moment longer than necessary. 'I'm OK, I promise. Please stop worrying.'

'Hey,' she said, affronted. 'I'll never stop worrying. I'm your best friend, remember? And I know you better than you know yourself.'

The sun is blazing in the sky as I walk down Greenwich Church Street, past the arched entrance to the bustling market and the prettily painted shops and on towards the DLR station. I can just see the mast of the *Cutty Sark* glimmering like a beacon as the sun hits it. I feel a connection with this historical clipper, her ropes and thin rigging woven like an intricate cobweb, a cat's cradle between the fingers of the three spiked masts that pierce the cobalt-blue sky. The mid-morning sun catches the diamond-patterned glass the hull is encased in, making it sparkle like a precious jewel. I walk around it slowly and it's like the present is fading away and the ship is being transformed into a working cargo ship. I imagine the sails flapping majestically in the ocean breeze on her maiden voyage to Shanghai. I'm reminded of Kieran as I stand here. Is it because of the naval uniform he's wearing in his Facebook profile picture; or is it that my subconscious knows he's a ship that's sailed and I should just stop thinking of him? I push him out of my mind (again) and start walking back down Church Street, so deep in thought that I don't look up as I step into the road. I gasp as I see a bus heading straight towards me. The driver honks at me and I leap back onto the pavement, my heart pounding as an image of the sign emblazoned on the side of the bus freezes in front of my eyes.

It's a giant advert for Greenwich University that says 'Join us today!' with a picture of laughing students. I whip my head round, watching the bus as it disappears around the bend. Then I feel my legs buckle and I sit down on a bench, my legs shaking uncontrollably as I hear Loni's voice in my head: *We always get shown the right path if we wait long enough, darling.*

I think of the UCAS form I filled in all those years ago, the one that had Greenwich as my first choice, until I changed my mind at the last moment and chose UEA because I didn't feel strong enough to leave home. Milly had told me not to be silly, that I *must* move in with her, but I said no quite firmly. I think she was as surprised as I was. She said I was making a mistake, and she was right.

But now an exciting thought occurs to me. What if I can go back and do it differently now? Finish my abandoned Garden Design degree, but this time in Greenwich, where maybe I should have done it in the first place? Then I wouldn't have met Kieran, I wouldn't have had that crazy summer, I would have finished my degree, maybe I would still have met Adam. And maybe, just maybe, I'd have actually married him because I wouldn't have had the same past, there wouldn't have been a Kieran to ruin every-thing. Because I'm starting to think that perhaps Adam and I weren't the problem: what happened before we met was.

I get up finally, my legs still shaking as I continue to walk, keep-ing my mind firmly fixed on that Garden Design course. I still have all my work zipped up in my portfolio folder at home. I could get Loni to post it to me and then send it all with my application. It's June now, maybe I could still apply to do just the third year of the course! Get a job to tide me over in the meantime, assist a garden designer or do something connected to garden design. After all, I may not have finished my degree but I have never stopped learning. I've read every book, watched every TV programme, been to every garden show. And I haven't stopped gardening either. When spring came, and after months of not leaving my room after Kieran left, I began caring for Loni's sprawling, unloved garden. Slowly, but surely I pulled up the weeds, untangled the climbers, cleared the beds, replanting and repotting until it was beautiful again. I brought it back to life, and it did the same for me. Then I transformed Milly's garden when I first moved in with her. And of course, the roof terrace at Adam's flat.

Being a garden designer is the only thing I've ever truly known would make me happy. I just stopped *believing* that I deserved to be.

I think of something Dad once said to me when I first showed an interest in gardening. I must have only been about four and I was helping him plant the strawberry and tomato plants in our veg patch.

You don't become a gardener, Bea; you're born one.

This is who I am and the sooner I accept that the better.

I feel something inside me stir, a long-forgotten feeling of certainty. I look up and see that I've stopped in front of a florist's on Greenwich Church Street. It's a slim, Victorian, red-brick building, unpainted, unlike many of the other shops, and I'm surprised that I've never noticed it before. But it has a pretty blue awning, and old-fashioned lead windows that have little glass baubles suspended from pieces of invisible thread in an arc. Each one has a single orchid inside, cut up to the petals and together they look like the path of a shooting star. Outside there are wrought-iron tables covered with pots of pretty sweet peas and lilac, small wooden stepladders displaying buckets of glorious hydrangeas, fat pink peonies and delicate roses, as well as vintage crates filled with shrubs and flowering plants. Above the awning is a sign with 'Cosmos Flowers' painted in pink lettering and surrounded by silver stars. I've seen that logo before somewhere. I think for a moment – it was on my wedding day! My bouquet and the buttonholes Milly picked up came in a crate with that painted on the side – but I've definitely never been to this shop before. It must have opened recently.

The door is open and I wander in, gasping at the delightful space with exposed brickwork and a ceiling hung with star jasmine and fairy lights that glimmer and twinkle in the space. I find myself drawn to the shop in the same way that I have always been drawn to gardens.

'Can I help you?' A girl comes to the counter from the back of the shop. She's wearing green gardening gloves and carrying a bouquet of peonies in a bucket. She's the definition of the word blooming: her face is blushed pink like a rose, her eyes are a stark delphinium blue against the thick black of her mascara, her hair is bleached the colour of daffodils and is scraped up into a bun as plump as the peonies she's holding, whilst tendrils fall around her face like catkins. She is stalk thin too, yet, when she steps out from behind the counter, a budding pregnant belly appears. She looks down at it and then back at me, her mouth curled into a rueful smile.

'I know it looks like I've just stuck a sodding football up there but I promise you it's a real baby. You wouldn't believe how many people said to me that I'd get some proper boobs now I'm up the duff!' She looks down dejectedly. 'So far, nada. Just *massive* nipples.' She gasps and flings her hand over her mouth. 'Too much information, right?'

I laugh and wrinkle my nose as I nod.

'Sorry,' she groans. 'This pregnancy has given me TMI Tourette's. I'll be telling you about my piles next!' I cough awkwardly and look around. That really *is* TMI.

'*Anyways,*' she says, without a hint of embarrassment, 'what can I do for you? I'm Sal, by the way.' She points at a badge on her chest and smiles.

'Bea,' I reply. 'Bea Bishop. Pleased to meet you.'

I glance around in delight. The shop smells so wonderful, of endless summer days and just . . . greenness. Permeating the air is the distinctive smell of hydrangeas and peonies and the intoxicating scent of sweet peas, roses and lavender.

I realise that I came in not intending to buy anything but now I'm here I want to get a gift for Milly to thank her for everything she's done for me.

'I'd like a bouquet of flowers, please.'

'I'd gathered that much,' she grins. 'Is it for a friend or a boyfriend?'

'My best friend,' I reply. 'She's been really good to me recently. I've moved in with her temporarily while I'm job-hunting.'

'Price range?'

'For my job?' I'm a bit taken aback. It's a personal question from someone I've just met. But she does seem very upfront.

'No! The bouquet!' Sal throws her head back and laughs.

'Oh, sorry, of course! Um, not too much, given I've just jacked in my job so . . . I don't know, £30?'

'OK, we should be able to do something lovely for that,' she says, clapping her hands and then resting them on her baby bump. 'If it's for a friend maybe you could start with a couple of stems of—'

'Actually I already know what I want!' I interrupt. 'Can I have some gladioli, please, and some purple irises and ooh a couple of these king protea?' Sal starts pulling out the stems and collects them in her hands as I direct her. 'If you could trim them, add some nice greenery, and maybe surround the protea with some softer flowers, that would be great.' I point at a bucket of long-stemmed flowers. 'These alstroemeria would be perfect.'

'Wow, you do know what you want!' Sal says admiringly as she plucks stems from buckets.

I laugh at the irony of what she's just said. 'Trust me, you're the first person who's ever said that to me.'

'You said you'd just left your job, right?' she asks, glancing back at me over her shoulder. 'What did you do?'

'Oh, I was just a temp,' I reply, embarrassed.

'And you left because . . .?'

'I want to do something I love,' I say with a newfound assurance. 'I'm thinking about going back to university to study garden design,' I add shyly, marvelling how saying it out loud makes it feel more real. 'I started a Garden Design degree years ago but unfortunately I left before the final year . . .' I trail off, not wanting to go into detail about why.

'I thought you seemed more knowledgeable than our average customer!' Sal exclaims, snapping her fingers and pointing at me.

I shrug modestly. 'I'm not *that* knowledgeable, I just know my best friend. And you should always choose bouquets that most closely represent the person you're giving them to, don't you think?' Sal nods emphatically. 'And gladioli shows strength of character and faithfulness and that just sums Milly up. King protea,' I continue, 'because it represents courage and resourcefulness. And alstroemeria signifies friendship.'

Sal stares at me for a moment and then frowns. She folds her arms over her bump and studies me. 'Are you one of those mystery shoppers?'

I laugh and shake my head.

She goes behind the counter and gets her scissors, still studying me suspiciously as she begins to arrange the flowers I've chosen.

'So are you local? I've not seen you here before . . .'

'No, well, yes, well not really,' I stammer. 'I mean, I used to live in Greenwich, years ago . . . and I've, well, I've moved back recently. I'm not sure how long for though . . . maybe forever, maybe not.'

'Not so decisive now,' Sal grins, deftly stripping off leaves. She pauses and looks at the bouquet before her. 'I'm going to add some eucalyptus to give the bouquet some extra girth.' She looks up at me and winks. 'And for you, there's no extra charge.' She grabs a generous amount and then begins winding twine around the bottom of the bouquet. 'That'll be £30, please,' she says, handing it to me.

'That looks amazing – thank you!' I exclaim, taking the flowers. I hand her the cash, feeling an unfamiliar sickness that comes with spending money now I don't have an income. Or Adam.

'Well, bye,' I say, feeling strangely sad to leave the shop.

'Hang on, Bea!' she calls out.

I turn back. 'Yes?'

'You don't fancy a cuppa, do you?' she says, a hint of desperation in her voice. 'It's very quiet today and well, this may sound a bit freaky-stalkerish and I totally understand if you want to leg it from the heavily pregnant, oversharing flower-shop owner, but I have a little job proposition for you, if you're interested . . .'

Chapter 22

I walk – no, I practically skip – to Milly's, feeling like life has just handed me a big unexpected chance – as surprising and beautiful as any bouquet of flowers.

'I need someone to help me out part-time until I have this baby, and then cover the management position full-time while I'm on maternity leave,' Sal had explained when we'd settled down with our tea in the shop's little back courtyard. I couldn't believe it when she told me that she's not just having a baby on her own – apparently she split from the father of her baby because he didn't want her to have it – but she's running her own business too. I'm utterly in awe of her. 'I was just wondering if, well, if you'd like to do it while you're waiting to start your garden design course? I'm desperate to hire someone but no one has had quite the right skills and then you came in and, well, it sounds crazy, but it feels like fate!'

It *did* sound crazy and I wouldn't have believed it if it hadn't just happened but, as I walk up the hill soaking up the delicate peachy-lemon late-afternoon sunshine, smiling at the pink and white blossom billowing in the summer breeze on the edge of Greenwich Park, my arms are filled with flowers and my thoughts are too. I'd tried to tell Sal that I wasn't qualified to do the job and that I didn't have any sort of certificate in floristry, or any training, but she'd just laughed.

'Bea, you've proved you know more about flowers in the last five minutes than most people that have worked here did in months! Besides, you don't need qualifications – I took on this failing business a year ago after doing loads of dead-end jobs. I had a bit of help from my dad to start with for the lease, but I've turned it around alone.' She'd stuck her chin in the air defiantly. 'None of my teachers seemed to see any potential in me, but just because I wasn't good at school didn't mean I wouldn't be good in business, so I trusted my instincts and proved them wrong. I've always been a people person and I've learned that in this trade all you need to do is to listen to and empathise with people.'

I shake my head and smile as I think about how she'd hugged me when I said yes to her proposition. *I have a job! And not just any job, a job that I'm actually going to enjoy! I can't WAIT to tell Milly!*

I also decide that it's time to start looking for somewhere of my own to live. The flower shop won't be paying much but I can always get an evening bar job or something. Meeting Sal has made me realise that I need to be independent. Loni was bringing up two kids alone by the time she was my age and Sal is embracing impending single parenthood without fear. I'm thirty – and I've been afraid of life for too long.

Sal and I had told each other our potted histories over the course of the afternoon – Sal popping in and out of the shop to serve customers in between me telling her my runaway-bride story. I even told her about Kieran. I don't know why but it was refreshing to say his name, to tell someone about him.

'Holy shit,' she said. 'It's so fucking romantic! I mean, your long-lost lover comes back to declare his undying love on your wedding day?' She sniffed and gazed down at her belly. 'The most romantic thing my ex ever did was offer to wear a condom, and he couldn't even get that right!' She grinned then, revealing dimples that reminded me just how young she was.

'So are you still in love with him?' she asked, taking a sip of tea.

I paused before shaking my head.

'Ahhh! You had to think about it then, didn't you! That means you think you might be. God, imagine getting back with your first love all these years later! Was he hot?'

I laughed and nodded.

'Is he still?'

I bit my lip shyly then nodded again.

'No middle-age spread or moustache, no grey hair, or worse, hair loss?'

I laughed again. 'No, I mean he definitely looked older, but it suited him . . .'

'Oh my God, you've totally thought about this, haven't you?'

I grinned, buoyed by her girlish enthusiasm. 'Only a teensy bit . . .' I admitted, holding my thumb and forefinger up.

After Sal had imagined a whole new future for me as Mrs Kieran Blake, she told me about the baby's dad, her 'sodding *useless* ex' (her words). 'He's not mature enough to deal with it, so good riddance to him. I'm going to make sure this baby has everything it needs. Besides,' she continued, 'I've got my dad to help me. He'll be a better male role model than my ex could ever be. He brought me up alone, so he knows what it's like.'

I'm still thinking about my chance meeting with Sal and the opportunity it has given me to take my life in a different direction as I unlock Milly's front door.

I look at the spare key she gave me and as I pull it out of the lock I make a decision.

I'm going to give Milly these flowers tonight, thank her and Jay enormously for putting up with me these past few weeks and then I'll tell her I'm moving out. I don't want to outstay my welcome when they've both been so kind. Like Sal I'm going to trust my instincts – and trust that fate will find me something quickly.

Chapter 23

'So, I actually have some news . . .' I say later that evening over dinner.

'Oh, that's funny, so do we.' Milly's eyes dart across to Jay who instinctively slides off his bar stool and takes his half-full plate over to the dishwasher.

'I'll . . . er . . .' he says, looking mildly panicked. A text message comes through on his phone. 'I'll just get this!' Relieved, he swiftly exits the room.

Adam, I presume.

'Shall I go first?' Milly and I say at the same time. We laugh awkwardly, unable to look at each other.

'Let me go first, I've been desperate to tell you this for ages,' Milly pleads. Calm, composed Milly looks uncharacteristically emotional. 'I'm . . . well, we're, that is, me and Jay . . .'

I smile. I'm sure she's going to tell me they're having a baby and I'm so happy for her. I am. I've just had this sense that she might be pregnant, I know she and Jay were talking about having a baby and things always happen quickly for Milly.

'I'm really happy for you, Mills,' I say brightly but she looks at me in confusion.

'I haven't told you my news yet!' she exclaims. 'The thing is, well, we're . . . moving to New York!'

'WHAT?' I stare at her, completely shell-shocked at this unexpected news.

Milly has always had her life planned meticulously. She doesn't like surprises, never has done. She's always plotted out her life perfectly. Marriage at twenty-seven, first baby at thirty-one, second at thirty-three. Retirement at fifty. I feel like the ground has been shaken beneath my feet. What will I do without Milly? I know I want to be independent, but I still need her. Especially now I've left Adam. How will I cope without *either* of my rocks?

'It's not forever. A year, maybe two.'

'B-but I thought you were settled here, you said you wanted to start trying for a family?'

'Well, I'm learning that, sometimes, plans have to . . . change. Not everything is as straightforward as you think. Life takes a different direction when you least expect it.' She glances away. 'Look, Bea, the truth is in Adam's absence George has promoted Jay to Group Managing Director in charge of overseeing the buy-out of a New York agency so Hudson & Grey can expand out there. It's a great opportunity for him and I have to support him right now . . . after all, one day he might be the main breadwinner.

'It doesn't have to, though, does it? I mean, you like the life you have!' I say vehemently. 'What about everything you have here, your career, your family, your friends . . .' I trail off without adding what I really want to say: *What about me?* 'What if . . . what if you hate New York? Your life has never had unexpected surprises or turns and that's good.'

She looks up at me. 'Is it?' she smiles. 'Sometimes I wonder if I've been so busy planning my life that I don't actually have time to live it. And New York's the most exciting city in the world.'

Milly gets up, walks over and puts her arm around me. I lean my head against her shoulder, trying not to cry.

'Exciting is overrated. What if you can't get another job and you're completely unfulfilled and miserable?' I'm clutching at straws and we both know it.

'Aren't you Little Miss Positive!' she teases. "I've already spoken to the other partners and it makes sense for me to transfer to our New York office and oversee the business out there. I'm just waiting for my visa to be approved. It's an adventure, Bea. Sometimes change is good. You should know that better than anyone ...' She gives me a squeeze. 'It won't be forever, I promise. Besides, you said yourself that you want to stand on your own two feet.'

'I do.' Those words again. 'I'll – I'll just miss you.'

'I'm sorry, Bea. I know it's bad timing. I feel awful ...'

'Hey, stop worrying about me,' I say shakily, getting up and clearing our plates so she can't see that I'm struggling to hold it together. 'I'm perfectly capable of looking after myself.' She doesn't need to answer for me to know that she doesn't believe me, and neither do I. 'And if you think about it,' I joke, as I walk towards the dishwasher, 'it's indirectly my fault that you're going. You might not have moved there if I had married Adam. He'd be doing that job, not Jay!'

She strides across the kitchen, takes the plates from my hands and stares meaningfully at me.

'You know what I think, Bea? I think sometimes things happen that are completely out of our control ... you can't do anything about it and no matter what you might have done differently, it might just have happened anyway.'

I wish I could believe that was true.

'I got a job today!' I say, wanting to change the subject, lift the mood. 'So I've decided I'm going to move out.'

'Oh no.' She shakes her head. 'Not on my watch.'

'You don't have to watch, remember?' I point out. 'You'll be in New York.' I swallow back the lump in my throat. Last time Milly left me to go to university I fell apart. What if it happens again?

'Exactly! I'll be in New York so you can flat-sit for us!' I gaze at her in disbelief and she stares at me from under her fringe like Cleopatra. 'Honestly, Bea, it would actually be really helping us out. We don't want to get strangers in, or get a letting agent to manage it, and we need to keep some sort of London base in case Jay or I need to come back for meetings. You'll be doing us a favour, keeping it occupied while we're gone. I've been planning on redecorating, smartening it up again so I can sell it at some point, buy somewhere bigger . . . and I thought perhaps you could help in return for living here rent-free? You know, spruce up the rooms with some paint over the next few months, and carry on doing the garden for me? It's already looking so much better, and it's going to be such a selling point. I'd be so grateful.'

Milly glances down and I know then that it's because she doesn't want me to know that she's trying to help me out. Part of me feels like I should say no out of principle. I mean I'm *meant* to be trying to be independent but I also know that what Milly is giving me here is a chance to make my new life everything I want it to be. Everything I've never felt I deserved.

And I *am* tempted. It means I can stay in Greenwich, work at the flower shop and save to go back to university. Once again, I feel like I've been given a second chance. How many people can say they get that? Elliot never had the chance to start over – thanks to me.

'Thank you,' I say to Milly as I hug her, forcing back my tears. She squeezes me tightly. 'Like I said, you'll be doing me a favour. I'll miss you though, Bea. You have no idea how much.'

'Me too, Mills,' I reply. 'Me too.'

July

Dear Bea

As I write this; our garden is awash with vibrant colour
and delicate scents. By the back door the flowers of the
morning glory with their distinctive heart-shaped
leaves and sky-blue petals come into full bloom in the
early morning. The sunflowers we planted together in
the veg patch turn their shining, golden heads to follow
the path of their namesake throughout the day. And, of
course, your favourites, the blooming honeysuckle and
sweet-smelling jasmine, cascade down the side of the
house. Ever since your mum told you that fairies love
to sip honeysuckle nectar you pluck some every day
after school and put it out for them on your doll's tea
set in the little dell at the bottom of the garden. Then
you sit amongst the foxgloves, phlox and hollyhocks,
your little tanned, grazed legs crossed, freckled nose
scrunched up in concentration , as you wait for these
magical beings to appear.

But while your thoughts may sometimes be away

with the fairies this month, don't forget to focus on the here and now. Sit outside, absorb the peace and stillness of the garden at the end of a busy day and there you will find new life blossoming before you. But beware the summer storm. When it happens (which it surely will) don't be afraid to go and dance in the rain.

Love, Dad x

Chapter 24

Bea Hudson is off to the in-laws for a Post-Honeymoon Luncheon (yes, that's its official title).

'Ad?' I call from our hallway, anxiously examining my appearance in the mirror and picking up my keys from the Danish console table. 'Are you ready yet? We don't want to be late.'

'Just a minute!' he calls back from the bedroom.

'OK! But don't be any longer,' I trill.

I'm trying not to get annoyed because we are still very much in the honeymoon period and I'm determined to prove to everyone, including myself, that we are going to have a blissfully happy marriage. And it *has* been perfect so far. Adam's surprised me several times by leaving work at a reasonable time, bringing home my favourite flowers – Cosmos, of course – and taking me on picnic dates. And I've cooked proper grown-up meals and served them on our fairy-lit roof terrace, where the scent of lavender and marjoram and honeysuckle accompanies our meals. Then we've lain in the hammock till late, drinking, laughing and talking under a canopy of sparkling stars and glittering lights from the city. I know being married shouldn't feel any different, but it does somehow. I feel like before, we were just two cut stems that had been put in the same glass vase. Now we are like plants that have been buried together so deep in the soil that they have become entwined at the roots.

So even though Ad only started getting ready ten minutes ago because he'd been caught up with a work call (on a Sunday) I didn't complain. And no doubt he will appear in minutes looking effortlessly sleek and handsome. Whereas I've spent two hours trying to make myself look acceptable and am now feeling like I need another shower thanks to this heat. It's not his fault that the thought of visiting his parents gets me so stressed.

I glance longingly out of the window. I wish we could be outside on a beautiful summer's day like this. Anything but spending an hour in the car in order to get to Adam's parents' Berkshire residence in time for our 'Luncheon'. And yes, it may be two months since we got back from Paris, but as George and Marion never tire of telling us, this is the first time they've been available. They are always busy, too busy for their only son, as far as I can tell. The only bright side of today is that, as bridesmaid and best man, Milly and Jay are also coming. I want to believe this is for our benefit, but I'm pretty sure it's because George knows that, with Adam and Jay both there, he can sneakily turn a family event into an unofficial work meeting.

I check my watch anxiously, wondering whether to call Adam again. Not in a nagging way, just a tiny little reminder that we need to, you know, go. Like, now. Marion is incredibly fastidious about appearance and style, not to mention manners and attitude. She takes pride in telling anyone who will listen that she has never dressed inappropriately, been late for an appointment, or left anything unattended. She is a minute-by-minute box ticker. She defines people as either go-getters – such as Adam's ex, Eliza – or 'wait-for-iters', such as me. It's never bothered me before but that was when she was just my boyfriend's mum. But now she's my *mother-in-law* and I realise she is going to be around *for the rest of my life* so I'm determined to find a way for us to get along.

I think I've started off pretty well too. I mean, I have a proper job now, and I've learned what not to say and do in her presence. From now on I will be the epitome of class and grace. I will still be me, but I will be a new and improved version. A more together, more grown-up, more go-getting Bea. More of a *Hudson*. Cool, calm, collected and . . . on time.

'ADAAAAAM!' I screech up the stairs. 'Come ON – we're going to be late!' I pause and clear my throat. 'Please?'

That isn't nagging. It isn't.

'OK, OK!' he laughs as he strides out of the bedroom and down the corridor as smart and cool as ever. He grabs his keys and wallet before giving me a kiss and then steps back to look at me.

'Wow. You look . . . different,' he says, raising a dark eyebrow, his mouth twitching at the corner.

'Is it too much?' I tilt my head and anxiously glance in the mirror at the floral pencil skirt I'm wearing with a white puff-sleeved silk blouse, a statement necklace and heels. I'm wearing my long hair up in a chignon – and I'm carrying one of the many horrible Stepford Wife designer handbags Marion has handed down to me over the years.

'No, it's nice!' Adam says, kissing my neck. 'Just not very . . . you. You know I prefer you in jeans and a T-shirt.' He starts untucking my blouse and I tap his hand away.

'It's for Marion's benefit though, not yours.' I smooth my hair in the mirror and try to ignore Adam's advances. 'I want to prove to her that I can be a perfect wife.'

'I'm pretty sure her idea of a perfect wife is very different from mine,' Adam murmurs, slipping his arms around my waist and then sliding them up and over my body.

'Control yourself,' I chastise playfully, batting his lips away and twizzling around. 'Or I'll be in trouble with Marion.'

'Just forget about my mum for now, you've been saying we haven't seen enough of each other recently . . .' Adam breathes. 'How about we do something about that right now . . .' And he unpeels my fingers from my bag, drops it on the floor and leads me back upstairs.

Two hours later, with slightly messier hair than I intended, we drive through the imposing electronic gates and up the enormously long driveway before pulling up in front of Adam's parents' Georgian mansion.

Milly and Jay's classic racing-green convertible Mini is here already and there are several other cars parked in the drive – which does not mean there are a lot of guests, by the way – George buys classic cars like most people buy new clothes.

Just then the front door swings open and Marion stands there in a wrap dress that somehow strikes the casual-chic balance that my outfit does not.

'*Finally!*' she says emphatically and throws her arms around Adam whilst I, sweating profusely, extricate the orchid I bought for her from the back seat and proffer it with a smile. Marion looks at me from over Adam's shoulder.

'My, my, you have got all dressed up for just a laid-back family Sunday lunch. Aren't you a little . . . hot?' She doesn't wait for me to answer, she simply turns to Adam and raises a thin, arched brow. 'You didn't tell her what I said, did you? That was just meant to be between you and me . . .'

'Mu-um,' he chides and shoots an apologetic look at me before she shoos him inside. He looks back at me from the hallway to check I'm OK and I nod. He blows me a kiss and heads towards the lounge where he knows George will be watching the cricket. Adam is always eager to spend as much time with his dad as he can in situations where he feels like a son, not an employee. It doesn't happen often.

I smile at Marion like a dutiful daughter-in-law, waiting to be embraced or at least made to feel welcome. Instead, she stands in the drive and appraises me, as if she's still considering whether to let me in or not.

'An orchid,' she says at last, finally taking the flower from my hand. 'How delightful! Is it from Tesco's?'

Tesco's? Surely she knows me well enough to realise I'm not likely to buy my flowers from a supermarket? I try hard to keep the smile on my face as I follow her into the vast chequered hallway, click-clacking self-consciously in my heels. Even though I've been here many times, I find myself examining the place again, like a tourist visiting a stately home. All over the walls and up the stairs are posters of the many famous ad campaigns George has run, as well as certificates of industry awards he's won and honours he's been given, and photographs of big social events he and Marion have gone to. I glance again over the photos of him receiving his knighthood from the Queen and his Ambassadorship of British Business. Every time I've been here it has astonished me that there isn't a single photo of Adam. I think of Loni's photos of Cal and me, in every room and hallway of her cottage almost like wallpaper. There are even a couple of photos of Dad – because she didn't want us to ever feel that we weren't allowed to think, or talk about him. And she didn't want us to forget what he looked like. But this home feels like an extension of George's office. I think of Adam's – I mean our – flat, the bare functional furniture, scarce photos and imposing 'work corner' that takes up a large portion of the lounge with a giant Mac screen almost as big as the flatscreen on the wall, the shelves full of books on brands and business – and no literature or fiction whatsoever. At times he seems so different from George, and then . . .

I walk into the lounge and am greeted by a wall of men staring at the plasma TV. Milly is perched comfortably on the arm of a chaise longue. She's wearing a loose, short, navy shift dress with tan sandals that somehow manage to make her look both more casual and more groomed than me.

'Bea!' she cries and envelops me in a hug. 'You're here!' she exclaims. Then whispers, 'Thank God.'

'Yes, here at last,' Marion adds with a laugh as she's followed into the room by a tray of Pimm's served by a member of staff.

'You look sensational,' Milly says and George turns round and acknowledges me with a wink. He's not an unattractive man. I can see where Adam got his looks from. But years of hard work and good living, eating in the best restaurants, the relentless socialising and drinking culture of the ad industry have definitely had an effect. He is red-cheeked, puffy-faced and out of shape – but he doesn't seem to see it.

'Hi, Mr Hudson,' I say.

'All right, Twinkle? You're looking an absolute sight for sore eyes, as usual.' George throws his arm around Adam's neck. 'I hope you're giving her what she needs, eh?'

'If you mean is he loving, honouring and obeying me, then he absolutely is!' I laugh. I know George can be intimidating, but luckily I've always felt able to handle him. Nevertheless, I grab a glass of Pimm's and down half of it. Something tells me I'm going to need it to get through this lunch.

What feels like an eternity later I fold my hands and rest them on the table as my dessert plate is cleared away. I sit back in my chair, looking around the stuffy, dark, wood-panelled dining room wishing that we'd been able to eat outside on such a glorious summer's day and wondering how much longer we'll have to stay.

I pull at the increasingly tight waistline on my skirt and fervently wish that I was wearing something looser like Milly. She looks amazing, I mean, she always does. But particularly so today. Her brown eyes are bright as buttons under her dark fringe, her dark olive skin is glowing.

'Well, isn't this nice,' George says, refilling every glass around the table and beaming at us all. George catches me looking at him and winks at me like he's a film star, not my father-in-law. I watch as he fills my glass to the brim. George doesn't seem to think any meal is successful unless half a dozen bottles of wine from his beloved cellar have been drunk.

Milly puts her hand over her glass just as he's about to pour, causing him to spill a little of the wine over the tablecloth. He curses and leans over her, dabbing at the red puddle. I try to ignore the fact that he is also trying to sneak a peek down the top of her dress. He's incorrigible.

'So,' Marion says officiously, her diamond-clad fingers clasped in front of her, 'there is actually a reason why we wanted you all to come here for lunch today.'

'To celebrate our very happy marriage?' Adam says and clinks glasses with me. Milly, Jay and George lean over to join in.

'Oh. Yes,' Marion says with a smile that doesn't seem to reach her eyes. 'Of *course* that, darling. But also, George has some other news, don't you . . .' She stares down the table at George who is mid-gulp of wine.

He looks around and stands up, wiping his mouth with his handkerchief as he does so. Adam leans back in his chair and crosses his leg over his knee. He looks intrigued, excited. Suddenly, I feel nervous.

'Obviously you're all aware that Hudson & Grey is at an exciting stage of expansion into the US and I recently led the
acquisition of an existing mid-sized agency in New York called
Friedman's . . .' George begins. Despite his alcohol intake he has
immediately gone into work mode, his red cheeks have faded,
his watery grey eyes have turned steely. In these moments I can
see the Adam in him. Both men are driven, determined gun-
slingers when it comes to making business decisions.

Everyone, except me, nods. I had no idea. I mean, Adam
might have mentioned some sort of US agency buy-out before
we went on honeymoon, but I was too caught up with the wedding and then going to Paris to take any notice. I feel a wave of
nausea, as though what George is about to tell us is going to fundamentally change the course of my and Adam's future.

'So,' he continues, 'you also know that Friedman's is big in the
New York advertising scene in a way that Hudson & Grey hasn't
ever managed to become. But I'm planning on changing that. In
acquiring Friedman's we are looking to branch into that exciting
market, bring some of their senior management onto our board,
and take some of our biggest London agency hitters out there to
ensure that Hudson, Grey & Friedman, as we will be known
from now on, will make a big splash Stateside. So . . .' He taps
his fingers on the table and I see Adam shift nervously in his
seat. 'I need to appoint some top-level positions that will lead
this next chapter in our agency's history.'

George turns to Adam, who is leaning forward eagerly, and
smiles benevolently at him. 'But who could possibly take us in
that direction, I asked myself. Who knows the company as well
as I do and would use their deep-rooted instinct to know exactly
what I want at all times, to second-guess me before I know what
I want? Do I know anyone with the hard Hudson drive, who will
work tirelessly, exhaustively to make this buy-out work? Who will

sacrifice their social life, their soul to take this company to the next level . . .'

He pauses to take a breath and I realise I'm hardly breathing. I'm at once imagining what will happen if Adam is promoted – and what will happen if he isn't. I'm not sure which would be worse.

'Adam, son, I'm promoting you to Group Managing Director, overseeing both London and New York during this transition!' George says. 'It will involve more work, more travel and more responsibility. You will be well rewarded, of course.' I look at Adam. He's happy. Of course he's happy. This recognition, this promotion, this kind of partnership and respect is what he's worked so hard for.

'Wow, Dad, I don't know what to say . . .' Adam gets up to hug George but at the same moment his dad leaves the table to get more wine. Adam looks lost for a moment, arms outstretched as he hovers uncertainly by George's chair. Then he sits back down in his seat next to me. When George comes back Adam tries again. 'I mean, I'm so glad you think I'm ready for this . . . I really want to prove to you that I'm worthy of—'

George cuts him off, holding up his hand and turning to Jay across the table. I can tell he's enjoying being the puppet-master at this lunch.

'As for you, my little gingery friend . . .'

I see Milly subtly clench her jaw. Her eyes flicker across at me and I know she's ready to hurl something at George. Milly does not find Adam's dad amusing. He's everything she hates about the type of people she has to deal with every day of her working life. And whilst *she* can handle being dismissed or patronised by yet another misogynistic man, she's super protective of Jay. He's more sensitive than she is and although he is brilliant at his job, famously winning the agency account after big pitch with his creative vision, he struggles to deal with George's old-fashioned, somewhat bullying management style. Sometimes I think Milly treats the people she loves the same way she does hedge funds; she spots potential, has a strategy to protect us from risk exposure, works out how to make us thrive in difficult economic climates. People like Jay and I need people like Milly who will drive us forward in our lives.

'. . . so,' George continues, 'I'm making you my new Executive Creative Director with a substantial pay rise and I'm doubling your hiring budget.'

Jay and Milly stare at each other in shock and George grins at them. 'Hire the best creative teams in to keep the London office on top. I want the awards shelf creaking by this time next year.'

Jay clears his throat and then coughs. I see Milly nudge him and then whisper something. When he doesn't speak, she does.

'The thing is, George, we actually have some news too,' Milly says briskly. 'As of next month I'm required to be in New York for an indefinite period. The sort of period of time that requires me moving out there.' My mouth drops open and I stare at Milly in disbelief. This is not how I expected to find out that my best friend is moving to a different city, a different *country*. She glances across at me and her soulful yet sharp dark eyes do their best to tell me she's sorry she didn't mention this major life-changing event before.

'An indefinite period? I don't understand. How does that affect you, or my business?' George directs this question back at Jay, ignoring Milly entirely.

'Well, sir,' Jay begins, pushing his glasses up his nose nervously.

'Because we're *married*,' Milly says, putting her glass down on the table. She takes a deep breath and glances at me as she delivers her next line. 'So if I have to move there, Jay does too.'

George grasps his wine glass and stares at her. 'Tell them no,' he shrugs at last and pours himself more wine. 'They'll soon find someone else.' Milly is staring at a mark on the tablecloth. I know she's trying to contain her annoyance as we're in his house. If this were a restaurant I dread to think what she would have said by now. 'Are you really going to let your wife's little job dictate the next step of your career, Jay?' George chuckles.

Milly visibly bristles, but then she just smiles as she puts her hand over Jay's and delivers her next line.

'I'm a partner in one of the biggest international asset management companies. Just to be clear, that means there *is* no one else. And besides, George,' she adds, 'my "little job" brings home more than double Jay's salary – including the pay rise you just offered.'

If I wasn't so upset at the idea of them moving, I'd cheer.

George's eyes widen a little and then he sits back and folds his arms as he appraises Milly with what appears to be admiration.

'Looks like we need to talk about this on Monday then, Jay.' He gestures at Adam to get up. 'Let's have some cognac in the library, son.' Adam pushes his chair out, glances apologetically at Jay and then follows George, who flings his arm round his shoulder as they walk out of the room.

Chapter 25

It's the Monday morning after the Sunday lunch from hell and I'm easing myself gently into the day with some Facebook action, having already wasted half an hour making tea and watering the window boxes by my brand-new permanent desk. I'm still trying to get my head around Milly leaving. She told me after we'd left Adam's parents' house that she could be in New York for as long as two years. Jay also told us he'd quit Hudson & Grey if they weren't able to offer him a new role out there.

'It's more important that I support Milly right now.' She and Jay had exchanged a glance and I'd presumed it was because he didn't want to slag off George in front of Adam.

I don't know why I feel so shaken up by their news, like I'm being abandoned all over again. It's ridiculous. I'm not twenty-two years old and on the verge of a breakdown any more. I don't need Milly's guidance. I can make good decisions on my own. I proved it when I married Adam. I'm a grown woman – a wife no less –with a life of my own and it's about time I stopped relying on her so much. But I can't shake this nagging feeling. Milly has always been the linchpin that holds my life together, and I'm scared that, without her, everything will fall apart. Just like it did last time. I don't understand why Milly feels the need to change the course of her life so drastically. Why can't things just stay the same?

'Bea!' Nick calls officiously as he strides across the office towards my new desk.

I jump a little and quickly flip my Facebook page shut. Nick may have been my friend before he was my boss but I want him to think I'm taking my new role seriously.

'Hi Nick!' I swing my brown swivel chair round quickly and cross my legs in what I think is a laid-back-but-in-control business pose. 'Do you want to touch base?'

Nick's lips twitch a little in amusement but I don't waiver in my seriousness. I'm determined to prove what a professional I am. So I smile a lot, say 'Sure, leave it with me' when I'm asked to do things and shout during staff meetings 'It's on my radar!', 'I'll have it to you by close of play!' and 'Team work makes the dream work' like I've heard the others do whilst inwardly wanting to shoot myself. It's like I'm on a mission to prove to everyone – including myself – that I can build a proper career. I can hit targets, make placements, go places. And I have been: in the last two months I've already placed enough candidates to hit the top of the target board – much to Tim's dismay. Nick keeps telling me how great I am, how perfectly I fit in and what an asset I am.

I pull at my tightly buttoned-up collar, suddenly feeling very claustrophobic, and smile at Nick as he hands me a piece of paper.

'Can you have a quick look at this, Bea,' he says, sitting awkwardly on the edge of my desk.

I throw a cursory glance over the piece of paper Nick has handed me.

'It's a new client who is looking to recruit an assistant to help him with a corporate project. It's not strictly our area, much more creative than our usual placements. Apparently we were recommended to him. Anyway, I think you're the perfect person to deal with it, given your background . . .' He smiles and puts his hands in his pockets, watching as I read the brief:

James Fischer Garden Design

Role: Temporary PA to the company director and head designer, James Fischer.

Term of employment: Six months. Start date: 1 September.

Job description: Working specifically on a large corporate garden design project based in Canary Wharf. The role is varied and includes general office and admin duties as well as assisting the head designer by contributing ideas, knowledge and old-fashioned get-your-hands-dirty-hard-work.

Requirements: Creative, self-starter graduate – preferably with background in garden design (but not essential). Passion for gardens a must.

'Are you OK, Hudson?' Nick asks. I know I've gone quiet, but I'm just focusing on swallowing back the aching disappointment and regret I feel as I read about what could have been my dream job. If only I'd made a different decision. 'Bea?' he repeats and I look up at him. 'I've given this to you because I know it's your area of expertise.' I look up hopefully. Maybe he realises this is my dream job and is giving me the chance to go for it. 'I mean, with your garden design and temping knowledge you're the perfect person to place this position!'

'Great!' I squeak.

'James wants a meeting to discuss his requirements in more detail and to look at initial candidates. Could you phone his office and organise a time some day this week?' As Nick walks away I place the job spec down on my desk, fold my hands over it and close my eyes so I don't have to look again at what could have been.

Tim's head peeks up over the desk. 'You OK, Bea?' he asks with a lopsided smile.

'Yep, good, thanks!' I lie. I keep rereading the brief of the garden design company position and mentally kicking myself. If life is all about timing, mine is definitely off. I feel like I've just been handed a golden ticket – and then been told to give it away.

Chapter 26

I'm sitting in the reception area of JF Design in Greenwich. I'm early because I want to look super professional and prepared but I'm trying to cover up the fact that I'm absolutely petrified. Since Nick gave me this contract to place I've pored over the company's website, looked at all its designs online and read up about James Fischer. He has won the Chelsea Flower Show Gold Medal two years running, and when I came across photos of his entry for this year, I couldn't believe it when I realised it was the same garden I'd considered my favourite when reading a piece about all the winners. This, for me now, is like meeting a pop star. I give myself a mental talking-to.

Let's keep this professional, Hudson! You need to impress him because you really want this job – I mean the commission from the placement.

I've already planned that Mr Fischer will spot me reading my notes when he walks in. But as the minutes pass, I find myself getting increasingly distracted. It is cool in here, the air con is on full blast as it is 30 degrees outside, but I feel stifled. My shirt buttons are too tight, this skirt too restrictive, the walls too close. My mind drifts away, taking me back to another time and place. I'm in Norfolk, a cloud-dappled sky above me, the smell of lavender and honeysuckle and jasmine under my nose. I see leafy pom-pom hedgerows along country lanes, scatterings of cowslips and dandelions bursting from patches of wild grass, fields of rape glistening after it's rained. I see climbing roses, fuchsia-pink achilleas lining borders, the delicate pincushion flowers of purple scabious at the bottom of Loni's garden. I have acres of space to think, to create. I'm in my element; there are no petty worries, there's none of the stressful hurrying that comes with city life. Then I find myself walking through endless fields along the coast with Loni and Cal, clambering over poppies and thistles, feeling the swish and swipe of long grass and heather against my bare legs, enjoying the warmth of the sun on my skin. They're laughing at me as I stop and study every single flower and bramble we pass, completely lost in my happy place . . .

'Bea Hudson?' a man's voice says. Startled, I jump up, simultaneously knocking over the water his receptionist had placed on the table next to me when I came in.

'Shit!' I exclaim, dabbing at the wet patch on the carpet. I look up at him and feel myself blush profusely. 'I'm so sorry, I didn't see you come in.'

'You looked like you were in another world.' He smiles and I relax a little. I note his friendly, open face, short dark hair that is closely cropped and flecked with silver. His nut-brown tan indicates a life spent outside. He's wearing jeans with a checked shirt tucked in that reveals a slight paunch – and that he doesn't seem entirely comfortable in. He pulls at his collar and I spot a gold wedding band glimmering on his finger as well as a leather necklace with a silver D hanging from it. Then he proffers his hand and I shake it nervously.

'I'm James Fischer. Very pleased to meet you, Bea.' We drop

hands and he gestures at the terrace outside. 'Listen, do you mind awfully if we go and grab a coffee outside? I don't think I can bear to be in here on a day like today.'

'That sounds like a wonderful idea,' I smile. 'I – I wasn't enjoying being inside much myself either.'

'I can't stand the city on days like this,' he says, strolling towards the door.

'It's so suffocating, isn't it?' I offer back conversationally as we walk along the river and head up to Café Rouge.

'That's exactly it! I'm afraid I'm a rather clichéd outdoor type,' he adds. 'Can't bear being inside too long, I feel as if it's sucking the life out of me. I'm sure it drives my staff – and my other half – mad. I literally have to leave the office every ten minutes just to get a breath of fresh air.' He leans forward and winks. 'Luckily I run the company so no one can complain *too* loudly. And my partner is a writer so he understands my prima donna-style creative urges.'

I smile in response, finding myself warming to him enormously. He pulls at his collar again.

'I probably shouldn't admit this but I was actually just daydreaming about my home county, Norfolk,' I admit shyly as we queue up for our coffees.

'I LOVE Norfolk!' James exclaims. 'I've been looking for a weekend place there for ages, in fact. I often think that there isn't a more beautiful spot in the world. And those sunsets!'

'I love them too,' I say. 'Along with the flowers in my mum's garden.'

'You sound like quite the gardening enthusiast,' James chuckles.

'Oh you know, in another life, perhaps,' I reply, opening my eyes as I suddenly remember where I am and what I'm meant to be doing.

'So, I understand you're looking for a personal assistant,' I say as we take a seat at a table outside, spreading my notes out in front of me. 'I'm presuming you are looking for outstanding organisational skills, proficiency in Excel, excellent time management skills, not to mention good communication skills . . .' I pause, confident I'm presenting him with exactly what he needs.

'Ye-es, I do require all that, this is a PA position after all. But anyone I employ has to have passion, enthusiasm and basically be an enormous garden geek, I think it creates good energy in the office. It's instinct I'm looking for.' He continues talking about his company for a while and he's so warm and dynamic, so enthusiastic about his new project that, once again, I find myself wishing I could rewind my life and go for this position.

He explains that a Soho-based media company has asked him to pitch for a project to design the 2,000 foot, 360 degree roof terrace at their new building near Canada Square in Canary Wharf, which they aim to be finished by March of next year.

'The best pitch will win the business. And the account could extend to their New York office, too. This could see JF Design go global! I don't yet have the funds to employ someone permanently, but, if we win the pitch . . . that could change.'

I smile politely as James tells me more – apart from who the company is.

'If I told you that, I'd have to kill you. Or at the very least, employ you.' He winks. 'I don't want to jinx it before we've even pitched for the project.'

It's like seeing a glimpse of my perfect life in a parallel world only visible through a kaleidoscope.

'So how long have you worked at Eagle Recruitment?' James asks.

'Oh, officially? Three months,' I reply. I never know how to answer this question.

'And unofficially?' he presses.

I blush. 'Seven years. I was a temp before I became a recruit-ment consultant.'

'The uncommitted type, eh?' he laughs. 'I was exactly the same at your age. Flitting from office job to office job, trying to make myself fit into the kind of career that everyone else thought I should have ...'

I'm panicking slightly that he has got the wrong – or should that be right – impression. 'I love my job, Mr Fischer,' I lie. 'I'm very passionate about it. In fact, I think I'm absolutely the *best possible person* – and indeed Eagle's is the *best company* – to find the perfect candidate for you.' I stop. Do I sound desperate, as if I'm begging? Oh God. I've majorly messed up here. I've been too relaxed, too pally. Nick is going to kill me if I lose this place-ment. The summer months are notoriously tough in the recruitment industry. Everything goes quiet until September and head office has given us unusually high targets this year.

I take another stab at clawing back credibility. 'In fact, as well as bringing you a selection of our best candidates I've also sent an email to the head of the Garden Design course at Greenwich University, asking for a list of their recent graduates. I'm expect-ing several recommendations. It's a very well-respected course, I know, because ... well, I just know.' I grasp the handle of my espresso cup when I realise I've talked myself into a corner. What was I trying to say? I know because I wanted to study there? Shut up, Hudson! You're placing the job, not applying for it!

'It is,' James smiles. 'I went there myself. I'm still a guest lec-turer in fact.'

'Oh, of – of course. That makes sense. I remember reading that on the biog attached to your Chelsea Flower Show garden.'

'Did you go?' James raises his eyebrows as he takes a sip of coffee.

'Not this year, ' I say sadly. 'I'd only just got back from honeymoon and couldn't take time off. But I saw it online.' I can't help but blurt out, 'I loved the way you created a contemporary garden that took inspiration from the past and the future. It was so clever and beautiful.'

'I wasn't wrong when I said you're an enthusiast!' James says with a laugh.

I waver for a moment, completely torn between spilling forth every single detail of my passion for gardening and staying true to the decision I've made.

Chapter 27

'You OK, pet?' Glenda says, appearing at my desk at the end of the day. I glance at the email of CVs I've put together for James. I promised I'd send a preliminary shortlist to him today, but I've spent all afternoon putting it off, instead composing an email in my head with a subject heading that says 'Re: PA Position – pick ME! ME! ME!'. I close my eyes and hit send. It feels like stabbing myself in the chest. I pick up my bag and start packing up my things.

'I'm OK, G.' I plant a big smile on my face as she stares in concern at me. 'You're looking lovely today,' I say, and she is, in a long, floral, pink-and-green dress with a matching pink cardigan and beads. I remember how when she first started she wore nothing but muted colours and old-fashioned tweeds. She said she'd always been too busy bringing up her boys and looking after her husband to think about herself.

'I'm going out,' she says shyly. 'On a date.'

'G! That's great!'

'I'm petrified,' she laughs. 'But there's no point sitting at home waiting for life to happen, you've got to get out there and grab it, right? I may be past my prime, pet, but I'm not dead yet!'

I gaze at her admiringly. Glenda's life has changed out of all recognition since her husband of twenty-five years died and she decided to go back to work. It's her first job since she had kids and she says it's given her a whole new lease of life. Nick has always been good at hiring what many people would consider 'outsiders'. I mean, what normal manager would hire a woman of almost fifty, with no experience, and then see her become one of the company's best consultants? Tim never thought he'd get another job after being made redundant from his banking job in the City. 'No one was employing guys like me,' he said. 'But Nick was willing to give me a chance, even though I was a complete knob in the interview ...' Jeeves – with his plummy voice and lack of academic qualifications – thought that no one would ever give him a job. And then there's me. With no degree, no decision-making skills and a history of depression, well, I'm practically unemployable. We're a rum mix, but Nick is obviously getting something right. Eagle's South Quay earns the most commission with the highest placement rates of all six City-based offices.

'You don't seem at all yourself,' Glenda says, resting her hand on my shoulder. I sigh and nod. 'Come on, tell Auntie Glenda all about it.'

'Oh, you know, I'm just feeling down because my best friend is moving to New York – this weekend is her leaving party,' I reply. It's the truth, sort of. I am feeling low about that.

'Oh, that's a shame, pet, but you can go and visit her, can't you?' Glenda says soothingly. Her accent never fails to calm me. When she talks I think of daffodils swaying in the breeze, their heads nodding like bells. 'And there's always Facebook!'

'It's not the same as living close by, though, is it?' I say and then I put my hand over my mouth as I realise what I've said. Glenda's sons live abroad – one in Australia and one in Canada – and she

is constantly resisting their demands to move over there, saying
she's too stuck in her ways. She also says having to constantly
save for the expensive flights gives her the incentive to earn more
commission. Nick is always good at giving her long holidays in
the summer. 'Oh I'm sorry, G, that was really insensitive of me ...'

'No no, not at all, pet. We've all got used to the distance.' She
leans forward and winks. 'No one wants their mum living on
their doorstep!'

I laugh and think of Loni. This is true. She would do my head
in if she lived too close. But I sometimes feel horribly far away
from her too.

'You miss them though, don't you, Glenda?' I ask. She looks
at me searchingly and then perches on the side of my desk. She's
told me she knew she had to do something different after her
husband died. Something just for her.

'Why, yes, of course, pet. All the time! But my boys, they're
grown-up, they have their own lives – and I need mine too. I put
it on hold for too long.'

'Do you regret that, then?'

Glenda looks out of the window and contemplates this for a
moment. 'Do you know what, pet, no I don't. I wanted to be a
full-time mum and I gave everything I had to those kids and my
marriage. Ewan and I had many wonderful years together, my
boys are happy and healthy and successful now and even though
Ewan is gone, my life isn't over. I've realised you can have many
lives within one life. There are many chances to start afresh.' I
look at her, trying to let this positive life view sink in.

'It just feels like whenever I make a choice a whole other life
is lost, you know? In moving away from one place, you also move
from your past. You take one job, you lose the chance of getting
another—' I stop when I realise I've been speaking my thoughts
aloud. 'Me and my navel-gazing! Sorry, G, just ignore me.'

She places a hand on my arm. 'You know, pet, if it helps at all, I don't think that the decisions you make necessarily close the door on a different future. I think that all paths lead to the same place in the end ...'

I want to believe her, I do. But Dad leaving and my summer with Kieran taught me that a single choice *can* change the course of someone's life forever. I give Glenda a kiss on the cheek in thanks and then I throw my bag over my shoulder and hurry towards the glass doors, suddenly feeling like I have a lot to think about.

Chapter 28

I'm lying in the hammock sipping wine and gazing at the city's constellation of lights, breathing in fragrant lavender as the balmy night air wraps me in its warmth. I've come up to our roof garden to think about what happened today. It's a place that always soothes me, helps me to get things in perspective. I wriggle up into a sitting position and look at my watch. Where's Adam? When he called at just gone 7 p.m. he said he was leaving the office and it's past 9 p.m. now. I know enough about Adam's industry to be sure that his delay is just due to some sort of account crisis. There's been a lot of them since he became Group Managing Director. My fears that this new promotion would mean less time for us together were not an exaggeration. I can't remember the last time he was home before 10 p.m. Weekends are now a blur of pitch meetings, Skypes to New York, occasional walks to get some fresh air before he has to write another presentation, or check in on yet more creative work. I've been trying to keep myself busy too – but my job is very much Monday to Friday, and Milly only has time for her move to New York these days. I realise my non-work life has always revolved entirely around Adam. I don't have any outside interests. I could go home to Norfolk, but the prospect of being there without him makes me feel anxious, like I could slip back into a bad place. I need Adam, probably more than is entirely healthy.

I feel Adam's presence before I see him, then he drops a kiss on my bare shoulder. I get the familiar buzz of electricity when he touches me and my brief annoyance melts away. His fingers brush the light material of the expensive new dress I bought with my new improved salary. I changed into it when I got home from work to remind myself of who I am and the life I have chosen.

'Are you OK?' Adam asks as we snuggle up on the couch in our lounge where we've retreated to after our (cold) dinner – and with a second bottle of wine. Candles are lit, soft music is playing and the grey blinds are open. Outside, the city seems to be pulsating with life; in here everything is . . . not flatlining . . . but it is ordered. Safe. Just how I like it, I tell myself. I nod, feeling satisfied, content, calm.

'Have you had a good day?' he says. 'I feel terrible that I haven't even asked.' We've spent the last hour or so talking about Adam's problems at work. He's told me how stressed he is because of the pressure his dad is putting on him. He said he's leaving on Sunday to go to New York for at least a week. 'The same day as Milly and Jay?' I'd replied, feeling my heart sink, and he'd nodded.

'It's a complete coincidence but I think we might even be on the same flight . . .' I forced myself not to panic, not to feel abandoned, like I'm being left – again – by the people I love. Adam's going to be staying in an apartment the agency has rented. He told me there is going to be a lot of toing and froing over the next few months but that he'd do his best to be with me as often as he could.

'I know it's not ideal,' he said apologetically. 'We should be spending as much time as we can together in our first year of marriage, but it won't be forever. And just think, with my pay rise we'll soon be able to afford to buy a house, maybe think about starting a family . . .'

'So what's been happening at work,' he says now. 'Any interesting contracts come up?'

'Oh you know,' I say, lifting my face up to his, 'same old same old.'

'Didn't you have a meeting with, you know . . . what's his name . . . the garden design guy?'

I nod, trying and failing to summon up a smile. 'James Fischer. Yep, I sent him a list of candidates and he's looking over them this weekend. So, you know – yay! Another bit of commission for me next week!' I raise my glass and take a long slug. Adam is looking at me strangely when I put my glass down. 'What?' I ask slightly defensively.

'Oh, I just thought, you know, you might be tempted to go for it yourself?' he says.

'Nope,' I reply briskly.

'Not even a bit?' Adam tilts his head and half smiles. 'Not one tiny little piece of you thought: I should consider talking to Nick about putting myself forward for it?'

I pick up my glass again and try not to respond too tetchily. 'No, what I *actually* thought was: I *would* have put myself forward for it . . . if I hadn't already decided to commit to Eagle's and make a proper career for myself.' I take another swig and look at Adam challengingly. 'Which I have, so . . .'

'But Nick is your friend and would understand that this is something you can't walk away from!'

I explain to him. 'I made a *decision*, Ad. Going back on my word would be like . . . it'd be like . . . retracting my wedding vows. You know: Oh sorry, Ad, here's your ring back, I'm afraid something better has come along!'

He shakes his head firmly. 'It wouldn't, Bea. It would be grabbing the chance you deserve. Opportunities like this don't come along every day – and they happen for a reason.' He takes my hand and squeezes it. 'To good people.'

I look at him longingly. I want to believe him so badly, but . . .

'If he hasn't already made a decision, change your mind. Talk to Nick. Arrange another meeting. Tell him how perfect you are for the job. Don't run away from this opportunity.'

I stare at Adam and can feel myself filling with not just resolve, but confidence. Adam always does this for me. His faith in me makes me feel able to do anything.

'You really think I can do it?'

He nods. 'I think you're *meant* to do it.'

August

Dear Bea

August is a time of transition. It provides the link between the secure days of summer and the onset of unpredictable autumn. Temperatures often remain high and inevitably some plants (and people) will show signs of stress. Often this is nothing that a holiday can't cure. But sometimes more drastic moves are required to ensure plants flourish.

No matter where I may be in the world and what beauty lies before me, I know I will always think of the majestic sight of the Norfolk coastline at this time of year. I'll only have to close my eyes to picture the purple halo of sea aster and lavender surrounding Holkham Bay, the spiky patches of shrubby sea-blite so characteristic of our coastline, and the bright yellow horned poppies, scarlet pimpernel and sea campion in full bloom. Norfolk will always be my home. And I will never forget it . . . or you.

Love, Dad x

Chapter 29

Bea Bishop is all over the shop!

'How are you getting on with those bouquets?' Sal calls from the shop front where she's getting all the buckets and displays ready for opening. I'm surrounded by stems, busily beribboning the last of the bouquets that are due to be delivered this morning.

'Just got one more to do!' I call.

It's amazing how I've settled into the swing of my new job. Sal has quickly given me more responsibility and I often arrive at the crack of dawn to receive and unpack nursery deliveries which then have to be conditioned, watered and arranged – or put in the refrigerator at the back of the shop. I print out the online orders that have come in overnight, jotting them down on our white board along with ideas to update floral plans and notes on any big events we're providing flowers for. Several corporate events companies in the area use us – as well as a local design company we have a close relationship with, not to mention catering companies and wedding planners who recommend our bridal bouquets and displays. So we're always busy, even when there are no customers in the shop.

I continue cutting back some yellow irises and thinking that, with her bright, bleached blonde hair and friendly, driven personality Sal's very much like this flower that symbolises passion. She loves her job and is brilliant at it. She attacks every single chore like she attacks the prospect of single motherhood, bravely and confidently and decisively. I think of Dad and how he used to explain to me in detail each flower, plant and shrub that grew in the garden, giving each one a story and a personality – and I remember my hunger to learn as much about them as possible. It's probably why I've always compared flowers to people. It's ironic that the only person I can't compare one to is Dad. Apart from the diary he's a stranger to me now. But I feel closer to him, doing this job, than I have for years. In unlocking my passion for plants and flowers after years of trying to do an office job, I've unlocked my memories of him too. It's starting to feel like fate that I found his diary and then this job.

I place my final bouquet carefully in a bucket of water and take my tea gratefully from Sal, who's on the phone to her dad. I stare at her for a moment as she tells him all her news. Maybe I find myself thinking of my dad more because Sal's is so present in her life. He rings her every day, no matter where he is. Sal said that he's been her rock ever since her mum died when she was fourteen. I can't imagine how hard that must have been for her. I mean, Dad leaving was tough but I was young and I had time to get used to it before I hit my teens. Plus, I always had someone to blame. Myself, mostly, Loni sometimes and, very occasionally, Dad too. But who can you blame when someone dies? I clutch the counter, feeling my legs weaken as an image of Kieran walking away from me, pushing his way through hospital doors and then disappearing into the black, black night, comes into my mind. I can't stop it, just like I couldn't stop his brother Elliot from jumping – or drowning.

The doorbell tinkles and I wipe my eyes on my pink apron and try to compose myself.

'Sal?' I call out, hoping that she can go. But she doesn't answer. I take three deep breaths before walking out into the shop with a welcoming smile on my face.

I let the customer browse the buckets and displays for a minute but I can tell he has no idea what he's looking for.

'Can I help?' I say in a warm voice and he turns and looks at me. I'd say he's in his early forties. He's tall and has that air of importance, of someone used to being in charge. I reckon he works in the City – he looks like someone Milly might work with. His watch is expensive and his suit looks it too. His face is drawn – maybe from tiredness, or misery, or both. His shoulders are steeply sloped and he looks thinner than he should. This is definitely a man under quite a lot of stress.

'It's my wife's birthday tomorrow and I – I need to come up with something pretty special. It's – it's not been a very good year for us.'

I nod. On my first day Sal told me all about the art of listening to customers. 'We're not just dealing with bouquets,' she'd explained. 'We're dealing with love and grief and thanks and joy and guilt.' Then she'd added, 'Remember, it's always easy to spot a man who's in trouble. The trick is to work out how much he's in and what you need to do to get him out of it.'

'I understand,' I say soothingly now. By the look of the man I'm fairly sure he's got something pretty big to apologise for. But I can't judge him. I have to remain neutral, friendly. 'Flowers are the perfect way to express emotion—' I put my hand over my mouth as he bursts into tears. 'Oh my gosh, I'm so sorry, did I – did I say something wrong?'

He rubs his eyes and shakes his head. 'No, no, it's not that, it's just that's exactly what I want to be able to say to her but I can't. Ever since we got her diagnosis, she won't let me tell her how much I love her, or let me care for her. She's just carrying on like everything's normal and I can't deal with it!' I glance anxiously at Sal who has peered out from the back. I can't believe I got this poor guy so wrong. I presumed he'd had an affair or something when he's actually just trying to care for his sick wife. I feel terrible.

I gently lead him by the arm to our consultation area, sit him down and prepare to listen.

'So why don't you start by telling me everything you feel about your wife,' I say softly. 'And together we'll find the right flowers . . .'

Chapter 30

At 7.30 p.m. I walk into Quo Vadis and head up to the elegant, art deco-style private room that's been booked for Milly and Jay's leaving party.

I hover by the doorway for a moment now, feeling overwhelmed by the throbbing mass of people here and wishing that Adam was by my side. I've never liked big crowds and never more so than now. Tonight I have to face up to the people I haven't seen since the wedding, Adam's colleagues who will all be here for Jay, friends of Milly's. Mutual friends of Adam and Jay's. Possibly George. After all, Adam's dad is known to never say no to a work night out.

I'm not going to feel sorry for myself though. Not after my humbling experience at work today. After all, who am I to wallow in my own mistakes when there are people in this world dealing with problems that they have no control over? Grief, illness, break-ups . . . Fleetingly, I wonder what Adam's doing right now. I still can't believe he's taken a sabbatical from Hudson & Grey. It seems so out of character. Milly told me that he's doing a road trip across America, taking time out to work out what he wants from life now the future he'd imagined has changed so drastically. I think of her and Jay's move to New York; it looks like things have changed for all of us.

I take a deep breath, think of Loni and try to channel some calming, yogic energy. But it doesn't help. I'm dreading this party and much as I would prefer to be anywhere but here, at the same time, I wouldn't miss Milly's leaving party for the world. She's my best friend and I'm doing this to support her. For once in my life I'm not taking the coward's way out.

I walk into the throng and quickly end up in the centre of the room, swallowed up by bustling, beautiful people. I edge over to the bar and stand on tiptoe for a moment to see if I can see Milly's bobbing sleek black hair amongst the crowd. I feel like I will be safe when I reach her, but all I can see are a mass of expensive handbags, sparkling jewellery and men in slick suits. I squeeze my slightly sweaty palms together and wish that I had seriously considered Milly's offer to borrow something from her wardrobe. I'd felt smart and summery and kind of . . . well, 'me' when I left the flat in faded jeans, a floaty top and gladiator sandals. I tied my short hair in stubby French plaits that I thought looked nice for a night out. I realise now that I seriously underestimated the dress code – and the guest list – for this occasion. Because all the great, good and glamorous of London's advertising, media, business and finance worlds appear to be here.

'BEA!' Milly calls. 'You're here!' I wave joyously as I see her pushing through the crowd, glass of champagne in hand. She looks beautiful in a billowing, empire-line maxi dress with gold jewellery and sparkling gold heels. It's not her usual style: she wears much more structured stuff, but it really suits her. I'm so relieved to see her that it takes me a moment to realise that the room has hushed and the atmosphere has grown what can only be described as hostile. That's when I see the staring faces, familiar faces I'd last seen smiling and wearing fabulous fascinators and top hats on my wedding day.

Milly envelops me in an embrace. 'Thank you for coming,' she whispers. 'I know how hard this must be for you.'

'Hard?' I whisper back. 'I'm Loni's daughter, remember? Attention-seeking, public-laundry-washing runs in the family!' I swallow, my fake bravado suddenly gone as I stare over her shoulder at the guests, most of them whispering loudly to each other.

Milly squeezes me and guides me over to the bar, away from her three female work friends who look like they are about to burst with undisguised glee that finally they'll get the gossip on what happened to my wedding. All of them are single and never went to the trouble of hiding their annoyance that someone like me – a lowly, unimportant, plain-looking temp – could bag a man like *Adam Hudson*.

'Just ignore them all,' Milly advises. 'You're here with me. Come on, let's get you a drink. Bubbles?' she says and I nod gratefully, thanking her with a smile for her kindness.

Five minutes later, Milly and I are safely ensconced in the corner of the room on a sofa. I can hear a conversation between two women standing to the left of us in which the words 'runaway' and 'bride' seem to be coming up regularly. I sink further down in the seat.

'They'll get over it if they see you're not bothered,' Milly says quickly and pulls me up. I remember her saying the same to me when she was trying to get me to go back to school to finish my A levels after my breakdown.

'Is Adam coming?' I ask as I rearrange myself on the seat.

Milly shakes her head. 'I wouldn't do that to you both. Besides, he's still travelling, but he promised Jay he'd come and visit us in New York.'

'Oh,' I say, feeling my heart sink unexpectedly. I have to remind myself it is a *good* thing that I don't have to face Adam tonight in such a public place. But I realise that it was him I was thinking of when I got dressed for the party. You don't spend seven years with someone and just switch off your feelings, even if you were the one who walked – sorry, *ran* away. 'You'll all be in New York together,' I point out to Milly miserably.

'So come over too,' she says impatiently. 'After all, there's nothing keeping you here now. You could still get Adam back, you know, it's not too late . . .'

'I don't want him back,' I say with an assurance I don't feel. 'I need to move on with my life.'

'If you say so,' she shrugs. 'But how exactly are you going to do that?'

'With my new job! '

She looks at me sympathetically. 'You don't have to pretend to me, Bea. I feel awful about leaving you like this. I know you're still having a hard time. I wish I could be here for you. Help you get back on your feet . . .' She studies me for a moment with her sharp gaze and her features soften. Milly is different with me than she is with other people. I know she's considered a bulldog at work – and with friends. She's impatient, stubborn, direct and yet with me – and Jay, in fact – she is softer, more forgiving, always prone to protection rather than attack. I don't know what sort of pathetic image I must display to incite this treatment – that's a lie, I do. But nevertheless I'm determined to prove to her – and myself – that I can go it alone.

'Milly, you have already done way more than I deserve. You're letting me stay in your old flat rent-free. Seriously,' I say tearfully, clutching her hand, 'I don't really know how I can ever thank you . . .'

'Don't!' Milly says, waving her other hand in front of her face.

I catch her hand and hold it as I look into her eyes. 'I'm going to miss you so much but I promise you, I *am* going to be all right.'

'I'll miss you too,' she says in a choked voice. Then she sniffs. 'Ugh, I cannot be seen crying in public. It'll ruin my ball-breaking reputation. And besides, we'll see each other soon. I'll pay for you to visit me . . .'

'I'll save up,' I tell her.

'On your flower shop salary?' Milly says doubtfully. 'I mean, I'm not being funny, Bea, but that might take a while.'

I bite my lip before I answer. 'Listen, I know I don't have a big salary Milly, but this job feels like the first good decision I've made in years. I really think that I might finally be on the right path.'

'Good,' Milly says but she doesn't look convinced. 'Well, I guess I'd better mingle,' she adds, standing up. 'Will you be all right on your own?'

'Tonight, or always?' I joke. She doesn't smile. 'Of course I will!' I say brightly. She looks at me, the worry evident in her eyes, then shakes her head and gets swallowed up in her party whilst I stand and look on, alone.

Chapter 31

I sit back on my haunches and gaze around me at Milly's garden. It's only been a week since she left but in that time the suffocating heat of summer has hit its height and I've made the most of my spare time away from the flower shop by being out here, taking solace in digging and weeding, planting and pruning. I gather up the cuttings and survey my work. I've fed the roses, pruned the early-flowering geraniums and pulled out loads of black vine weevils. I've hoed bare patches of soil, cut back overgrown bushes and perennials and tended the flowering clematis – I couldn't help but think of our roof terrace, and wonder if Adam had remembered to do the same. Then I remembered he wasn't even there. He'd gone.

I'm soccer-punched by a memory.

'I can't believe he's gone!' Kieran sobs as I stroke his hair, my own tears and the sterile hospital smell almost choking me.

I blink and come back to the present. In the last few days I've been getting more and more of these flashbacks to the night Elliot died. I try to push the memory away.

'Focus on the flowers,' I murmur to myself. Ever since I moved in three months ago, found Dad's gardening diary and began digging the earth out here, I've felt like I'm digging through my past. I glance down at the little blue book lying by my side, the pages fluttering in the breeze. Dad's slanted scrawl and diagrams are as familiar as if they were my own, even though I hadn't seen them for years until I moved back here. I pick up the diary and clutch it to my chest and then to my nose as I inhale the musty scent of memories.

I catch a glimpse of the platinum ring I'm wearing on my right hand. I tentatively put it back on when I found it again in the suitcase along with the diary. It is Loni's wedding ring. The one I'd stopped her throwing in the sea after she kicked Dad out. The same one I'd worn for a year after Kieran left as part of our promise not to forget each other.

I take it off now and roll it between my thumb and forefinger as I think about Kieran turning up at my wedding. Was I too quick to send him away? Should I have given him more of a chance to talk? Listened to him, like I listened in the shop to the man who was nursing his sick wife?

I put the ring back on, marvelling at how it feels at once unfamiliar yet comfortable, as if it made an invisible impression when I wore it for that year, a groove on my skin that has never gone away, despite the time that has passed. Putting it back on is like opening up the portal to my past. I close my eyes, thinking about the days of that summer that Kieran and I spent counting the many reasons we were meant to be, honing our love story like we would be telling it for years to come.

'I wasn't going to come here this summer, you know,' Kieran had said one afternoon when we were lying on Wells beach, in front of one of the little beach huts, pretending we owned it. He rolled onto his stomach, displaying his oak-brown back, and gazed up at me through his eyelashes. His eyes were hypnotically green; I remember thinking that I could lose myself forever in them. 'Elliot got us jobs at this pub in Devon but on the day we were meant to drive down from where we were staying in Dorset, I turned the camper round and headed in a different direction. Completely spur of the moment.' He blinked at me, lashes brushing his dark skin as he lit a cigarette, exhaling the smoke as easily as he'd told the story. 'It was like I was being pulled by a magnetic force. Then, when I met you, I knew what, or rather who, it was I'd been drawn to . . .'

'I wasn't meant to go to the beach party that night,' I continued. 'But Loni ended up inviting a load of her cronies over. Cal was at college and I just felt this urge to go for a run on the beach . . .'

'You looked so sexy in your Lycra!' Kieran laughed, dropping a kiss on my chest.

'I heard my name being called. Then I saw you, sitting playing the guitar, and I knew, I knew I wouldn't be leaving any time soon . . .'

'I couldn't move when I saw you, let alone leave. It was like the sole purpose of my summer was to meet you,' Kieran told me as I stroked his golden-streaked hair. Then he sat up and kissed me, pressing his lean, half-naked body against mine so I sank into the sand. I loved how urgent, how full of need and desire his kisses always were. In that moment I knew my life had entered a new dimension: my sleepy, cosseted Norfolk existence had been sparked into life at last. It scared me, but it made me feel alive too. I didn't need anything other than Kieran to make me happy now.

My phone rings and I pull it out of the pocket of my jeans.

'Hi, Loni,' I say in a voice that does not sound like my own.

'Bea, my darling! It's been aeons since we last spoke! A lifetime! Too busy shaking off the shackles of your boring old existence to call your poor mum?'

'I've just been busy,' I say tightly. I pause and look at my right hand and then at the diary on my lap. 'I'm finding my world, Loni, and with all my heart giving myself to it,' I say softly. 'Just like you've always told me to. I'm taking a leaf out of your book – literally.'

'That's what I like to hear! As long as you know that I'm always here, darling. You're never alone, remember that. Even in your darkest hours there is always a light to aim for – isn't that what I've always told you? And hasn't it always been true? Last time you thought your life was over, you moved to London and met Adam. And now, you've got yourself this wonderful new job and I'm so proud of how strong you're being, darling. But that doesn't mean you don't need help. When your dad left—'

I don't let her finish. 'You became the woman you were meant to be. What was it you said after Kieran dumped me, Loni? "You don't need a partner, just your pride." Leave before they leave you – that was the message, right? And that's what I've done with Adam. Left before he left me.'

Loni is uncharacteristically quiet for a moment. 'But Adam would never have left you, darling, surely you know that? And that wasn't the point I was trying to make all those years ago. It wasn't *your* fault that Dad or Kieran left. Your dad adored you. And Kieran – well, those were pretty extenuating circumstances. He had just lost his twin, my pet. He just wasn't in the right place to love you . . . you have to stop blaming yourself.'

I think of Kieran standing before me on my wedding day. Did he come back because he's in the right place now? I think of the time ball in Greenwich and envision it dropping now, making everything clear for me to see. Kieran being there was a sign that it was time for us to give it another chance. To try again. A fresh start. That's what I've always wanted. Maybe this is my chance to fix what happened in the past. Why didn't I see it before?

'I'm sorry but I really have to go, Loni,' I say urgently. And I end the call.

I stand for a moment as the penny – time ball, whatever you want to call it – drops, over and over again. I've been in denial these past few months. Could it be that I left Adam because I'd never stopped loving Kieran? I throw my gloves off and run back into Milly's flat.

I strip off quickly and get in the shower. I feel like I want to wash both the dirt from the garden and what I've done to Adam away. I loved him so much but I've never stopped thinking about Kieran. A guy I hadn't seen for eight years and who I spent just one summer with. It's madness. I feel like I'm being haunted by my past, and the more I try to throw myself into this new life, the more it takes me back to my old one. Kieran's brought everything flooding back. I'm living back in the place where I came to recover after it all happened which means, logically, the next step is returning to Norfolk to see if he's still there. It feels like everything is leading me to that summer, to him – and that terrible night.

And I don't think I can ignore the signs any longer.

I get out of the shower and grab my phone, open Facebook and before I can talk myself out of it, I scroll through my messages until I find the one he sent me after the wedding. And without thinking, I quickly write and send a reply:

Kieran, I'd really like to see you ... if you still want to, that is? Bea.

Chapter 32

I am brushing my teeth, trying to avoid looking at my phone resting on the side of the sink. I tell myself firmly that I'm not going to obsessively wait for him to respond. He might not see my message for days. He might have forgotten all about the one he sent. It's been months after all . . .

It's been years since he left, we didn't forget about each other . . .

I look in the mirror. Time seems to slip away as I realise how similar I look now to when Kieran left. I'm much leaner (break-ups do that to a girl), a fact offset by the short haircut I gave myself the day after I ran out on my wedding and which I know makes me look younger. I've acquired a light tan from afternoons spent in Milly's garden and a generous sprinkling of freckles, the like of which I haven't seen on my skin since I left Norfolk. I may not look as polished as when I was with Adam, but I look more like me.

I pick up my phone and, holding it between my chin and my chest as I tie up my towel and pick up my clothes, I head out of the bathroom, every step feeling like a tread back to the past because I can't stop myself thinking about Kieran. Suddenly I feel like the last few years haven't happened and when I close my eyes I can see us together, Elliot sitting between us as we drove along endless expanses of country roads, free to go wherever we liked, do whatever we pleased, our whole future ahead of us. I drop my clothes and phone on the bed in the spare room. It is still yellow – the colour I painted it when I first moved in. It wasn't really in keeping with Milly's minimalist style, but she understood I needed to wake up to brightness. Suddenly I have an idea. I throw open the little suitcase I've kept here all these years, pull out my old Monet prints, and grab the Sellotape from downstairs. Then I spend a happy hour covering one of my bedroom walls with them. When I'm done I step back and fold my arms, looking at them happily.

I glance at my phone to see what time it is. My heart thuds as I notice a red icon over my Facebook app. I have a message. No, he couldn't have . . . not already. Could he?

With a trembling finger I tap the blue icon with the white F.

Bea, I'd really love to meet up as soon as possible. I'm here in Norfolk if you're planning on coming here soon? Just say and I promise I'll be there. Now I'm back, I can't bring myself to leave . . . K

I read the message over and over again, trying to quell the fear and excitement and sickness that I'm feeling just by having this briefest of contacts with Kieran.

Oh God, I can't do this. I shouldn't do this. It isn't right, is it?

Suddenly all my decision-making skills have deserted me again. I sit on the bed and stare at my phone and my eyes naturally settle on certain words: 'really love', 'I'm here', 'I promise I'll be there'.

He is saying everything I dreamed he would for the entire year

I waited for him. Yes, it's seven years later than expected but better late than never, right?

With my heart beating a dance anthem in my chest I write his name:

Kieran

I stop, hovering over the letters. I delete his name and add another word:

Hi Kieran

I delete it.

Dear Kieran

I'm trying not to seem too keen but at the same time I feel that, having waited years for this, I can't wait a moment longer. Don't think about it! I tell myself. Respond to him with the same spontaneity that you did half an hour ago!

Kieran, I'd love to see you, too.

I just want to get some answers, I tell myself. I'm not still in love with him.

I'm coming back to Norfolk at the weekend.

Another pause. I wasn't planning to, but he isn't to know that. And I *did* promise Loni I'd visit soon.

Shall we meet up then? Bea

Is there a please in that question mark? A plead? Kiss or no kiss after the name? STOP OVER-ANALYSING!

I hit send and within seconds a reply appears:

I'd love to. Where shall we meet? Saturday is the anniversary of . . . well, you know. K x

How could I ever forget? Part of me feels that the stars have aligned to bring us back together eight years to the day that we were torn apart by his brother's death. There is a beautiful symmetry to it that seems in keeping with the two versions of my life that always seem to be running alongside each other. Before and after Dad left, before and after Kieran – and now before and after Adam.

With a jolt I look back at the phone and realise that Kieran's waiting for my reply. I cling on to my phone tightly, feeling this renewed connection to him. He's back, and he's been waiting for me a long time.

And I think I'm finally facing up to the fact that I've been waiting for him, too.

Chapter 33

I arrive in Norfolk two days later to a half-hearted welcome from Loni, who opens the door looking very tired and on edge.

'Oh Bea, it's you.'

'You could try and sound a bit more pleased to see me,' I say, kissing her lightly on the cheek and stepping inside. There's lots of chat and laughter coming from the conservatory. 'Guests?' I ask.

'Of course! Did I not mention that my latest retreat group would be here? It's their last night tonight. We're just about to have dinner and set fire to our inhibitions that we've written down on pieces of paper. Come on through.'

I follow her reluctantly, trying not to step on the long silk scarf that has unwound from her neck and is trailing behind her on the floor, and doing my best to disguise my disappointment. All I wanted was to get in my PJs, have a glass of wine and a catch-up with Loni. Not share her with ten other people and be given the third degree. Not to mention third-degree burns, judging by her latest crazy therapy game. However much I want to be annoyed that Loni didn't tell me there'd be a house full of people, I don't allow myself to be surprised or upset. Even though she is technically on her own, it is rare to find Loni by herself.

The house is a mess and Loni seems very distracted, nervous almost, as she leads me through to the conservatory.

'This is such a nice group, darling, I'm so glad you'll get to meet them. There are a few old faithfuls but also some rather nice new faces that I've really loved getting to know . . .' She lets her sentence drift away and she looks over her shoulder at me. She seems on edge about something but I can't work out what. It's not like Loni at all. She's usually so calm and laid-back. I do sometimes worry that she may be finding her relentless workload too much. She's definitely lost weight, and whilst I admit she looks good on it, it is rather worrying. Cal has voiced his concerns recently, too. I know she looks good for her age and we all think of her as much, much younger. But she's nearly fifty-five now – she's not invincible . . .

'Come on through and meet everyone,' Loni says and when she smiles at me I decide I have nothing to worry about. The same sparkle is still there, the brightness in her eyes, the same spirit and determination – even more so perhaps. Loni is tougher than all of us. She isn't ill and I'm sure she doesn't need help. She's made her living out of needing no one. But I resolve to keep a careful eye on her anyway . . . just in case.

I hover by the doorway as she flounces into the conservatory. The room has been lit by a circle of tea lights, her guests are sitting on the floor in the lotus position and there is a low Moroccan coffee table in the middle upon which sits a big earthenware casserole dish with the lid on but which, from the smell of it, holds something spicy and exotic. Everyone is clasping little earthenware cups of red wine, or sangria or something, and a distinguished-looking older gentleman is handing out vegetable crisps and houmous.

'Welcome to our last supper,' he says and I roll my eyes when I realise that Loni's guests are all passing around bread and breaking it between them. 'I'm Roger, a friend of your mum's.'

'Don't be shy, come and join us, darling!' Loni says quickly, her eyes flickering to him and then back to me. 'Let me introduce you to *all* my friends.'

She and Roger sit down next to each other, almost at the same time, in the lotus position like everyone else. She adjusts her knee so it isn't touching him and I see him glance at her. I should let him know he doesn't stand a chance. Loni never goes for anyone who has paid to come on a retreat. She says it sets a bad precedent. And besides, he's way too old for her. The last time she was with someone her own age was . . . well, Dad. And he was actually fifteen years older than her. He left her when he was forty-seven and she was thirty-two, which means he'd be seventy now. I do this sometimes. Work out his age, try to guess where he might be in the world, if he's remarried, how many children he has, what he does for a living. If he's still alive. Sometimes I'm struck with this deep-rooted fear that he is miserably lonely, ill, or even worse dead, but then I can equally imagine him being alive and blissfully happy and with a family he dotes on.

Two versions of his life, and both are equally painful to me.

'Well, thanks so much for the invite, Loni, but I've just got here so I think I'll, you know, just leave you to it.' I smile. 'I just wanted to say hi really. So hi! I hope you all have fun . . .'

I start backing out of the room, desperate to escape. I've seen enough of Loni's retreats over the last twenty years to know that these events mostly involve aged divorcees spouting Buddhist quotes about life paths and making your own journey and being happy to be on your own, until an occasional devotee – who hasn't quite found peace with their single status yet – starts slagging off their ex saying what a shag-a-round, money-stealing, soul-sucking life form they were. And then the whole thing turns from some hippie Zen-like experience into an anger-management session. I don't want to be here when Loni explains that I'm her runaway bride daughter. I'll probably be mobbed.

Having made my excuses, I gather up my things and make for the caravan in the garden. It's been parked there for years. We used to take holidays as a family in it, and then, after Dad left, there weren't any more holidays. It just sat here, abandoned, until I adopted it as my own. The house was always so full of people that as I headed into my late teens I found it harder and harder to share Loni and her worshippers. Here in the caravan I could find peace to think, dream, and design. And then, when I met Kieran, I used it even more.

I need some space to think about my first proper meeting with Kieran tomorrow. As I try to drift off to sleep on the bunk bed, Kieran is in my mind. He is all I can think about. I need to see him again, to move on from where we parted. I feel myself drifting back . . .

'Kieran, there's something I have to tell you.' My voice is carried up on the wings of the seagulls' cry and then dropped in the ocean. 'I need you to understand what happened that night between Elliot and me.' He's followed me here to Holkham beach where I've run to after the funeral to get away from the scent of lilies, of death. I'm standing on the sand dunes being blown by the unseasonal winds that have continued to batter the coast since Elliot died in the storm two days before. I've come here because I want to be battered too. I want the sea to swallow me, just like it has Elliot. I deserve it.

I look at Kieran who is standing with his hands in his pockets, gazing out to sea. His eyes have clouded over like the sea froth at the shore and his long hair is framed by a halo of sea-lavender that now, suddenly, looks more like a wreath. Never again will I think of this coastline and be able to see anything other than a dead young man and a lost love.

Kieran doesn't have to look at me – or speak – for me to know it's over. I haven't told him the truth about what happened with Elliot and me. I can't. But I know that something died between us when Elliot did. Kieran's leaving me. And it was nobody's fault but my own. Please don't leave me, I know you blame me and I understand, I do . . .

He grasps my arm tightly and pulls me to him. 'This wasn't your fault, OK? You tried to save him . . .' I brush my face against his neck, inhaling the scent of him. 'It's my fault he died – and that's why I have to go.'

'I don't think I can live without you . . .' I gasp, barely able to breathe.

'Don't say that,' he says, his breath warm against my hair. 'Don't ever say that. Of course you can live without me. I'm no good for you. Not right now.'

'So let me come with you,' I beg, my fingers clawing his back like I'm trying to cling on to a rock face.

'No!' He breaks away and turns his back on me. He looks like a lost soul again, a broken being, in his black suit, his hair blowing out like entrails. And I want him more than ever.

'You're better off without me. I don't want to drag you down, like I did Elliot. This was my fault.'

'It wasn't!' I cry. But he isn't listening to me.

'I know the doctors said it was the impact of his skull on the pier that killed him, but I as good as dragged him under those waves by encouraging our crazy lifestyle . . . and dragging you into it too.'

'Kieran.' I dart forward and clutch his arm. 'Listen to me, please.'

He turns to me again and I see that tears are streaming down his face, falling from his cheekbones like bodies from a cliff edge. 'I don't know what I'm going to do without him, Bea . . .' It's like he doesn't want to acknowledge it. He doesn't want to face up to the fact that I'm the one who did this. I should have died that night on the pier. Not Elliot. I don't deserve to be here.

I sob as I gaze at him and then up at the dark, dark sky.

He envelops me in his arms, comforting me when it should be the other way round. We cleave to each other as the wind swirls around us, as if we're in the eye of a storm. Kieran pulls away at last and holds me by my shoulders.

'I'm not going forever, you have to know that, OK? But I need to become a better man before I can be with you.'

'No – no you don't, Kieran . . .'

He kisses my lips lightly to silence me, a gentle graze that steals my voice. 'Just listen to me, please, Bea? It wasn't your fault.' I sob then because I know I can't change his mind. He pulls out a ring and holds it in front of me before slipping it on the third finger of his right hand. 'This is a promise to you that I'm yours, and as soon as I can – in a few months, a year, max, I'll come back for you. Wait for me, please?'

I gaze at him and he looks at my hand. I know what he wants me to do. I take off the wedding ring I have worn around my neck since Loni tried to throw it in the sea and I slip it on the same finger on my right hand.

'One year,' he repeats. 'One year and I'll be back for you.'

'Do you promise?' I plead.

He smiles wistfully and nods. 'You'll wait for me, won't you? I need to know you'll wait.' I nod and he kisses me and then pulls away. 'Until then promise me you'll do everything to make the most of your life. Do it for me – but mostly do it for Elliot. Goodbye, Bea,' he says. And then he walks away, striding across the beach, head bowed, into the wind.

Chapter 34

The following morning feels unbearably long and I mostly spend it watching Loni pack and repack her carpet bag of books and notes, a picnic blanket and yoga mat and wait anxiously for her to go out. She goes upstairs and gets changed three times. The first time she comes down in a long, plunging, crimson, crepe-effect maxi dress that doesn't look at all yoga-friendly to me, then she changes into some more suitable leggings and a vest top. But one look in the mirror and she disappears upstairs and comes down twenty minutes later in a pair of patterned jersey trousers and a bright pink T-shirt with matching fuchsia lips and her hair piled up on top of her head. She leaves the house at this point only to come back thirty seconds later, pretending she's forgotten some important notes. I watch as she grabs an enormous pair of beaded earrings and notice her hands are shaking a little as she puts them on in front of the hallway mirror.

I make a note to look 'the shakes' up later as a possible symptom for something. Now I'm here I can understand why Cal is so worried. Loni might look amazing but she really isn't herself.

'You look . . . nice,' I observe as I lean against the kitchen doorframe and munch on my toast. I am hoping to instigate a conversation about her health.

'I could say the same about you,' she replies, staring deliberately at the floaty embroidered top I'm wearing with some cut-offs. I've spent ages styling my hair and putting on make-up. It's been so long since I've really bothered about my appearance – my wedding day, I realise – that I'd almost forgotten how.

'What, me? Must be the Norfolk air!' I reply, retreating into the kitchen to put more toast on the grill in the Aga – even though I can barely eat what I've already made, just so she doesn't see me blushing.

'So, what are you up to today, darling?' she calls as she *finally* puts her bag on her shoulder and starts heading for the front door.

'Oh, you know . . .' I follow her just so I can check she actually leaves this time. 'I'm just going to hang out here. Maybe potter around in the garden a bit. It needs some serious TLC.'

'Oh, yes,' Loni says distractedly, as if noticing the patchy grass and wilted, overgrown beds outside in the front garden for the first time. 'I haven't got out there much recently. Just haven't had the time, or inclination . . .' She trails off. It feels like she's forgotten what she wanted to say.

'Are you all right, Loni?' I ask in a more confrontational tone than I intended.

'Fine, darling! Fine fine fine! Just, you know, busy as ever. And you know the garden has always been your forte. It's never really looked the same since you left here. I try, you know I do, but I just don't have green fingers like you do . . .' She trails off again but this time I know exactly what she wanted to say. Dad is the elephant in the room here. Loni has always told me I'm just like him. I sometimes think he is what always comes between us, that he's the reason I don't have the easy relationship with Loni that Cal does. I can't forget that she made him leave us and I feel like I'm a constant reminder of the man she's always wanted to forget.

She turns and kisses me on the cheek and I rub it petulantly, knowing she's left a bright pink lipstick impression there. 'I'd better go. Are you sure you'll be OK on your own?' Her blue eyes widen with worry.

'I'm your daughter, remember?' I say wryly. 'We both love being on our own.' She doesn't look satisfied. 'I'll be *fine*, Loni. Stop worrying.'

She opens her mouth but then closes it as if she's had second thoughts about what she wanted to say. I glance at my watch anxiously as she wafts another kiss in my direction, before heading out into the bright sunshine.

I only exhale when I close the door behind her. 10.50 a.m. Ten minutes before he's due to arrive.

I dash through the hall and back into the kitchen and throw my breakfast plate and mug in the sink that is already piled high with washing-up. Then I run upstairs, grab a brush and some lip balm, spritz some perfume and rebrush my teeth. For the third time. My heart is pounding as I thunder back downstairs.

I hear a car pull up and I dart into the lounge as if there are hot coals under my feet. I slide along the wall and stand there for a moment with my eyes closed as I hear the crunch of gravel beneath his feet and then a short, sharp knock at the door.

Oh my God. He's here. He's actually here.

After all this time.

Chapter 35

He's standing in the doorway as if he's never been away, smiling lopsidedly, causing lines to appear around his mouth. Oh God, his mouth. I daren't look at it and in fact I can't because I can't drag my eyes away from his eyes, the dark murky memories reflected back at me in the green pools of his irises. In one glance I am lost again. I blink and force myself to look down and I see he is holding out a bunch of hand-picked wild-flowers.

We don't speak for what feels like an eternity, both of us clearly lost in the same moment. Remembering not the day we last saw each other on the beach at Holkham after the non-wedding – but the day we left each other behind. I can't help it. I'm being carried back on a tidal wave of memories from eight years ago and I have to fight my way back, to stay afloat in this moment, not drown in the past.

'Hi, Bea,' Kieran says now. His voice is deeper than I remember.

'Hi.' It comes out as a whisper. We stare at each other again as if trying to convince ourselves that this is really happening.

'So,' he says. 'Shall I come in?'

I shake my head and his face drops.

'Just in case Loni comes back . . .'

He smiles. 'Ah, I'm still your dirty little secret, am I? Some things never change.'

I blush and feel my skin prickle with – what – embarrassment? Lust? Shame? I don't know. 'Where, then?' he says and I shut the door behind me and lead him through the house and out into the back garden and towards my caravan, where we spent many nights together.

'This brings back memories,' he says. I don't reply. I feel like I'm walking the line between two completely different times.

As we step inside it feels like we're stepping into the past and suddenly I question my decision to come here. The space feels too small, too intimate. I move back from Kieran, who feels too close. He seems to take up more space than he used to.

'Tea?' I ask as I turn and grab the kettle, trying to silence the pounding of my heart.

'If you spike it with some sort of relaxant.' He laughs and rubs his hand over his head bashfully. 'This is really weird,' he observes.

I smile, in spite of myself. 'It's kind of like, where do we start . . .?'

He goes and sits down on the sofa by the window. He folds his hands on the table and stretches his legs out. I avert my gaze, busying myself with tea-making.

Eventually I sit opposite him, slide his tea across the table and instantly take a sip of mine to give my lips something to do other than talk. 'Hot!'

'Just what I was thinking,' he grins cheekily. 'Not being married really suits you.'

'I was talking about the tea!' I blush but I feel a flood of pleasure anyway – quickly followed by one of guilt.

'So . . .' He smiles. 'How have you been?' he asks. 'You know, since . . .'

'The wedding? Fine,' I answer quickly. 'Really good, actually! Just trying to work out what happens next, I guess.'

'And have you?' he asks meaningfully, gazing at me intently. I shrug and look down. 'Worked it out?'

'What about you?' I ask shakily. I'm trying not to look at the ring that is still on his finger. I'm not wearing mine. I didn't want to give him the wrong impression. This meeting is just my way of answering some questions, getting some closure. That's what I keep telling myself anyway. 'What have you been up to . . . for the last eight years?' I work hard to keep my voice even. I don't want to sound accusing.

Kieran gazes across at me. His lips lift into a lilting smile. 'I guess you could say I've been all at sea since I left you.' I don't reply. 'I joined the Navy, Bea.'

I try to fashion a look of complete surprise to cover up the fact that I want to reply 'I know'. I realise I've known it ever since I saw his Facebook picture, I just hadn't properly acknowledged it as I'd been too busy trying not to think about him. But it makes sense. Kieran, the uniform, the sea, being close to Elliot . . . Of *course* he joined the Navy.

He smiles at me and nudges my foot with his. 'You thought I'd been bumming around for years, didn't you?'

I nod. It feels easier than telling him the truth. That I knew. I've always known, really. Just like I've always known that he didn't come back because, no matter what he told me at the time, he blamed me for Elliot's death and couldn't bear to be with me after that.

'I did for a while,' he grins. 'After I left I travelled around the coast, you know, working at campsites and in bars, catching up with old friends, kipping on people's floors, heading my way

south down to Dorset and then Devon and Cornwall. Everything I used to do with Elliot. It was hard without him. Nothing
felt the same even though I wasn't doing anything differently. By
winter I'd saved up enough money to head abroad so I went to
Thailand. Elliot and I had always said we'd go there together and
I needed to have experiences to take me away from the memories but keep me connected to him. I backpacked for about three
months then went on to Bali and got some bar work before
going to Australia.'

'Sounds fun,' I say with a forced smile.

'It wasn't,' Keiran says wryly. 'The further away I got, the
worse I felt. Nothing had changed and yet everything had. It was
coming up to a year since I'd left and I had my ticket booked to
come home.'

I swallow. 'So you had planned to come back, then?' He nods.
'So what changed?' I am trying to keep my voice even, my tone
interested, but not eager. Or desperate.

'I flew back into Heathrow all ready to come back to Norfolk,
to come back to you.' He glances up at me and his green eyes
bore into mine. 'You have to understand what a mess I was, Bea.
The year away hadn't helped me at all. I felt like I'd done nothing, learned nothing from Elliot's death, I was in a state –
mentally and physically. I was ashamed of myself. I wanted to see
you so badly but I knew I'd let everyone down – me, you, most
of all Elliot. I didn't know what else to do though, it hurt too
much to be away from you . . .'

I blink and look away, I feel like I'm having an out-of-body
experience, listening to him fill in all the gaps.

He rubs his hand over his head again and suddenly I long to
do the same. To touch him, feel the realness of him. I force
myself to focus on what he's saying.

'I got off the plane with my rucksack on my back not knowing who I was any more, or what I could possibly offer to anyone. But then, as I was walking down the corridor, heading for customs, I saw this advert in the airport for Royal Navy recruitment and it just hit me. That was what I had to do. I went straight into the internet café at the airport, filled out a form online and then bought a ticket and got on a bus to Portsmouth to sign up. I didn't even unpack or think about coming home. I was determined that this was the only way that I could make sense of my life and Elliot's death.'

I stare at Keiran and he looks back at me meaningfully. All that time he'd been trying to find himself, make sense of everything that had happened and make a better life for himself.

'I've been in the Navy for five years now,' he says proudly. 'I'm a CPO – a chief petty officer – which means I basically do a bit of everything. I'm a jack of all trades, but I have a team of guys – about sixty or so – who report to me.' He laughs because my mouth is agape.

'I love it. I get to mould the younger officers coming in and really guide them. It's given me a purpose, you know?'

'Saving lives,' I add and he looks at me meaningfully.

'I knew you'd understand,' he says softly and reaches over and squeezes my hand.

'But what about you?' he says, shifting in his seat.

I don't know how to follow Kieran's story. 'The usual,' I mumble. 'I moved to London, got a job as a temp, met Adam – my hus— My boyfriend— My . . . ex . . .'

As I stumble over my words I fold my arms and pull my mouth wide into a smile. I don't want him to know how nervous he makes me. 'Kept temping, had fun, got engaged and then . . . well, you know the rest.' I blink quickly and go on, 'But since that day I've left my temp job and got a job in a flower shop!' Kieran nods slowly, he looks surprised and I suddenly realise that, even though this is a big deal to me, it must sound completely pitiful to anyone else. My life seems so small. But it's all I can cope with.

Kieran frowns and in that moment he looks so grown-up, so mature and responsible I barely recognise him. 'You're not a garden designer? But I thought that was your big dream?' He looks around the caravan, then. My drawings, notes and designs still line the wall. Loni has never taken them down. This caravan is like a shrine to my ambition. Suddenly it feels incredibly suffocating in here. Like I'm locked in the past and I can't get out.

I drain my tea and stand up. 'Shall we go somewhere?'

Kieran nods as he stands up too. 'You always did hate being cooped up inside.'

We walk around to the front of the house and I see his bright yellow VW camper van parked in the road.

'I can't believe you still have this ancient heap of crap!' I exclaim, laughing as I look at him and then running my fingers along the side. I close my eyes, feeling the summer at my fingertips. We did everything in this thing. And I mean, *everything*. I blush at the memories and turn my back on him.

'Shhh!' he chastises and then rests his hands over the passenger-seat window and leans his lips into it. 'Don't listen to her.' He turns to me and grins. 'She's very sensitive about her age, you know.' He strides round the other side of the camper van and slides into the driver's seat before flinging open the passenger door.

He starts the engine and after a few hiccups she purrs into life. 'That's my girl!' he murmurs, stroking the steering wheel. 'She does it for me every time,' he says and he winks at me. I cross my legs and fold my hands in my lap. I hope I'm not drawing attention to the shiver of longing I just felt down there. I uncross them and sit on my hands.

The sun is beating down on the van as we pull out onto the road, and casts a gilded glow on the fields and trees we pass, making everything look like it has been woven with gold. I feel I've been transported back to that summer when we'd drive along the coast, me squeezed between Elliot and Kieran, off on our adrenalin-fuelled adventures. Sometimes I'd drive as they slept, preparing themselves for the next base or cliff jump or caving expedition or set of waves to surf. Then there were the nights spent curled up in the back with Kieran as Elliot slept in a tent, or under the stars, or somewhere else entirely. Often we didn't know where. It felt like we were having the time of our lives.

I shiver and Kieran brushes my knee with his hand. 'Are you OK?'

'Yes,' I squeak. 'I'm fine. This just . . . brings back some memories.'

He nods. 'I know. It's why I couldn't get rid of the van. It's everything I loved about that summer. When I'm in it I can access all the happy times . . . instead of the . . . Well, you know.'

I nod. 'We had a lot of fun, didn't we?' It comes out more of a question than the statement I intended it to be. I realise Kieran's hand is back on my knee and he squeezes it. I inhale and move my leg slightly. He takes his hand away, but his touch is still burning my skin. 'Where are we going?' I ask, my voice sounding unusually raspy. Suddenly it feels like a much bigger question than I intended.

'I thought we could walk along Blakeney Point, for old times' sake.'

We used to go there a lot. Just us, no Elliot, no collection of crazy friends. We'd lie amongst the grasses, Kieran reading poetry to me, telling me about his awful childhood in care and how he had realised at a young age that, with his background, books were his only passport to a better life.

'Do you remember the twilight date we went on?' I say with a smile. 'You "borrowed"' – I make inverted commas with my fingers – 'a boat from Morston Quay and took me to see the seals.'

'Oh God I did, didn't I? I got in so much shit for that. Another part-time job I didn't last a week at!' Kieran throws his head back and laughs and I join him. I remember how much I loved his don't-give-a-shit attitude. It made me realise I'd always cared about everything far too much. Especially since Dad left. I was sick and tired of thinking so much, worrying about everything, wishing, wondering ... Kieran didn't think, he just did. I remember now how he broke into the beach hut we'd spent weeks pretending we owned. The night we had in there was one of the most romantic and magical experiences I'd ever had. He didn't wait for life to happen to him, he made my life come alive and I loved it. I love ... loved him. Past tense.

'So, er, tell me about the flower shop,' he says to change the subject. I hate how suddenly it sounds more like a lowly part-time job than the start of a new life.

'It's great. But it's not all I'm doing,' I add defensively. 'I plan to go back to university to finish my degree, too.' For some reason I care what he thinks of me now. I feel like such a failure. I don't want him to think that way too.

'You didn't graduate?' he says, his voice full of surprise as he stares at the country road unfolding before us.

'I never went back after that summer,' I say quietly. 'I missed my final year. I just couldn't bring myself to go back after ...' My sentence trails off and I look at Kieran. He's biting his lip as if he has something he needs to say. God, those lips. I remember now how, even in profile, I always found him hypnotic.

I wish I could tell him that my life ended when he left me. And then ended again when he came back on my wedding day.

But I know how unfair that would be. None of this is his fault.
I remember now how impossible it was to get mad at him or
Elliot. They used to just smile languidly, their identically long
eyelashes weighing down their eyelids until anyone's frustration
at them subsided. I was completely under their spell.

We arrive at blustery Blakeney Point, a national nature reserve
which is a spit of shingle and sand dunes, but also salt marshes,
mudflats and farmlands, and home to colonies of harbour and
grey seals that tourists come to see. We park up the van and walk
past the distinctive blue visitor centre with the curved roof, along
the north-facing sea point. It's unusually peaceful here today. The
wind has picked up, but the sun is still burning brightly in the
sky. I become aware not just of Kieran's presence, but the *pre-
science* of our being here together, by this sea, today. The eighth
anniversary of Elliot's death. We walk along the shingle, and I
find myself silently naming the wildflowers I spot on the dunes,
just to calm my nerves. *Sea campion, glasswort, yellow-horned poppies.* All the flora my dad had pointed out to me as a kid.

'Why did you contact me, Kieran?' I say quietly when I run
out of plants to spot. He doesn't answer. I try again. 'And more
importantly, why did you come to my wedding?'

He stops and turns to face me. 'My ship was just passing, I
guess.'

I hit him on the chest with sudden, unexpected furious indig-
nation. 'Seriously? That's the best you've got? You were
PASSING!' My hand burns and I try to cover up the fact that my
face is doing the same by turning away. 'You *pass* by a pub and
pop in, Kieran, you *pass* by a beach and decide to go for a surf,
you don't pass by a church and decide to go in and watch a wedding!'

'Better late than never, though, right?' he says hopefully and
I give a short, sharp, surprising burst of laughter before hitting

him again. He grins and holds my wrists against his chest. 'OK, OK!' he says. 'You got me.' He takes a deep breath and I swallow. I feel a sense of both panic and relief as I feel his heart beating against my hand. I can't breathe. Not just because I'm about to get some answers, but because I'm so close to him.

'I – I saw on Facebook that you were getting married . . .'

'How?' I shoot back, not looking up. 'We're not friends on there.'

'You don't have your privacy settings set up,' he says, 'so I could always see your status updates. You're not exactly a shy social networker, are you, Bea?'

I glance through my eyelashes in embarrassment and step away from him, thinking of the hundreds of status updates and photos I've posted over the years. Has he seen them all? Then I ask myself a deeper question – did I purposely not set my privacy settings because deep down, I hoped he would see them?

'Anyway, I looked you up a lot, just to see how you were . . . if you were still the same or if, you know, you'd settled down.'

'And there I was thinking you'd forgotten all about me,' I say, bending down and plucking some sea-aster out of the grass and twirling it between my thumb and forefinger.

'How could I possibly do that, Bea?' Kieran murmurs. There is a pause. A beat. A look of understanding between us. 'What did you do?' he adds. 'After I'd gone?'

'Do you really want to know?' I say and he nods. I stop midstep, blinking up at the blue sky as a load of people pass by us. I wait until they've gone before I speak.

'I waited, OK?' I reply, turning to face him. He rubs the back of his neck with one hand and I see a sad mist has formed in his eyes. 'For a really, really long time,' I continue. 'You said you'd be back after a year.'

Kieran sits down in the grass, resting his wrist on his knees as he gazes out to sea. 'I needed more time. I was a mess after the funeral.' He glances at me with such sorrow that I sit down beside him and take his hand.

'This time of year is always hard.' I look at Kieran anxiously. 'You must miss Elliot so much.' He hides his face with his arm then, before swiping a hand across his forehead.

'I'm sorry.' I instinctively put my arm around Kieran and then we fall into each other's embrace and it's like the years have melted away. Being held by him is exactly as I remember. It's like we have one heartbeat. 'I'm so sorry ...'

'I struggled too, you know,' he says at last. 'I realise now that running away wasn't the right thing to do. I tried to justify my actions. I was so confused. I missed you so much, but I knew that us being together would have been much worse than us being apart. I was determined to do my own thing, to make up for what happened ...' We look at each other and I feel like my heart is breaking. After all this time, it is still so raw. 'I just wanted to make up for what was lost by living this amazing adventurous life. We'd made a promise after all ...' He glances down at his ring – the ring he said he'd wear until he came back. And he did. I blink and look away.

'I see you don't wear yours any more,' Kieran says softly.

'You may have noticed that me and rings don't seem to get on,' I retort wryly.

'I've never taken mine off,' he says poignantly.

'I wore it for an entire year,' I say. 'You can't blame me for giving up ... after *eight years* ...'
He holds his hands up. 'I know, I know. I don't want to make excuses. I wanted to come back, so many times, you have to know that ... but joining the Navy, it felt right. It was what I had to do.'

I feel ashamed then, for being petulant about him not coming back when he was doing such a positive thing. 'I still can't believe you're in the Navy,' I say, forcing myself out of the past and back into the present. 'Isn't it dangerous? Don't you ever get scared?'

He nods. 'Sometimes. But I like fear, remember?' He smiles. 'And this kind is healthy, it's for the good. Besides, being scared reminds me I'm alive. I mean, what is a life without risks, eh? Or am I talking to the wrong person about that?'

'You don't have to tell me about taking risks! It was a pretty big risk running out on my wedding, wouldn't you say?' I stand up and begin to walk, stuffing my hands in my pockets.

'Not if you knew it wasn't right,' Kieran calls matter-of-factly. I turn around and glare at him as he walks towards me, each crunch of shingle bringing him closer. 'What about the rest of your life from now on? You've never really been one to live dangerously, have you? I mean, when was the last time you did something to push yourself ...' He brushes his hand over his head and raises an eyebrow.

'When I left my temp job!' I say quickly.

'Ooh, *crazy*,' he teases. And suddenly I snap.

'Go on, mock me, go right ahead! But why do you think I'm so careful, huh? I spent a summer not caring about anything apart from you. I took a risk on *you* and then I took another stupid, irresponsible risk that night on the pier ...'

'Bea, come on, you're not still blaming yourself for that, are you?'

'Of COURSE I am! Your brother died and it was all my fault.'

'I thought we'd dealt with that!' Kieran says, reaching for my hand. 'You couldn't have stopped him jumping in that night any more than I could have stopped myself falling in love with you!'

I snatch my hand away. 'Love? Is that what you call it?' I laugh. 'Yes, you said you loved me, but you also told me you'd be back in a year. What else did you expect me to think other than you couldn't bear to be near me after what had happened?'

He tries to embrace me but I hold my hands up and shake my head, trying desperately to compose myself.

My hands are trembling, so is my voice. 'So, you know, maybe you should revise your definition of the word "risk". Because I've just walked away from everything, a whole life I've spent seven years building, and I'm sorry if that isn't exciting or "risky" enough for you but . . . but it happens to be one of the craziest things I've ever done!'

He touches my shoulder gently. 'I'm sorry.' I try not to notice how gorgeous he looks when he's apologising. 'I didn't mean to upset you. I don't have any right to make a judgement on your decisions. I just hate to think that you didn't finish your degree because of what happened that summer. You inspired me so much because you always knew exactly what you wanted. You made me feel so sure of everything I did. You knew who you were and where you were going in a way that neither Elliot nor I did. The version of you I saw at the beach after your wedding wasn't the Bea I remembered. She wasn't even remotely the same. I guess we've both changed though,' he says softly, his fingers lightly grazing my wrist.

I don't say anything; I'm too busy fighting back tears.

'I think it's time I went home,' I say at last. 'Okay,' he sighs. 'I'll take you home.'

I don't go home though. Kieran convinces me to go for just one drink with him. He always was incredibly persuasive. And then one drink turns into dinner, which turns into an evening drive to Sheringham and a long walk on the beach. After our tense conversation we have relaxed in each other's company and it is nearly midnight when we pull up in front of Loni's house. He switches the engine off and I'm about to get out when he grasps my arm. I turn to face him and see him gazing at me intensely; his green eyes are shining in the soft glow of the van's lights. 'Please can I see you again, Bea?' he says. 'I've loved being with you today so much.'

I look away. I've spent years dreaming of a moment like this, but now it's real, I'm terrified of what might happen if I see Kieran again. In theory, this should be it. I have my closure. He's told me why he didn't come back, he's said he never blamed me, and done it in such a way that he might even have finally convinced me. And yet I know I can't say no to him. Am I being drawn back to him because our twenty-something selves were right? We *are* meant to be?

'I'll call you,' I say and I turn away from him and open the camper van door. The air is still balmy, despite it being so late. I must be too, to consider seeing him again. I look back at him leaning over the passenger seat, one arm stretched over the steering wheel. I'm trying not to notice how his tan sets off his eyes in the dark, how plump his lips are, how sinewy the muscles on his bare arms. It takes me all my strength to simply smile and turn to get out. But before I can he jumps out of the van and runs around to my door.

I stumble a little in my hurry and he catches me, his arms strong as they slip around my waist. There is a pause, a beat, a spark when it feels like we are being drawn together by a magnetic force. I find myself touching his cheek, I close my eyes and it feels like I'm twenty-two again and I've just met him at a beach party and he's brought me home and I'm standing here, desperate for him to kiss me – but utterly petrified at the same time. I remove my hand quickly as if I've been burned and open my eyes in time to see him lower his face to mine but I pull away just before our lips meet.

I've waited years for this moment, but suddenly it feels too soon.

I brush past him. He calls out, a hint of desperation in his voice this time. 'Bea, please, can I see you again soon?'

I turn and smile at him. 'Goodbye, Kieran.'

He presses his fingers to his lips and then brushes them lightly over mine. 'It's not goodbye, Bea. Because that means going away and I promise you, I'm not going anywhere this time . . .'

I walk away backwards, unable to unlock my eyes from his. Then, when there is enough distance between us, I turn and run towards my childhood home, my feet pounding the gravel and an intense burning sensation rippling through my body, feeling more alive than I have for years. I get to the front door and put my key in the lock. As I turn it, I glance round and see him leaning against his camper van, silhouetted by the light of the moon and the stars.

Chapter 36

The light from the computer is casting an eerie blue glow across the room matching the violet hue of dawn. Loni is asleep, or out – I'm not sure which. All I know is the house was dark when I got back and I was relieved. The last thing I needed was the third degree from her. Kieran is my secret for now.

I wasn't able to sleep. I lay awake for hours; my brain was wired, my heart pounding, my head full of thoughts, reliving the day I'd just had. At 5 a.m. I finally gave up tossing and turning and crept downstairs to make myself a cup of tea, tidy up the bombsite in the kitchen and check my emails on Loni's computer.

Obviously I've found myself looking on Facebook. Again. I'm just about to write a little cryptic status update when I spot a new update from Milly:

Milly Singh has got some BIG news. Huge, in fact.
1 hour ago, New York.
27 likes.

I comment immediately:

Bea Bishop: OK, OK, you can't post something like that on Facebook and not expect this ... SKYPE CALL IMMEDIATELY!
Milly Singh: Dialling you now! X

I reread Milly's status update as I wait for my best friend to appear before me. Has she been promoted? Has she got a new apartment? Is she coming *home*? The last is wishful thinking. I have been trying not to dwell on how much I miss her. Milly and Jay leaving has felt like the last link to my old life with Adam has been completely severed.

I find myself getting distracted waiting for Milly to call and the unbearably slow Wifi. I stack four old, dirty coffee mugs, turning up my nose as I do so at all the mess whilst also trying not to look at the Post-it notes on Loni's computer that say 'Sex for the Over-Sixties – book eleven title?' And 'How to Get Old Without Acting It'. She also has her favourite Buddhist life mottoes stuck to the pin board directly behind the screen. 'To dare is to lose one's footing. Not to dare is to lose oneself.' I stare at it for a moment. It seems horribly appropriate given Kieran's observation on our date yesterday. No, not date. A casual meeting ... Anyway, whatever it was, he was right. I have been so risk-resistant, so unwilling to do anything remotely daring, to stand on the edge, to risk failure, or worse, falling, that I've completely lost sight of who I am and what I really want. I feel like I have sleepwalked through the last eight years, guided with my eyes closed and my instincts switched off by people who were fully engaged with life. First Loni and Cal, then Milly and finally, Adam. I knew it was happening, of course. I welcomed it, in fact. But that doesn't mean it always felt right.

It took Kieran showing up on my wedding day to make me

turn my back on my safe, secure life, my risk-proof future, and find the courage to be myself. To make my own choices.

I smile to myself as I cast my mind back over the last twelve hours. Strangely, seeing Kieran has made me finally make peace with what I did to Adam almost four months ago. Marrying him would only have ended in disaster. I wish I'd seen it before we got to the church, but better late than never, I guess.

A loud ringing emanates from the computer telling me Milly is making contact. I feel nervous as I press accept call. I realise I haven't spoken to her properly since she moved. Somehow we haven't yet got in synch with the time difference. Whenever I phone her, she seems to be otherwise engaged and the one time we have talked, it was a three-way conversation with her and Jay – against a backdrop of a dinner party they were throwing for Jay's new colleagues at their swanky Manhattan loft. As a result, since she's been gone she hasn't just felt far away geographically, but emotionally too.

It sounds childish but it's felt like she's been keeping her new life a secret from me . . .

I gasp and put my hand over my mouth as a surprising, beautiful image fills my screen. Not of Milly's face, but her bare belly. She is standing sideways and all I can see is a tiny bump, the merest hint of a protrusion on her slender frame.

'MILLY!' I scream, watching my face drop with shock. 'Oh my GOD! You're PREGNANT!' Her grinning face appears now, she's nodding and I'm crying. I'm just not sure whether it's happiness for her, or sadness for me. I knew our dream of sharing this next stage of our lives was over when I walked away from Adam. But this is the confirmation of just how different our lives are now.

'Oh, Milly,' I sob and then I add, 'I'm so HAPPY for you! You're going to be a *mum*!'

'I think you'll find it's *mom* over here,' she says wryly, executing a perfect New York accent. I notice that she looks exhausted.

Hang on, what time is it over there? I quickly work it out. 6 a.m.
here is . . . God, it's 1 a.m.

'Hey, shouldn't you be in bed? It's the middle of the night over
there, isn't it?'

'No rest for the wicked,' she says wearily. 'I've just got in from
work.'

'But you shouldn't be working so hard in your condition,
Mills!'

'You sound like Jay! I'm pregnant, not an invalid,' she snaps and
then rubs her forehead. 'Sorry, sorry, I'm just tired. And hormonal.
Turns out I'm definitely *not* one of those women who has loads of
energy and glows throughout pregnancy. I feel like shit, in fact.'

'You'll start feeling better soon. Everyone says the first few
weeks are the hardest. You'll soon get that Milly Singh spring
back in your step again when you hit the second trimester . . .'

'Maybe.' She looks down, away from the camera. 'Look, I
know I should have told you this sooner and I'm sorry I didn't,
but there never seemed to be a good time . . . what with . . . you
know, everything that's happened.'

She doesn't need to say 'With you and Adam'. I know that's
what she means.

'But I'm *in* my second trimester, Bea.' She looks at me with a
mixture of nerves and defiance. 'I'm nearly sixteen weeks . . .'

I quickly do the maths in my head and then gasp again.
'That's nearly four months! So h-how? WHEN?' I'm struggling
to let this all sink in. Not only is Milly pregnant, but she's been
pregnant for months and not told me? I know she said she didn't
feel there was a good time . . . but what did she think I'd do?
Have I been such a bad friend, so selfish and obsessed with my
troubles that I was *living* with her and still managed not to notice
one of the biggest changes of her life? I let my mind rewind and
I suddenly recall her uncharacteristically shovelling leftovers into

her mouth, turning down top-ups of wine, then there was the comment at her party about how Jay might one day be the main breadwinner. What else have I missed, what else has been happening around me while I've been so wrapped up in myself?

I think of how Loni and Cal have been begging me to come home. I think of how tired Cal looks and how worried he's been about Loni. And I resolve to start being more present in their lives. I've been so focused on my world that I've missed the changing seasons of theirs.

Milly smiles sadly, she seems embarrassed somehow. 'Well, I'm pretty sure I don't have to explain to you how, but as for when . . . well, um, it was your wedding night, I think. I didn't tell you earlier because I thought it would upset you . . .'

'Upset me?' I pause for a moment. Perhaps a beat too long but only because I need time to process this news. I'm happy for her and Jay, I really am. 'Milly, of course I'm not upset,' I reply at last. I try and think of something to say to make it sound more convincing. Not for the first time, I wish she was here so I could talk to her face to face. I'm worried my happiness is being lost through the computer screen.

'I'm so happy for y—'

'Are you sure?' she interrupts uncertainly.

'Yes!'

'Sorry,' we say in unison. 'You go,' she says, waving her hand.

'No, you.'

We laugh uncomfortably and I break the awkward moment.

'I mean, at least this means something good has come out of this whole sorry mess!' I catch sight of my face again and I can see how unnatural and strained it looks. 'Just think, maybe if I *had* married Adam you wouldn't be pregnant!' I force out a little laugh.

'I'm pretty sure it would have happened on your wedding night anyway. We'd have been so full of happiness – and champagne –

it would have been a given!' Milly smiles. 'But in this case, I think we were so shocked by what had happened we needed to reassure ourselves that everything was OK with us. We'd spent all afternoon and evening comforting Adam in your bridal suite; it was stressful and emotional, and when we finally got back to our room we just . . . well. I don't need to say what we did.' She looks down at her tummy.

I nod. Milly had often complained that she and Jay got back so late from work and were so knackered that sex had fallen low on their agenda. She'd never doubted the strength of their marriage, but I'm sure what I did would have made her feel insecure. Adam and I met at the same time as they did – the four of us have always been each other's relationship barometer. Milly always said she loved how little pressure Adam and I put on our relationship, how easy and slow it was. Whereas I admired how certain she and Jay were about each other. How they wanted to settle down immediately. Get married and now, have a family . . .

I feel a wave of sadness at the thought of the baby Adam and I will never have. And then I have a word with myself. This isn't about me. It's Milly's moment.

'Do you have a picture? You know, a scan, of your baby?' I ask. She nods and smiles and pulls one out. And there it is. I lean forward to get closer to the screen. I can't believe I'm looking at Milly's baby. It is wonderful – and I'm crying with joy for her, and yet it also feels like yet another line she has crossed, like we're in two different worlds.

'It doesn't really look like a baby. More like a freaky little gremlin,' she says. But her voice is bursting with a pride that belies her words. 'I've actually got something else to tell you, Bea.'

'Is it twins?' I joke. 'You can't possibly have two in there. I get a bigger bump after eating my dinner than you have right now.'

Milly doesn't laugh. 'It's got nothing to do with the baby. It's –

well, it's Adam. He's here at the moment. He's actually been staying with us for a while. He's taken a New York stopover during
his travels.'

'Oh,' I reply quietly. For a moment I imagine it is Adam and
I out there together, married and on a transatlantic mini break.
We'd probably go out every few months to see them ... maybe
book a holiday together in the Hamptons next year or take a US
road trip together. In this version of my life, I wouldn't have lost
the two – three including Jay – best friends I've ever had. A different choice, but the question is would it have been a better life?

And then another thought occurs to me. 'Is he there, in the
flat right now? While I'm talking to you?'

'What?' she exclaims. 'GOD, no! I wouldn't do that! What do
you take me for? Look,' she sighs. 'I didn't want to tell you
because I knew you'd feel left out. And I didn't NOT want to tell
you because I don't want us having secrets, but with the baby and
everything ...'

Then it hits me that Adam will have known about Milly's
pregnancy before me. And this thought fills me with unprece-
dented sorrow. I mean, in what freakish universe does Adam
know that my best friend is pregnant before I do?

I pick at some invisible fluff on my pyjamas as I try to think of
something to say to Milly. It never occurred to me when I split up
with Adam that I might lose my best friend too. But now I can see
it all unfolding in front of my eyes. The three of them together, in
New York, maybe they all go out to a bar and a cool restaurant,
Milly brings a female colleague as 'company' for Adam. Or Jay does.

Oh God, Eliza Grey. Suddenly I am hit with a wave of jeal-
ousy that takes me by surprise.

I have no right to feel jealous, I tell myself sternly. But it
doesn't help.

'So, is er Adam, has he been ...' I trail off, too embarrassed to voice my concerns to Milly. What I want to say is *Has he been seeing anyone else while he's been out there?* Instead, I go with the more acceptable, 'Has he finished his sabbatical?'

'You could say that,' Milly says carefully. 'He's left, you know. He told George he doesn't want to work for him any more.'

'Oh,' I say, utterly dumbstruck. I can't believe it. How could Adam have left? Adam's life IS Hudson & Grey. I don't think he knows what to do or who he is without it.

'He told us he doesn't know who he is without you. So he's taking some time out to find himself again, without any other distractions.'

I stare at the the screen in front of me, unable to process this information. I have never considered that Adam might be struggling without me. I always thought I needed him far more than the other way round. I am trying to imagine Adam, my strong, incisive, stoical Adam, in a world where he isn't working and I realise that, even though I'm happy for him, I feel . . . sad. I wish I could see him relaxed and carefree, travelling across America. I hope he's enjoying being unshackled from the pressures of working for his dad, living the kind of life that he'd never had the opportunity to consider before. I hope he does work out what he wants. I realise that the fact he's in New York means that what he wants definitely isn't me. I think of the Facebook messages we exchanged just a few months ago. We've both moved on, just like we knew we would.

So why don't I feel happier about it?

Milly and I talk for a bit longer, about sonograms and ante-natal classes, buggies and other baby stuff. Then we say goodbye quickly, both desperate to get off the phone and back to our new lives. In different time zones. And what appears to be increasingly different worlds.

Chapter 37

'Morning!' calls Sal, smiling broadly at me as I push open the door on Monday. I'm immediately engulfed by the fragrance of flowers and earthy wet flower-shop scent. I loved being back in Norfolk, seeing Kieran and catching up with Loni and then having dinner with Cal. So much so that I've promised I'll visit more often. I won't be full-time here until Sal goes on maternity leave. In fact I've already decided to go back home this week. It's not because of Kieran – I want to spend more time with my family. Well, that's what I'm telling myself.

'How was your weekend?' Sal asks as she puts out the buckets of flowers.

'Great!' I reply. 'Brilliant, in fact. Just what I needed . . .'

This is true. I feel so much better for spending some time at home. Hearing Milly's news made me realise just how much I've been neglecting my family. I can count on one hand the amount of times I've seen them in the past year and I feel horribly ashamed. Not least because Cal and Lucy could do with some help. They're both clearly exhausted. They don't have the benefit of on-hand babysitters. There isn't a limitless fund for nights out. Loni babysits when she can but she has so many evening events lined up they have to book her well in advance. I'd been putting off going to Norfolk because I didn't think it would help me to be there, but I'd been so obsessed with my own needs that I hadn't considered that *I* might be able to help *them.*

Maybe that's why Loni was so ridiculously thrilled when I told her I'd be back in a few days when she drove me to Norwich and dropped me off at the train station.

'You're coming back in DAYS, not months, darling? What a JOY!' she exulted, pulling me into her bosom and kissing my head fervently. The tight hug Cal gave me on the platform told me he was happy too.

I'd glanced up at Loni as we'd said goodbye and was surprised to see the glimmer of tears in her eyes and I'd felt more ashamed of myself than ever. We're not the closest mother and daughter in the world but she's all I have and I know I've neglected her.

'I'm so glad. I'll have to change some plans though,' Loni said, more to herself than to us.

'Oh yeah, G-LO?' Cal answered teasingly. This is the nick-name Loni gave herself because she didn't feel old enough to be called 'Grandma'. Cal has taken to using it, too. 'Got a proper boyfriend, at last? Someone you *make plans* with? Have you finally decided it's time to settle down?' He'd rubbed his chin thoughtfully. 'It makes sense – I mean, I've hardly seen you recently . . .' He was teasing her and we all knew it. Usually Loni laughs along, but not on this occasion.

'No, darling!' Loni snapped, flicking her chin up defensively. 'You know I don't plan on settling down! Why shouldn't a single woman of my age have some fun? Just because I don't want a life-partner doesn't mean I shouldn't be able to have SEX.'

She said this word so loudly that a gaggle of passing passengers turned to look at us. I blushed and begged her to lower her voice. But she refused. 'Don't be such a prude! Sex is the best way of being in the moment, of being in the flow of life without thinking of the past or worrying about the future.'

'Aside from just, you know, being happy on your own . . .' I offered.

'Well yes, but that's just *dull*!' Loni exclaimed. 'Honestly, you two, if you'd listen to me more often . . .'

'Hear that, sis? Listen to your wise old mother,' Cal said affectionately, giving Loni a squeeze. 'You go slag it up reet proper!' he added in a broad Norfolk accent and Loni whacked him.

'That's not what I'm saying,' she chastised him, and grinning he threw his arm around her.

In that moment I felt so happy to be with them that I knew I'd made the right decision to come back more often. I got on the train not feeling my usual sensation of guilt and relief and like the odd one out, but soothed, healed.

Maybe Loni was right, I thought as she jumped up and down on the platform, waving a tie-dyed scarf at me as the train pulled away. Maybe it was time for me to get back in the proverbial saddle. I thought of Kieran and then quickly pushed him from my mind.

This wasn't about him . . . was it?

It's a question I've been asking myself after the text conversation we had that left me unable to sleep last night. I felt like a teenager again as I lay on top of the covers in Milly's flat, the hot, humid night only adding to the excitement I felt every time my phone beeped and a new message from him appeared.

What are you doing? K xx

I replied instantly, my fingers moving deftly across the phone keyboard, hovering over the x before pressing it.

Nothing. x
What about now? x
Still nothing . . .
Not taken any risks recently then, huh . . .? ;-)
Depends what you mean by 'recent' . . .
Fancy taking one with me? x
I'm texting you, so it looks like I already am . . . x
I mean taking a leap. An actual one.
So do I.
Together. This week? x

I paused for a moment and my phone buzzed again.

I'll pick you up from your mum's on Thursday. All will be
revealed then. x
I'm not that sort of girl. x
Ha ha. Shame . . . xx

That was followed by another text.

Question. What are you most scared of?

I looked at the ceiling, struggling to know how to reply
without revealing too much. I'd finally settled on just one
word:

Falling.

He responded within a second.

You should never be afraid of that. xxx

I suddenly realise I've been daydreaming in the back room for nearly ten minutes. I unhook my bag from around my neck, with shaking hands take off my denim jacket and go into the shop. I'm horrified when I see that Sal is crouched down, trying to drag an olive tree in a heavy earthenware pot out onto the street.

'Let me do that!' I exclaim. 'How many times do I have to tell you to stop lifting heavy things,' I scold. We have quickly settled into roles that involve me nagging her like a concerned mum and running around after her whilst she protests at my help.

'I'm not ill, you know, Bea,' she says, heaving and exhaling so that wisps of yellowy blonde hair fly up around her face, like rays of sunshine. Her comment instantly makes me think of Milly and of how similar my old friend and my new friend are. Headstrong, decisive, straight to the point. I think of Milly, my best friend, four months pregnant and Sal, now nearly seven months gone. I feel a now familiar sense of being in some sort of new, parallel universe. One where everything has changed.

'So, any gossip?' Sal asks meaningfully.

I smile. I can't tell anyone else, so why not her?

Chapter 38

'SURPRISE!'

'Oh my GOSH!' Glenda cries, dropping her handbag as I hand her the bouquet of flowers Nick ordered for her fiftieth birthday and asked me to deliver personally. I convinced Sal to close the shop early and come with me too so I could introduce her to my friends. The shop has been quiet this month; London is on holiday.

'Oh Bea, it's gorgeous!' Glenda exclaims and she kisses me on the cheek.

I smile as I look at the bouquet. There's a single yellow zinnia there because she chose it for her husband's funeral and it symbolises daily remembrance. Then I've added some golden yellow alstroemeria (*friendship and devotion*), some bright, late-blooming azaleas (*maternal love*) and sunflowers – because other than daffs, I can't think of a bloom that better represents her.

'Oh Bea, they're beautiful, pet!' Glenda says, her eyes filling with tears. 'And a yellow zinnia ... I—' She gets all choked and envelops me in a warm, perfumed hug and then turns to Sal and beams at her. 'It's *so* lovely to meet a new friend of Bea's. Thank you both so much for coming.'

'I wouldn't have missed this for the world, G,' I say, giving her a tight squeeze as Nick brings out the cake he's had made in the shape of her name, iced in colours of the Welsh flag and with five sugared daffodils with candles in stuck on top – 'I couldn't fit fifty,' he'd said – and we all sing 'Happy Birthday'. The entire room bursts into applause.

She pulls away and wipes her eyes.

'Here, G, let me put those in a vase for you,' Tim says, slipping his arm around her. 'I'll make some more tea while I'm there.'

'I'll help you!' Sal says a second later and scurries after him. 'Watch out,' she warns him as he fails to hold open the kitchen door for her. 'Lady with a baby coming through!'

'Oh, shit, babe – and er, baby, I'm so sorry!' Tim gasps. He turns around and stares at Sal's face and then her stomach in horror. He looks mortified as he holds the door open. 'I didn't realise you were behind me.'

'Hard to miss, aren't I?' Sal says, clasping her tummy. 'I'm ENORMOUS.' She edges past him.

'You look . . . lovely.' She stops and looks up. He towers over her but they stare at each other for a moment and in that second I experience a strange sensation that my old and new lives are crossing and whole worlds are changing.

September

Dear Bea

So here we are in September; the lazy hammock that swings between the staunch tree trunks of summer and winter. Your well-tended flowers and shrubs are mellowing out this month, giving a colourful climax to their end-of-season show. As the month goes on and the days begin to shorten, you'll notice a subtle muting of colour; bright pinks and yellows are replaced by darker cerises and burnt-biscuit golds. Clouds of Michaelmas daisies drift across borders, swarms of sedums and hordes of helianthus, too. The approach of autumn brings a second flowering to shrubs and trees, providing a flush of bloom that brings to mind the renewal of old romances. Notice, too, the burgeoning bellies of frothy pink or white gypsophilia or 'baby's breath' that will suddenly appear.

You may find yourself locked in a back-to school mentality that prompts you to sharpen performance, passion and prospects in preparation for a big professional change. Now is certainly the time to establish a new lawn. Ground should be properly prepared and levelled first to form a firm surface on which new seeds can flourish. Dig up those roots and transplant evergreens; you will soon see how they flourish in a new position. Sow hardy annuals that you know you can always rely on to bring colour and depth – but remember to plant new bulbs too.

After all, Bea, the garden is always evolving and so should you.

Love, Dad x

Chapter 39

Bea Hudson is finally making the leap.

'I still can't believe it's your last day,' Glenda says mournfully, stroking the dark green leaves of the jade plant I gave her for her birthday last month as I continue packing up my desk. It is said to represent the joy and energy of friendship and is considered lucky. 'I'm going to miss you so much. We all are.'

'Me too, G. ' I glance around the office that has been my career foster home for seven years – and my real home for the past four months. I can't believe it's only been three short weeks since I walked into Nick's office and told him I wanted to go for the temp position at JF Design. It was Adam's idea. He was the one who got excited when the candidate James had chosen unexpectedly dropped out because she got offered a full-time position somewhere else ('How many more signs do you need?' he'd said). I'd finally listened to him, because even I couldn't run away from this opportunity a second time.

Nick had immediately called James who'd been thrilled that I was being released from my contract and said he'd love me to work for him.

'You've always been on borrowed time here,' Nick said when he ended the call that changed my entire career future. 'I can't ignore the signs any longer that you're way too good for us.'

And now, my last day at Eagle's is drawing to a close. Everyone starts gathering around my desk, plastic cups of sparkling wine in hand, bowls of crisps and a Colin-the-Caterpillar cake spread out on the table, and I realise how much I'm going to miss every single one of my colleagues. I look around at them all now, taking in their beaming smiles, their genuine happiness for me. Even when I was a temp I always felt like I knew the staff of Eagle Recruitment pretty well, but really I just flitted in and out here like a honeybee, pausing to get my fill of friendship nectar before buzzing off to whatever soul-sucking City office had hired me for the week or month. I thought I liked it like that; surface friendships were safer, after all. But now I realise I made assumptions because of that. I thought Glenda was a lonely widow. But now I know her better I realise she is the busiest, happiest woman I know. She's making the most of her new beginning. No living life in the past for her. And then there's Tim . . . after Nick's speech he's gone back to work dutifully, even though it is long past 5 p.m.

'All right, Timbo?' I say congenially as I pull my chair round to his side of the desk. 'Looks like you're hard at it . . .'

He sits back in his chair, stretches and grins. 'Always, babe, always. Got to make hay while the sun shines, can't keep a good guy down, no rest for the wicked, et cetera et cetera. Have you come to tell me how much you're going to miss me and that you've secretly been in love with me all this time?'

'Of course I am. I mean, what woman could possibly resist you?' I grin back.

He exhales loudly. 'I know, it's a burden. I just feel sorry for you being married to that, frankly, embarrassing specimen of a man that you call a husband. I mean, tall, handsome, rich, clever, bloody nice guy . . . honestly, what *do* you see in him?' He winks and I drop a light kiss on his cheek. At which point he blushes profusely. I have always known Tim isn't quite the ladykiller he pretends to be.

'Here.' I hand him the bamboo plant I've been holding.

Tim takes it and studies it for a moment. 'Thank you, Bea, it's er, very green. Should I munch on it like a panda?'

I laugh. 'I know you're not really a flower guy, Tim, but bamboo plants represent joy and wealth. They're also meant to bring luck. I thought it would be a good charm for you to have on your desk.' Tim acts like he's Mr Chilled but I know he's pet-rified of losing his job, of losing everything again. That's why he works so hard, that's the need for all the bravado . . .

Tim gazes at it then looks back at me. His eyes appear to be watering a little.

'Don't you dare cry on me, Timbo,' I threaten, punching him lightly on the shoulder, and he sniffs manfully and shakes out his shoulders.

'You're a good friend, Bea. You really do deserve every happi-ness in the world.'

I smile, trying to believe that's true.

Chapter 40

It's late when I get back to the flat, and I'm tipsy on both happiness and alcohol. Nick and the gang gave me such a lovely send-off; we went to the pub and drank Prosecco and played drinking games and they all made me promise to stay in touch.

Nick even took me to a quiet corner and spent ages telling me how much he was going to miss me, that I'd always inspired him to think bigger, to look for more in life, and told me earnestly that he would always be there for me if ever I needed anything at all . . .

I'd given him a grateful hug. 'Thanks so much, I'll never forget what you've done for me. You're the best boss ever and I'd work for you again in a heartbeat.'

He'd mumbled something about not meaning a job.

I call out to Adam, my voice echoing around the stark grey walls of the flat. But there's no answer – he's obviously working late. Again. He's already been to New York twice in the past month and I can count on one hand the evenings we've spent together. I'm trying to be understanding – I know his job is highly pressured and I know he's not exactly happy about how much it is taking him away from me, but I am upset that he hasn't thought that I might want to celebrate my last day at Eagle's with him. I was hoping he'd turn up at the pub as I'd specifically told him this morning that's where we'd be. Glenda was very excited about him coming. She's always loved Adam. Said he's 'a keeper'. I throw my bag down on the granite island unit that is – as ever – completely spotless. Sometimes I have this urge to whirl through the flat like the Tasmanian devil, messing everything up to make it feel more homely.

I open the fridge and peer inside woozily, gripping the door and the side feeling like I might fall into the icy depths otherwise. I haven't been shopping this week and Adam has been out at client dinners most nights so all there is is a couple of M&S meal-for-one selections. I pull out a Gastro Fish Pie, stab the lid with a fork – almost spearing my hand at the same time – and bung the pie in the microwave before grabbing my new *Gardener's Monthly* from where the cleaner has left it on the coffee table. I'm thinking about redesigning the roof garden slightly. I flop down on the couch and switch on the TV and start channel-hopping.

Moments later the door opens and I scramble up to a sitting position as Adam comes in.

'Hi,' I call as he throws down his bag and heads straight for the fridge. 'Good day?' I ask. He grabs a bottle of beer, pulls open a drawer, grabs a bottle opener and slams the drawer shut again. Then he opens the bottle and takes a long swig before walking over to the lounge area and starting to look through the pile of post I took my magazine from.

'A kiss for your wife wouldn't go amiss,' I say pointedly.

Adam comes and plants a kiss on my forehead. 'I'm sorry. It's been a hell of a day.'

'I've just got back myself from my leaving do. You know, the one you were meant to be at,' I say to his back as he heads for the other sofa.

He looks round, immediately contrite. 'Shit, Bea, I'm sorry. I've been on a conference call to New York all evening. How was it?'

'Fine, good, fun,' I say succinctly. 'You were missed though.'

Adam groans and collapses onto the sofa. He takes another swig of beer then closes his eyes, the bottle resting on his stomach. I don't think he really heard me. 'As well as dealing with all the shit in New York it turns out Dad also expects me to oversee the office move from Soho to Canary Wharf, and brief the designers. Plus we have to find new premises in New York – which is a nightmare. Not to mention that we have a couple of big pitches on and I'm expected to hire some more senior staff in two different countries. I've tried to tell Dad that I can't take it all on alone, but he just reels off examples of when he was starting the agency and all the sixteen-hour days he did, and how our generation don't have the same work ethic. I don't know what he wants – blood, I think.' Adam exhales and rubs his forehead and goes to get up. 'I've got to do some more work now, in fact.'

'But it's nearly midnight on a Friday night!' I exclaim. 'What can you possibly do at this hour?'

'Dad's given me the task of briefing the garden designers who are pitching for the urban roof terrace contract. To be honest I haven't got a clue where to begin. It's really not my area of expertise.'

'Well, why don't you ask an expert?' I say, walking over to him and pushing him gently back on the sofa before sitting on his lap. He smiles wearily as I gaze up at him. God, he looks exhausted.

'Like who?' Adam replies, adjusting his position. 'Sorry, Bea, can you just move a bit, my back's really hurting . . .'

I lift myself up so he can sit up and then slide in next to him. 'Oh you know, Ad, someone who has been passionate about garden design all her life, who transformed your very own roof terrace, who reads gardening magazines obsessively, who did a degree – well, almost did a degree – in garden design and who, as luck would have it, is about to become an assistant to one of the best garden designers in the country! Need any more clues?' I give him a Cheshire cat grin and prod him. 'The woman you love, the wife you married, the person you know best in the world . . .'

Adam shifts awkwardly on the sofa and I move to give him a bit more space. 'Oh Bea, that's really very sweet of you, but I can't discuss this with you.'

'Oh. OK. That's OK. I understand.' I get up. But I don't understand. Not really. I don't understand why he can't talk to me, why we're so distant and why he doesn't seem to notice. Maybe it's all the alcohol I've drunk tonight that's making me overreact but suddenly I feel unanchored, unmoored – like I'm drifting, no, *we're* drifting apart. We should be closer than ever – we're still newlyweds, for God's sake – but each new pull on Adam's time seems to pull *us* further apart. I thought this would be the perfect opportunity to help him with his work – something I can't usually do – but even though this is my area of expertise, he still doesn't want to let me in. I walk back over to the kitchen to make a cup of tea. I feel like he and I are on opposite sides of the same line and we have no idea how to cross it.

'I need to Skype New York,' Adam says a moment later, his voice piercing the uncomfortable silence that has descended on our flat.

'Fine.'

I look over my shoulder as he heads for the bedroom with his laptop. He opens the door and stops to look back at me as if he's about to say something but obviously he changes his mind because he then disappears inside, shutting the door firmly behind him.

Chapter 41

'How's your first day been then, Bea?' James asks sweetly as he walks up to me.

'Amazing!' I reply with a gigantic smile. It is 4.30 p.m, and my brain feels like it's about to explode with all the information I've absorbed. I want to impress James, I want to show him that his instinct was right; he made the right choice. Luckily my temping background means that I'm used to first days and having to learn new information at speed. But today has been different: exciting, invigorating, stimulating, inspiring. I've felt carried on a wave of certainty that this just feels right; that my working here is meant to be. I spent the first hour this morning setting up my stuff on my desk under one of the beautiful big skylights that flood light into this open-plan loft space. The view is incredible and it feels *great* to be back in Greenwich even if it is for work. I realised when I stepped out of the DLR just how much I miss Greenwich, and I couldn't help reminiscing about the days living with Milly in her flat opposite Greenwich Park. Moving there brought me back to life again after a terrible time. Milly looked after me, made me realise that I had a chance to start again. I remember she said I was like Bambi at first, all wobbly legs and afraid of the world, not knowing which way to turn, constantly worrying about falling. But Milly convinced me I was strong enough to start looking for a job so I signed on to Eagle's as a temp, I met Adam and I didn't wobble any longer, because he began to carry me.

Through the skylight I can see the impressive English baroque twin façade of the Old Royal Naval College designed by Sir Christopher Wren and the masts of the *Cutty Sark*. And if I look through the window at the back of the office and stand on my tiptoes I can just make out the Royal Observatory on the hill. I feel inspired simply by being here, back in a place I love, surrounded by green space and culture and history. For the first time in my life I was in the right place at the right moment and I am so grateful for this opportunity. Now I just have to prove myself worthy of it – and I really think that I can.

Maybe that's down to James's easy, encouraging management style. Maybe it's the way I've been welcomed into the small team with open arms. There are only three staff here – excluding James and me – Jack, Chris and Georgie. All in their early thirties, all super friendly and welcoming, all passionate about gardens and creating beautiful, inspiring outdoor spaces for their clients.

This is my world now. It is a thought that makes my head spin and my happiness levels soar.

'Are you feeling a bit overwhelmed?' James asks. I realise I must look pretty gormless, siting here grinning inanely at him.

'No, no!' I exclaim. 'I'm so happy that I'm here, I – I still can't quite believe my luck,' I add quietly. 'I kind of feel like this shouldn't be happening to me. Like I've stolen someone else's life.'

It occurs to me that I should thank my lucky stars that I have Adam. Without him giving me that nudge, I wouldn't be here now. It does make me wonder what I'd do without him, where

I would be. A picture flashes into my mind of him standing alone in a church doorway watching as I'm driven away. I shake my head, trying to banish the dark thoughts that sometimes close in. It doesn't bear thinking about. I know I'm just feeling a bit vulnerable because we're not spending enough time together. I resolve to change that. After all, Adam is a guy, maybe I need to make the effort more . . . I tune back into James in a bid to tune out my worries.

'No such thing as luck, Bea,' he laughs. 'In your own unique way you have worked hard for this position. Your years of temping have prepped you well – as have your own personal design projects. Your roof terrace, your friend's garden, your mum's garden . . . all irreplaceable experiences in my opinion. And the fact that you seem to have read every garden design book going, know more about horticulture than most grads, have been to lots of garden shows and most of all spent your life gardening . . .' James pauses and gazes kindly at me. 'Well, let's just say I much prefer taking on people like you who consider this a way of life, not just a job.' He goes over to the cooler and gets some water. 'Take my partner: he calls himself a writer, even though he's not published, because he writes every single day. It's the same thing, isn't it? I mean, you may not have been paid for it before – but it seems to me that you've been a garden designer your whole life. It's just taken you a while to believe it!'

He sits down in his chair and smiles at me and I nod, trying not to weep at his lovely words: that would be a major no-no on day one. Or day two or even week two, I tell myself sternly.

'Now, I want to talk to you about this big corporate project you'll be assisting me with. I wanted to give you the day to settle in with the team, find your feet around our progammes and systems – the position is an admin one first and foremost – but the pitch for this project is at the beginning of November and I like

to consider every member of this company a creative contribu-
tor. And this could be a game-changer for JF Design. If we win
it, it will be this company's biggest and most ambitious project
yet. I want you to read over the brief so you can get a real sense
of who the client is and what they want and then bring your
ideas to our brainstorming meeting. I value everyone's opinions
on this team; there is no hierarchy in creativity, as far as I'm concerned. The ad agency we're doing the roof terrace design for is
going to be moving into this building near Canada Square in the
spring.' He points at a map and then looks out of his window
across at the City as if visualising it on the skyline. 'This means
if we win the project we will have approximately six months from
the design process to finished product. We won't be able to start
planting until the beginning of March at the earliest as the office
won't be ready till then – and they will be showing the new
office space and terrace at a grand opening party at the end of
March. All the measurements are on the plans.' He hands them
to me and I cast my eyes over them, my heart thudding to what
feels like a standstill when I read the company's name printed
at the top of the page.

Hudson, Grey & Friedman.

I feel a flush of panic. That's Adam's agency, but how . . .? Did
he . . .? I'm struggling to hide my shock. How can I work on this
project when I'm married to the MD and am the daughter-in-law
of one of the partners? Did Adam know about this? Do I tell
James? Oh God . . .

'Do you want to take some notes?' James prompts.

'Oh, er, yes, of course . . .' I blush as I pick up my pen and
notepad. I'm scribbling down as James speaks, all the time wondering how to tell him. Will it compromise my new job, or
Adam's job, or JF Design's pitch?

'With any project, I always imagine I'm designing it for the core client,' James explains, 'which is often very hard with corporate projects when there is no single vision and no chance to get to know them well.' I blink and smile weakly, unable to tell him just how well I know them. 'In this case,' he continues, 'Hudson & Grey is very much the vision of the two men – George Hudson and Robert Grey – who started it, but we won't be dealing directly with them. They've recently bought out a small but successful New York agency and there are plans for Europe and Hong Kong next. This design could well become a blueprint for their international offices. That means designing a space not just for the company's group identity, their culture, but for their clients too. Their MD has made it clear in my initial briefing that this will be both a work and entertaining space so it has to be functional but inspirational.'

The MD? So Adam and James have met. There is no such thing as coincidence. I start thinking about all his pushing for me to go for this job. Has he been pulling strings? Did I even get this job on my own merit?

'Right, I think that's enough to take in for one day!' James smiles, his hands clasped over his knee, gold ring glinting in the sunlight streaming through the loft windows. 'This project is very important, Bea. I'm going to need your one hundred per cent effort and energy, OK?'

'I – I guess so, ' I reply uncertainly. 'I mean, yes, of course.' I know I should tell him but I'm scared I'll lose this opportunity . . . I don't know what to do.

Make the right choice.

'Is there a problem, Bea?' he asks gently. I take a deep breath and then imagine myself closing my eyes and jumping in at the deep end. I have no idea if I'll sink or swim.

'Not exactly, it's just . . .'

Chapter 42

Adam's mobile rings once and then goes to voicemail. I throw it down in frustration and run my hands over my head. It's 6.47 p.m. and I'm still at the office. Even though it's only my first day I'm staying late as a) I want to make a good impression and b) I have no one to get home for as my husband has gone AWOL. I've left him so many messages to call me but haven't heard back. I've wanted to talk to him about this project so much but I also wanted to stay late at the office to start jotting down my ideas and sketches for the brainstorm. James had been amazing when I told him about my connection to Hudson & Grey.

'I didn't know, James, I promise. I'm so sorry. I'll understand if you want to terminate my contract immedi—'

'What? No, don't be silly, this whole city is nepotism incarnate!' He'd winked and I'd exhaled. 'Why don't you talk to your husband and see if he can ensure everyone else at the agency knows and is fine with it. We'll just have to go all out to impress them even more and prove we don't have any unfair favour. Are you up for that?'

I'd nodded, thrilled and relieved that he'd been so understanding.

I've spent the last couple of hours making sure I'm ahead on my more menial tasks, organising James's diary, filing invoices and bills from suppliers before putting my mind to creative ideas for the project that will bring green to the grey landscape, fun to a functional working space. Now I know it's an ad agency – and not just any agency, Hudson, Grey & Friedman – I feel like I instinctively know what will work for it. I'm thinking shelter and surprise, strong lines and symmetry, perennial plants and physical features . . .

I pause with my pencil hovering over my pad, tapping it against my mouth. James made it clear he just wants creative input. I don't have to worry about building regs, planning permission, fire escapes, other safety issues – or even cost. He'll be covering all the technical aspects. It feels like a test, and one that I'm determined to pass.

I think of my and Adam's roof terrace at home, the things we love, the mistakes I made with it and what I learned through the design and planting processes, and I scribble down a few ideas for texture and lighting. I think of all the gardens I've endlessly studied from the past few Chelsea Flower Shows – especially James's one from this year – and I jot a few more ideas down. I think of all the posh private London bars I've been to with Adam. Shoreditch House, Century, Boundary, Sushisamba at the Heron Tower, Vista at the Trafalgar Hotel – all with rooftop bars. And then a less polished, much more urban space – Frank's Café in Peckham, the cool cocktail bar where the Eagle's gang went for drinks last summer at Tim's suggestion. They all have unique styles, vistas and clientele – and have incorporated clever tricks to make the space work for big groups of people.

I write 'What do they want?' at the top of a page and scribble everything down James told me about using it as a public – and a private – space. I think about seating areas, work areas and entertaining areas. I think about some practical elements – electricity, lighting, storage, water, shelter – as well as ease of movement between inside and outside. I think it should feel like an extension of their new offices, but for it to feel separate too. I close my eyes then, I start forming the ideas in my head, lost in a whole new world that feels so incredibly comfortable.

I finally get home at 9 p.m. to find Adam there, sitting working on his laptop on the sofa. He barely looks up. 'You're back! How was your first day?'

'Great, really interesting,' I reply evenly. 'Did you get any of my calls?' I put my bag down, flick on the kettle, go to the fridge and pull out the milk to make a cup of tea.

'There's a bottle of champagne open – I thought we could celebrate,' Adam says, not answering my question and beckoning me over to the sofa. I put the milk back, get out the champagne, pour myself a glass and go and join him. He leans over and kisses me quickly on the lips before looking back at his laptop.

'So tell me what you've been doing. General admin and photocopying, researching and making tea?' He glances up and chinks my glass.

'No actually, I'm helping James with a really big project he's pitching for . . .'

'Oh?' Adam says. 'That's great! So, er, do you know what it is?'

'It's a corporate project, a company that has recently grown and is moving offices from Dean Street in Soho to Canary Wharf and its new building has a 4,000 square foot roof terrace.'

I watch Adam carefully as he swallows back his champagne, hoping that he'll admit he knows. He doesn't. I push back a wave of anxiety. Why isn't he being truthful with me? He must think I'm a complete idiot.

'It's your agency, Adam, don't tell me you didn't know,' I say wearily, getting up and walking over to the window. The blinds are open and the city is sparkling below, an intermittent blue glow from Canary Wharf flashing in the distance like it is measuring the countdown to our confrontation.

'Huh! What a coincidence, hey?' he says quickly. I turn around, suddenly furious at him.

'Come on, Ad, stop treating me like an idiot,' I say in exasperation. 'I know you've known all along. You set this whole thing up, didn't you?'

He doesn't reply. He's staring purposefully down at his trousers. I take it as an admittance of guilt.

'Oh Adam . . .' I rub my forehead. 'Why didn't you tell me? I might have been better prepared then to deal with it when James said who the project was for.'

'I just didn't want you to think—'

'What? That I couldn't get a job without your help?' I interrupt. 'Too late for that.'

'No! Of course not!' he protests. 'You got this job entirely on your own merits. Yes, I met James to brief him on the contract, but I didn't ask him to give my wife a job! All I did was mention Eagle's when he said he was looking to take on a temp to help with the project.' I stare at Adam, feeling like a puppet whose strings are constantly being pulled because I can't cope with doing anything on my own. I'm a thirty-year-old woman and I need to start taking control of my life.

Adam gets up and walks over to me. I stiffen when he slips his arms around me. 'I know how talented you are, Bea, and I knew you wouldn't go after a job like this yourself because you're too scared of failing,' he murmurs. 'I just saw an opportunity for you to do a job you might love and made sure it was put in your path. I think you deserve that, I just wish you did too.' He pauses and shakes his head. 'I just want you to be happy, Bea, that's all. And I'm not sure I've been managing to make you feel that way recently.'

I stare at Adam, a lump forming in my throat because he's right. 'I miss you, Ad,' I say thickly. 'I feel like we've drifted apart since we got married. You're barely here, and when you are your head is still at work . . .'

'I know and I'm sorry,' he says defensively, turning away from me. 'God, don't you think I miss you too? I feel terrible that I never see you. I wish we had time to just hang out together, but it's not like I'm doing anything other than work really hard, is it? I mean, I don't go out, unless it's for work, I don't have any hobbies, I don't see my friends – I don't *have* any friends outside the agency any more. I live and breathe it because I have to. It's our future, Bea. Don't you see? I'm doing all this for us. For our kids, to give them the kind of life that my parents have given me.' He sighs deeply in frustration. I realise again how exhausted he looks. 'I feel like Dad is testing me, pushing me to my limits right now because he wants to know that I share his vision.'

He looks up at me pleadingly, but his jaw is tensed, his mouth pulled into a hard line. 'I owe it to my dad to do everything I can to prove to him that I'm the right person to take the agency forward. I need to make him proud, you know how important that's always been to me.'

'I know, Ad,' I say softly, taking his hand and pulling him towards me. I don't want to fight any more. 'I understand, I do. I just don't want you to lose sight of who you are and what you want because, well, we only get one life, don't we?'

October

Dear Bea

Whilst October was once my favourite month, now when the world is adorned in a last explosion of colour, I will always see autumn as a symbol of my one chance of happiness going up in flames. From now on, October will be the 'lost' month; when leaves fall to the ground like tears, the amber sunlight loses its warmth and the garden becomes desolate and bare. In October I will think not of the beauty that I can still see, but of what I can't.

But you, Bea, you have an endlessly bright season ahead of you. One filled with family, love and laughter. It is the month that you celebrate your birthday so it should be lucky for you, always. It is no coincidence that your birth flower is the cosmos, the Greek word for harmony or ordered universe. Follow the right path and the earth and stars are yours, Bea, always remember that.

Love, Dad x

Chapter 43

Bea Bishop is feeling adventurous.
13 likes, 3 comments.

I stand and gaze out of Loni's back door at the horseshoe-shaped garden which has exploded in a spectacular wave of bountiful autumnal colour. It's glorious, and right now there is nowhere I'd rather be than here. I've decided to spend my two days off from the flower shop in Norfolk this week, partly to do what I'd promised Cal – to spend more time with Loni, but also, somewhat selfishly, for myself.

I've been here a lot lately and with Loni so often out (I have no idea where and she's cagey when I ask) I've been finding myself tending the garden, nurturing it like I am my memories, pulling away at the weeds, cutting back the undergrowth, untangling the deeply embedded roots. But as much as I love it, it is particularly hard to be here at the moment, because no matter what beauty the season brings, October will always be the month my dad walked out.

My phone buzzes and brings me back into the present: Kieran. I smile as I open up his text.

Ready for the next stage of Operation Adventure? K x

I feel a rush of excitement and fear as I reply.

Ready as I'll ever be. x

I think of our dates, no, our meetings, that Kieran has christened 'Operation Adventure'.

The first time we met up after Blakeney, he drove us in his VW to Thetford Forest, a man-made pine forest that sits on the border of the south of Norfolk and the north of Suffolk.

It had soon become clear that Kieran hadn't brought me to the forest to walk – at least not on the ground.

'High wires?' I'd gasped as he led me to the little wooden hut with the sign 'Go Ape' emblazoned on the front.

A girl wearing a green uniform smiled broadly at us. 'Are you doing the Tree Top Adventure today?' she said.

'Yep,' he grinned at her, and I noticed her swoon a little, then he glanced at me as he rubbed his hand over his head so his hair bristled like soft suede before he leaned in towards me. 'See what I meant when I said we'd be taking a leap?'

'I'm not sure I can do this . . .' I said nervously, backing away. 'I don't do heights, or leaping, not any more.'

'And look where it's got you, Bea.' He looked at me apologetically, realising he'd hit a raw nerve. Then he added pleadingly, 'I promise you it'll be fun. You'll be all rigged up properly – and just think about the views across the canopies of all those pine trees. I thought it'd be right up your street.'

'My street tends to be firmly fixed to the ground,' I replied stubbornly.

'And you're happy with that, are you?' He fixed his eyes on me intently. As I looked at him, I felt my knees go weak, and not just because of the prospect of walking a high wire.

'Come on: you Jane, me Tarzan?' I laughed as he beat his

chest. 'I'll be with you all the way,' he murmured, taking my hand.

Moments later we were standing on a platform, high up in the treetops, enveloped in a mossy green cloak of leaves, autumn sunlight filtering through like a path of molten gold.

Kieran was behind me, his hands rested gently on my waist. 'You can do it, Bea, I know you can do it. You're completely safe, you're not going to fall. No one is going to let you fall. Come on, just close your eyes and imagine yourself at one with the forest. The trees are your friends. And I'll be right behind you. One jump and you'll be safely at the other side.'

And maybe it was the warmth emanating from his hands, or his choice of words, but before I knew it I'd shuffled to the edge of the platform, closed my eyes and felt my stomach give way and my heart leap into my mouth in a way I hadn't experienced for a long, long time. A quarter of the way across the zipwire, I screamed a high-pitched scream that seemed to bounce off the trees and echo in my ears. But it wasn't a cry of fear, it was pure unadulterated joy.

Then I stepped back and waited as Kieran swung across. In the distance and suspended in the air as he swung at speed towards me, he looked like the same person I knew eight years ago: a twenty-five-year-old guy with no fear and no regrets and who I loved because he was brave enough to take on the world his way – and gave *me* the confidence to do the same.

The following week, I was back. To see Loni and Cal, I told myself. But I couldn't kid myself any longer. After just two meetings, I needed to see Kieran as desperately as I'd needed to run away from my wedding six months before. I'd gone back in time, to a point in my life when I didn't care about the future or the past; I was living only for the moment, every single moment that I shared with Kieran, like I was all those years ago. I didn't care that my dad had left me, only that I'd found Kieran. I was happy to throw everything away for him, to travel the coast with him and watch him surf and cave, bungee-jump and tomb-stone, do all those things he and Elliot and his groups of friends loved. It absolutely petrified me to watch him throw himself from cliffs and bridges, quarries and harbour walls, but I wanted to be with him, so I supported him. I just didn't tell anyone what he was doing. I still remember Loni's words when she first met Kieran.

'I understand the attraction but please be careful, darling. I'll always support you, whatever path in life you choose. Just don't be led too far down someone else's.'

I hear the sound of tyres on gravel and glancing back at Loni's empty house and with a pounding heart, I take a deep breath and prepare to take the leap once more with Kieran.

Chapter 44

'So what are we doing today?' I ask Kieran, biting my lip and tapping my fingers on my knees as we pootle along the country road behind a tractor, 'Green Day' seeping through the van's old speakers, reminding me of Elliot who used to sing all the lyrics to 'When September Ends' at the top of his voice. I really want us to overtake the slow-moving vehicle, to feel the wind in my hair and that rush of adrenalin that I've grown used to feeling when I am with Kieran. He, however, seems perfectly content to just amble along in second gear.

I'm trying really hard not to think too much about the fact that Kieran hasn't shown any interest at all in kissing me since that time late at night in front of Loni's house. His eyes haven't lingered on my lips, his mouth hasn't once hovered that tiny bit too close to mine. In fact, whilst it seems that the intimacy, the honesty and the friendship have grown equally between us over the last few weeks, the sexual tension has plateaued. I want – no I need him to kiss me so I know just what we're doing here.

'What do you want to do?' Kieran asks now with a friendly smile.

There's a beat while an answer pops into my mind that I know I would never say.

'It should be something involving a leap, right?' Kieran continues. 'Although I take it you're not ready to jump out of a plane yet, huh?'

'Definitely not!' I exclaim. 'You may have got me swinging like a monkey through the trees, but I won't do that.'

'No you won't do that!' Kieran sings in a cheesy rock voice and laughs. I can't help but think of the first line of that song title. *Would I do anything for love? Do I love him?*

Kieran glances at me. I pull my Parka tighter around my body and nestle my mouth in the collar. After an Indian summer the temperature is beginning to drop. Winter is on its way. A new season before a brand-new year . . .

'So, how about trying to find your dad?' The words are thrown out carelessly. It feels like they have tied a noose around my neck, tightening so much I can't breathe.

He brakes suddenly as the tractor in front indicates a right turn and he instinctively puts his arm across my body as I find myself flung forward. I grip the dashboard tightly. My knuckles are white as if I'm about to jump myself and Kieran slowly removes his arm. He looks at me and places his hand lightly on my leg. I look at it, because I can't look at him. I feel like if I do, he will see everything I'm feeling illuminated in my eyes.

We've talked a lot about ourselves over the course of our last few meetings. More than we ever did when we were together. Back then it was all fun and thrills: the future, not the past. We knew a little of each other, but we wanted to live in the present. But this time, I've told him more about my dad, my lifelong feelings of loss and abandonment, about my complex relationship with Loni, and my inability to make decisions or commit to anything since Elliot died. He in turn has told me more about his childhood being pushed from pillar to post, first the foster home and then the care homes, how it was always just him and Elliot and how he's never got over losing him. He's also told me about the naval rescue operations he's been involved in, how he served in the Iraq War in 2008, about his inability to commit to relationships, and his complete apathy at discovering his father was still alive and living in Ireland.

'Bea,' he says softly. 'You say you've always wanted to know your dad. But as far as I can tell you've always been waiting for him to come and find you. So why not take your life into your own hands now and try to find him?'

'Because . . .' I stop and try again. My voice is shaking. 'Because . . .' I can't finish. I don't have a reason other than what the small seven-year-old girl inside my head is screaming: *Because it's his job to find me; he's the one that left!*

'I know you think that it's his move,' Kieran says. 'But you've been waiting for that move for over twenty years. And you know what they say, the definition of madness is doing the same thing over and over and expecting a different result.'

'I – I . . .' I stutter. He is way too close to the bone.

Kieran pulls up onto a grassy verge, cuts the engine and turns to look at me. 'I know exactly how you feel, Bea; I mean, me and you, we're just the same. You think you're defined by what you have lost in your life and that's exactly how I felt when I lost Elliot. But I've learned that the only way to change that is to take charge of the future.' He takes my hand and squeezes it. 'I did that when I joined the Navy. How about you do the same by trying to find your dad?'

'You're right,' I say at last. 'I know you're right. But I'm so scared, Kieran. I'm afraid of him not being alive, of him not wanting to see me, or me not liking what I find. I've built him up in my head until he's almost become the missing half of me.

At the moment, that half is made up of my good memories of him. But what if seeing him destroys them all?'

He glances out of the window and then gazes back at me, his eyes not just looking at me, but through me. 'Surely it is better to know and be disappointed, than to never know and always wonder?' Kieran says softly. I stare at him, unable to breathe. Is that why he came back? Because he wanted to know about us? Has he always wondered too . . .?

I force out some words just to break the intensity of the moment. 'So what do I do? Where do I begin? I don't know where in the world he might be . . .'

'You should start by going to his last known address in this country.'

'That would be the place he moved into when Loni kicked him out.' I've always known this because I'd seen an address written on a box of belongings Loni had delivered the week after he'd gone. But he didn't stay there long. Loni told me it was just a stopover before he left for good.

'Where was that?' Kieran asks now.

'Cley-next-the-Sea.'

He starts up the engine, glances in his rear-view mirror and does a three-point turn. 'Do you remember the address?' he says over his shoulder.

'What, wait – but we're not doing this now, are we?' I say, somewhat startled.

'No time like the present,' he says with a grin and I cling on to my seat, my heart thumping as he puts his foot down and we speed off.

Chapter 45

As we approach the small village of Cley-next-the Sea I find my mood dampening like the marshes that surround it. When Loni told me years ago that he'd stayed here briefly I found it hard to understand. The village is less than fifteen minutes from Holt; if he lived so close, why didn't he come and visit us? Surely the reason he would have moved here was so he could still be an actively involved parent to me and Cal? But why move here temporarily, and then move away? It didn't make sense then – or now.

I have so many questions, I realise. Questions I have put to the back of my mind for years because Loni has always made it clear that there was nothing more to know. She didn't like being married to Dad, he was old and set in his ways. He fell in love with her spirit and sense of adventure but when they had kids he wanted her to be the archetypal stay-at-home mum. He hated her going out, didn't like her friends, or her wild spirit. They battled on for a few years until finally she told him she wanted to go it alone. Then he moved out to a friend's place before heading off into the sunset to make a new life for himself. End of story . . . Whenever I'd question it she'd tell me that he didn't want to leave but she was adamant. That he tried living close by but couldn't cope with seeing her make a new life for herself without him.

So I've just silently blamed her all these years for taking the decision out of his hands, for not giving us any other choice. And then I've waited for him to make the choice to come back.

I can't believe I've been waiting all this time. Doing nothing. Letting other people's decisions mould my life. It wasn't even me who tried to find him when I got engaged, it was Adam.

Adam. His name pops into my mind and with it an explosion of memories and pain. Right now, I don't know which is more painful. Being left, or leaving someone who loves you.

'You OK?' Kieran says. Small, grey, fast-moving clouds are sweeping across the marshy landscape like liquid mercury, the sails of the windmill marking the picturesque village like an X marks the spot on a treasure map. I can't believe I've never thought to try this before. I mean, what if the clue to Dad's whereabouts for the past twenty-three years have been here all along? I used to come to Cley a lot – there's the Garden Centre on the Holt Road that I worked part-time at when I was seventeen after I dropped out of my A levels; I got all our plants for our garden from there. It gives me shivers to think I might have driven past the place that would have told me where Dad was.

I texted Loni on our way here, asking her for Dad's old address in Cley, and she replied with it instantly. So quickly she clearly didn't need to go hunting for an old address book. She must remember it off by heart. She texted again, moments later, unable to resist sending a follow-up: *Why do you need it, darling? Are you OK?* I haven't replied. She's always worried about me. It's the curse of being a parent – particularly a parent of someone prone to depression. I'll explain everything when I go home later. She has a right to know. Just as I have a right to know where my dad is.

After driving down the tiny high street, past a series of small shops, including Crabpot Bookshop, a cute little place selling second-hand books and where, I now suddenly remember, Dad used to buy a lot of his gardening books, we get to Beach Road and pull up in front of a small flint cottage, overlooking the marshes.

I look at the brightly painted front door, glance at Kieran who smiles and squeezes my leg. I try to disguise the shiver that travels through my body as I slide out of the van.

Walking up the overgrown path I feel like I'm treading in my father's old footprints. Is that where he came with his suitcase of clothes, after leaving us? Will I find a clue here that will tell me where he's been all these years and why he didn't come back?

I knock on the front door; a tentative, apologetic rap, and then I wait. I look up at the cottage that appears in dire need of repair. Has it been neglected by just one owner over several decades? An owner who may know where my dad is.

I wait breathlessly and then, just as I'm about to give up, the door opens a tiny bit and an old man with small, inquisitive eyes gazes at me suspiciously through the crack.

I think I'm about to find out.

Chapter 46

'So?' Kieran says when I get back into the van half an hour later.

I don't say anything for a moment. I'm still recovering from the shock that this has been so easy. That finding some answers to my dad's disappearance has been on my doorstep all along.

I nod and smile weakly. 'You could say that.'

'Holy shit, it wasn't him, was it?' he says, his mouth dropping open in shock.

'No! God, I would have ... I don't know what I would have done. No, it was this sweet old guy in his late seventies who gave my dad a place to stay. He's a priest at St Margaret's Church in Cley. He said Dad had always been a good friend and came to him after he left us. Dad told him he knew he couldn't be with us any more but that he didn't want to be too far away either.'

'How long did he stay?' Kieran asks as he pulls onto the road.

'Not long. Just under a month. Father Joe said Dad wouldn't tell him exactly what had happened, but he said he was incredibly low. He felt he was being punished but he couldn't explain what he meant by that. Father Joe said all he could see was a weary man who loved his family and was deeply ashamed by the breakdown of his marriage. Dad told him that he didn't want anyone to know where he was.'

'Was your dad religious then?' Kieran asks.

'I don't know,' I reply. 'I mean, Loni's always said he struggled with her Buddhist beliefs but I don't remember him being a particularly active church-goer. As far as I can recall he always said gardening was his religion.'

'So did this Father Joe have any idea where your dad went afterwards?'

'California,' I reply, dully. I'm still in shock. As is Kieran who gapes at me. 'Yep. Middle-aged family man who gets kicked out of family home by bonkers Buddhist wife hides away in priest's house in sleepy Cley-next-the-Sea for a month and then jumps on a plane to Los Angeles . . .'

'Whoa!' he exclaims gleefully then resets his expression into one of more appropriate concern. 'Why?'

'To fulfil a lifelong dream of becoming a movie star? To join a monastery? I don't know . . .' I gaze out of the window, irritated by Kieran's reaction.

'So did he leave a forwarding address?' I nod and turn over the piece of paper Father Joe gave to me. 'Some place in Orange County.'

'So what are you going to do next?'

I shrug. 'Google it, I guess.'

'We could go,' Kieran says excitedly, his green eyes shining like a cat's. 'We could turn this into an American road trip. Just think, me, you, Route 101. Now *that* would be a leap.'

I laugh nervously. 'Let's not get ahead of ourselves.'

'Suit yourself,' Kieran shrugs, gazing back at the road. 'But the offer is there. I could extend my leave from the ships. And you did say you wanted more excitement in your life . . .'

A contemplative silence descends over the van and as the road curls and coils ahead of us I can't help but wonder, did *I* say I wanted that? Or did Kieran?

Chapter 47

It's a briskly chilly Saturday morning and I'm lost in my thoughts as I weave through pretty cobbled back streets and through Greenwich market which is already bustling and heady with the scent of spices and incense. I walk down the tiny passageway past the independent shops and out onto Church Street.

I pull my phone out of my pocket, scrolling through the perfunctory birthday messages from my friends on Facebook. I know I have no right to but I can't help but feel Adam's absence today. I think longingly of how he'd always take the day off work – a treat in itself – and would wake me up with a special birthday breakfast in bed of pancakes, fruit and coffee and we'd stay there for most of the morning before he took me out for a surprise. Sometimes we'd head out of London in the car to a hotel, or he'd drive me to Kew Gardens, or to a National Trust house for lunch. Adam loved my simple tastes and I loved how relaxed he became when I took him out of the high-powered, money-and-status-obsessed world he'd been brought up in. Out of London, our differences were pruned back and it was then that we seemed most compatible. We laughed about the same thing; talked about the same goals – kids, living in the countryside, working for ourselves. Adam would open up about the things he loved: art, travel and history. He once even admitted that he wished he'd studied History of Art at university, like he'd wanted to, instead of being pushed by George into doing an advertising degree.

I miss him, I realise with a sharp jolt. I miss him a lot.

I walk towards the flower shop, and am surprised to see the 'Closed' sign on the door. It's past 7 a.m. – Sal had told me to have a lie-in this morning but I can't. I'm always up early, desperate to fill my day with the one thing that is finally right with my life – work. If not in the flower shop, then in Milly's garden. I've realised just how much my happiness depends on me doing the thing I really love. And I want to make sure it is part of my life every single day. It is better for my head and heart than any amount of therapy.

My mobile rings as I peer through the window; all the lights are switched off.

I glance at the caller ID. 'Hi, Lon—'

'Happy birthday to you, happy birthday to you! Happy birthday, my darling beautiful daugh-ter, happy birthday to you. And many mooooore!!!' she trills. No matter how lonely I feel, Loni is always there.

'Thanks,' I say with a smile.

'So how is my gorgeous girl on her special day? What are you doing, darling? Anything nice? I'm off to do some T'ai Chi on the beach now and I'm even considering a cheeky little skinny dip to get the old toxins out of my skin. I can't believe you're thirty-one,' she gasps. 'I look too young to have a daughter your age!'

'And I feel too old to have a mum who looks as young as you!' I say warmly. 'I'm fine. I've just got to work.'

'Oh Bea, why don't you hop on a train and come here after

you finish at the flower shop? Let me look after you. We can go for a long walk, have some proper time together.'

'I don't know,' I say, racking my brains for an excuse. 'I think I just want to be on my own.' Even as I'm saying these words I know they're not true. Besides, I've had no luck finding out any more about the address. Perhaps this is the perfect opportunity to ask Loni. She knows my birthday always makes me think about my dad.

'Nonsense!' Loni says. 'No daughter of mine is spending her birthday weekend on her own. I had plans but I can definitely rearrange for you . . .'

'What plans, a retreat?'

'What? No, just, I'm seeing a . . . *some* . . . friends. But they can wait. I'll cancel everything to see you, darling. So how about it? Please? Pretty please?'

I laugh, steam-rollered by Loni's energy and enthusiasm.

'OK, I'll get a train tomorrow.'

'Such a JOY!' Loni squeals. 'I'll tell Cal.'

'I don't want any fuss—' But she's already rung off.

Yes, she can be overwhelmingly full-on and her crazy life often gets in the way of our relationship but she always makes me smile.

I open the door into darkness. The flower shop smells dank and heady with the scent of pungent autumn flowers. Even without seeing them I can smell gerberas and chrysanths, dahlias, rosehips and seeded eucalyptus as well as the sweet smell of the carved pumpkins in the windows. Suddenly the lights ping on and I find myself surrounded by laughing faces as not just Sal but also Nick, Glenda, Tim and Jeeves all stand singing their little hearts out and holding out a cake with my name spelt in beautifully iced flowers on the top.

I blush as I blow out the candles and clap them all for their singing.

'And many more!' finishes Glenda in her best Welsh soprano.

'I can't believe you're all here,' I say, turning and wagging my finger at a guilty-looking Sal and Tim who have clearly conspired to get everyone together.

'You can't be mad at me; I might get upset and go into labour prematurely!' Sal says, holding her hands up.

'Please don't do that,' Tim pleads, his face a picture of panic, and everyone laughs.

'Your birthday breakfast is served,' Nick says with a bow, coming out of the kitchen with a tray of pastries. 'Now for your gift,' he says as he rises up again. 'This is a joint present from all of us.'

It's a beautiful coffee-table garden design book. One I've been wanting for ages.

'Oh, I love it,' I say, beaming at everyone.

'Open the card!' Sal chants and I tear it open. I laugh as I read the front. 'Born to garden, forced to work'. Inside it is another card.

'It's membership to Kew Gardens!' I exclaim. 'This is perfect.' I smile at Nick and then at them all, genuinely touched by their thoughtfulness. 'Thank you, everyone!'

I arrive on Loni's doorstep after lunch the next day. All the way here I've been trying to work out how to tell her that I want to find my dad. I thought she'd confront me about it on the day I texted her for his Cley address, but she is so preoccupied these days that if she had wanted to know why, she certainly wasn't bothered by the time I got back. I'm worried that explaining what I want to do might lead me to tell her that I'm seeing Kieran again. And I'm just not ready to do that.

Besides, Googling the address Father Joe gave me did provide me with some answers. Albeit confusing ones. I discovered it's a residential home in a city called Garden Grove, north of Orange County. Aside from the name, which I could instantly see would appeal to Dad, it made no sense. He was forty-seven when he left us; old, by Loni's standards – and in my and Cal's recollections – but certainly not ready for an old people's home. Besides, the place didn't become one until three years after he left us. Before that it was privately owned. Maybe Dad had just gone for a holiday to visit a friend. Maybe he'd moved out there for good. I'm not sure I'll ever know. I keep mulling over Kieran's idea to fly out there together as part of 'Operation Adventure', to do the crazy Californian road trip. But aside from my financial circumstances (my part-time flower shop wage definitely won't cover a flight to California – not to mention a couple of weeks off) I'm sure there must be a better way. I know I could ask Loni, but surely if she knew where he was she would have told me? Then there's the other question that's been niggling me. Loni still uses Dad's name and she's never divorced him. She's always told Cal and me that she tried for a while to trace him so she could send him the divorce papers. We told her that there are ways to divorce a missing person but she said it didn't seem that important 'It's not like I'm ever going to get married again.'

'Bea, darling?' Loni says, looking at me in surprise as she opens the door, as if she's forgotten she has a daughter at all. Her hair looks wilder than usual, like it's been given some sort of electric-shock treatment. And she doesn't appear to be dressed in actual clothes, just a dressing gown that's she's obviously hastily pulled on in a hurry over her knickers and a yoga vest.

'A hello would be nice,' I say, leaning forward to cover her up. After a beat, she gathers my face in her hands and kisses me enthusiastically.

'You're er, early, come in!' she says, glancing up the stairs before ushering me into her chaotic house. 'I was just about to do some yoga.'

'Is that what they call it these days.' I smile, dropping my bag in the hallway. She's acting like a teenager caught having sex by her parents.

'Yes, darling, it is,' she says, wagging her finger at me. 'Although admittedly that is the umbrella term and there are lots of different trendy methods like vinyasa and ashtanga and Bikram, so people nowadays often refer to those rather than the overall discipline itself...' Loni's eyes flicker upstairs again and she shuts the door to her office as we pass and then envelops me in another hug. 'Oh what a joy it is to see you! Now, what shall we do first? A little mother–daughter meditation and then a long beachy walk? We could take a trip to ...' Loni tries to stifle a yawn. 'Oh dear, sorry, darling. How rude of me!'

'You look tired, Loni,' I say anxiously, studying her. Although I wish I looked as good when I'm knackered. Her bright blue eyes are shining and she can't peel the smile from her face.

'Me? What? No, I'm fine! Just ...' She yawns again.

'Do you know, Loni,' I reply, glancing through the kitchen and out to the garden where I can see the leaves of the red Acer brushing against the window, 'why don't you go and have a lie-down. To be honest all I want to do is potter around in the garden for a bit.' This is true. As soon as I got here I felt the familiar pull to the garden. It is where I feel happy, whole. And I know there is so much to do out there still. I've neglected it – and Loni – for too long.

'OK, well, as long as you're sure.' I can see that Loni looks relieved. 'A little nap will be lovely and it means I'll be completely re-energised to go out for your birthday dinner later. We'll have a proper girl-on-girl catch-up later.'

I stifle a chuckle. 'Girl *to* girl, Loni, girl *to* girl.' and she bounds upstairs.

Columns of apricot sunlight are streaming across the garden. I feel the crisp autumn air on my face; it pinches my skin pleasingly as if reminding me that I am awake, alive. I have survived. And I am ... content. Happy, even. As the thought enters my head I feel a wave of surprise. I never thought it was possible to be so happy on my own. Not without Adam and Milly, not without people propping me up. But in the last few months I have completely turned my life around, changed the course of my future and I've done it all on my own. And what I've learned is that I needed to go back to my roots. Plant myself back in the past, back home here with my family, in the place I love, and with the people I love. Loni, Cal, Lucy, the twins – and Dad? I think of the cottage in Cley and how I'm one step closer to finding him. Do I want to go any further down that path? Or should I stop, turn away now in case it leads to yet more heartache?

I focus on keeping my mind in the present; on what is making me happy in the here and now. My job. My family. This garden.

Kieran. I smile to myself as I grab my tools from my caravan and set to work in a better place – the best place – I've been for years.

Chapter 48

'Well, isn't this nice, darling? It's always a joy to have my baby girl by my side!' Loni says emphatically over the gentle noise of chat and laughter in the King's Head, the pub in Holt we've always come to for family occasions. She smiles as she looks at Cal, Lucy and the twins. 'I can't help but be gloriously happy that Bea is here on her birthday. In the bosom of all her family, just like she should be.'

Cal puts his arm round Loni and Lucy and smiles. I look around the warm, timber-beamed pub but can't help feel like there's something missing. We didn't see them often but Adam loved my family. He revelled in the affectionate chaos that was my relationship with Loni and Cal, the arguments and constant teasing yet affectionate banter. He said it was an atmosphere that was so different to that of his own family. He'd find it hilarious when Loni wrote yet another article about her sex life, making me find humour in something that had previously only held embarrassment. He'd point out that she did it to earn a living, that I should be proud that she had a life outside her kids, that she'd been incredibly brave to start again in her early thirties as a single mum. His views – and his presence – had stuck together my torn-up past and stitched over the hole in it where my dad should have been. I'll always love him for that.

I smile at everyone chatting happily around the table and then glance at the other diners, listen to the hum of music in the background, the distant thwack of snooker balls in the bar beyond. It's reminding me of the many evenings Kieran and Elliot spent here. Drinking, playing pool – Elliot and I against Kieran, just to make sure Elliot didn't feel pushed out. We did that a lot, Kieran and I, to include him and not be too couply around him. He and Elliot were all the other had and he made it clear he didn't approve of me. I had no interest in coming between them. It was only when we were alone that Kieran and I told each other how we really felt, whispering long into the night about our dreams, our newly formed future together.

A bottle of champagne arrives and Cal makes a great show of popping the cork. He stands up and raises a glass.

'Here's to Bea, my big sister. I'm so glad you're here . . .' His sentence drifts off and I can see he's choked. His words are a reminder of how close I once came to not being here. I smile gratefully and reassuringly at him.

'There's nowhere else and no one else I'd rather be with right now. Thank you for always being there for me and helping me through a . . . another tricky year.' I raise my glass. 'To family.'

'Family,' everyone echoes.

Just then my mobile rings and when I see who it is I show the caller ID to everyone and gesture to them to start eating then weave my way out of the pub and into the dark street.

'Milly!' I answer, my delight at hearing from her evident in my voice.

'Happy birthday, babe! How are you?'

'Old!' I laugh. 'Single, old and back home with my bonkers family. But surprisingly good.'

'Oh, I wish there were two of me.'

'There are,' I joke. 'Remember?'

'I don't mean the baby! I just mean I'd do anything to be back there with you now. I know how much you must be missing Adam.'

'I'm fine,' I say emphatically. And I'm surprised to find I mean it. I miss him, obviously. I have done for months. But now? Now, well, I'm stronger, I guess. Maybe because Kieran's here. I don't have to deal with the ghosts on my own. 'Besides, you don't really want to be back here. You spent your teen years dreaming of getting out.' Milly always said she felt like she spent her entire childhood in Norfolk waiting for her life to begin elsewhere. 'You're in New York!' I exclaim. 'Living your dream!'

'Oh yes,' she says. 'That's right. I'm Melanie Griffith in *Working Girl*, Diane Keaton in *Baby Boom* . . .'

'Soon to be Sarah Jessica Parker in *I Don't Know How She Does It?*' I add, and feel my heart contract with longing. In another life perhaps.

'Just what I've always wanted – to be a Hollywood film cliché!' Milly whoops. 'Not that I feel very Hollywood right now. Just kind of fat . . . and tired. Anyway, what about you, what have you been up to?'

I think of all the time I've been spending with Kieran and my mission to find Dad. Neither of which I feel I can tell Milly about in a phone conversation. 'Nothing much,' I lie. There's an awkward pause. I hate how much we can't tell each other these days.

'Oh, right.'

Just then I see a dark figure walking down the street towards me. My breath catches in my throat as I look at him. He's wearing a navy military coat with the collar pulled up around his neck and a beanie slung low over his forehead. His green eyes are glistening in the darkness and he's wearing that lazy, sexy smile of his.

'Actually, Mills, I really have to go. My meal's on the table.'

'OK, well, happy birth—'

'Bye, Mills. Love you. Talk to you soon!' I say hurriedly and press call end and stuff my phone in my coat pocket just as Kieran leans in and kisses my cheek.

'Hey, you,' he says. 'Happy birthday.'

'What are you doing here?' I ask, glancing nervously inside the pub.

'I just had a feeling you'd be in town. I wanted to see you on your birthday.' He's slurring slightly, I notice.

'I'm with my family,' I say, looking up at him meaningfully. He knows I don't want them to know about us, or our search for my dad at the moment.

'Come see me after?' he says softly. 'I promise we'll have more fun than you're currently having in there.' He winks at me and I feel my stomach bubble up with excitement.

I'm unable to tear my eyes away from him. 'I have to go, Kieran,' I say apologetically, reluctantly. 'My family are waiting for me.'

'No they're not.'

I turn quickly and look at Cal who is standing in the doorway. His face is thunderously dark, and he's gazing furiously at Kieran. It's clear he has recognised him immediately. 'I think you'd better come inside, Bea.'

'Isn't she old enough to decide that for herself?' Kieran puts his hands in his pockets and smirks challengingly at Cal.

'She certainly doesn't need *you* to help her.'

'I am here, you know, guys!' I turn between them, feeling furious that they're treating me like I can't make decisions on my own. 'Cal, go inside. I can handle this.'

I wait for him to leave. But he just folds his arms and stands next to me like a security guard. I glare and turn back to Kieran.

'I'll see you *soon*, Kieran,' I say evenly, trying to talk to him with my eyes. Cal has no right to treat Kieran like this. He wouldn't, if he knew the truth.

'Bye, Bea,' Kieran murmurs, then adds, 'Remember what I said . . .' He looks at me, eyes struggling to focus. He holds up his hand in a half-salute, half-wave before he turns and walks away. I'm about to reply but Cal drags me back inside. Just then, my phone buzzes in my pocket and Cal storms off ahead. I look at the message.

I'll be at the beach. Please come. I don't want to be alone. K x

Chapter 49

I find it hard to finish my meal after that. Cal is glaring at me across the table and I refuse all offers of more alcohol. I've never been a big drinker . . . and Loni knows that when I'm feeling emotionally fragile I steer clear of anything that might give me a high and then bring me to a crashing low. I know it's wrong, but I use it as an excuse to leave as soon as the bill is ordered.

'I don't want to push myself too much. I'm er, feeling like I need to be by myself for a bit.'

'Alone?' Cal says darkly.

I glare at him.

'Oh darling, are you sure?' Loni says. 'It's a bit late.'

'I'll be fine. And I'll be home soon. Probably before you!' I smile. 'Um, can I take your car please, Loni?' She hands me her keys, clearly relieved that I'm not planning on going for a walk on my own.

'Of course, darling. We'll get a cab. I've probably had a couple too many to drive anyway!' She giggles and Cal folds his arms and stares at me.

Just as I'm opening the pub door I feel my arm being tugged back and I turn around.

'You're crazy if you let yourself get involved with him again after what he did to you.' Cal's features are distorted with worry. 'Please don't go to him . . .'

'I know what I'm doing, Cal.'

He shakes his head, and as he does it's like a sand timer has been tipped over and he is no longer a twenty-eight-year-old father of two but the fifteen-year-old boy who saved his sister's life. 'I won't let you do this, sis. I can't,' he says determinedly.

'Please, Cal, you have to trust me. I promise I know what I'm doing. I'm thirty-one years old. You don't have to keep being my superhero . . .' I see that tears have sprung into his eyes and I pull him into a hug, feeling a wave of remorse for what I put him through all those years ago. 'I'm sorry, Cal. I promise to take care.' I kiss him on the cheek and he releases his grip. He's still standing at the door as I get into the car and start the ignition.

I pull in at the car park next to Kieran's yellow camper van, grab the flashlight I know Loni keeps in the glove compartment and get out of the car. The wind takes my breath away. The sky lies above me like a gown of deep royal blue, stars are scattered like sequins upon it. I begin to run towards the beach, flicking on my torch and allowing myself to be blown across the dunes.

'KIERAN!' The wind is so strong my voice is instantly swallowed by it.

I whip my head round, desperately trying to look for any sign of him. Where is he?

'KIERAN!' I yell again. I begin to run, my mind a whirl of anxiety.

Why did he come here when he's been drinking? What was he thinking? He wouldn't have done anything stupid, would he? I remember how, when Elliot died, I felt drawn towards the sea. On bad days I felt like it was seducing me into thinking that it held all the answers, that my future lay with it, not here on solid ground. It was part of the reason I didn't leave Loni's house for so long. I was scared of what I might do. The sea seemed to call me, each wave telling me that I could breathe within it. Become one with it. That it was the only thing powerful enough to carry me. I couldn't rely on Cal and Loni forever, it sang, my moods, my incapabilities were only holding them down, drowning them. Loni would never love again while she had me to look after and I was stopping Cal from ever being allowed to be a kid. But the strong, supreme sea would lift me to a place where I would always feel like I was surfing, cruising, swimming, not sinking. Is that why Kieran came here? To be closer to Elliot?

'Kieran!' I shout again, almost choking on the panic, the memory of just how close I had come to believing the dark, swirling shadows in my mind. And then I see him. He is sitting in the dark near the shore, his beanie pulled down over his forehead, and I can see the orange glow of a cigarette or joint being lifted to his lips. I stumble down the sand dunes towards him. He doesn't turn as I call him. I slide onto my knees and throw my arms around him. I feel the weight of a bottle pressed against my back, the cold, wet sand seeping through my jeans. I can smell whisky on his breath.

'I didn't think you'd come. I thought your family would convince you I'm a bad influence and I'd never see you again.'

'I'm a big girl, remember?'

He looks at me then and I shiver and stand up, pulling him up with me. My skin burns as we clasp hands. I don't know if it's because of the cold, or the heat between us. 'Besides,' I add, 'they didn't stop me last time.' Kieran takes a step closer and slips his arm around me. I look up at him. Our lips are inches apart. 'I don't need anyone to tell me what to do,' I murmur.

'Not even me?'

'It depends what it is,' I shoot back teasingly.

'Take your clothes off.' He eyes me challengingly, his eyebrows raised.

I pause and bite my lip and then stick my chin out and fold my arms with a defiant smile. 'I will if you will.'

Kieran smiles lopsidedly and begins undoing his coat. I mirror his movements and without taking my eyes from his I start peeling off my clothes layer after layer before I can change my mind. His eyes are burning into mine, keeping me warm from the inside out. I throw my pieces of clothing at his feet one by one. Parka, jumper, jeans, top, T-shirt. Then when we are both in our underwear, he grabs my hand and we begin to run, laughing and yelling at the tops of our voices as we head for the sea.

We dive into the water and I gasp with shock as I feel it suck me into its icy mouth, the roar in my ears drowning out the noise in my head. For a moment I give into it, feeling it encase me in its cold grip as my head disappears beneath the surface. Is this how Elliot felt?

Seconds later I break the surface and come up for air blinking and spluttering. My lips chatter uncontrollably as I get my bearings in the darkness and see Kieran next to me, his face lit up by the pale moonlight. He stares at me solemnly, shivering as he treads water just inches from me. He is trying to speak, but it is so cold, he can't catch his breath.

'I – I wish I hadn't stayed away for so long,' he says at last. I nod. We don't touch or kiss, we just stay like that for a moment, bodies submerged in the icy waves, our eyes locked. Two people forever linked by their past and now desperately trying to work out if they have a future together.

Chapter 50

When I get back to Loni's, I slink in through the back door, avoiding any floorboards that I know will squeak. I notice there's a ghostly, greenish light coming from the kitchen and I freeze to the spot and try to hide in the shadows as the door swings open.

'You're back, thank God!' Loni cries. I turn and look at her. She is wrapped in a silk gown, her silvery hair coiled like Medusa's around her head. 'Where have you been? Oh darling, you're blue with cold!' She hurries forward and envelops me in her arms, my teeth chattering against her shoulder. She hustles me up the stairs.

'Let's get you in a hot shower, darling. I'll get a towel warming on the Aga and make you a hot-water bottle.'

Fifteen minutes later I arrive in the kitchen in my PJs and dressing gown, clutching the hot-water bottle she's made me.

The kitchen looks like a bomb's hit it and Loni is standing in front of the Aga, hastily stirring some milk that is slopping all over the sides of the pan. 'I've got some hot chocolate on. You look like you could do with one,' she says shakily, turning her head and gazing directly into my eyes as she continues stirring. She always makes eye contact when she's having a conversation because she believes it shows that you are giving the other person your 'full engagement'. She says years of running her retreats has taught her that the worst thing you can do is not listen to someone properly. 'It leaves them feeling desperate, alone, like even when they're opening up about themselves, they're not being heard.'

'Th-thank you.' Despite my hot shower and warm clothes I haven't been able to stop shivering since I dried off in Kieran's camper van before driving myself home. It didn't scare me that he was drunk. What scared me was that I didn't care. I hadn't felt so reckless for a long time.

'Cal told me who you'd be with . . .' Loni keeps stirring fervently.

'H-he had no right to,' I reply.

She swings round and I see she is crying. 'Of course he did! He's worried *sick* about you. We all are!'

'You don't have to be, Loni,' I say evenly. 'I know what I'm doing.'

'Do you, darling? Do you really?' She turns away and pours milk into two mugs and stirs them. I see her take a deep breath before she brings the steaming cups over to the table. She gazes down at me and I see that her hands are shaking uncontrollably. Is this all because of me? Have I worried her this much? I didn't mean to.

'I know you don't want to hear this. I know you think you're old enough to handle it yourself, but as your mother I have to say this. Be careful, darling. I know how fragile you are.' She pauses and blinks as if to gather herself. 'I – I just don't think seeing him can be good for you right now . . .'

'I understand why you feel like that, Loni, I do.' We often talk like this to each other in 'counsellor chat' as we call it. Lots of starting sentences with 'I feel' and 'I understand' and 'I know'.

It's partly to do with her job, partly to do with my illness. 'He's making me face up to things. Things I've run away from for years.'

'Like what?' Loni tries and fails to keep the disbelief out of her voice. I know only too well how she felt about Kieran.

'Like Dad.' The words drop like rocks from a cliff edge.

She stares at me for a moment, a kaleidoscope of emotions flickering through her eyes.

Then she rubs her hand over her eyes, exhaustion evident on her face. 'That's why you wanted the address.' I nod. 'You really want to find him after all these years?'

'I've never stopped wanting to find him, Loni!' The words burst from my lips, like a fountain of frustration. 'I need to know what happened to Dad after he left. It's my right; I deserve to know.'

'If that's how you feel then I'll support you, you know I'll always support you.' She pushes out her chair and stands up, turning away from me. 'One question. If you find your dad, will that be it for you and Kieran?'

I don't say anything for a moment. 'He isn't what you think he is, you know. You've got him all wrong. Everyone has.' I want her to understand. I feel like she might be the only person who will. 'He knows me better than anyone. I don't have to pretend with him. I can just be me, the version of me I don't think anyone else wants to accept. Including you . . ..'

She turns around suddenly and grasps my hands. 'I know you have history together, darling, but trust me, you can't build a relationship on memories, no matter how hard you try. A relationship has to keep evolving, through the good times and the bad, or there is nothing. *Noth-ing*.'

'What can you tell me about making relationships work, Loni? As far as I can see you've run away from them your whole life.

Clearly I'm my mother's daughter . . .' It's a low blow. She doesn't respond. She just looks at me sadly.

'Do you know where Dad went?' I ask challengingly.

'I promise I don't, Bea!' she adds.

I wish I believed her, but I'm starting to feel like my whole life has been a lie.

November

Dear Bea,

So the days are shortening, the colours of autumn fading and the last of the late flowers dying, which means a long, cold winter is about to be born.

I'm already tired of the endless darkness of the days. I long for light. I know it is the cycle of nature; this is a season that brings excitement and joy to many (Fireworks! Crackling fires! Christmas coming! Snow!) but even so, I find I have no desire to witness the bare trees, shivering in the cold. I don't want to feel the icy grip of winter's fingers clinging to my skin, nor watch as it relentlessly kills off everything that is bright and beautiful in the world.

So instead I'm drawn to warmer climes where I can always feel the welcome breath of the sun on my skin, wake up to hot, bright mornings and languish in the long, lonely days that won't allow me to retreat inside or to hibernate from my life choices. Sometimes, I fear I will have run from so many winters that I'll no longer enjoy the summer. I won't get the lows, but nor will I experience the highs. For how do you compare the radiance of a sunflower, when you no longer see the snow? How can you enjoy sunshine, when there is no rain? How can you truly live life when you have turned your back on it? But I have no other choice. I hope you will understand and be able to forgive me one day.

Love, Dad x

Chapter 51

Bea Hudson is petrified. I feel like I'm about to throw myself off a cliff without a parachute.
13 likes, 4 comments.

I pick up my pace as I walk through Soho towards the office of Hudson, Grey & Friedman. It's a cold, rainy November day and I'm desperately trying to hurry in my heels towards Adam's agency on Dean Street. It's the day of the pitch and I'm meeting James here. Adam sent me a good luck text from New York this morning. He's been there for the past few days, but luckily I've had my own work to keep me busy since James told me he wanted me to present with him at the pitch. I stand in front of the modern glass façade and glance up at the neon H&G sign in the window that is lit up in light bulbs while I wait for him to arrive.

I can't believe I'm about to do this, I'm excited but terrified about presenting to Adam's peers. Adam's reassured me that he's talked to the partners and everyone knows and is fine with the fact that James employed me to work on this project without knowing who I was, and that I took the job not knowing who the project was for.

The last few weeks at work have carried me through a tricky time at home. Adam is hardly around, and while I do feel that we've reached an understanding about where our lives are right now, I can't help but feel like we're always on opposite sides. Winning this project is my only chance of crossing the line. Surely it'll bring us closer if I'm working for the agency? We'll have common ground at last.

As for today, I feel like I'm in a dream and this isn't really happening. I mean, I'm a *temp*. I should be back at the office, filing, taking phone calls, doing the admin. But my role has grown in the weeks since I shared my ideas at the team creative meeting. James was really impressed. He said I had a natural flair and innate understanding of concept and design that he hasn't seen in anyone for a long time. He's been giving me more and more to do, managing the budget and ensuring we stay true to the design objectives. Last week he brought me into his office and told me how pleased he'd been with my work and how pivotal my ideas had been in locking down our creative concept.

'I'd like you to present with me next Monday,' he said as I stared at him open-mouthed. 'You have become a key part of this project and obviously you have a remarkably instinctive understanding of what the client wants.' He winked. 'Not that that is anything other than a happy coincidence but we may as well utilise it, right?'

'But—'

'Ah-ah, let me finish,' James said, holding his finger up. 'So, I thought we could play this presentation as a two-hander. I will cover the more technical aspects after you've talked about the creative concept – particularly the central design feature which was, of course, entirely your idea. And a brilliant one at that,' he adds.

'But I can't, I have no exper—'

'I wouldn't ask if I didn't think you were more than capable. Bea,' he said earnestly. 'I honestly think you're the best person for the job. You've become more than an assistant on this, Bea; you've fundamentally shaped the whole design. I know you're worried about what people think but the truth is, I need you. Right now, I'm thanking my lucky stars that you crossed paths with me and, nepotism or not, you've more than proved yourself.'

I see James approaching and I wave, finally feeling ready to show everyone what I can do.

'Are you ready?' James smiles, brushing down his navy blazer and picking fluff from his trousers as we stand in the meeting room, waiting for the agency members to come in.

I nod, glancing down at my notes then around nervously to check everything is in place. The big meeting table has been pushed to the back of the room and four empty chairs sit in front of a small podium and a big white screen.

The door swings open suddenly and Robert Grey, George's partner, strides in, his PA following behind him. He's in his late fifties and looks movie-star good for his age. He has silvery-grey hair and a deep tan and the easy air of someone who has always been at the top of his game. I take a sharp breath but he is too busy tapping out an email on his phone to acknowledge us. Given Eliza's history with Adam, I'm pretty sure I'm not Robert's favourite person in the world. I've only met him a couple of times, but he came to our wedding, so he's bound to recognise me. I feel like running out of the room already.

The door opens again and a tall, thin, dark-haired man strides in, grinning broadly and showing off a set of gleaming white teeth.

He introduces himself as Maxwell Friedman and I realise he's the head of the American company Friedman Media that Hudson & Grey have acquired. That leaves one empty chair. I feel my stomach tighten as the door opens and a woman walks in.

Her long, poker-straight, perfectly blow-dried hair billows out behind her as if there is an invisible wind machine following her as she greets the two men, laughing and joking before seamlessly moving into some business chat. She takes a seat and looks directly at me.

It's Eliza Grey.

At that moment George ambles in. Eliza immediately goes and kisses him on both cheeks. She whispers something in his ear and George's eyes flicker up at me and his mouth slides into a giant smile.

'Bea!' he exclaims. 'Wonderful to see you here. Looking forward to hearing all the plans!'

Eliza carries on whispering. I wish I could hear what she is saying. Then she smiles imperiously and folds her arms, leaning back in her chair as if to say, 'This is going to be fun.'

I gulp and step forward onto the podium next to James who has already begun his spiel.

'Good morning, my name is James Fischer of JF Design and this is Bea Hudson' – at the mention of my name Eliza leans over to Robert and murmurs something – 'who is part of the design team.' If she's trying to unsettle me, it's working. 'As you know, we are here to talk you through the design concept for this exciting, innovative urban roof space for the new London office of Hudson, Grey & Friedman. Bea is going to talk you through our creative vision, showing you the design layout and planting plans. We've also made a scaled-down mock-up to show you at the end. Then I'll talk about the more technical elements – the lighting plan, the hardscape features, in other words the walls, fences, safety, irrigation issues, and our planned budget and timescales. I do want to say that this concept has been inspired entirely by your vision, your business. We want to create somewhere that will best exemplify the outstanding creative output of the agency as well as continue to inspire everyone who works here. Take it away, Bea!' He smiles and steps back off the podium, to some encouraging applause. Eliza's is more of a slow handclap.

'H-hello, everyone,' I say, my voice shaking with nerves as I click the first slide in my presentation. 'As you know, I have a personal link to this incredible company, one that I believe has helped us to shape this design into a true representation of your vision. I hope you will see how hard we've worked to that end and how inspired we've been by you as a company . . .' I smile confidently as I prepare to continue, suddenly feeling for the first time since I met Adam that I really belong in his world.

Chapter 52

There's applause from the handful of people in the room when I finish my part of the presentation and I feel excitement course through my body. I did it! And not only that, I did it well! I remembered everything I wanted to say, added a few good ad libs and kept everyone engaged throughout. I step down off the podium so James can take over. The loudest applause is coming from George. I smile at him gratefully and James gives me an encouraging squeeze on the arm. I'm still shaking as he steps up to the podium.

'Thank you, Bea. Does anyone have any questions before I go into some of the more boring technical detail, the structural considerations for such a project and so on?'

'I have one,' Eliza says silkily and we all turn and look at her. 'Firstly, thank you for your ideas. I think I speak for all of us when I say they are very impressive and completely on brief for this company. Now, as the Account Director from the New York office, I've flown over to ensure that the design we choose can be rolled out internationally, because we are also hoping, in the next three or four years, to expand into Asia and Europe. Obviously with such an important project, we've been seeing other design companies too. Can I ask what credentials you have that would make us give you this project?'

James smiles winningly and launches easily into a sales pitch about the extensive merits and awards he's won and the outstanding profile of JF Design. I smile shyly as George gives me a thumbs-up and I turn and focus my attention on James.

When he's finished Eliza looks pointedly at me. 'And what about you?'

'Well, I really think our design fundamentally gets to the heart of your company's core vision,' I begin. 'And I believe that . . .'

Eliza holds her hand up. 'I don't want company principles now. I mean what is your background?'

'Oh, er, JF Design is an award-winning garden design company renowned for its work with corporate companies. We have a client list that includes—'

'Yes, yes, so James said,' she interrupts sweetly. 'But I mean *yours,* specifically. You.'

'Bea's a design consultant,' James says, stepping forward. 'I employed her to work on the project because of her obvious creative talent.'

'Of course! And your experience is?'

'Well, I – I . . .' I stutter, looking at James for support. 'I don't have any.'

My face is burning as I look at the floor. I feel humiliated, not just for me but for James. I've ruined his chance of winning this contract. I should have known my place, not tried to step out of the life I'd cultivated and into Adam's. This isn't my world. Only my loyalty to James is stopping me from running from the room, and keeping me rooted to the spot.

Then James begins to speak. 'She may not have much experience, but in a few short weeks Bea has proved herself to be utterly indispensable. I believe in nurturing talented garden designers like I do plants. Bea may be a seed right now but I can tell just how much she's going to grow. As you can see from her incredibly astute and innovative ideas, Bea is immensely talented and an essential part of this project. I certainly wouldn't have been able to create this design without her.'

Eliza opens her mouth to speak but she's drowned out by the sound of George clapping loudly. He stands up.

'Well, I think that's enough questions! Eliza's right . . .' I feel my heart plummet to my feet. 'This *is* the most exciting and innovative design we've seen and it fulfils the brief – and then some. In other words,' he grins, 'when can you start?'

And with that he thrusts out his arm and shakes James's hand, and then mine, dropping a kiss on it before striding out of the conference room, followed by Robert and a chastened, miserable-looking Eliza. I blink, unable to believe that really just happened. As the door swings shut behind them, James and I throw our arms round each other and jump up and down. I can't remember the last time I felt this happy.

Chapter 53

I wake up and see I have a DM on Facebook from Milly asking me to go and check on her flat. It's still empty after they moved out three months ago and I seem to have taken on an unofficial security role, popping in every now and then just to check that everything is OK. I don't mind, it gives me something to do – especially because Adam is in New York, again, and will be there until the end of the week. I haven't spoken to him in days, not since I told him we won the pitch. I was hoping winning the contract would help. He'd been so positive and supportive about it all, I thought he'd be thrilled, but he seemed underwhelmed when I told him we'd won. 'I knew you would!' is all he said, which had annoyed me. Didn't he realise what a big deal this was for me? 'Why, did you fix it somehow?' I shot back teasingly, but he didn't find my joke funny.

'No! What? No!' He exhaled, a long sigh of frustration. Our conversations are like this a lot now. Defensive, unnecessarily confrontational, snappy.

Since then we keep missing each other, sending texts at odd times of the day because of the different time zones, leaving messages on voicemail. It's like no matter how hard we try, we can't get our lives to align.

I step out of Greenwich DLR and I think of the Royal Observatory, peeking up over the hill. It's as if my world and Adam's have split and we're on opposite sides of the meridian line. I shake my head. I don't want to be negative or sink into dark thoughts. I think of what Loni always tells me to do when I start feeling low. 'Do a Gratitude List, darling,' I hear her say in my mind, 'and remember what the Buddha said: "You have cause for nothing but gratitude and joy!"' She's right. It always works. I start counting my blessings: my great new job, my family, my friends, and of course, Adam. He is not my father, I recite in my head. He is not my father. He won't leave me. He *hasn't* left me. This is just a little blip in our relationship and one we can overcome.

I set off down Greenwich Church Street, enjoying getting lost in the busy Sunday morning bustle. At least there is company in my solitude here unlike the grey, empty void that is Canary Wharf at the weekend. There's a commotion behind me and I see the door of a shop burst open and I take a step back in surprise as a woman clutching her stomach and groaning staggers out and then leans against the window with her back to me. I run over to her immediately. 'Are you OK?'

She bends over and exhales loudly, clutching hold of my arm. 'I'm fine, thanks! Just a few little contraaaghhhhhhhhh . . .' She roars for at least a minute and then looks at me and smiles bravely as she pants and gets her breath. She looks young, early twenties, I'd say; her bright blonde hair is pulled up in a big messy bun and she looked flushed. 'Contractions.' I glance down and notice her swollen pregnant belly. 'No need to panic though!' she says cheerily as she catches sight of my horrified expression. 'I've got it all under control! Plenty of time really, they've only just staaaar . . . oh here's comes anotheeeerarghhhhh!'

I stare at her, feeling utterly useless and panicky as people stream past us, apparently oblivious to a woman in labour. I am desperately hoping one of them will realise that I do not in any way have this under control.

'Are you on your own? Shall I call an ambulance?' I ask when she's finished screaming. She smiles at me and shakes her head. She seems to be taking this whole being-in-labour-on-her-own thing completely in her stride. 'Honest, I'm fine! I reckon I'll just get the bus down to Queen Elizabeth's. I've got plenty of time. The contractions have only just started coming really. Oh hang on—' She holds her hands up and I notice that a tiny bit of panic is etched on her young face. 'Oh-oh mooohhaarghhhh! Oh shit, here comes another. Gurghhhhhhhhhhh . . .' She crouches on the pavement and groans, rocking backwards and forwards on the soles of her feet.

'ARGHHHHHHHARGGGH,' she cries, lips pointed to the sky like a werewolf.

I bend down next to her. 'And breeeeeeathe!' I say, trying my best to remember what Loni used to say to me when she wanted me to calm down. And in swwiiiiiiiii and out swooooooooo! Everything's going to be OK . . .' I trail off.

'Sal, my name's Sal. Thanks,' she says gratefully. I stand up and gaze up and down the road and then back at the shop to get my bearings in case I have to call a cab company. I suddenly recognise the name and the logo with the smattering of stars. And then, in the distance, I spot the orange light of a free taxi. I sprint into the road with my arm stretched out yelling 'TAXI!' at the top of my voice, thanking my lucky stars – and the cosmos – for being on my side for once.

Chapter 54

The taxi swerves into the forecourt of Queen Elizabeth's Hospital. The pregnant girl – Sal – is gripping my knee tightly. I know she's having this baby on her own because she soon told me that the father of her baby was 'a sodding useless idiot who fucked off'. Her words. She's much calmer now but every time she has a contraction – or we go over a speed bump – she squeezes me so hard that I've ended up crying out in pain with her.

'Don't come out yet, little fella, don't come out yet!' I say, wincing as she has another contraction.

'What makes you think it's going to be a boy?' Sal says, as she closes her eyes ready for the next one.

'Just a hunch,' I shrug, mouthing 'Ow' silently as she squeezes my knee again.

'Oh God, I wanna puuuuushhhh!' Sal screams suddenly.

'DON'T!' the taxi driver and I both yell.

Several hours later, I walk out into the waiting area having just witnessed the most incredible thing I've ever seen. I get a cup of water from the dispenser and sit down, trying to process what I've just been a part of. Watching a baby come into the world was every bit the miracle that people say it is. I don't even have a connection to this child, but I felt this instant urge to protect him – and his mum – and to be there for them. I can't explain it, but I felt like I'd known her forever. So when Sal had begged me to come in with her when we arrived at the maternity ward it felt totally natural to agree. 'I can't do this on my own,' she'd sobbed. 'I thought I could but I'm really fucking scared. I know it's a lot to ask, but will you come in? Dad's stuck in traffic and might not be here in time, and I know it sounds crazy but I feel like you were meant to pass by when you did . . .'

'Of course I will,' I'd said and given her a hug. She was eight centimetres dilated when we arrived and I relayed her birth plan to the midwives, fed her Jelly Babies and Ribena from her hospital bag after each contraction to give her extra energy, allowed her to lean on me when she wanted to stand up, and helped her breathe through the pushes. I didn't even leave when her dad eventually arrived as by then it was too late – Sal gave birth to her baby a second later. It was like she had been holding on, just waiting for her dad to walk through the door.

'It's a boy!' he had said, his voice cracking with emotion. He stroked Sal's wet hair and kissed her on the forehead as she held her newborn son. 'A beautiful baby boy.'

I'd stepped back, looking at the three of them, a family. Not a complete one, but a family nonetheless. I'd smiled as I'd witnessed this beautiful scene: a father rushing to his daughter's side just in time to see two generations of a family become three.

'I'm so glad you got here in time, Dad,' Sal had sobbed.

'I wouldn't have missed it for the world,' he'd replied. I'd slipped out of the room then, wanting to leave them to have their moment alone. But also because I wanted to take a moment on my own, add this experience to my Gratitude List.

December

Dear Bea

Here we are in the bleak midwinter and even though Christmas is nearly upon us, the world around you may seem barren, empty of promise, devoid of colour. Don't sink into the cold earth. Try to remember that one of the great benefits of winter is that without all the flounce and frippery, you can see the bare bones of your garden and work out what you have to do to make it flourish in the future.

Easy for me to say, right? On the contrary, at times it felt to me as if all I could ever see was the bare bones. I felt like I'd be working tirelessly, exhaustively, on my hands and knees turning and pruning old ground, raking away the mulch and trying to plant new seeds of positivity amongst the mature shrubs. Maybe the problem was I was always looking down at the earth, because no matter how hard I worked, or how much time I spent out there, I just couldn't appreciate the brightness and the beauty of what I'd planted any more.

I hope you are always able to see the splendour surrounding you, Bea. Remember to shake off the snow sometimes, clear the paths of overhanging branches that may obstruct your journey and always, always look up.

Love, Dad x

Chapter 55

Bea Bishop is back at the mothership for Xmas. Crackers definitely included.
22 likes.

I hear the crunch of gravel as another car pulls up in Loni's drive that's already crammed full of cars. I'm lying on the floor in her spare bedroom where Neve and Nico are repeatedly trying to stick bits of Duplo in my ears, armpits, nostrils and mouth or whatever orifice they can find.

'Aaargh!' I laugh as Nico and Neve jump on top of me giggling whilst shouting 'Bum Bum!' as they try to roll me over. I tickle them until they squeal with glee and then wriggle up into a sitting position. I've been getting a much-needed niece fix and doing my Auntie Duty on Christmas Day by entertaining them while Cal and Lucy cook a feast fit for fifty. Loni loves Christmas. She always has done. I smile as I think of Christmases past. We always started the day with it just being the three of us, then as the day wore on more and more people would arrive, clutching food and drink, musical instruments and party games. Loni has always loved opening the doors to anyone and everyone at this time of year. As well as close family and friends and people from the village, she invites people she's met on her retreats, recently divorced and sensitive about their first Christmas alone. By the evening the place would always be alive with laughter and chatter, fairy lights glittering in the garden, mulled wine being made by the gallon. I'm not sure if Loni knows how many people's festive seasons she has transformed. It's kind of amazing to think of the impact she has made. I hate that I've been doubting her influence on mine because of Dad. I need to talk to her. But I just haven't found the right moment.

.It's evening, but we've yet to have dinner, and downstairs a bunch of drunk, aged, mistletoe-clutching singles are roaming the rooms whilst Pink Floyd pounds out of the speakers. I glance at my phone. There's a new text from Sal, wishing me a Happy Christmas, and I ping her one back sending lots of love to her and baby Aaron. I've only seen her a couple of times since she went into labour at the shop and I took her to the hospital. I actually really miss her. It's amazing how quickly she's become such a big part of my life. It makes me wonder, sometimes, if we would ever have met if I hadn't run away from my wedding. I feel like my job at the flower shop – and her friendship – has really saved me. Especially since Milly moved away. I can't imagine a life where I don't know Sal now. I'd love her to have come here today, but I know she was looking forward to her first Christmas with her dad and the baby. Another car pulls up outside and I glance at the girls who are both sitting astride me again, bouncing up and down repeatedly, giggling hysterically between my gasps.

The twins stop mid-bounce and try to peer out of the window. 'Adam here?' they ask hopefully, in unison.

'No,' I reply sadly. 'Adam's a long, long way away.' Even though it's almost eight months since I last saw him, he's never far from my thoughts. Especially since Kieran left after my birthday. He had to go back to the naval base in Portsmouth and his absence has left a space in my brain that Adam has filled.

'Where's Adam gone?' Neve demands, prodding a finger in my chest. 'Where. He. Gone?'

I open my mouth and close it again. I think of Loni trying to tell Cal and me that Dad wasn't coming back and it's then that the words come, words that she said to me over twenty years ago.

'Sometimes grown-ups are a bit like flowers,' I say quietly. The girls look at me silently, their angelic faces displaying rare graveness. 'And they have to find a new place to be planted because they weren't growing very well where they were . . .' I trail off as the memory of Loni saying the same words to me reverberates around my head. The twins look up at me blankly. 'Gardening analogies not working for you, huh?' I smile tearfully and then feel a sharp jolt of pain in my stomach.

'Ow!' I remove the red brick Neve is trying to shove in my belly button and she gazes at me with her soulful blue eyes as if she is about to say something world-changingly wise.

'Bum-Bum-Bea,' she says, trying to get me to roll over so she can insert something in another crevice.

'BEA!' I hear Loni shout as the music is turned down momentarily. 'There's someone who wants to see you!'

'BEAAAAA, come downstairs!' Loni calls again.

'OK, OK, don't get your yoga pants in a twist,' I mutter and I descend the stairs slowly, freezing to the spot when I see who is standing at the front door.

'Kieran?' I glance at Loni and then at Kieran nervously. 'I – I didn't expect to see you here!' My smile is fixed on my face as hordes of people swirl around us in the corridor, talking, laughing, looking at Kieran, staring at me.

'I'm full of surprises,' Kieran grins, his evergreen eyes boring into mine.

'You certainly are,' Cal pipes up, stepping out of the crowd and onto the bottom stair protectively, creating a barrier between us. 'Still don't have a home to go to, huh?'

'Cal!' Loni chastises, eyeing me warily as I push my brother out of the way and walk towards Kieran. 'That's no way to treat a guest of Bea's. Come in, Kieran, please, and you're welcome to stay for Christmas dinner if you like.' If she is surprised or displeased to see Kieran she isn't showing it. Maybe after the chat we had on the night of my birthday she realises that things are different this time and that being with him is helping me, healing me almost.

'Come in, grab yourself a glass!' Loni says warmly. I smile at her gratefully.

I take Kieran's arm – mostly in a show of defiance to Cal. I know he's just trying to protect me, but he's judging Kieran only from his experience of him in the past. Doesn't he realise that people change; everyone deserves a second chance. After all, not all of us can be Superheroes like Cal.

I can feel Kieran bringing out my rebellious streak again. I should be anxious about him being here, but I'm not; I feel invigorated. He makes me feel like I'm living my own life. Not everyone else's version. He makes me feel brave. Defiant. In control.

I lead Kieran through the crazy, bustling house, squeezing past Loni's cronies who are laughing and chatting at the top of their voices. Out of the corner of my eye I see Cal shake his head, like I'm some sort of errant child.

'I didn't mean to interrupt your Christmas dinner,' Kieran says with an apologetic smile.

'Most people have eaten by 8 p.m. on Christmas Day,' I laugh. 'But then again, most people don't have Christmas at Loni's.' He slips his arm around me and I flinch a little at his touch. It feels too intimate somehow, even though the last time we were together we were almost naked in the sea. Despite that, we still haven't kissed. I had panicked and run out of the water, desperate to find the shore.

'I thought I'd left it late enough. I just really wanted to see you. It's been too long. I hated going back on the ship. I've spent every moment in the last six weeks wanting to be back here, with you.' He starts to take off his coat.

'Oh, no don't bother taking it off!' I say quickly.

A flicker of hurt flashes across his face. 'Oh, right, yeah, sorry. I'm not staying . . .'

I tut and smile, touching his arm gently with my hand. He's always been oversensitive. 'No, that's not what I meant. Look!' We walk into the conservatory where the glass doors have been pulled back, letting floods of cold, wintry air into the room. Heat lamps are blasting out hot air and some sensible guests are huddled around them, but the rest don't seem bothered by the cold. They must have been at the yoga disco. It is bonkers being outside like this but it is also incredibly beautiful.

A line of trestle tables leads all the way out into the cold, frosty garden. Fairy lights are draped all around the conservatory and the garden beyond so the whole place twinkles like stars. About thirty or forty people are milling around, wearing festive hats with their coats and scarves. In the centre of the line of tables is a turkey, a gigantic ham hock and a suckling pig, as well as a heap of knives and forks, loads of bread rolls, home-made chutneys, apple sauce and cranberry sauce, along with five different salads and four different types of potatoes. A wintry wind is whistling around us, but everyone is so well inebriated no one seems to care. Loni always says each season should be celebrated and that feeling the cold air on our skin helps us feel alive. In one corner is a giant urn of mulled wine, there are bottles of home-made elderflower wine and a vat of Loni's special sloe gin-and-rhubarb punch. There are no chairs, just a stack of paper plates and cups.

'Welcome to A Very Crazy Loni Christmas,' I smile as we grab plates and pile food upon them. We watch as Loni, dressed in a full fake fur over an Aztec-print pantsuit, circulates , hair spiralling in the wind, her peals of laughter bouncing off the trees.

'So what happens now?' Kieran asks. I'm not sure if he means right now, or with us. I go with the most comfortable version.

'It's Christmas, and you're at Loni's so there is only one thing to do.'

'What's that?'

'Get drunk, of course!' I lead him over to the urn of mulled wine.

'Sounds good to me,' he grins.

We jump as Cal calls for silence by banging a giant Indian drum and Loni is lifted up on the shoulders of a man to shouts, cheers and applause.

'Who's he?' Kieran asks, nodding towards him as he takes a sip of warm wine.

I shrug disinterestedly. 'He's been to several of Loni's retreats. He's called Roger, I think.'

'Well, Roger looks like all his Christmases have come at once,' Kieran drawls and he nudges me.

'Attention, please, everyone!' Loni shouts, waving her arms. 'I just wanted to take this moment to say a few words of thanks for what we all have – and what we're about to receive . . .' Everyone bows their head.

'A prayer?' Kieran scoffs. 'Really? I didn't know your mum was religious.'

'She's not,' I reply somewhat defensively.

I think of Adam and how he never questioned Loni's weird ways, he just accepted them, even though they were as far removed from his own upbringing as they could possibly be.

'Merry Christmas, everyone,' Loni says as she ends her prayer. 'Now, let's have some fun!'

'Oh God,' I groan as there is a whoop of excitement as Loni starts a conga.

'Let's go somewhere quiet.' Kieran slips his arm around me and he nods towards the swing seat at the bottom of the garden.

I look at him and he is staring at me with such intensity and devotion and a kind of desperation that I know that, even though my instincts are telling me not to, I can't resist. I have never been able to resist Kieran.

Chapter 56

We sit next to each other, clasping our warm mulled wine as we observe the party in silence: the dancing, laughing people, the twinkling lights, the stars blinking above us, the fire blazing in the fire pit, the guy with the guitar who is playing folk songs. Kieran's hand is next to mine and slowly, slowly, he curls it around mine until our fingers are entwined. I don't move, or breathe. I can't. I feel as if the last eight years have fallen away. I remember how being with him always felt illicit, dangerous, exciting, just like it does now. I'm not being the good girl any more.

But does it feel good?

I glance across the garden and see Loni standing in the doorway of the conservatory. She rests her head against the doorframe and I stretch my neck, trying to see why. It isn't like her to be on the sidelines. Then I see someone next to her, placing his arm around her shoulder. And she leans into him for a moment. It's Roger.

Kieran follows my line of vision.

'Looks like your mum may not be so anti-relationships after all,' he says, nodding at Loni just as Roger whispers something to her. She shakes her head, and pushes him away gently. I'd told

Kieran how worried I was about Loni's tiredness, her lack of interest in the house, or work, the fact that she'd lost weight. If she didn't look so well I'd have taken her to a doctor by now. 'She's not ill,' Kieran continues, a mischievous tone to his voice. 'She's in love.'

'No,' I say quickly, more to myself than to Kieran. 'She couldn't have fallen for someone after all these years. Loni doesn't do love.'

'What about you, Bea? Do you do love?' Kieran says huskily, turning me to face him.

I look down, unable to return his intense gaze and wanting to look back at Loni who I'm more preoccupied with right now. 'I – I don't know, I mean, I just . . .'

'Bea,' Kieran says, lifting my chin gently so I have no choice but to look at him. 'I can't go on like this much longer, being with you and not saying how I feel. I know you're scared and uncertain, I know being with me is an enormous risk but I came back because no matter how hard I tried I've never been able to forget you. I'm not the same guy that left all those years ago and I hope you can see as clearly as I can that even though I've – *we've* – both changed there is still something very special between us.'

I'm trying to breathe, but I feel like there's no oxygen left. I feel dizzy with confusion. After all, this is everything I spent years wanting to hear but now he's saying it I feel like I'm submerged in a sea of doubt.

'I need to know where I stand. I need you in my life and I need to know if you feel the same.'

'Kieran.' I manage to say his name but then stop. It feels like a dream. All of this feels like a dream. As if there is another version of me, one who never left Adam, who is happily married and settled and who isn't here, obsessing about my long-lost dad and seriously contemplating being with my first love again even though it went so tragically wrong last time . . .

'I know you're very confused,' Kieran adds quickly. 'And I know I've brought back a lot of painful memories you wanted to forget. We both stayed away from each other for so long because of them. But no matter where we go, or who we're with, or how far we try and pull ourselves apart we're always going to be drawn back to each other again. We're meant to be, babe.'

I open my mouth to reply, but as I do, Kieran lowers his lips to mine and I realise that he is going to kiss me. It is a moment I've waited so long for and yet, now that it's happening, I know that it signifies an ending, not a beginning. He kisses me with such longing that I know in this one moment he is transferring all of his feelings of – not love, it doesn't feel like love – pain, loss and regret to me. I understand. Finally I understand. As we kiss I feel as if our lives, our worlds are reshaping, merging until what has been is no more. The darkness that shrouds us both is circling and joining, as if it is burying us. I realise that this is what I've always been running away from, this darkness that is known only by Kieran and me. And as I pull back from him my world re-forms. I open my eyes and I see Kieran looking at me and feel that my path is completely illuminated and for the first time I know exactly what I want and where I want to go. The past is gone, there is only now left.

I pull away and jump up from the swing seat as two figures appear out of the gloom. I squint when they call my name.

'Milly! Jay!' I gasp. 'Oh my God. I thought you guys were in New York!' I step towards them and glance guiltily back at Kieran. They're standing looking between me and Kieran, clutching a bundle of perfectly wrapped gifts. Milly is wearing a bright red swing coat that emphasises her bump. Her beautiful, newly rounded face is a picture of shock, annoyance, disbelief and disapproval.

'Cal said he saw you come down here. Is everything all right?' She looks at Kieran and then at me.

'Everything's fine!' I exclaim, standing up and throwing my arms around her. 'I didn't know you were coming!'

'I can see that,' she says coolly.

'Hi.' Kieran waves at Milly and smiles at her charmingly. But she ignores him. Kieran does the same to Jay, but he ignores him too. Credit to Kieran, his smile doesn't waver but he does drop his hand.

'Milly, you remember Kieran.'

'I do. Unfortunately.'

'Milly!' I say warningly.

Kieran steps forward and slips his arm around me again. I flinch slightly – especially when I see how angry Milly looks. 'I should probably go,' he says.

'There's a surprise,' Milly murmurs. He glances at her and I see a flicker of annoyance in his eyes but then it is gone.

'Merry Christmas, Bea. I'll see you soon, yeah?' He kisses me lightly on the lips. I smile weakly and then watch as he heads off into the darkness.

Milly and Jay's disapproval is weighing heavy in the night air and I know I shouldn't let them see that I'm watching him go, but I can't help myself. I feel like I've just made a momentous, life-changing realisation.

'Are you going to tell us what the hell is going on then?' Milly snaps.

I turn to face her wearily. 'No, Milly, I'm not.' I don't want to have to defend myself any more. I know what I'm doing. At last.

'Why not? We're best friends – you should tell me everything, right, Jay?'

'I think I'm going to leave you girls to battle this out on your own.' He backs away quickly and then heads over to the heaving table of alcohol.

'I can't believe you're seeing him. When are you going to give up on this crazy version of your life you've opted for that exists entirely in the past and instead get back together with the one person who is right for you?' Milly's voice has become ear-piercingly high-pitched. I look at her, astonished by her vehemence.

'I threw away my chance with Adam a long time ago. You need to stop obsessing about the past and move on.'

'Like *you* have? With him?' She jerks her head round to where Kieran disappeared into the darkness.

'Like we *both* have. Adam's travelling, having a great time, meeting people, I'm sure he's forgotten all about me . . .'

'That's where you're wrong!' she continues, her brown eyes shining passionately. 'No matter where he's gone or what he's done, he's never forgotten you. In fact, he's been waiting for you, giving you space to come to your senses as well as trying to make everything better for you!'

I shake my head, unable to deal with this version of events.

'He's left his job, Bea, he's changed his entire life for you, and not only that, he's spent the last few months trying to find your dad for you. And he's done it too – look!'

I blink at her, unable to take in this bombshell. I look down at the envelope she's handed to me that has an address in Baga, Goa written on the front. I open it up. Inside is a letter from Adam and I scan his words quickly, barely able to take them in.

'After you ran out on him and, apparently, went back to Kieran, Adam decided that, in order for you to ever be happy with him, or anyone else – he had to help you find your dad,' Milly explains gently. 'He knew you wanted him there at your wedding, but he also knew you'd never decide to find him yourself. He's spent the last few months tracing all the places your dad

moved to since he left Norfolk and then he's gone to each place
to try and track him down for you.' She stops and stares at me,
panting a little from the exertion of her speech. 'Now try and tell
me that isn't just the most romantic fucking thing you've ever
heard?'

I open my mouth to speak but I can't. She leans against a tree,
like she's been deflated of every last bit of energy.

'*That's* what he's been doing these past few months, Bea,'
Milly says quietly. She looks up at me sadly. 'And all the while
you've been acting like a reckless teenager, shagging around with
Kieran!' She shakes her head and rubs her stomach. 'I don't
understand, Bea. I don't understand why you would go back to
him after what happened. His brother *died* because of him ...
you nearly died, too ... and then he dumped you!' I stare at her,
shocked, as I see her eyes fill up with emotion. Milly never cries.
'When you were with Kieran I was so scared I'd lose you, Bea, so
scared that you would do something stupid and I'd never see you
again. You had been depressed before, but when you met him it
was like you didn't give a shit about life any more. You were scar-
ily reckless, crazy, in fact. You said that he understood you better
than anyone. But he didn't. He brought out the worst of your illness but made you feel like it was the best. Please don't get back
with him, Bea, please ... I'm begging you as your best friend –
you have to listen to me ...'

I look at the point in the distance where Kieran disappeared
and then at Milly. I fold up Adam's letter and put it back in the
envelope. I want to tell her that I haven't done anything except
try to work out who I am and why I've made such bad choices.
I want to tell her that seeing Kieran again hasn't been a mistake.
I needed to be with him because I needed to make peace with
what happened between us all those years ago. But I also want to
tell her that doesn't mean I want to be *with him* now.

The opposite, in fact.

Because when he kissed me just now I knew with absolute clarity that Kieran wasn't The One. He never has been. No matter how much I've tried to convince myself over the past few months that this could work, it has never felt right. He's a piece of my past, nothing more, nothing less. I was over him a long time ago. I just haven't ever got over what we *went through* together. It's not him I've been obsessed with all these years. It's what happened that night on the pier. It's not love I've been feeling, it's guilt that he lost his brother and it was my fault.

And then there's Adam. All this time I've been picturing Adam living this great new life without me. But instead he's been trying to help me find myself from afar. Even after what I did to him on our wedding day. The truth is I wasn't running away from him, I was trying to run *to* my long-lost dad. It's all I've been doing since the day he left us. Searching for him, in the place where we shared our love of gardening, in his old diary and in Kieran: why else would I choose the kind of guy who I (and everyone who loved me) knew would leave me one day? Just like Dad had done.

And I've realised now that none of what has happened this year – running away from my wedding and revisiting all the choices in my life and making new ones – has been about choosing between Adam and Kieran. It has been about finding my dad.

'Bea?' Milly says, stepping away from the tree. 'Are you going to say anything? Surely you can see what an idiot you've been?' I stare at her dumbly and she groans in frustration. '*God!* You are infuriating! I've come all this way to stop you throwing away your future and you haven't got anything to say?'

I begin to cry then because here in my childhood home, the place where both my dad and Kieran are tangled in the roots of my past, the realisation of what I've thrown away hits me. I ran away from Adam but he's *never* left me. He's been here for me all this time without me even knowing. Adam, my strong, loyal, patient, encouraging, kind, understanding Adam. I miss him so much. Everything I thought I knew, every choice I've made has just been dug up and turned over and now all that's left is a bare plot of earth where I know Adam should be.

'Adam loves you, Bea.' Milly clasps my arms. 'He always has done. I just wish you could see how much. I know it's none of my business and I'm sure you wish I would just butt out, but I can't allow you to throw everything away. You're my best friend, Bea. I care about you so much and I just want you to be happy!'

'Milly,' I say at last. We're both crying now. 'You've always believed you've known what's right for me and I've always followed your advice. But this time I need you to know that the one thing I've learned in the past few months is that I *have* to make my choices on my own . . .'

'Bea, I know, but please not Kieran—'

I take her hands. 'If I make a mistake, it'll be my mistake,' I say firmly. 'You have to just trust me, OK?' I look at her, willing her to understand what I'm trying to say. *Let me make my own choices. I promise I'll make the right one.*

She groans again. She's always been stubborn.

'I mean it, Milly, it's my life and—'

Suddenly she slumps to the ground. I crouch down next to her.

'Ohhhh,' she gasps.

'Milly, is it the baby?' I demand.

'Yes, no, I don't know, it's too early . . . ohhh!' She looks up at me and her dark eyes are pools of fear. 'She's not due for another six weeks!' I stand up and look manically around the garden, not moving from Milly's side. Why can't I be more like Cal? He'd know exactly what to do.

'Jay!' I scream and he turns and then bounds over, putting one hand on her tummy.

'Milly, is the baby coming?'

She closes her eyes and nods, unable to speak for the pain. Jay looks up at me desperately. It's so dark but I can see that Milly's face is ghoulishly pale, like the moon shining above us.

'CAL!' I scream and I see my brother turn and gaze into the distance. He sprints over and throws himself into full paramedic mode whilst phoning the hospital. As he does, I have a flashback to that night, fourteen years ago, when he came into my room and found me semi-conscious, surrounded by paracetamol bottles. He wasn't a paramedic then, but he was my hero. He acted fast, phoned the ambulance and kept me conscious until they arrived. I have no doubt he saved my life. I stand back now so he can get to her, completely petrified for Milly and Jay. Thankfully moments later an ambulance screeches down the road and pulls into the drive.

A hushed crowd has gathered around us as two of Cal's colleagues rush over and Milly is gently lifted onto a stretcher, flanked by Jay and Cal. I grasp her hand. 'It's going to be OK, Milly, everything's going to be OK, I promise.'

'I can't lose this baby, Bea,' she says, staring at me with wide, fearful eyes. 'I don't know what I'll do—'

'You won't lose the baby,' I say firmly, my cold breath circling hers. I glance up at the stars that are just visible. 'There is no way in this world that's going to happen.' I see one star twinkling brighter than the rest and I wish with everything I have that it is the one that will carry Milly's daughter into this world safely. 'I think she just wants to meet you a little sooner than you'd planned.' I smile tearfully, trying to hide my fear. 'She's her mother's daughter. Very decisive and totally in charge . . .'

'Or an insufferable control freak,' Milly says weakly. And then she closes her eyes and is taken to the ambulance.

I watch it reverse down Loni's drive and with red lights flashing, it speeds off into the dark, dark night and only then do I begin to cry.

It feels like an entire lifetime has passed when I finally allow Loni to lead me inside.

Chapter 57

It's 11 p.m. and Loni and I are alone. Her guests have either left or crashed out in the various guest rooms, outhouses and random caravans that are parked in the drive. I'm sitting in front of the fire with a blanket wrapped around my shoulders, not speaking, just slowly sipping the brandy she gave me. We're still waiting to hear from Cal. I can't stop thinking about Milly and her baby. I feel like what happened is my fault – if we hadn't been arguing maybe she wouldn't have gone into premature labour ...

'It's not your fault,' Loni whispers, as if reading my mind. 'You have to stop blaming yourself for everything.'

I lean my head against Loni's chest and stare at the flickering flames. I remember that we sat like this a lot in the year after Kieran left and I was living at home. I close my eyes, enjoying the warmth of Loni's embrace. It feels good being here with her. Just like the old days. Back when I wanted to hide away from the world.

'Do you think I made the wrong decision by leaving Adam?' I ask her falteringly. I'm thinking of his note, which I still have in my pocket. I'm thinking about everything I have felt about Kieran in the past few months, and how confused I've been, and how completely certain I was that it was Adam I wanted when Kieran kissed me.

'Do you want to know what I think?' Loni says softly. 'I think you've been incredibly brave in trying to face up to the things that stopped you from truly giving yourself to Adam. You have found a job you really love and the kind of independence you've never had before, and that can only be a good thing. I think there were lots of things you needed to confront that Adam, without realising, protected you from. I think the decision you made on your wedding day had nothing to do with you and him and everything to do with what had happened in the past. You know, darling,' she says gently, kissing the top of my head lightly, 'you've always been so quick to blame yourself. But what you don't often realise is that there is a trail of decisions that other people have made. It was the same when Len left . . . When I told Cal he'd gone he was upset, but he accepted it was your father's decision. But you,' she strokes my hair, 'you were convinced that you'd driven him away, that it was *your* actions that led him to leave us.' Loni shakes her head sadly as she gazes at me. 'You became so introverted, so full of guilt, unable to articulate your thoughts or feelings, and I had to battle to make you see that his leaving had nothing to do with you. You always focus on the final event: Len leaving, Elliot jumping off the pier, Milly's premature labour . . .' She lifts her hand and continues stroking my hair, until her hand comes to rest on my forehead, the warmth of it soothing the swirling current of guilt and shame I've spent years trying to live with. 'I just wish you'd be kinder to yourself and realise that the universe doesn't fracture, the stars don't split because of one decision you make, Bea. Life goes on, just in a slightly different way.'

'Like without Dad,' I say quietly. I can see the path opening up in the conversation before me. This is my chance to talk to her about what I've been hiding from her for weeks.

I'm sick of secrets. Sick and tired. I pull out Adam's note and show her the address on the front. Loni gazes down and I see her blue eyes darken as she stares at it. She doesn't say anything at first. She just keeps staring, first at it, and then out the window, as if she's looking for something. Or someone.

'Of course,' she murmurs.

'Loni? Do you recognise this address?'

'He always loved Goa,' she says quietly. 'It's where we were when we conceived you. It's where he was happiest.'

I pull out another piece of paper. This time the one Father Joe had given me. 'This is where he went after Cley, Loni. Do you know this place too?'

Loni looks down, nods, and then looks at me, her eyes full of torment.

'What?' I ask desperately. 'What is it?'

She closes her eyes and inhales deeply. I can see her hands are shaking. 'It was a Church-run treatment centre for depression. I only know because when your father and I were travelling we lived just down the road from it on a commune in Garden Grove . . .'

The words hit me like bullets. Dad suffered from depression. Just like me. I feel at once like my world has split – and come together, the information fitting into the jigsaw puzzle of my life perfectly.

'And you knew he'd gone there all this time?' I say.

'No!' she exclaims, clutching my hands. 'No, I had no idea. Honestly, Bea. I knew he went to stay with his friend in Cley, but then I – I never heard from him again. Bea,' she pauses, 'Bea, darling, I think it's time I told you the whole truth.'

I pull away from her. 'I thought you just did. You didn't

know he'd gone to that depression clinic. That was the truth, you said.'

She nods slowly. 'It was, but there's more . . .'

A silence descends, one that hangs heavy in the room like a mist over the ocean. It is stifling, sucking the air out of me. I feel like I'm walking a tightrope between the past and the future, and whichever way I fall I'm going to get hurt.

'Tell me what happened,' I say. 'I need to know, Loni. Stop protecting me. I'm not a child, I'm not *ill* any more, just sick, sick and tired of not knowing. I can cope with the truth. I'm stronger than you think,' I say firmly, then I soften my voice. 'I'm your daughter, after all . . .'

She clasps my hand and stares at it. 'I wasn't bored in my marriage, Bea,' she says at last. The words come out in staccato, like she has to force each one out, her breath raspy as if she's struggling to get air. 'I didn't kick him out. I was devoted to Len. I loved him with every ounce of my being but I didn't always understand him.'

Her eyes glaze over and I see she has been carried away on a wave of memories. 'We were so happy, darling; he said I was the light of his life, the one person who made him happy. I was twenty and I loved being in love with such a kind, wise, sensitive man who believed the whole world revolved around me. I knew he'd been ill, but I thought it was all in the past. At that time in my life, I truly believed I could keep him lifted and his life filled with love and light. We travelled for a year or so around California, China, Bali, Thailand, India and when I fell pregnant with you, we came home, got married and Len began teaching again at the university. And then Cal came along too and for a few years everything was perfect. He said he felt that he'd finally found his place – and peace – in the world. But then, he became more distant. I remember being worried that he might have been having an affair but I knew he wouldn't do that to me. He stopped communicating. He stopped working. Some days he wouldn't get out of bed. The only thing that seemed to make him happy was gardening. He spent more and more time outside and less and less with us. I could see I was losing him to his illness again.'

She looks at me tearfully. 'You quickly realised the only way to be with him was to be out there too. You used to work together out there for hours, side by side. I honestly think you were the reason he stayed as long as he did.'

I stare at her in shock, my head reeling with all the new information.

'I loved him so much, Bea, you have to understand, but I just couldn't get through to him any more. I'd have moments when I thought I was making a breakthrough. Days when I would see my old Len again; but then he'd disappear behind another wall and I'd be left to carry on alone. And then one day he disappeared for good. Packed a bag and walked out, no warning, no note. All he left was that gardening diary for you.'

I stare at the floor.

'But you knew he went to Cley . . .' I say at last.

'One of his friends from the church he went to told me. I went straight there and knocked on the door for ages, but Father Joe explained Len wouldn't see me. He just asked me to bring a box of his stuff which I did. When I went back a week later, Len was gone. I was told he hadn't left a forwarding address.'

'Why didn't you tell us before . . . why did you make out it was your decision?'

'I wanted you to have the opportunity to have a relationship with him if he chose to return. And for him to have a second chance of being the father I always knew he could be. I loved him, Bea, so very much.' Her voice cracks with emotion.

I stare at Loni as if I'm seeing her for the first time, not as the relentlessly happy and upbeat social and spiritual whirlwind I have always known her to be, but as an abandoned woman, who has spent years keeping everything together when her whole world had been torn apart.

'I blamed you. I blamed you for something that wasn't your fault,' I manage at last.

'I didn't care, darling!' Loni says, enveloping me in her arms and allowing me to bury my head in her chest. 'I was strong enough to take it. I knew that being here, able to look after you, to love you every single day, would mean that you'd love me unconditionally even if it meant that sometimes you hated me too. But your father was the centre of your world, you adored him, and I didn't want his leaving us to change your perception of him. He was a good man and a great dad, but he was ill. I just wish I could have helped him more . . .'

'Like you helped me,' I say quietly. She stares at me and takes my hand. It feels warm against mine and I close my fingers around hers as I think back to my teens and early twenties, the hours, days, months, years spent battling my own demons. The dark thoughts that came swirling in on me in the middle of the night, exaggerating every tick of the clock and cannibalising the things about myself I didn't like, telling me I wasn't good enough for Dad, that I wouldn't be good enough for anyone or anything. That I was ungrateful, useless, that mine was a waste of a good life. I remember the feelings of inadequacy and misery that caused me to crash spectacularly out of my A levels and take an attempted overdose of paracetamol. Then there were the doctors trying various sleeping tablets and antidepressants to get me back on track before Loni demanded that we use a more holistic approach. She changed my diet, encouraged me to start exercising more; I began running along the coast every day with Cal, Loni never far away in her car, ready to pick us up as soon as I'd run myself to a happy place. She got me doing her garden – the one part of our home that had been neglected since Dad had left. I got my place on the Garden Design course at UEA in Norwich. I felt if not always happy, then stable, steady, calm. It was like I'd accepted my past and begun to embrace the future. It was not an exciting life but it was all I could deal with. It was enough.

And then, two years into the course, aged twenty-two, and finally feeling that I knew where I was going, I met Kieran and I fell again. And then the accident happened.

Now I ask myself, was this how Dad felt when he left us? I feel like my world is cracking once again and as I look up at Loni I suddenly realise what I must have put her through. But she didn't give up on me. She picked up the pieces after my A levels, and after Kieran had gone, and after I left Adam. She cocooned me in the house like it was a womb, nursing me back to health – again and again.

'I can't imagine what you went through when Dad left. I – I just wish you'd shared it with us.' I break down then. 'I'm sorry Loni, I'm so sorry . . .'

'Shhh, it's not your fault, darling. I should have told you the truth about your father sooner. I – I wanted to make it easier for you kids . . . I thought knowing would make it worse. You were so similar to him that I wanted to give you the best chance of living your own life; I didn't want you to think that your fate was fixed because of what your father was like. I realise now I made the wrong decision.'

I want to tell Loni how selfless she's been, how stable and strong. That I don't know where I'd be without her.

'I know, Loni, I know you've always done what you've thought was right. I understand why you didn't want to tell me the truth. He was ill and if I'd known that when I was ill it would only have made it worse. But I do want – no, I *need* to find him. I don't think I'm ever going to move on in my life until I do.'

She nods. 'I'll help you find him, Bea – I promise.' She grasps my face and rests her forehead against mine.

I wrap my arms around her and nestle my face into her neck, buoyed as always by her strength and support.

Chapter 58

It's New Year's Eve and I'm standing opposite Cromer Pier, feeling like I'm walking the line between past and present. I've just been to see Milly and her beautiful baby daughter in the hospital. After a week of bed rest and being kept on a drip, Milly gave birth to Holly Rose this morning at 12.01 a.m. Five weeks early and a very healthy 5lbs 2 oz, she is as beautiful and as full of spirit as her mum; the first picture Jay took of her shows the determination clenched in her fists, her screaming mouth, her soulful eyes. A new life born on the eve of a new year. It doesn't get more hopeful than that.

Distant thunder rumbles like cannons being fired. A storm is on its way and even though everyone else appears to have sensibly stayed indoors I knew after seeing Milly and Holly I had to come here tonight. It's the one last place from my past I have to revisit before I can move on. I haven't seen Kieran since Christmas Day. He texted a few times and wanted to meet up but I made various excuses. I've spent the last week just with Loni and Cal and it's only now that I feel ready to face up to all this. They know I'm here and they know why. No more secrets.

I look up at the pier entrance. The neon lights around the

'Christmas Seaside Special' sign are switched off, the twin domes of the booths that remind me a little of the old Royal Naval College frame the stretch of the pier. Tomorrow the town will be packed full of people watching fireworks light up the pier. For now there is only the sound of waves thrashing against the stilts that separate this ancient structure from the angry sea, and the rain pounding against the pavement. Just like it did that tragic night eight years ago. I'm here because I need to let go. Of it all. My guilt about Elliot's death . . . and Kieran. It's the right kind of day to put ghosts to rest.

I walk round the curve of the sea wall and look down at the pier. Instinctively, I glance back over my shoulder and see Kieran appearing through the mist. Somehow I knew I wouldn't have to wait long to see him. He's lost in thought, his head buried in his hood, eyes staring at the pavement as if searching for something, or someone. He's not even noticed I'm here.

I step out in front of him and touch his arm. He looks up, scared, expectant, hopeful – and then I see a flash of disappointment which he tries to hide.

'Bea, I wasn't expecting you to be here . . .' Kieran leans forward to kiss me.

I pull away guiltily. I don't want to give him the wrong idea.

'Is everything OK? I mean, I don't know what's happened since Christmas, but I've missed you.'

'Have you?' I ask him. 'Have you really?' He stares at me, hurt and confused. I look out over the sea wall; I can feel him next to me, waiting. 'I've done a lot of thinking, Kieran, trying to work out what it was that drew us back together. And I realise that I've been in denial all these months, wanting it to be love, hoping it was love, trying to make it feel like love.' I turn and look at him. 'But it wasn't love, not for me, and – and I don't think it was for you, either.'

Kieran's about to protest but I put my hand out to stop him. 'Please, just hear me out. This wasn't love, Kieran. It was guilt. Guilt and sadness and loss and longing. We were trying to cling to each other because we felt in some small way it would bring us closer to Elliot and lessen our guilt, because no matter what anyone tells us, both of us blame ourselves for his death.'

'But I told you that night I didn't think Elliot's death was your fault and that's never changed!'

'I came between you ...' I say. 'Because of me *everything* changed.'

He lifts my chin with his forefinger and looks deep into my eyes. 'You don't see it, do you? Elliot was never going to grow up or calm down and until I met you, nor was I, Bea. He jumped, Bea, *he jumped.* You have to stop believing that you caused Elliot's death, and start believing that you saved *my life.*' He takes my hand and as he does I feel another piece of my pain drift out to sea. 'That's what *I* realised when I left you that summer. Losing him and being with you made me see there was a future for me different to the one that had been mapped out before. I stayed away for so long because I wanted to be sure I was worthy of you, not because I blamed you.'

As I look at him the present falls away and I see him as the lost, reckless boy he was when I met him.

The sky has turned black now, the sea is like a serpent wriggling beneath us, rising up against the side of the pier. It's as if it senses that we are old prey and this moment, so like the one eight years ago, is another chance for it to claim us as its own. Every rise and fall of the waves feels like it's trying to curl itself around us and drag us down, swallowing us whole like it did Elliot.

I should be scared of being out here in this storm but I'm strangely calm. It seems right for us to be here now. Like this was all predestined. This meeting, this moment, this weather so like it was that night. In a strange, sick kind of way, it is perfect.

Kieran stares out to sea and when he speaks his voice is loud above the wind and rain. 'I convinced myself I was doing something big and brave and important when I joined the Navy. Something that would make me feel close to my brother. But the truth is that I've never stopped drifting. The only place I have ever felt anchored is with you . . .' He steps towards me, his eyes glistening brightly. 'I *am* in love with you, Bea. I always have been.'

'Kieran—' I begin, but he pulls me to him.

'Come on, Bea, let's do what the universe has been telling us all this time and be together!'

A flash lights up his eyes and I turn and see lightning slice the sky down to the sea as if it's splitting the world in two. Immediately afterwards another forked streak of lightning shoots out, like a serpent's tongue.

'No, Kieran,' I say softly, putting my hand against his chest as the mists clear and the world becomes one again. Kieran tilts his head back and stares up at the stars and then down at the sea that claimed his brother.

'We were kids then,' I tell him. 'Stupid kids who experienced something wonderful and then something terrible together. It isn't me you miss, Kieran. It's not me you've come back for. I think you know that . . .'

'I miss him so much, you know, Bea,' he says quietly. 'Every single day. It feels like a piece of me is missing and no matter what I do or where I go, I can't find him. I thought if you and I were together, at least it would make what happened that night make sense. It was all such a waste.'

I put my arm around him and squeeze him tight as I rest my head against his shoulder.

'I just want to turn back time, Bea. Relive that moment. Press rewind and do everything differently, you know? Make different decisions.'

And I do know. A calm has settled over the sea and over us. Neither of us will ever get over Elliot's death. We will always blame ourselves, but being together again would only make it worse. I kiss him on his cheek. We both know this is goodbye.

'Will you be all right?' I ask, stepping back from him.

'I'm just going to stay here a little while longer,' he says. His voice is soft, distant, like he is already a long, long way away. Part of me wonders if he has ever really been here. In body, maybe, but not in spirit. That was lost the night he lost his twin.

It is his brother he's wanted to be with all these years, not me.

And it's Adam I want to be with now.

It has always been Adam.

January

Dear Bea

A new year is upon us. Despite the bare branches of the trees, the spikes of spring shoots shimmer in the frosty sunlight bringing promise of new life. Holly bushes are heavy with ice-covered berries, glazed like frosted sweets, swathes of early snowdrops carpet the earth, nodding their white, honey-scented heads like brides at the altar. Maybe this isn't enough to coax you from the warm comfort of your home but that's OK. Just as we use this time to reflect on the past year and make resolutions for the one to come, we should reflect upon our garden. We might want to make big changes, like reshaping beds and borders or removing dominant, long-standing features. After all, sometimes a reshuffle is long overdue . . .

If you decide to make these changes, you may find it hard to see clearly through the wintry mists as they descend upon you. There have been times when I have felt that everything is so dark my life will always be devoid of colour. It is tempting to hibernate, to hide away from the world until you can see the promise of sunshine again. But if you brave the bad weather and you feel like the relentlessly inhospitable wind is pushing you to the edge, trust that there will always be something or someone there to soften your fall.

Love, Dad x

Chapter 59

Bea Hudson is looking back and thinking ahead. May this year brings hope, health and happiness to everyone I love.
29 likes.

New Year's Day at the Hudsons' is exactly as it always is. Overblown, inflated, obese in its spread and yet anorexic in its atmosphere. The dining room is cavernous and cold. The four of us are seated around a giant table that has been lavishly decorated with their best silver and china, and large sprigs of spiky greenery. A sparsely decorated spruce stands in the corner on some sort of plinth, like a piece of art rather than a piece of nature. A chandelier dangles precariously low over the centre of the table, reflecting our faces back at us a hundredfold as if trying desperately to make us feel that there are more of us in this enormous dining room. I so wanted to make today a happy occasion and start the year in the right way. Christmas was . . . disappointing. Adam worked so late on Christmas Eve that we didn't make it to Loni's for the usual family festivities. He told me to go on my own because he didn't want to spend hours in the car when he only had two days off, but I couldn't imagine being there without him. I can't go home because I'm still scared of seeing Kieran. No matter how hard I've tried, I haven't forgotten the way he turned up at my wedding, or the Facebook message he sent. Anyway I didn't want to be apart from Adam when I felt like I'd barely seen him all year. So we stayed at the flat, just the two of us, with our little, last-minute tree and the lavish presents, using them to make up for what was lacking in our marriage. We'd gone shopping on Boxing Day because it was something to do, and it meant we didn't have to be alone in the flat, trying to paper over the cracks of our relationsip with festive wrapping. And now we're here.

I look at the giant bird in the middle of the table and the elegant trimmings around it, and take in the fact that the four of us are sitting here in silence. For a moment I'm struck by a longing to be at Loni's. There were times when I was growing up I wished there were fewer people around, that the house was quieter, calmer, more contained. I felt like Loni was filling every square inch of space to fill the void that had been left by Dad and I resented her for it because no one could ever replace him. I thought that being with a complete family on special occasions like this would show me exactly what I'd been missing. But now I realise that all it's doing is making me appreciate what I have. Yes, Loni is unconventional, yes, our family gatherings are wildly different, but at least they are fun, informal, happy. Loni's energy is always spent trying to making other people happy – including me: it's been like a life's work for her.

And the funny thing is, I realise I have never asked her if she is happy herself.

Suddenly I have an explosion of images in my mind of New Year's Days past, one after another. I smile as I see Loni, when we were kids, dragging me and Cal into a conga round the house, Cal in his little superhero outfit, both of us squealing with laughter and feeling like the joy of the party the night before was spilling into another day. There was the New Year's Day in Thailand with Loni when we were teenagers, and the one when she allowed Cal and me to have a house party with our friends.

Now here I am celebrating with my new family, the complete, 'perfect' family I've always wanted. Except they're not so perfect. I'm beginning to think there's no such thing.

'For what we are about to receive may the Lord make us truly thankful . . .' Marion says piously. I'm not religious but I close my eyes and think of Loni and Cal and say a silent prayer of thanks. Then I vow to myself to go home and see them.

Adam's mum claps her hands and smiles. 'It is customary for George to say a few things before we begin New Year's lunch. George?'

'Thanks, Marion, I do indeed want to mark this special day with a few choice words that will best summarise our year.' Marion nods and adjusts her neckscarf as George stands up, looks at us all, clears his throat then raises his glass and bellows, 'Bottoms up!'

I stifle a laugh as Marion gazes at him furiously. 'That's it? Seriously, George, that is all you have to say about a year that saw our only son do such a marvellous, life-changing thing as' – Adam takes my hand as if to acknowledge what Marion is about to say – 'become MD?' I keep the smile on my face, waiting for her to mention me, us, our marriage.

She doesn't.

'Oh for Christ's sake, Marion, can we eat some of this food?' George refills his glass, downs half of it and stands up to carve the bird as we watch silently. I think of Loni's New Year's Day Ritual Carving Ceremony with longing. Everyone around the table cuts a slice and makes a wish for the person next to them.

I realise what a wonderful uplifting way it is to connect every-one and start the meal.

'So, Adam,' Marion says. 'Do fill us in on what's been going on at wor—'

'Shall we each make a wish first?' I ask, cutting in with a bright smile as everyone looks at me blankly. 'No? OK, cracker then?' I say weakly, lifting a posh Fortnum & Mason's number. I'm desperate to make some noise, to break the cycle of con-versation, to make them all act differently, think differently. To stop them treading so carefully down the line they've drawn. The one that keeps them all at arm's length from each other, that favours reserve over emotion, that erects perfect façades to dis-guise messy emotions, a line that always falls on the side of work, not life. Not love.

I glance at Adam and wave the cracker under his nose but he ignores it so I put it back on the table, lift my glass and take a long swig. If I can't beat George, I may as well join him.

After lunch we retreat with brandies into what Marion calls the 'salon' which is weird because a) they are not French and b) there are no visible sinks or other hairdressing implements in the room. Despite her name for it, this is a surprisingly homely room and the one I feel the most comfortable in. It has a big open fire – this time with logs flickering away merrily – that reminds me of home. I sneakily stand next to it before sitting down. What occurs to me as Marion joins me on the sofa is that even though Adam and I both come from a family of three, Adam's family seems so much smaller than mine.

'So Bea,' Marion says conversationally, legs crossed at an angle to face me, head tilted to indicate interest. 'Tell me, girl to girl, wife to wife. You must miss Adam terribly when he's away, hmm?'

I take a sip of my drink. It burns my throat. 'Of course,' I reply hoarsely. 'Every day. But I know it won't be for long . . .'

'Oh!' Marion claps her hands and smiles at me whilst somehow managing to not look pleased at all. 'So you're happy to move to New York now that Adam's role means moving there permanently?'

Suddenly the room shrinks, conversation stops and everything seems to go into slow motion.

'Mu-um!' Adam exclaims.'I haven't told Bea yet.'

He sits forward on his sofa and stretches out his hand to me, like a policeman trying to entice someone, about to jump, back from a sky-rise window ledge. 'Bea, I was going to talk to you when we had a quiet moment but I haven't had a chance . . .'

Marion folds her arms and stares at us, as if she's preparing to watch a tennis match.

Adam glares at her. 'Can we have some privacy, please?'

'Oh darling, if we stay we might be able to help you sort this little misunderstanding out,' she says, resting a hand on his arm. He instantly shakes it off.

'I think you've done enough,' he says warningly.

'I'm just trying to help—'

'Please will you just stop interfering!'

I've never heard Adam talk to his mother like that. George has already retreated from the room but Marion is standing with her mouth open.

'Oh that's charming. Well, Adam, if you don't want to have perfectly *valid* parental guidance from your mother and father who have done nothing but love and *guide* you throughout your life, then that's absolutely *fine*,' she says, then flounces out of the room.

I see that Adam is shaking and I want to go over but I can't move. I'm in shock.

A silence descends as we're left alone.

'That went well,' he murmurs. Then he looks at me. 'Bea, I'm so sorry, I promise I was going to tell you . . .' he says, stepping towards me.

'*Tell*. That's an interesting word,' I reply evenly. 'When *were* you going to *tell* me, Adam? Because you clearly didn't intend to *ask* me.'

'I was just waiting for the right time.'

'How long have you known?' I ask.

He doesn't answer straight away. He just rubs his forehead and slumps down on the sofa. 'Not long.'

'How long?' My voice is calm, smooth, even though I'm a bubbling volcano of emotion.

'Dad told me when he made me MD that it would involve a move out there.'

I stare at him incredulously but he won't meet my eyes. 'That was six months ago! Why didn't you tell me then?'

He doesn't look at me, he can't. His grey eyes are fixed on the floor. 'I didn't want to worry you unnecessarily. I thought the less time you had to think about it, the easier it would be for you. I know how anxious you get.'

'So when *were* you going to tell me?' I press, a dangerous edge to my voice.

He doesn't move for a moment and then he pulls an envelope out of his pocket. It's gift-wrapped, with my name on it. He hands it to me and I look up at him before I rip off the paper furiously. Inside are two plane tickets, for the 5th of January.

'Four days?' I say quietly, my voice shaking. 'You were going to give me four days' notice to completely uproot my life and move to a different country? To leave the first job I've ever had that's made me happy? To say goodbye to my family and my friends? And you thought that would be easier how exactly?'

'I didn't think it would be easy.' Adam looks up at me beseechingly. 'But I also knew you wouldn't cope with the alternative. I knew you'd just refuse to go. You've always hated making decisions, you haven't ever been able to cope with change. Our relationship has always worked by me organising everything, making the decision and then presenting you with a fait accompli . . .'

'Like when you arranged for my current job to land on my lap at Eagle's?' It is a cruel jibe and he gazes at me reproachfully. He looks in pieces. Have I done this to him?

'I've only ever wanted to make you happy, Bea,' he says wearily. 'You know that I'd do anything for you but sometimes I don't get to make decisions because I don't have a *choice*.' He bangs his fist on the arm of the sofa and then raises it to his forehead, closing his eyes as if to calm himself down. 'I *have* to move to New York, Dad made that clear, or I'm out of a job, out of the company and out of his favour.' He continues sorrowfully, 'I thought it'd be good for us, Bea. A fresh start . . .' For a moment he looks so confused and hurt, so uncharacteristically vulnerable that I want to melt into his arms, to tell him that I trust him and that I'd go to the ends of the earth with him. But I can't. He must see me wavering, however, because he takes that moment to get off the sofa.

'You'd love it out there, Bea, I know you would,' he says, approaching me with his arms outstretched.

'I know how much you miss Milly,' he says animatedly, 'and I know how many opportunities you'd find for yourself out there . . .'

'Work Adam' has taken over now, the guy who is used to problem-solving, leading people, making creative decisions, selling a product to people. I realise how much of Work Adam I've had at home recently. And it occurs to me that I don't like that version of him very much. 'I know you'd love the city too,' he continues seamlessly. It's like he's doing one of his pitches. 'I know how much you'd love Central Park – there's even a Greenwich Village, Bea! You've always said you miss living there – now you can but in New York! And really, be honest, is there anything keeping you here?'

'How about my *job*?' I look at him in disbelief, my frustration growing at the fact that he doesn't see the problem. He can't see that I can't just up and leave. I don't want to . . .

'You can do the same job in New York!' he exclaims. 'You can work on the new office out there. I could talk to James, see if you can work on the project out there—'

'Stop trying to control everything!' I yell and he steps back as if thrust by the blast of a cannonball. I put my hands up at my temples to drown out the noise of my fears. 'Just STOP IT!' I begin to cry. 'You think you can fix everything, don't you? You thought you could fix me, well you can't! So why don't you just go, go to New York, leave like everyone else always does. It looks like you've been building up to it from the moment we got married.' He comes across the room, tries to envelop me in his arms but I push him away like I've been trying to do for years. The barriers are up and the fears I've been trying so hard to ignore flood out in force. I knew I didn't deserve to be happy. Adam is too good for me. Adam steps back and walks over to the fireplace and leans his forehead against it.

'I'm not trying to fix you, Bea,' he says quietly. 'I love you. But I – I also know that because of what you've been through . . . in the past . . . with, you know, your . . . illness, that you're scared, no you're fucking *petrified* of taking a risk and jumping into the unknown. But I'm here for you, Bea. I'll always be here for you . . . no matter how much you try to push me away.'

He breaks off and I close my eyes and take deep yogic breaths like Loni taught me, trying to contain the panic and confusion I feel. Everything is crashing down around me. Everything I thought I had built. I'm standing on the edge of that pier again and I can feel myself wanting to disappear beneath the icy cold waves. I open my eyes and look at him as if for the first time.

'I won't let you fall.' Adam comes forward, reaching out to me again. 'You can trust me.'

I hold out my hands to stop him. 'That's the problem, Adam. I've spent the last seven years trying to pretend that I don't believe you're going to leave me one day and it is exhausting.' I think about how hard I tried not to fall in love with him, not to move in with him, not to marry him. Every time I took a step forward I hoped it would wipe out my uncertainty. But it didn't. It hasn't. I know he's a good man and I know he wouldn't intentionally hurt me. But I also know that every man I've ever loved has left me. It's just a matter of time before he does too. It is as certain as the leaves falling in autumn.

'I'm not like your dad, Bea,' he says reproachfully.

'No,' I say before another thought occurs to me. 'But maybe I *am*.'

I feel the certainty growing in me now as my heart is shrinking, shrivelling like skin in water, and I am pushing away from the edge where I have been standing for so long. It's not Adam, it's me.

He moves towards me again. 'I know you're scared. I know you find it hard to make decisions, take steps forward but that's OK. I'm here, Bea, I'm here and I want to make you happy. I know I can make you happy,' he says determinedly. 'If you'll just let me.'

'No, Adam,' I say evenly. I feel light, like I'm floating above this moment, the free before the fall. 'You don't know what you want. Every single step you've taken so far in your life has been determined by what your parents want for you. You're married to your work, not me.' I pause and take a breath as I walk towards the door. With each one I have to force myself not to turn back.

I feel like I'm swimming against the current; no matter how fast I paddle I'm being drawn back to the other side. But I know I have to keep going. When I'm finally there I reach out and grasp the handle, like I'm gripping the shore, all the time the waves are trying to pull me back. I need to let go. I need to let him go.

'This isn't the life I want, Adam, and do you know what? I don't think it's what you want either. If you did, don't you think you would have worked harder at *us*?' I hold my hand up. 'Don't answer, I know you won't admit it because you don't want to acknowledge that the one decision in your life you actually made yourself was *wrong*. There was another life out there for you that could have made you happy. Another *wife* . . .'

Adam shakes his head, tears forming in his eyes. 'If that's really what you think, Bea, then you don't know me at all.' He leans his hand against the wall and bows his head. His wedding ring glistens back at me and suddenly it looks completely incongruous. Like it was never meant to be there.

'And it's why I have to leave,' I say. 'I'm sorry, Adam, but I can't do this any more.'

I don't look back as I walk out of the door.

I can't. It will hurt too much.

Chapter 60

As the taxi speeds me back to London I pull my phone out of my bag. There's only one person I want to talk to. One person whose advice I need in this situation. I scroll through my phonebook until I get to L and press call.

'Hello, this is Loni Bishop wishing you SUCH JOY this New Year!'

'Loni?' I say, my voice cracking.

'Bea?' I begin to sob at the sound of her voice. 'What's wrong? Is it that Marion woman? What's she said to upset you this time? I swear if she—'

'I-it's not Marion,' I stammer, 'it's me. I – I've left Adam.'

'Oh darling . . . where are you?'

'In a car on the way back to our flat. I'm going to pack some things and then I wondered if – I wondered if I could . . . come home?'

The flat seems cold and unfamiliar when I walk in. It feels like I've been away for months even though we only left it to go to Adam's parents this morning. *Was it really only this morning?* I'd called Milly after Loni. She seemed to take the news pretty badly, crying out as if in pain when I told her what I'd done. I knew she loved Adam and me but it had seemed a bit extreme. It took me a moment – and hearing Jay shout 'Hospital, please!' to what was obviously a taxi driver – to realise that her reaction was due to the fact that she was having contractions and the baby was coming five weeks early. I'd been horrified that I'd potentially caused her more stress.

'Please, forget about me and Adam. Focus on you and your baby. We'll work it out. I'm sure we will ...'

'You'd better,' she'd panted tearfully. 'Or you'll have me and this baby to answer to. You guys are our number one choice in godparents ... I'll call you.' And with that, my best friend had gone.

I drop my bag on the floor and slump, unable to carry the weight of my body and what I've just done any longer. I feel so distant, so far away from everyone, so alone.

I gaze at the simple hi-tech décor and suddenly feel like I'm in a hotel room. None of this feels familiar. It's like I've had an extended holiday for the past seven years in a place where I never expected to stay for long. It's beautiful, comfortable, safe, but not mine.

I get up and wander listlessly over to the sideboard in the lounge. On it are two photos in frames; one is of me and Adam, taken at his thirtieth a couple of years ago. He's wearing a dinner suit and is laughing at something I've said. We look so happy. I pick it up and stroke my finger over his face. I feel a stab of shame and remorse so stomach-searingly awful that I crouch down. I miss Adam. I hate being here without him and can't bear the thought of not seeing him, holding him, talking to him, loving him again. I know that he didn't mean to hurt me. He did what he'd always done, made decisions that he thought were best for us, because I became incapable of making them a long time ago. I'm just surprised he stayed with me for so long. 'I'm sorry,' I whisper into his picture. 'I'm so so sorry.'

I go to the bedroom and I throw some clothes, a handful of books and CDs into a medium-sized suitcase. As I easily zip up all my worldly possessions, it occurs to me that I don't own anything that isn't transportable. Have I been waiting for this moment all along? Waiting to run away, just like my dad?

I walk back into the lounge and take one last look around. As I do, the fire exit steps appear in my peripheral vision. I know I should just go, but as well as feeling this centrifugal pull to leave, I feel an equal and opposite desire to stay. I turn to the steps. I want to go up there, to have one last look at the view from the roof garden, but if I do I'll never be brave enough to leave. I can't go on as I am, charging forward pretending that everything is OK. Ever since I fell over in that church I've been desperately trying to carve a new life for myself, and wipe out everything that happened before. My illness, my insecurities, my need to find my father, and my mistakes. But I'm sick of hiding my past, sick of feeling so guilty, sick of believing that everyone I love is going to leave me and sick of not knowing where to go with my life.

I have to face up to what I've spent so long running away from.

I have to go home.

Chapter 61

I gaze out of the car window and into the yawning darkness of the Norfolk countryside where I'm sure I can hear the sea calling and the marshes sighing. Cal drove up to London to pick me up, arriving just over two hours after I called Loni and then driving us straight back to Norfolk. I tried to tell him how grateful I was, how he and Loni had always been there for me and how sorry I was for neglecting them. He wouldn't let me finish. Which was good because I couldn't, I was crying too hard.

'My Superhero,' was all I could manage.

'You looked after me for my entire childhood, sis,' he said in a choked voice. 'I'm just glad to still have you in my life.' He blinked quickly then he stretched his hand out and squeezed mine. 'I love you, sis. We all just want you to be happy.'

I look up at the moon that has replaced the sun and think of it endlessly circling this planet like a clock. I have kept the exterior version of my life ticking over for so long, but now I just want to muffle the persistent thudding in my ears is growing louder. Thankfully soon I will be wrapped in the comfort and security of Loni's warm, Wifi-less house where the rest of the world will retreat back into the darkness, ticking onwards as my own life slows and slows and slows to a standstill. We are only ten minutes away now and I am feeling a sense of calm acceptance. Norfolk is where I belong, where I've always belonged, where life is slow and expectations are low. Where I can walk for miles alone without having to make a single decision. Not like in London where I was constantly trying to prove to everyone including myself that I was someone I'm not, pretending that I could cope just to keep everyone happy. For a while there it had worked; I'd done a good impression of a functioning human being in my smart clothes and heels, with my happy marriage and my dream job. But it was all a façade: it couldn't last because nothing can last until I face up to my past.

The radio is emitting a low hum, a countdown of the biggest hits of the past year. I absent-mindedly look up the definition of 'countdown' on my phone.

Countdown: an arbitrary reliving of past events as time ticks forever onwards.

I've given up moving forward; leaving Adam and coming back to Norfolk is proof that the best thing for me is to submerge myself in the past once and for all.

Something clicks in my brain. Ticks. That's what I have to do.

'Turn left!' I cry out suddenly as I spot a signpost. The clock is ticking urgently.

'What? Why?' Cal says, startled.

'Just do it, please,' I beg. 'I need to make a detour, Cal. Now.'

He flicks the indicator and as I hear the tick-tick-ticks inside my head, like my very own countdown, I stare at the road ahead.

The one that is taking me all the way back.

Chapter 62

'What are we doing here?' Cal pulls up on the seafront and stares at the pavilion and promenade in front of us, worry etched tellingly on his face.

It's 9 p.m. and Cromer is eerily quiet; a ghost town after the action and excitement of New Year's Eve last night, and the annual fireworks that would have taken place earlier this evening. I imagine everyone is at home, recovering from the storm that thrashed the coast last night – not to mention all the celebrations that a brand-new year brings. Strange to think I'm here on the other side of them, the storm, the year. I am walking my own line, as usual. Everything is calm. I am calm.

'I just want to walk on my own for a bit,' I say lightly, opening the car door and breathing in the fresh sea air. 'Is that OK?'

'I don't know, Bea,' Cal says; his face looks tense in the harsh light of the car's interior. 'You won't—'

'Do anything stupid?' I shake my head and smile in what I hope is a convincing way. 'Of course not. I'm not a kid any more, Cal.'

He looks into my face. 'I'm coming with you.' He unclips his seat belt and goes to open his door. 'I don't want you to be by yourself.'

I put my hand on his arm to stop him. 'No, please, Cal. This is something I need to do on my own.'

He stares at me for a moment, his bright blue eyes full of fear and uncertainty, and then he looks away and takes his hand off the door handle. 'OK, you can go on your own but you can't stop me staying here and watching you from the sea wall, OK?' He folds his arms determinedly and in that instant I see the serious, determined, responsible and stubborn kid he's always been.

I nod and then I lean in and quickly kiss him on the cheek before I get out and slam the car door shut behind me.

The wind steals my breath as I leave Cal and make my way to the pier forecourt that has a large compass landscaped into the ground. I shiver and pull my thin city coat around me tightly. Is this the kind of day to put ghosts to rest or to unleash them? I haven't been here for eight years but at the same time I feel like I was here yesterday. I can hear echoes of my past whistling in my ears and I can see shadowy images of me and Kieran everywhere I look. For the first time in years I allow them to flood my mind instead of trying to drown them out. I allow myself to think of how Kieran came to my wedding, and to dare to wonder what might have happened if I hadn't married Adam that day. Would I have dealt with everything that had stopped me from being able to let go and be happy? Would Kieran and I have talked, put the past to rest and then walked away from each other again? Or is there more to it? Did I turn away from my destiny, that day? Or did I make the right choice . . .

I turn, half expecting to see one of them approaching. But I am alone.

I stand in the middle of the compass with my shoulders

hunched and my hands dug deep into my pockets. The compass feels like a symbol of where I am in my life right now, and of how indecisive and directionless I've been for so long.

I wander over to the flint wall and have to steady myself as I sit on it because the wind is blowing with such force. I pull my hood up and look at the side of the pier that Elliot jumped from on that fateful night. Then I look down at the beach and feel giddy and sick when I remember how I sat there, wrapped in a tinfoil cloak, shivering, sobbing as the paramedics ran their tests on Kieran and me. He was in shock. They'd done crazy things like this before and had always survived. He and Elliot always survived, he said. He was wrong.

It was my fault. It was all my fault.

I step tentatively onto the pier now. I'm afraid the boards beneath my feet are going to give way and this time I will be plunged into the icy depths, not by choice, not through daring, but because I deserve it.

Looking round I see the silhouette of Cal leaning against the sea wall. One hand is raised over his eyes as if he is looking out to sea. But I know he's just looking for me. Looking out for me, as always. He was there that night too – a student paramedic working with the Ambulance Trust. I was amazed as I watched him spring into action when they found Kieran and me huddled with Elliot's body. Trying to save a life, not throw it away.

I cling to the rails, gripping so hard that my knuckles go white, and as I gaze down into the swirling, icy froth I think of the recklessness, the pure selfishness and stupidity that made me clamber up onto the side that night, feeling like I was invincible. That I was a survivor. I wasn't drunk, it was worse than that. I was completely deluded; blinded by what I thought was love, but was actually self-destruction. Only once Kieran had left did I realise how close I'd come to losing everything. It made me lose faith in myself completely.

And now, being back here eight years on, with my brother watching me carefully and Loni waiting for me to come home, I realise I've never been alone. I've always had people who loved me, who would never ever leave me. Loni, who made it her mission to nurture my happiness and help me deal with each day: giving me the garden to look after, filling my days with yoga, running, meditation – and the house with life, love and laughter, and then using what she'd learned to forge a whole new career for herself. Cal, ever the paramedic, always looking out for me and making sure I didn't have to deal with anything that might tip me over the edge.

Then there's Milly, who's never left my side, even when I dropped out of school, coming over every day after school when I was lying on the sofa to tell me what had gone on. Even when she went away to university, she would write me endless letters, telling me how much fun we'd have together once she'd graduated. Then when it was clear Kieran was never coming back, she forced me into the glare of life by moving me to London, but always kept me safe, making decisions for me, encouraging me to start temping, being gentle when she needed to, forceful when necessary.

And finally there's Adam. I wish I could turn back time and tell him I was wrong. He *did* fix me, he saved me. I look at Cal who is still gazing anxiously in my direction, poised as if ready to spring into action at any moment. I want to call out and tell him that he needn't worry because I don't want to jump any more. I'm not the same girl. I crossed that line a long time ago, chose a different path. The right path. All I have to do now is get back on it.

I look down at my hands gripping the rails of the pier and realise just how much I have changed. My life is no longer determined by the list of people who have left me, but by the ones who have stayed. It has been for a long time. I just didn't see it. My phone buzzes in my pocket and I pull it out. There are twenty texts, all from Adam. Each one says the same thing.

I love you Bea and I'm never going to leave you. x

I raise the phone, nuzzling it as if it is his cheek, tears staining the screen. When I think what I have put him through over the years we've been together and yet he's never lost faith in me, or us. I look at my engagement ring and my wedding ring. They are shining brightly in the darkness, auras of Adam's love and protection. He's always known that I am prone to emotional instability, that I find it hard to cope with life, that I push away happiness because I don't feel I deserve it. It's why he never took no for an answer every time he proposed. It's why he organised the wedding because he knew I couldn't cope with the enormity of it. It's why he arranged for James to contact me. He believes in me so he makes decisions for me when he knows I'm too scared to take a risk. It's probably why he didn't tell me about New York. He isn't a control freak; he keeps me moored, bobbing on the waves, whilst trying to steer me towards a happy future. Our future.

I wish I'd told him – and Loni and Cal and Milly – what had really happened that night but I was too ashamed. I jumped before Elliot, not because I was reckless, or depressed, but because I wanted to prove that I could. It was a stupid snap decision. The wrong decision. I wish I'd trusted them all more. They would have understood. Adam would have told me it was OK, he would have pulled me out of the murky depths of my guilt and made me see that Elliot's death was a tragic accident. I feel like I can hear him whispering to me on each whip of the wind that it's all right, it wasn't my fault.

Suddenly Kieran's voice comes into my head, a déjà vu moment, like an echo of a time before, or a life not lived.

It would have happened anyway, Bea! You have to stop believing that you caused Elliot's death, and start believing that you saved my life.

I put my hands over my ears because suddenly I can hear everyone in my head. Loni telling me we make our own paths and that we can't save other people, only ourselves. Milly telling me that the main thing she's learned from years of working in finance is that the only thing worth investing in is love. Dad telling me in his diary to always look up and ahead, not down and back. And Adam telling me he loves me over and over again. I think of the compass I was standing on earlier and how it felt like a symbol: one life, so many different directions. The infinite What Ifs we live with every single day. The possibilities at each pole, the confusion at the crossroads, the excitement when it feels like life is going our way, the sorrow when it doesn't. And that's when I realise no one ever truly knows where they're going. No decision is easy. Loving, or leaving, saying yes or no. We can waste our lives wondering if we've made the right choices; or we can own them. Stop looking at the other routes and just follow our inner Siri, or in my case, listen to Loni and realise that being happy is the only decision we really have to make.

I look up, thinking about my dad all of a sudden. I may never know if his choice made him happy, but I have to stop letting it make me miserable. He left his diary for me to help me to come to terms with his choice. So, for the first time in ages, I take my long-lost Dad's advice and gaze at the infinite galaxy of stars shimmering above me. I realise then that I have to trust my instincts. Follow the path my heart has taken me on so far and know that, no matter what detours I may make, I will always end up exactly where I'm meant to be. I just have to trust myself.

And with that, I turn my back on the pier and my past – ready to embrace the future I'm now completely certain I want.

February

Dear Bea

The winter is nearly over and all around you new shoots of promise are beginning to appear. It's time to come out of hibernation, to stop thinking of your garden as bare and see what is growing beneath your feet, what has been there all along. You will see drifts of dwarf iris and early crocuses piercing the earth, not to mention beautiful, bright cyclamens and camellias rampaging through the garden like Pink Ladies on an adventure. Soon the wild narcissus – a flower that grows best in the sun – will parade its golden petals once more before the other perennials that always seem overshadowed by it.

There is much to do in the garden this month, but I see February as a comma, a pausing point, a breath between a hard winter that is on its way out and a spring we're waiting to meet. Maybe you are not ready to forget what has gone before, you are still feeling the effects of being out in the cold for so long, but I'm sure there are also moments when the pale sunshine touches your face and you can sense brighter days ahead.

I don't have to be with you to know you have such a bright future before you, Bea.

Love, Dad.

Chapter 63

Bea Bishop is Going to Goa (Goaing?)
9 likes, 1 comment.

As my taxi pulls into the airport I notice that there are thick, bulbous clouds hanging like blimps in the gun-metal grey sky. The day feels broodingly heavy like a sullen teenager desperate to unshackle him or herself from their studies and sod off to sunnier climes.

I climb out of the cab and the taxi driver smiles as he hands me my backpack from the boot and waits for me to scrabble about in my purse for the fare. He's been a good companion, chatty without being intrusive, offering more personal information than he took. I've heard all about his two adored teenage daughters, how much he worries for them and how he insists on picking them up when they're on nights out, no matter what job he's on – or where it's taken him.

'I'd go to the ends of the earth for those two,' he'd laughed at one point, glancing at me in his rear-view mirror as I'd smiled weakly at him, as if he was assessing whether I'd caused my father as much concern. It had sent a pang of pain through me to know the lengths some fathers go to for their children.

Then I'd comforted myself with the thought that Loni had done the equivalent of running solo around the world for Cal and me. And after all that, she's still supporting me in my quest to find Dad. Even though I can't imagine what it's doing to her.

This trip was Loni's idea. After I'd shown her the address of where Adam had traced Dad to that Milly had given me on Christmas Day, she'd taken everything in hand, made me organise a week's holiday from the flower shop. I told her I couldn't, not when Sal had just had her baby, but Loni went ahead and called her and Sal told her immediately that of course I should go. She said that her dad would happily run the shop for the week I'm away. So Loni booked me a ticket and arranged for me to stay with an old friend of hers.

'And you don't mind? You won't mind if I find him and manage to build a relationship with him?'

'Oh Bea, you don't know how much I wish that for you, what *joy* I would find in that!' Loni's eyes had filled up then and I'd cried and hugged her tightly. 'Remember, darling, to dare is to lose one's footing momentarily, but not to dare is to lose yourself.'

'Thank you, Mum,' I said quietly. Calling her that made me wonder when I had stopped using that word. And made me want to start using it again.

'Ooh don't call me that, you make me sound so *old*!' she said, kissing my forehead, and I laughed. But I noticed her eyes were glistening with tears. Had that been another adapted story for my benefit; she making it look like she didn't want to be called Mum, when actually, she found it hurtful that I didn't call her that? Or was it her choice? I'm amazed that one person could protect another so fiercely that they wouldn't care about hurting themselves. She is incredible, and part of me wishes that she was coming with me on this trip.

Cal hadn't been interested, even though I asked him to come. 'I understand why you want to, sis,' he said. 'But I'm not willing to leave Lucy and the kids to go on some wild goose chase. This is your journey and I hope meeting him helps you see what I've always known. That our childhood, our lives have been the best version they could be because of the choices both he and Loni made.' He stopped then and I saw him get a bit choked up.

The terminal is abuzz with excited holidaymakers; couples looking to escape the cold British weather (and no doubt their respective families) after the long Christmas break, parents with young kids on half-term in search of winter sun. Others probably off for fabulous city breaks or going back home to their own countries after a Christmas in the UK. So many people looking to escape their lives – or return to them.

I'm not entirely sure which I'm doing.

I gaze up at the departures board as people stream past me and I get momentarily tangled up in a family or a conversation. I feel like a bobbin, spinning uncontrollably in the effort to keep still as everyone else seems to weave easily around me. The electronic letters on the board are clearly spelling out destinations and flight numbers and gates but they blur in front of my eyes and I suddenly feel completely overwhelmed by this journey I'm taking alone. What am I doing flying to India to find a man I haven't seen in over twenty years to see if he can find the answers to my life? I wish Adam were here; he'd make this better, I know he would. I want to tell him everything I've gone through since last April to get to where I am now. I want him to know that I haven't forgotten him either, that he's always been there, that it wasn't him I was running from – or our relationship. I was running back to everything that had happened before. I've tried to get in touch with him since Milly told me what he'd done for me, but he won't answer my calls. Milly says he's out of the country but I think finding my dad was his final act of altruism, helping me because he still thinks I can't help myself.

I head for the check-in desk slowly and take my place at the back, feeling self-conscious in my solitude and yet empowered by what I'm doing. I'm in control for the first time in my life. I hear a commotion from the automatic doors but I don't turn around. I just want to focus on getting to the front of this queue, get through the gate and onto the plane. I'm worried that if I turn around I'll make a run for it (it is my party trick after all), get in a cab and go back home.

'Mind out of the way, please! Lady with a lot of luggage on her way through!'

I turn just as she appears like magic at my side.

'Ta-dah!' She presents herself with a little shimmy, jewellery a-jangling in time with her body.

'LONI?!' I gasp as she plonks down her rucksack, takes off her fedora and shakes out her batshit-crazy hair as she grins at me.

'The one and only.' She bows as what feels like the entire queue, the entire *terminal* of travellers, turn and look at her. She is dressed in a floor-length tie-dyed skirt that she's wearing with battered old boots she's had since the 1970s. On top she's wearing a white vest – and a loose-fitting jumper that has slipped off her shoulders. At least six necklaces adorn her neck, she has on gigantic hoop earrings and rows of beads are wrapped around her wrist. She's also wearing an Afghan coat. She looks incredible.

'What are you doing here?' I gulp.

'I'm coming with you, of course, darling!' She laughs, throwing her arms around me as my jaw drops open. She pulls back and strokes my face. 'How could I miss the chance to show my baby girl a place I've loved for years, that runs through my blood and yours, through my work, my every breath! I want to support you, to be there for you when you meet your dad . . . this is just as much my mess as his.'

I'm about to speak but she holds her ring-covered fingers up. Only one finger is bare. Her wedding ring finger. I clasp her hand.

'Loni, you don't have to do this. I know how hard it's going to be for you.'

'I want to do it,' she replies. 'Not just for you, I'm not a total martyr.' She winks and I can't help but smile. '*I* need to. I've realised that I can learn a lot from you, my darling. I need to face up to my past before I can move on, too. Roger – you remember Roger, don't you, darling?' she says coyly. 'He was there at Christmas. Beautiful man, silver hair, voice like silk, moves like Jagger?'

I see she is blushing – I have never seen Loni blush.

'Well, it would seem he is rather interested in me . . .' She leans forward and whispers in a voice louder than most people's shouts, 'And not just sexually! He wants a relationship. You know, to be serious, go steady or whatever the word is these days. But anyway, I can't, you see. I haven't been able to let myself fall in love with anyone since . . . well, you know. Since your dad left.'

I nod and take her hand. I can see she's finding this hard to talk about.

She clears her throat and smiles. 'In many ways I've been in limbo as long as you have. I've just got better moves . . .' She throws her head back so her hair almost brushes the floor and starts displaying some of them. The people in our queue begin to clap and she stands up and puts her hands in prayer position and bows before looking back at me.

'So, I've decided I need to be as strong, brave and forgiving as my daughter.' And she wraps her arms around me and presses her cheek against mine.

'There is no map in this life, Bea, only your own inner compass. *Samskara saksat karanat purvajati jnanam . . .*' She laughs at my confused expression. 'It means, through sustained focus and meditation on our patterns, habits and conditioning, we gain understanding and knowledge of our past and how we can change the patterns that aren't serving us to live life more freely and fully.' She slips down her sunglasses over her eyes but her trembling lips give her away. 'And I haven't lived as freely or as fully as I've pretended to since your father left.'

I swallow and nod as the group in front of us leave the desk and we are called.

We step up to the desk and place our passports and tickets in front of the bemused-looking woman.

'We're going on a life-changing trip,' Loni informs her proudly.

'How nice,' the woman says politely. 'Are you sisters?'

I laugh and go to say yes – just as Loni taught me to do as a teenager, but she gets there before me.

'No, actually, this is my daughter.' She takes my hand and squeezes it gently as she turns to look at me. Her face is awash with pride. Then she turns back and lowers her sunglasses as if revealing herself like a celebrity to the check-in girl. 'Now be a darling, will you, and see if we can have a cheeky little upgrade?'

Chapter 64

When we pass through Goa airport it is more hectic and overwhelming than I ever imagined. The heat is engulfing, sweat drips off my back almost immediately and Loni and I are swamped by men trying to grab our bags, shouting, trying to get our attention, but Loni deals with them all firmly. Then she puts her arm around me, lifts her chin and ushers us through to find the pre-booked car she ordered.

She has already come into her own: on the eleven-hour flight she pulled out various snacks and gave me a herbal sleeping tablet that I referred to as a horse tranquilliser when I woke up because it knocked me out immediately. God knows what was in it but I slept better on the plane than I have for weeks. I came to as we were descending into the hazy Indian heat and I felt like something momentous was about to happen.

And that feeling continues as Loni and I climb into a white mini-van and we set off towards Baga, where Loni lived with my dad many years ago when they were young and in love. And where she's told me I was conceived.

So if I wanted to go back to where it all started, there is no better place than this.

Loni is quiet for once, gazing out of the opposite window. There's only the sound of the wheels on the road, Indian music playing from the radio and her bangles jangling as our car bounces through gigantic potholes on the wide road. The arid, heat-soaked countryside stretches as far as the eye can see, only punctuated by the buzzing of small motorbikes whizzing by, with helmetless, shirtless Indian men driving them, sometimes with girlfriends riding pillion, their colourful saris billowing in the breeze. Occasionally I gasp aloud and close my eyes as giant lorries overtake cars and seem to head straight for us. It seems the rules on these roads are that there are no rules. It's frightening and invigorating all at once. I have never been anywhere that has felt so alien but at the same time so alive.

'Are you OK?' I nudge Loni.

She turns and gives me a fleeting smile. 'I just feel like I've slipped through some sort of vortex and you're my only proof that the last thirty years ever happened. Nothing has changed here, and yet everything has.' She squeezes my hand and smiles wistfully.

'Is this going to be too weird for you?' I ask. 'Seeing Dad, I mean? Maybe we shouldn't do this,' I say quickly, suddenly feeling my old panicky, indecisive self returning. Loni shakes her head and puts her arms around me. 'Darling, we're not backing out now. No more running away, hmm? We both need to do this.'

Forty-five minutes later we are cruising down Calangute Road and into a bustling street awash with colour and noise and smells that attack every one of my senses. I've never seen so many people in such a small space. Cows wander in front of our car as motorbikes weave past. Palm trees, market stalls, shacks and whitewashed houses line the street. At one point an elephant strolls past. My neck is aching from craning to see in every single direction. I have never seen so much life, and so much poverty. We finally pull up in front of a small, white, colonial-style guest house that has a rickety old sign with *Sarah's* in gaudily painted italics.

Loni gets out, pulls out a handful of rupees that makes our driver smile, and thanks him. He gives us our luggage and sets off in a cloud of red sand.

'Come on then, darling,' Loni says, excitement visible on her face. 'Let's get checked in. There's so much I want to show you!'

It's nearly 7 p.m. by the time we leave the guest house but the heat has barely subsided. The reason it has taken us so long to get out is because I had to take two showers. The first was to wash off the journey, the second to cool down from the heat. Loni was waiting in the little courtyard garden, chatting to 'Sarah', the somewhat grumpy Indian owner, who of course remembered Loni and had instantly become a different host entirely. As I hovered in the doorway I saw that she was excitedly gesticulating to show her delight at seeing Loni again whilst Loni must have been giving her a potted history of the last thirty years. They were murmuring quietly and I heard Loni say, '. . . although he did give me two wonderful gifts.' Then she turned and gestured to me, hovering on the step.

Sarah ran across to me, clasped my hands and shook them enthusiastically. 'You most welcome here in Baga. We love English. We love your Loni. Your mum is good and old!'

Loni stood up and rolled her eyes. 'A good old *friend*, you mean, Sarah. Honestly!' But she put her arm around Sarah and laughed to show she was teasing and Sarah's face wrinkled like a prune, her bright brown eyes glimmering as she grinned at me. 'Sarah has already told me that Len has come to Baga regularly in between other travels for many years and stayed here. But this last couple of years he's stayed longer and now has a place up near

Anjuna beach. She says he's well known in the area and that we'll find him easily.'

Loni nodded emphatically as Sarah relayed a new barrage of information. 'He likes Goa. It feels like home to him. And then old British women like him. Him very popular with older women. Though he keep himself to himself. They swamp him like flies round the sacred cows on Baga beach. They think he is some sort of god.'

Loni raised her eyebrows and flashed me a wistful smile. 'Sounds about right. Your father was a very attractive, sensitive man.'

'So,' Sarah continued, 'he goes to the market on Wednesdays. You find him there.' I felt my heart tilt and tip at the thought that tomorrow I might finally see my dad.

We arrive at Baga beach just as the sun is setting. Loni drags me straight over to a shack with tables right on the beach and orders two beers and a selection of traditional Goan dishes that she promises me I'll love. Then she pulls her chair next to mine and nods over to the ocean.

We sit in silence as the sun that hangs like a gold pendant in the sky slowly dips down into the water and sets the sky alight, sending a flame of colour across the horizon and making the sea glow ultraviolet. I feel humbled by the sight and so grateful to be here with Loni that tears prickle my eyes and make my throat ache. Even if I don't meet Dad I know that I'll never regret coming here. As I look around, I'm trying to get to know him already, to see this place through his eyes. This is where he decided to put down roots after all: it's his chosen garden, so different from Norfolk. Just as the city I chose to move to was so different from Norfolk too. I feel like I already have so much in common with my long-lost dad; I'm just not sure how much of it is good. Aside from both of us being prone to depression, we have both tried to make new lives for ourselves because we couldn't cope with – or didn't think we deserved – the one we had.

'Are you OK?' Loni asks gently. 'What are you thinking about?'

I take a sip of beer. 'Adam. I miss him so much, Loni.'

She nods and touches my hand. 'I know, darling.'

We watch a family of four on the beach, just by the shore, cast in black silhouette. They all hold hands as the sun slips away, the tip of it glowing gold like a doubloon before disappearing behind the horizon. I know that both Loni and I are placing ourselves in that picture as if in a snapshot of the family we could have been.

'Do you ever regret marrying Dad?'

Loni leans forward and cups my face with her hands. 'How could I? Bea, you have to know that my life has been such a joy because he gave me you and Cal. I've always felt like I could cope with anything as long as you two were OK.' Her eyes mist over. 'That's why I found that summer so hard, when you were with Kieran. I could feel you drifting away from me – and then, that night I got the call from the police and I was driving to the pier to collect you, I was scared to death that something had happened to you and I swore if you were OK, I'd never let you out of my sight again. When Kieran left I was so relieved, even though I knew how heartbroken you were. I knew he wasn't bad, but he wasn't good for you either. But instead of helping you to brush yourself off and start again, like I should have done, I smothered you. I took you to the doctor's, he prescribed antidepressants and I was relieved, Bea, I was so relieved. Even though I have never thought they were the answer, even though I could see they were stripping you of your confidence, your ability to make decisions, your desire to get up and try again, I was so grateful to still have

you that I welcomed the dull calm that came over you. I didn't
care that you had dropped out of university, that you weren't
going out and that your life had been reduced to lying in bed or
on the sofa, watching old films with me. I didn't care because I
still had you. I could look after you. I could keep you safe with
me.' Tears are streaming down her face now and she doesn't even
bother wiping them away. It's like the floodgates have been
opened at last. She doesn't have to pretend to be strong any more.

'It's OK, Loni, I understand.'

I've seen her in a whole new light since I discovered the truth
about Dad. A whole new *life*. One where she is a woman who
had her heart broken but who couldn't fall apart because of her
two kids and so came up with a way to manage her heartbreak
in a positive, inspiring way. She did everything she could to bring
us all out of a terrible situation and give Cal and me the best
chance of happiness. She protected us, yes, but she protected
Dad too. She knew enough about being a parent to realise that
being there meant taking the good and the bad from us and
knowing that both would be calibrated by her unconditional
love. I'm in awe of her. With her books and appearances and
retreats she's been a role model to thousands of people: finally I've
realised she's *my* role model too.

And I've also realised that the reason Cal and I began calling
her Loni wasn't because we didn't love her like a mum. It was
because 'Mum' just wasn't a big enough word for what she was
to us. What she *is*. She hasn't ever just been a mother, she's been
a father, a teacher, a counsellor, a sister, a saviour. My saviour.

'You really loved him, didn't you?' I observe now.

'Oh so much,' she says vehemently. 'I remember sitting here
in almost the same spot watching that sunset for the first time
with your father and thinking that I couldn't imagine ever wanting to be anywhere – or with anyone – else.'

'So why did you leave here?' I ask. 'If you both loved it so much? Do you think if you hadn't made him come back to England you might have been happy here together?' I'm clinging on to long-lost possibilities like they're life-rafts. What could have stopped Dad from leaving? What was their alternative ending?

Loni takes a sip of beer and shakes her head. 'I've realised that I couldn't have saved him. Our relationship wasn't enough.'

'Like me and Kieran's.' She rests her head against mine. 'What do you think Dad's going to say, when he sees us?' I ask quietly. I realise that I'm scared.

'I don't know, darling, but no matter what, we're in this together, every step of the way.'

I look at Loni and nod. 'I wouldn't want it any other way.'

Chapter 65

The next morning I'm sitting on my balcony, staring down at the dusty road, when Loni knocks on my door, resplendent in a bright pink kaftan and sandals. Her hair is pulled up to the top of her head and she has wrapped an aqua scarf around it.

'Morning, darling, are you ready then? Have you eaten? Shall we go? We should probably go early, don't you think?' She's anxious, restless, she can't keep still. 'Come on, darling, what are you waiting for?'

I drag myself inside reluctantly. I'm tired and sluggish after barely sleeping last night. Not that I'm not used to feeling it. I'm accustomed to long, dark nights spent alone with my thoughts. I've suffered from insomnia throughout my life. When I was eleven and had just started secondary school I went through a phase when I couldn't sleep because I was worrying about my GCSEs. My insomnia increased in my teens until I was lucky if I slept at all. I'd just lie there all night, heart racing and fears swirling round in my head like sea monsters.

Last night, like back then, my mind was whirring like ticker-tape, one thought after another. I kept going back and forth, rewinding and fast-forwarding through every memory I had of my dad and then playing out every possible scenario of what might happen when I saw him today.

Today.

'Are you ready?' Loni asks.

My face is scratchy with heat, my hair limp and my shorts and vest top already damp with sweat. I have spent the last hour getting ready but I couldn't feel less ready if I tried. Frankly, I just want to run away. But that's always my default setting. And today I'm going to meet the person who made me this way. I take her hand and we walk down the simple white-washed corridor through the small reception area and then out into the dry heat of the morning.

'What's that?' I say, pointing at the moped parked outside.

'Our wheels for the day!' she exclaims. Then she hitches up her kaftan and throws her leg across the moped as if it is some kind of Harley-Davidson. She looks so funny, her generous frame swamped by swathes of pink material which almost hide the moped entirely. She starts the ignition and revs the tinny engine and winks wickedly at me. 'Come on, my girl, are you ready to burn some rubber with your mama?'

I fold my arms and shake my head. 'I'm not getting on that thing with you. No way.'

'I'll take it slow, I promise,' Loni says. 'It'll be an adventure! And remember, I used to ride one of these here all the time so I'm not exactly a novice. Let's live a little, Bea, or should I say *Thelma*,' she drawls in a Texan accent. It was one of the films we watched over and over again the year after Kieran left. It was Loni's very unsubtle way of wanting to empower me with stories of women going it alone. I'm not sure she'd thought through the driving off the cliff climax though, bless her.

'I can't believe I'm doing this,' I sigh as I go and sit behind her. I cling on to her waist tightly and squeeze my eyes shut as she revs the engine and then we both squeal as we jerk forward with three little jolts. Loni presses her foot down really hard and we set off . . . at about 10 mph.

I burst out laughing as we pootle along the dusty road. 'Wohoooo, this is craaazy, Loni!' I yell. 'You're so WILD I can't deal with the speed!'

We jump and jolt along the road with me laughing hysterically as Loni desperately tries to control the moped.

'I can get some speed in this thing, just you watch!' She revs the engine and then promptly stalls our moped in the middle of the road.

I burst into fresh peals of laughter. I lean my head on her back, crying now with laughter as she tries the ignition again. I turn my head just as a cow pauses next to us, watching us as if we are a little passing road show.

'Mooo!' it says encouragingly which makes Loni jump. The engine starts again suddenly and we skid around in a circle as the cow scampers out of the way with another, more indignant, moo.

We set off again, the moped spluttering and phut-phutting its way along the road, red dust flying up alongside us as Loni whoops and punches the air. I yell words of encouragement as we reach speeds of at least 15 mph.

'Are you sure we should be driving like this?' I shout in my best Geena Davis impersonation. 'I mean in broad daylight and everything.'

'No we shouldn't but I want to put some distance between us and the scene of our last GODDAMN CRIME!' Loni stands up as she shouts Louise's line, she whips her scarf off her head and hands it to me and I hold it aloft as she pushes her foot down and we drive down the road, screaming and laughing our way to Anjuna.

I'm not sure if I can ever remember a time when I was happier.

Chapter 66

Anjuna market is in full swing when we arrive half an hour later and I'm fervently wishing that I hadn't encouraged Loni to try and get here faster. I wish we were back on that moped, going in the opposite direction. As if sensing this, Loni links my arm as we enter the market on the beach and I feel that familiar sensation of being pulled forward and back. I need to see my dad but right now I just want to run away. Again.

The Goan sun is beating a relentlessly intense heat down on our backs as we find the relative shade provided by the canopies of the market stalls. But the heat, coupled with the smell of incense and spices, the noise of drums and music and chatter is still utterly overwhelming. There are rugs spread out over the sand with palm trees as shelter, their sellers sitting cross-legged in front of their wealth of goods: rows upon rows of necklaces, beads, opaque stones, plaited bracelets, trays of silver and gold jewellery. I have never seen such colour, so much merchandise, so much *life* in one place. Women in bright billowing saris, displays of traditional Indian puppets, canvas bowls of colourful spices, row upon row of moccasins, T-shirts, rugs, lanterns, vases and hand-crafted statues. There's a moment when I stop and close my eyes for a second and apart from the heat, with the hustle and bustle and delicious smells and noise, I feel like I could be in Greenwich market.

Loni and I weave our way through the market for a while, browsing the stalls and pretending to be having some sort of leisurely mother–daughter experience, buying beads and a beautiful shawl each, when we are just trying to delay the moment as long as possible. And the stall-holders are so excited by what seems to be our obvious Western riches that we feel guilty not buying something before enquiring if they know Len Bishop.

We draw a blank from the first few we ask. They just gaze at us and shrug. I'm not sure if it's because they don't speak English, they don't know Len – or they just don't want to tell us where he is.

It's nearly lunchtime and I'm feeling faint with heat, tiredness, disappointment and dehydration. Loni points to the shade of a palm tree, just beyond the market, and we buy some water and some fruit and head towards it.

'It was a bit of a long shot, I suppose,' Loni says as we walk sipping periodically from our water bottles. 'I mean, I guess he could be anywhere. We could try again tomorrow . . .'

'Or we could just give up,' I say wearily, leaning my head back against the tree and closing my eyes. 'I'm beginning to think this wasn't such a good idea after all. I mean, I'm pretty sure he won't want to be found. We could just spend the rest of the week relaxing, spending time together – right, Loni?'

I open my eyes and see that Loni is now standing in front of me. One hand is resting on her hips and the other is resting on the top of the straw hat she bought from a stall. 'Loni?' I repeat. 'Did you hear me? I said it doesn't matter . . .'

She doesn't reply at first. Then she points into the distance. 'He's over there,' she says softly. 'Len is over there . . .'

I scramble to my feet and stand next to her. I lift onto my tip-toes and shield my eyes from the sun to see if I can see what she is looking at. I feel like a kid who has lost her dad at the beach but as my eyes search desperately for him I realise I don't really know what I'm looking for. It's been almost twenty-five years. He could have changed beyond recognition.

Loni grabs my hand and starts walking quickly towards him. I have no choice but to go with her. I'm hopping over the burning hot sand, pausing to try to put my flip-flops back on. She weaves through some market stalls then stops suddenly so I almost bump into her. When I follow her gaze I see a man: correction – an *old* man sitting in front of some paintings. It's a shock, even though I have always worked out exactly what age he would be as every year of my own life passed. He is a seventy-one-year-old man now and he looks it. His face is thinner and longer than I remember, like it has been stretched with sadness over time. He has a deep nutty tan and long pigeon-grey hair that's parted in the middle and pulled back into a ponytail. He's wearing khaki shorts and a linen shirt open halfway down his chest. I can see that despite his age, he has strong athletic calves just like me. He has expressive hands too – artist's hands. He is talking to someone, laughing and gesturing. I feel I can understand what he is saying without hearing a word.

It's my dad. My dad. I stare at him, studying him like I might study myself in a mirror. Do I look like him? We have the same hands, and his eyes are dark like mine. I look more like him than Loni and Cal, I note.

I *am* more like him than Loni or Cal.

'It's him.' These words are in my head and come out like a sigh, so softly that for a moment I think I uttered them. Then I realise it was Loni.

She grasps my hand suddenly as if we're standing on the edge of a cliff and she's scared of letting go; not because I might fall, this time. But because she might.

'I can't believe it,' she murmurs. I let her make the first move. Suddenly this feels as much her moment as mine. She walks towards him. With every step we are going back ...

'Len?' She stands in front of the stall like a bright sunset. I can see her hands are shaking. He freezes, then turns slowly and looks directly at her. Instinctively I step back and then dip to the side of the stand so I can observe.

'Loni?' he replies. His voice is an echo of my lost memories.

I stare at him, looking not just at him, but this life he is living. The life he chose over us. I notice he is sitting at an easel and a half-painted landscape picture is on it. There is a photograph clipped to the top of the easel; his subject, I presume. Loni always said Dad was very creative. He taught History of Art, he painted, he enjoyed sculpture, gardening. 'Anything that involved his hands and his heart,' she once said. His stall is full of canvases, paintings of the English countryside and coast. My eye settles on one in particular, a painting of a horseshoe-shaped garden. A soft golden autumn sunlight is filtering through the willow tree. Under the tree, there is a figure, kneeling, her hands in the earth, her face looking up to the sky. It looks familiar, like the drawing in the front of my diary.

I put my hand over my mouth as I recognise the figure; the little girl is me.

Loni and Len are still standing opposite each other. It's like there is an invisible line between them that neither dares cross.

Len speaks first. 'You found me.'

'I didn't,' Loni replies. A flash of confusion flickers over his face and I suddenly see myself in his distant expression and uncertain gaze. 'Bea did. She has been waiting for you to come back for years. She was the one who decided it was time.'

'Bea.' He moves his head quickly, his eyes combing the market for me. 'She's here?' He looks back at Loni and I can't tell if it's hope or fear in his eyes.

I step forward slowly out of the shadows, one foot in front of the other towards him.

Everyone and everything has melted away and it's just me, on my path, walking towards my dad. I feel like I'm walking a line, a tightrope between the past and the present. I can't believe this is actually happening. I've imagined this moment so many times, the last one being my wedding day. I had pictured him reaching out to me as I ran into his arms, but also him seeing me and then just walking away. One moment: two equally possible outcomes.

He's squinting at me now as if he's struggling to make me out. Then I see him gasp and put his hand in front of his mouth.

Finally I'm standing before him but I don't run into his arms like I always thought I would. Instead I take Loni's hand and stare directly into my dad's eyes. I can see myself reflected in his irises, not just my silhouette but my soul. It's like we are one. There's a sadness, a loneliness deeper than any garden well in them and I can't bear it. I can't bear to see it in him because I know it's in me too.

There are tears, but it is he who is crying, not me. I want to comfort him but I can't. He's a stranger, a man I don't know. He holds his tanned, liver-spotted hand up and I notice it is shaking. 'I'm sorry. I'm OK. I'm OK.' He repeats this as if he's trying to convince himself. He pulls a bottle of water out of his pocket and tips a couple of tablets into his hand then shakily swallows them.

He smiles at me weakly. His eyes are watery, not with age or regret, but disconnected somehow. Like they know no great waves of happiness or sorrow, just the peaceful lapping at the shore of emotional equilibrium.

'Dear Bea,' he says softly, as if practising how the words sound on his lips. As he does I can imagine him saying them aloud all those years ago when he wrote my garden diary. 'Dear Bea,' he repeats. 'You're here.'

Chapter 67

We leave the market and go to a beach bar and find a quiet spot in a corner. I'm glad we're on neutral territory; it was strange enough to see Dad's humble little stall, I don't know how I would cope seeing where he lives.

The fact that the three of us are sitting around a table is almost too surreal to deal with. This is not helped by the fact that there appears to be a cow lying feet away from us, sunbathing next to a group of tourists.

'So, you're a painter,' I say as three beers are placed in front of us by a man with a bright white smile. My question plants itself awkwardly between us. It is small talk and yet it comes out punchy, confrontational: sitting opposite him it feels like I'm interrogating him. I take a sip of beer to relax me, the cool but sharp taste piercing my throat and hopefully allowing my conversation to flow more freely.

'It's a little hobby,' Len says, twirling his bottle on the table. 'I paint the places I love. It makes me feel at home when I am far away; I find it therapeutic.' He squints at the label and deep chasms appear around his eyes.

'Do you work?' I ask briskly. I bite my lip immediately. I don't want to challenge him, I want to understand him.

'Bits and bobs, Bea. Bits and bobs. Other than my stall I have my pension, I do some volunteering, I teach English to foreign students.'

'Do you live here permanently?' Loni asks. Her voice comes out as a squeak. She clears her throat and takes a swig of beer. I'm glad it's not just me who's nervous.

His eyes settle on her; they seem to come in and out of focus as if he is in turn seeing her now and remembering her back then: before the time ball dropped, and after.

'Permanent isn't a word I have ever got along particularly well with.'

'Me neither,' I butt in and he looks at me, nodding as if understanding exactly what I'm saying. I look down at the table, buoyed by an acknowledgement of the connection I've always thought we would have. 'I ran away from my marriage too,' I blurt out suddenly. 'On my wedding day. I ran away because I'm just like you, Dad . . .' The sentiment slips from my mouth but falls into a void. 'I'm just like you,' I add quietly when he doesn't say anything.

It's like he hasn't heard me. Or doesn't want to.

'So I'm here for a few months of the year,' he says conversationally as if I haven't spoken. 'Well, until monsoon season anyway.' I feel like my heart has been thrown at some rocks. He doesn't want to know. He doesn't want to accept that I'm like him. 'I can live a simple lifestyle here for very little money – the silver rupee is strong, you know!' He pauses as if waiting for us to acknowledge this little joke but then continues quickly as if scared of the possibility of silence. 'Most of the expats here are in our sixties and seventies. It's all very *The Best Exotic Marigold Hotel* really!' He laughs hoarsely and Loni and I force one out too; I notice how his eyes don't twinkle like Loni's naturally do. They are still; not quite tranquil, more ... inert.

No one knows what to say next and the longer the joke seems to be laid out in silence, the staler it becomes. He looks away, his gaze settling on the horizon as if he'd rather be anywhere but here. I glance at Loni. She hasn't taken her eyes off him.

'Why, Len?' she says at last. 'Why did you go?'

He doesn't answer for a moment, like he is lost in another place. Another time.

'I couldn't cope,' he says simply. 'I couldn't cope with the life we had and I couldn't cope with the guilt of what I knew my staying would eventually do to you. Leaving was the only option. It was that or ...' His voice croaks and cracks and he closes his eyes and takes deep restorative breaths. Suddenly it feels like he's no longer here. That this is just an imagined, transient moment and if I make a sudden movement it will be gone.

'You still practise meditation then,' Loni says, her voice soft, soothing, maternal. 'I'm glad.'

Len looks across the table at her and now I feel like I'm no longer here. This moment is for them. 'It's one of the many ways in which you helped me, Loni. Learning meditation with you was one of the best things I ever did.'

I think of Loni when I was ill, our daily mantras and meditations, my runs, the yoga, the gardening. Did she do it all – learn it all – for Dad? It all feels too familiar. Suddenly, without thought or intention, I push my chair out and I stand up. I can't be here. It's too hard.

'Bea?' Loni cries and grabs my arms. 'Are you OK?'

'I can't do this ...'

'Shhh, Bea, it's OK.' She holds me and we sink back down into our seats. Len looks at me – with sorrow but also detachment.

Loni puts her arm around me. 'I think we both know why you

left, Len,' she says shakily. 'But what we'd really like to know is why you never came back.'

He gazes at us both as if he has searched for the answer to this question for a long time. It feels like a lifetime until he speaks again, and when he does it is in a choked raspy voice.

'Like I said earlier, I – I couldn't cope and I just knew you could live a better life without me.'

'That wasn't your decision to make,' Loni replies, holding me tightly. We're like one now, she and I. She is carrying me. She has always carried me. 'Len, I loved you. I'd have done anything for you. If you'd just *talked* to me about how you were feeling I – I could have helped more ... we could have had counselling, I would have done anything!' She sobs suddenly, overwhelmed by the pent-up emotion of twenty-four years. 'I needed you,' Loni says tearfully when she has composed herself. 'We needed you. All of us. No matter how capable I appeared I needed you because I *loved* you. I loved you and would *never* have left you. I'd have done anything to make you happy.'

'And what about *your* happiness? If you'd have sacrificed that, then what?' Len shakes his head firmly. 'I could see that being with me was sucking the life out of you. You had already done everything you could to make me better, but I couldn't expect you to keep throwing your energy into me when there were our kids to think about. I tried so hard to be the husband and father I wanted to be but every moment I spent with you all was also spent trying not to drown, to keep my head clear and my thoughts and emotions positive. I loved you all but I felt so weak all the time. But you, you ...' He looks at Loni and sighs, then says, 'You were so strong. And the kids were always so happy around you; no matter what else you were dealing with, you were always silly and light-hearted and fun, you were always running around at the beach, making them laugh. I was useless, good for nothing.'

'You weren't useless – you were a husband, a father! I told you, they needed you – we all did!' Loni says, and peels her arm from around me and slams her hand on the table. Len doesn't flinch.

'No, Loni, I wasn't fit to be called a parent. I could barely cope with getting out of bed each day.' He rubs his forehead and when he looks at me again I feel like I can see him clearly for the first time. Not as the picture book father I've been so desperate to remember, but the man – the raw, real, flawed man that he has always been.

'You have to know how hard it was to leave you. It wasn't a decision I made lightly. For a whole year I kept putting it off, I'd wait until after Christmas, then Valentine's Day, then Easter, then the summer holidays and Bea's birthday. Bea, you and me, we always had this special connection . . .'

He trails off, staring at me as if he's trying to light our family circuit again but I look away. It's too painful to look at him. I don't feel any connection, just sorrow. I'm not stuck in the past any more. I'm right here in this moment; one I hope is going to finally allow me to let him go.

'You were my little shadow, my little climber, do you remember?' I smile politely but I can tell he doesn't expect an answer. He isn't seeing me as a thirty-one-year-old woman. I'm frozen in his memory as his seven-year-old child. 'We used to spend hours outside, pottering around in the garden, you made me laugh every day, you brought the sun out when my heart was drowning in rain. You were my shining star when the sky was black. Every moment I spent with you was another day of my life saved. But then there were other days, dark days, when nothing could pull me out of the shadows, even you. I was so scared I was going to drag you down with me. I could see my anxiety reflected in your eyes, your sensitivity simmered on your skin. You walked around as if you had the world on your shoulders. I felt that I'd done that to you and

I couldn't bear it. I knew I needed to get help and I hoped that doing so would allow me to be the father I wanted to be to you and Cal. I went to California to try and sort myself out. I thought being out there would remind me of happier times, would make me strong enough to return. But in the six weeks I stayed there I realised that I wasn't strong enough, or brave enough, so instead of coming home I moved on. I left because I wanted you both to cling to Loni's comet, not plummet to earth with me.'

His words make my heart break in two. 'So why did you leave the day after my birthday?' I ask tearfully. It is so long since I spoke that my voice sounds thin, reedy, childish. Childlike. 'How could I possibly move on with my life when every year I got older was a reminder of another year that you hadn't come back?'

'I'd used every ounce of strength and resolve I had to get through your birthday with a smile on my face. I wanted to see your little face as you woke up that morning, I wanted to be there to watch you open your presents, to see your party, watch you blow out your candles. I had spent an entire year writing the garden diary for you and when you unwrapped it, I knew it was the right time to go. I stayed that night, but was too scared to stay a day longer in case I totally fell apart. I just couldn't risk it.' He shakes his head vehemently and his ponytail swishes behind his neck.

'Instead *I* did,' I say quietly. 'Fall apart, I mean. Not that day, not even that year, just gradually, I completely fell apart . . .'

Len gazes at me, not with shock or empathy, just with the blank gaze of an old man. I stare at my fingers that are twisting and coiling with anxiety. I glance across the table and see Len is doing the same. I pull my fingers apart.

'Maybe I wouldn't have become ill if I'd had you in my life,' I challenge. I want to hurt him now. I want to force him to see the similarities between us.

'No.' He says it fervently.

'How do you know? You made a decision that affected my life forever – you can't ever know now if the opposite decision would have been better or worse!'

'I can, Bea,' he says quietly. His voice breaks and Loni looks at me worriedly. She clutches my hand again and I feel like her warmth, her spirit and strength is flooding into me. 'I can,' he repeats, 'because my dad – your granddad – suffered from depression too.' I stare at him but once again he isn't seeing me; Len is lost in another time. 'My dad, he – he was never a strong man, or a happy man. He suffered like I have suffered. But he stayed, he pretended he was OK, he tried to disguise himself as a functioning human being by pushing himself to do more than he was capable of . . .'

I swallow as Loni squeezes my hand. 'But he stayed, Bea, he honoured his commitment to his wife and kids. He tried so hard to make it work but he couldn't cope. He just couldn't cope.'

'What happened to him?' I whisper, but I think I know.

'He . . . he committed suicide.' Len's words fall like rocks from a cliff and I feel myself slipping too. Back to the year when I was doing my A levels and Cal found me, in my bedroom, surrounded by coursework and revision cards and several empty bottles of paracetamol. He and the paramedics he'd called saved me that day. He was only fifteen and he had to watch me being dragged into an ambulance to have my stomach pumped. He always says, though, that it was the moment that made him decide what he wanted to do with the rest of his life. He wanted to save lives. It's the only thing that has ever helped me make sense of what I tried to do. My selfish, stupid act has effectively saved hundreds of other people through my brother.

I feel Loni grip me tightly. My breath has grown short, I'm panting with the pain of my past – and my dad's.

'I was eight years old,' he says. 'Just eight. I'd seen far too much and had felt too much responsibility for a man that I now accept I could never have saved. I didn't want that for you,' he says, reaching across the table for my hand. He looks up at Loni. 'For any of you. It was my destiny, not yours, and I had to do something to break the cycle. Make a different choice. I knew my illness was too strong and I couldn't deal with the guilt of dragging you down too, like my dad did with me. Every year you got older was a reminder of how similar I was to him, and when you turned seven, I knew my time had run out. I had to choose a life where no one had to be responsible for me and where I didn't have to be responsible for anyone.'

I feel like my heart is breaking for him, but Len seems emotionless. 'Aren't you lonely? Do you miss us?' I say in a small voice.

'This is the only way I can live, Bea,' he says firmly. 'It is half a life, but it is better than none.' He smiles at me and I allow him to take my hand. 'I can't regret my decision because seeing you today is proof that I made the right one.' He looks up at me then, his eyes watery with what-ifs. 'I've never stopped thinking about you all, I've spent days, weeks, months wondering what would have happened if I had stayed. Would life have been different – not for me, but for you? But – my resounding answer has always been no.' His words are broken and disjointed. I want to comfort him, to say something to make him feel better, but I don't know how. Is this what I would have always felt? At once responsible and helpless? What would it have been like to always feel that I was trying to keep my father from throwing himself from the edge? Is this how Loni has always felt about me? I feel a new wave of wonder for her; this buoyant, compassionate woman who did everything to keep her family afloat even when disaster struck. I'm so lucky to have her. I look at her and see she has reached out across the table to Len and taken hold of his hand. She stares at it for a moment before raising it to her lips.

He closes his eyes, a serene smile appears on his face and suddenly the years melt away. When he opens his eyes again he looks at Loni like a husband, not a stranger. 'I never really left you, not up here. Never up here,' he murmurs, tapping his temple.

'I never left you either,' she says tearfully.

'I think it's about time we did, right?' And she nods and rests her cheek against his hand and they sit there for a moment. It is the goodbye she never got to say.

She's seen her alternative ending, and she knows it isn't the one she was destined for.

'So where do we go from here?' I ask, breaking the moment and at once feeling like the child I used to be, squeezing in between my parents' cuddle. A silence falls over us all as he looks at us both. The sun beams down on us relentlessly and suddenly I feel like I can't sit here for much longer. As he stares at me I get the impression he's storing my image for the future but strangely, I feel OK with that. I think it's time to say goodbye too.

I pull a book out of the pocket of my shorts and place it on the table in front of us.

'I brought this with me because I wanted you to know that you've always been a father to me, even after you left.'

He blinks as he looks at the book and then he slowly untangles his age-spotted hand from Loni's and gingerly strokes the blue diary with the gold embossed letters.

'You've used it?' His voice is hopeful, his eyes are shining for the first time.

I nod quickly. 'As a child, and more recently I turned to it when I really needed some guidance. I've had a pretty tough year—' I stop. I don't want to burden him with my problems. 'Having this – having you with me has made it easier. Thank you.'

He nods and a tear falls, a raindrop in the vast ocean. He swiftly brushes his fingers across his eyes and then slips his hand into his pocket and pulls something out and holds it out to me.

I recognise it immediately. It's a piece of blue card, crudely folded, with 'I love you, Daddy, always' scrawled on the front in crayon. I made it for him on my seventh birthday so he would have a piece of my happiness too. With tears blurring my eyes I open it. Inside is a flower I'd pressed for him. It's a forget-me-not.

'I've kept this with me every day for twenty-four years, Bea. In this gift you allowed me to leave but you gave me a little piece of your heart to take with me. I want you to have it now because it isn't possible for me to ever forget you. I think this version of you, this loving, hopeful seven year old, belongs with the version of me you have of me there.' He rests the card on top of the book. 'The dad who loved you to the ends of the earth but who knew, if he left you with Loni, she would lift you up to the stars.'

Chapter 68

The sun is starting to set again as Loni and I head back to Baga on the moped. There's no whooping and squealing from us this time. Just the noisy whirring of the little engine phut-phutting down the potholed roads. Neither of us feels the need to talk over what just happened. I cling on to Loni's waist and close my eyes as the warm breeze tickles my face, the sun healing all the hurt that has gone before. Suddenly I am aware of my weight, how heavy I have felt for so long and how strong she has always been. She pulls up in front of the beach, like I ask her to. I want to go for a walk.

'You know, Bea,' she says as I get off the moped. 'The one thing I've learned from all this, it is that happiness is the only choice in life you ever have to make. Don't turn your back on it again, darling. You didn't need to find your dad to be happy. You needed to find—'

'Myself?' I ask. She lets go of the handlebars and takes my hands. She stares at me and suddenly I feel closer to her than ever before. I smile and she kisses my forehead maternally.

'I think you've done that already. I've been so proud of you this year, for being brave enough to start again. But now I think it's time you found someone else, someone who has always loved you without suffocating you, who can hold you without carrying you, who has given you back your life and who has shown you what true happiness can be . . .'

I swallow back my tears as I say his name: 'Adam.'

She nods.

'You don't think it's too late? That he's given up on me?'

She shakes her head and smiles. 'You never give up on the one you love, darling. But sometimes you have to spend an awfully long time waiting for them . . .'

She looks out at the ocean. It occurs to me that's what she's been doing for years. Filling her life with work and people and laughter and more work to hide the fact she's been waiting for Dad. It's why she's never divorced him. She's been waiting for him to come back as much as I have. She turns and looks at me.

'I think you're ready now, darling, ready to live the life you've always been heading towards. This is your time.'

I watch her as she zips off, arm raised, her crazy curls billowing behind her, looking exactly like Susan Sarandon, and I feel an enormous wave of love.

I look at the card in my hand that my seven-year-old self made as I walk down to the sea, turning it over and over, exploring both sides of it. I feel myself transported back to that time before he left us, when I was a little girl with a world of happiness before me. Can I be that girl again?

A warm wind has whipped up and clouds are moving quickly across the sky, the sapphire ocean rippling calmly beneath it. I walk barefoot across the beach and towards the shore. The sunset has set the sky ablaze and as the tip of the sun sinks out of sight, I note that its last impression before it disappears is a ring of gold: a wedding band dropping into the ocean. I sit on the beach and gaze at my bare left hand, thinking both of the marriage I threw away – and the wedding ring Loni tried to throw into the ocean after Dad left. I pull out my phone because I want more than anything to talk to Adam. I know I can't but maybe, just maybe, this time he'll answer. His is the first name in my phonebook and before I can think twice I hit call.

'Hi.' I hear his voice and I freeze because I didn't expect to hear it. The phone continues to ring and it is then that I think it either a figment of my imagination or that he has been conjured from another world and dropped here so I can tell him exactly how I feel right now.

I turn around and stare at him in disbelief. A smile spreads across his lightly tanned face. His dark hair has grown and there is a smattering of coal-dust stubble over his chin. We just stand looking at each other for a moment, like neither of us can quite believe the other is real. That this is actually happening. I feel like I'm on some sort of parallel universe. One where miracles exist. He is here. The only man I have ever really loved and ever truly trusted, the only man I can imagine sharing my life with is standing here in front of me.

'I came as soon as I knew you were here,' Adam murmurs. He has changed in the ten months since I last saw him. I note how his hair tickles his neck and forehead, his eyes look less tarnished grey; instead they are shining as brightly as the stars that will soon come out above us.

'B-but-how?' I can't take my eyes off him. This feels magical, miraculous, a coincidence conjured out of dreams, or written in the stars.

'Loni told me you were coming to Goa,' Adam explains with a smile. 'And she said she'd make sure you came here tonight.' I look back at the dirt track where Loni's moped disappeared five minutes ago and laugh. Not a coincidence, then, a set-up. He steps towards me and I notice how the twilight makes him

appear almost ethereally handsome. Even though nearly a year
has passed, he looks younger than I've seen him look for years.
His smooth edges have been roughed up, like they've been
rubbed out and drawn in again with less controlled and precise
edges. He doesn't look like he is trying to trace himself into an
image of his father any more. He looks like his own man.

I can feel myself blushing as he sits next to me, and I stop
breathing momentarily as his leg brushes mine. The air is rich
with aromatic smells – but all I can smell is Adam's scent. It is
more powerful, more intoxicating than anything nature could
create.

'So did you find him?' he asks. He tilts his head as he makes
circles in the sand with his fingers.

'No,' I reply and his smile breaks in sympathy before I add,
'You did.' I put my hand on top of his and have to stop myself
from passing out. 'I met him today, thanks to you.'

'That's great, Bea, really great!' he says softly, clasping my fingers. My skin burns, like it is fusing with his. I'm having to tell
myself to breathe. I feel like I'm standing on the edge of a cliff,
but for the first time I'm not scared of falling.

'I don't know how to thank you, Adam,' I say. 'For doing all
that for me, for searching for him after everything I put you
through . . .' I blink back the tears I know are about to come. 'I'm
so, so sorry.'

'I understood why you did it.' He squeezes my fingers. 'I've
always understood you, Bea. I feel like my heart knew yours
before I ever met you.' I nod and hiccup a little because I agree
but I can't speak and we both laugh. 'So, did he give you all the
answers you wanted?'

'Some. Enough. Meeting him made me realise that I shouldn't
be so focused on the people who left me, but the ones who've
always been by my side . . .'

'Like Loni,' he says with a smile.

'And you,' I murmur, gazing into his eyes.

He runs his fingers through his hair and glances up at the stars that are appearing in the sky, little lights flicking on, one after another. There's a moment of silence as we stare at the dark horizon in front of us, trying to work out what to say, where to go next. I can tell Adam doesn't know and for a moment I feel scared. But then I realise it's my move. He's so used to sorting everything out, making it OK. But I'm determined to do it this time. I go to speak but as I do he turns and I can see his face is taut with anguish. 'Bea, I came here because I needed you to know how sorry I am. I should never have forced you to get married when you weren't really ready. There was stuff you needed to do and I never really understood that. I thought it was all about going forward, ticking boxes, getting results. I never stopped to think that it might not be the right time for us, that there might be things I needed to do, too. I only realised that once you'd gone.' He looks at me and his solemn expression pierces my heart like an arrow. 'You know, I thought your leaving me on our wedding day was the worst thing that could ever happen to me . . .'

'I'm sorry,' I interrupt, unable to stop myself. 'If I could go back—' I stare at Adam. I want to say that if I could go back I would do everything differently, but the words won't come. Because I wouldn't do anything differently. I couldn't. I realise that this is the journey I had to take to get where I am now. I wasn't ready to marry Adam a year ago. That hasn't changed. But now I have faced up to everything that went before. Everything that was stopping me from completely letting go and moving on.

'If you could go back you wouldn't change anything?' he says, finishing my sentence. 'I know. I wouldn't either.' He smiles gently, sorrowfully almost. 'It's fine, honestly it is, Bea. I know now you made the right decision for both of us.'

'Oh, yes, yes, I suppose I did.'

My heart sinks like the sun, disappearing into a dark horizon. This is not how things were meant to turn out. It's ironic that I've realised he's the only man I want to be with at the same time he's realised I'm not the one for him. I feel like I can already see his life diverting from this path; this is a crossroads moment and it seems we're going in opposite directions.

'You were right. I'm thirty-three years old and I'd never taken any time to work out what I wanted from my life,' Adam says, his jaw set in a determined line. For a moment the new, laid-back Adam is gone and all his inherent Hudson-ness is back. The seriousness, the ambition, the determination.

There is a distant rumble of thunder; the inevitable storm after a hotly anticipated day. It doesn't feel foreboding, more like a welcome break from the heat. Soon it will all be over and a new day can begin.

'It's OK, Adam,' I say bravely. 'Honestly, you don't have to explain. I understand.' I go to stand up but he catches my wrist. I feel that his fingers are creating an invisible band of gold like a bracelet. Or a ring, No matter what, my heart will always be his. I will never stop loving him. I will never forget him. I place my hand on my pocket and think of the card that's hidden in there.

'No, let me finish, Bea, please,' he begs. A small flash of distant lightning lights up the horizon like a firework. 'I've come here to tell you that I want to change. I want to live a different life.' There's another fork, brighter this time, bolder. 'I want to be the kind of man that *I* can be proud of, not that my mum and dad can be proud of. And I've spent the last ten months trying to work out who I am. For the first time in my life I've been free to make my own decisions and I'm so grateful, Bea, I'm so grateful, because if I hadn't, well, I don't know where I would have ended up . . .'

With me, I think sadly as the ground beneath me shakes along with the thunder rumbling above. *You would have ended up with me.*

I reach over and take his hand, feeling the tears roll down my face as I prepare for our inevitable goodbye. I shouldn't be this upset. After all, it was my decision that brought us here. I squeeze his hand to let him know it's OK. I can take it.

'I know who I am now, Bea, and I am even more certain of one thing . . .' He pauses and looks at me and I have to stop myself from throwing myself into his arms and begging him to give me one more chance. One more chance at happiness, that's all I want. 'You see, since you left me I've realised that the one decision, the single life choice I made on my own, was actually the *right* one.'

He smiles, his lips drawing up into the shape of an anchor and raising my hopes from the bottom of the sea.

'So?'

He reaches up to my forehead to brush the hair out of my eyes as the rain begins to fall. 'Bea, you are the one certainty in my life, the one decision I made on my own, and you are the one thing I've never *ever* had any doubt about.'

I sob then and cover my mouth with my hand, unable to believe that this is happening. His hand cradles my head until our foreheads come to rest against each other.

'I can't change the past, but I need you to know that I am going to work really hard at living a different life in the future. I've quit Hudson & Grey, Bea. I'm not on a sabbatical, I've gone for good.'

'What are you going to do?' I ask. My tears are mixing with the warm rain on my cheeks and his hand moves round to brush them away before cupping my chin.

An easy, lazy smile spreads over his face and lights up his eyes so I feel like I can see the stars reflected in them.

'I don't know. Set up my own business one day, but maybe I'll just freelance till then . . .'

'You'll be a temp!' I snort, laughing a little through my tears, and he joins in.

There's a crack of thunder and he instinctively puts his arm around me, our mouths meeting just as the lightning splits the sky.

'I've loved you from the start, Adam Hudson,' I say when I finally pull away.

'And I've never stopped loving you,' he murmurs.

He lowers his lips to mine again and as the lightning crackles above us he suddenly breaks away.

I can see he's torn, unable to trust that I've made a decision. 'I don't want to put any pressure on you, Bea. I mean, maybe we should just take it slowly—'

I put my finger in front of his lips. 'I'm in charge, OK?' I say softly and he looks into my eyes searchingly then nods.

I take a deep breath and look at Adam, really look at him. He's not the strong, confident man I've known for over seven years. He doesn't know what he's doing with his life any more. This Adam isn't perfect; he's not always certain and he does make mistakes. And the truth is I love him more than ever.

'There is something I want to ask you,' I say slowly, assuredly. 'Obviously you can take your time, because this may seem a little crazy, but I have to trust my instincts . . .'

'I'm ready,' he says.

I take a deep breath, teetering on the edge before the words fall from my lips. A risk, yes, but one I'm ready to take.

'Adam, will you marry me?'

He looks at me for a long time before he answers. And in that moment I've already lived both different scenarios. I have imagined me laughing and crying as he says yes and throwing myself into his arms. I've also imagined the alternative. I realise I am OK with both. I've made my decision. It's up to Adam now. Whatever he says, yes or no, stay or go, I do or I don't, I know I'll survive. What will be, will be.

It is only when his lips have melted into mine and he is murmuring my name over and over again that I realise he has already decided.

'Is that a yes?' I laugh, grasping his face and gazing into his eyes hopefully.

'Of course it's a yes, Bea!' he laughs.

'And you're certain you want to go through it all again?' I look at him, trying to search for the doubts that I know must be there because he wouldn't be human if there weren't, 'Aren't you worried I won't make it down the aisle?'

A whisper of a smile tickles the corner of his mouth before he replies.

'Yes ... but I think I'll take my chances.'

March

Dear Bea . . .

. . . . and dear March, do come in! I'm so glad to see
you. You're always the turning point in the year: as
nature is stirred into action by warmer days, so you
inspire us to start the hard work again. It's a busy
time for a gardener, but Bea, know that however manic
life might seem right now, very soon you will get to
celebrate the culmination of years of your hard work. I
know you have spent a long time grafting, turning
over soil, planting new bulbs, cultivating new life. I
wish I could be there to see what you have achieved. But
I know you will always have an appreciative, adoring
audience to witness your accomplishments. And I
know that now spring has begun in earnest you'll
barely remember the cold days that fell on your
garden. You'll look down and instead of bare ground,
you will see the hardy perennials that are already
pushing their way back into your life again after a

long, hard winter. They are the ones to focus on, Bea, not the ones that didn't make it.

I love you so much, Bea. I always have and always will.

Love, Dad x

Chapter 69

Bea Hudson is on top of the world.
34 likes.

I stand on the corner of Canada Square and look up at the impressive new building where Hudson, Grey & Friedman will now be based.

It's small compared to the skyscrapers that surround it and is dwarfed completely by the gargantuan Canary Wharf Tower. With its four-storey glass exterior and exposed roof with the glass spherical ball at the centre, the agency's new home looks like a small 'i' in the middle of a word full of capital letters. But it stands out, because of that very fact.

I feel goosebumps prickle my arms despite the unusually warm March evening. It has surprised me that there has been no snow this year, no late frosts, or winter winds. The daffodils appeared early as did the crocuses and the cherry blossom. Spring arrived in February and has simply stayed.

I'm nervous about tonight not just because it is the official unveiling of the roof terrace project, one I have played a significant part in, but because I'm convinced Adam will be there. It will be the first time I will have seen him since I left his parents' house on New Year's Day.

The last two months have felt interminably long without him. When he called me at Loni's after I got back from the pier I told him that I was wrong to run away, I just needed space to see what it was I wanted. And I knew that I wanted to be with him. I've only ever wanted to be with him. But he wouldn't listen. He told me that I'd been right. He told me that he loved me and that he wanted to be with me but that we can't be together until we've worked out some other stuff. Then he told me he'd handed in his notice to his dad and had decided to go away for a while. 'Not for long,' he'd added quickly. 'I'm not leaving you, Bea, I told you that. I'm never going to leave you. I just need to find myself first.'

'How long will that take?' I asked, feeling myself wobble but knowing that it was the right thing for both of us.

'I don't know; a few weeks, maybe a month or two. I just want to take some time out to work things out and I think you should too. But I promise I'll be back, Bea.'

A memory washed over me then, of Kieran saying the same thing. But this time I knew it was different. I trusted Adam. I had faith in us. 'Will you be OK?' he asked, and I looked out into the garden.

'Of course I will. I've got the roof terrace project to throw myself into and a university application to fill in. Besides, I'm kind of used to being left on my own. I don't want to go back to the flat though without you. Milly has said I can stay at her place temporarily and I'm going to take her up on the offer . . .' She'd told me this the day she'd come home from the hospital with baby Holly Rose. She was been born five weeks prematurely in a hospital in Brooklyn and Milly had already extended her maternity leave to six months from the statutory three you get in New York, and asked them to transfer her back to London.

'I feel like this is where I'm meant to be. I had this terrible urge – a pain that almost felt like a contraction – because I missed my family so much. And you, of course. I have the rest of my life to work, but I won't get this time back with Holly. Nor will my parents. I want to be nearer home so I can really enjoy my maternity leave, spend it with the people I love. Work understand, they have no choice really. It's my decision. And what's the worst that can happen? I get the sack and end up working for another hedge fund . . . or,' she added, 'I set up my own company. You know, I've been thinking about using my skills and time to invest in something good.'

'Like what?' I asked.

'I don't know,' Milly mused. 'Charities. I thought maybe I could set up a kind of "Philanthropy in the City" group run by ex-City women, for various good causes. Weirdly, Marion inspired it. I mean, I know she's a pain in the arse, but she actually does loads for charity and this would be a way of incorporating my skills. Encouraging investors to give a percentage of what they earn on their hedge funds to charity. There are a few companies who do it already but I'm sure there's room for another . . .'

'It's a great idea,' I said. 'I mean, you're a natural at helping people. You've always been there for me. Plus you're very persuasive.'

'Is that code for bossy and controlling?' She laughed and I joined her.

'Sure is.' I heard Holly gurgle then and suddenly I'd felt something deep within me, an ache, a pang, totally soundless but at the same time louder than anything I'd ever heard. As loud as a ticking clock. I imagined the time ball dropping again. Another sign.

Adam had suggested we rent our flat out. 'Then when I get back maybe we can look for a new place, somewhere we both want to live, somewhere with a garden that will be great for, you know ... starting a family. It will be different, this time,' Adam had said softly. 'I promise.'

I glance back over my shoulder as if sensing his presence. But there's no one there. A young couple, about my age, are walking down the street, their arms wrapped round each other, and seeing them makes my heart expand. They look so right together. Like nothing could ever break them apart.

I go inside and get in the lift that will take me to the top floor. I feel like my life is at its highest pinnacle. I'm teetering on the brink of a new world, one that I'm completely ready for.

As the doors open into the glass sphere that is set into the centre of the roof terrace I can't help but gasp with pride at how my and James's vision has been brought to life. Under the convex dome of the glass roof arched trellises form an inner dome and a fragrant floral canopy is woven up them. The flowers that grow on the trellis can be seasonal but for tonight we decided on red, star-shaped cosmos. This was both a nod to James's Chelsea Garden but also to me because it's my birth flower. I also like how their red leaves make the glass sphere look even more like the Royal Observatory's time ball. It was, James says, one of the concepts that had won us our pitch. The glittering night sky is just visible through the flowers now so it looks like stars upon stars – and the roof has been designed to open on sunny days like the petals of a flower.

I step outside the glass sphere and onto the terrace. People are still running around, checking up on things, and I get caught up in a few last-minute adjustments, electrical problems and a couple of other design issues to deal with. As the decks clear ready for the first guests I look around and realise that everything has come together on time. There are not many things I have been certain of in my life, but for some reason with this I always knew it would.

On the terrace we have embraced the work/play/day/night themes to create a completely original space that is breathtaking.

The 2,000 square foot glass walled-space has been lined with trees and planters and in the centre is a 'Grow your own herb tea and juice bar'. Lemon and orange trees, chilli plants and a herb garden have been sunk into the middle of the beautifully designed brushed concrete bar and there are ten Eames stools either side of it, in front of each one is an iPad dock. The idea being that the agency staff can come here first thing in the morning, pick their own mint for tea, or camomile, or lemon, and make their own breakfast beverage. Underneath the bar is a locked cupboard full of alcohol so in the evenings and for special events it can be transformed into a cocktail bar.

Uplit silver birch trees and grasses give the effect of living wallpaper. In one corner, in front of the modern terrazzo furniture, there is a contemporary water feature made up of a moss-covered hour glass shape with the front cut back to reveal the Perspex tubes inside where water runs both up and down. It has been designed to remind the staff of the passing of each hour, the toing and froing of time, even when they are relaxing on one of the built-in recliners.

'Pretty impressive, for your first project, Bea.' James folds his arms as he stands next to me, smiling at a waiter who offers him a glass of champagne. He takes a sip and rests the glass on his elbow.

I turn and smile at him. 'I've loved every moment, James. Thank you for giving me the opportunity . . .'

'I'm just glad we crossed paths when we did. It's a shame it's

all over really, isn't it?' he says, giving me a sideways look. 'I'd like
to give you more opportunities, you know, take you on as a permanent assistant . . .' His words hang in the cold, night air like
stars.

'Thank you,' I say gratefully after a moment. 'But I've decided
I really want to go back to university to finish my degree. I'm not
sure how much longer I'll be living in London.'

I think of my twenty-two-year-old self and how I became paralysed by my mistakes, unable to trust in any of my decisions. Even
the right ones. And much as I love this job and it's been hard
knowing I'll have to leave it behind, it's country gardens I love and
gardens I want to design. It's time to go back to my roots. 'I've
been accepted by UEA in Norwich to do my final year and complete my degree – thanks to this job. I start in September.'

'Not Greenwich?' he says in surprise and I shake my head.

'They couldn't fit me in, and besides, I have this real urge to
go home. I realise I've been fighting it the whole time I've lived
in London. I've been trying to resist the pull back to the wide-
open skies and beaches – and, of course, my family . . .' I smile.
The ones who have always been there at every turn. Now I've
faced up to my past, finally told them about what happened
that night on the pier, I can stop running scared. I'm not going
to get sucked back to the past. I'm not going to get ill again. I'm
not the same person I was before. Life has moved on, *I've*
moved on.

James hugs me and gives me a paternal squeeze. 'I don't
blame you, it's a very special place. And at least I'm not losing
you until September. I'll have you for another six months, right?'
He smiles. 'And you're welcome to assist me as part of your
final-year project. Or look for an office for me in East Anglia,' he
adds teasingly. 'I've wanted to expand the business for a while so
I can do bigger, more horticultural, countryside-based projects.

It just hasn't been the right moment till now as I just haven't known who to do it with. What do you say? It feels like fate, doesn't it?'

I nod delightedly as he flicks a switch so the terrace is flooded with warm light just as the first guests come trickling through.

An hour later and the party is buzzing. Champagne and canapés are whirling around the room in an endless cycle, a hundred guests are moving easily around the space, and I've lost count of the amount of compliments James and I have received. He keeps coming up and telling me of yet another corporate company who want us to transform their outdoor space in Soho, Hoxton, Chiswick, Pimlico, Poplar. I've chatted to Adam's old colleagues who have all lavished praise and thanks on me. They can't hide their surprise that the temp has turned her life around. Most of them have asked if Adam will be coming tonight and I had to tell them that I don't know.

I think he will, I feel he will, and I trust my instincts. I just don't *know*.

Chapter 70

Bea Bishop is on top of the world.
34 likes.

It's still dark when I wake up and it takes me a moment to get my bearings. My entire body is encased in the kind of warmth that only comes from having another person spooning you. The weight of Adam's arm lies across my body like an anchor. That sums up how I've felt in the weeks since we got back together in Goa: moored. He nuzzles my neck and I turn over so I'm facing him. His exhales are long and deep which tells me he's still asleep. He's always been an easy sleeper and that hasn't changed, but while I've always tossed and turned, now I'm finding myself waking up in the exact same position I fell asleep in. It's as if even in sleep I know that I'm exactly where I want to be.

We have been inseparable since that night on the beach b⸱ after staying on there together for an extra week to talk about ⸱ future, we decided we couldn't move back to Adam's flat. In⸱ we've been staying here at Milly's. It's convenient for work⸱ the flower shop but we've also been going to Loni's on ⸱

off. I've loved showing Adam around the Norfolk coast; he's been
getting to know my home – and my family – better. In all the
years we were together, we only went to Loni's a handful of times.
I was too scared of facing up to everything.

Not any more.

I look at the clock, see that it is before 5 a.m. and I close my
eyes again. But I can hear my brain click into gear, the ticking
sound of my thoughts going round in a circle. I haven't slept past
5 a.m. for weeks despite staying up till the small hours with
Adam most nights. It's like the days aren't long enough to catch
up on the year we've lost. We find ourselves going to bed, talking, kissing, laughing, making love and then talking some more.
We're not the same couple we were when we first got together
because we are happier individuals than before. It is that which
makes this feel like the best possible kind of new relationship. We
don't have that awkwardness that comes with unfamiliarity – the
threat of a silence that needs to be filled, the urgent desire to
impress which makes you act unlike yourself. But neither are we
making any assumptions about each other. We have unearthed
our roots, repotted ourselves and are growing together now,
instead of apart.

I lie with my eyes closed for a few minutes, allowing my
breath to coincide with the rise and fall of Adam's, giving me the
sensation of floating in water, bobbing over waves. And I find
myself, for a moment, being drawn back into the past again like
I've often been since I took Adam to Cromer and told him the
truth about what happened that night on the pier. It's as if now
's all out in the open, I'm no longer too scared to remember and
h time I cast my mind back, the details come more clearly and
a let go of what happened a little bit more.

pitch dark, the town is deserted and the rain is lashing down
'ripping off our bodies. Everything is wet, hair, cheeks, noses,

necks, arms, legs, but we don't care. We are immune to the elements, impervious to the sensation of anything outside of our bodies.

'I NEED MORE!' Elliot shouts to us above the wind, emptying the last of the vodka from the bottle into his mouth and swallowing it down like a gull devours a fish before throwing the bottle into the sea. He staggers sideways towards Kieran and me who are kissing on the pier, saliva mixing with rain, hands fumbling, our lust fuelled by the elements as much as the alcohol we've consumed. Elliot bumps into us as a crack of thunder and a bolt of lightning split the sky above.

Kieran and I break off reluctantly as he leans over the rail. We watch as he climbs up so that he's standing on the slippery railings like a tightrope walker. 'YOU CAN'T FUCKING TOUCH ME!' he shouts at the sky. 'I'M INVINCIBLE!' I lose my breath as I watch him, even though I have seen him pull crazy stunts like this, anything to get a thrill bigger than the last. Elliot doesn't scare easily.

I gasp and put my hands over my mouth as there is another clap of thunder. The earth itself seems to shudder and Elliot wobbles precariously on the rail.

'Woah!' he yells and then he jumps back down onto the pier, laughing and whooping at the top of his voice. Kieran and I look at each other and we roll our eyes parentally and a moment passes between us, this understanding that we're in the same place. He kisses me gently but Elliot pushes us apart like a kid trying to squeeze in on his parents' cuddle, thrusting his closed hand in front of our noses and then opening his palm to reveal three small blue pills.

He looks at us both, his eyes flicking back and forth manically. The Joker-style smile still on his face. He's off his head. He has be all night.

'Fancy a piece of heaven, guys?' he says, kissing each pill and ing at us both. 'Kieran got them, didn't you, bro?' Kieran's eyes apologetically to me and I know that I wasn't meant to learn

Elliot grabs my wrist, prises open my palm and places one in it. Then he tosses one to Kieran, who catches it with ease.

'On the count of three,' Elliot says, 'we throw our heads back and swallow, OK? The Three Musketeers, right? All for one and one for all! Ready? One!'

I watch as Kieran immediately closes his hand over the pill he's holding. Then he flicks it into the sea.

I do the same and we take each other's hand and smile.

'Pussy,' Elliot spits.

'Call me what you like,' Kieran says evenly.

'I wasn't talking to you.' Elliot opens his eyes and gazes at me challengingly with his dark, nettle-green eyes – complete with sting – that tell him apart from his brother. I want so much for him to like me but the closer I get to Kieran – the further I get from Elliot.

'You're out of order.' Kieran steps forward and pushes his brother.

'I'm just trying to find her wild side for you, bro, I know how much you love girls like that.' Elliot looks at me and raises his pierced eyebrow. 'I'm SURE she must have one! You wouldn't be with her if not . . .' He pauses and grins. 'One, two, three!' he shouts and he closes his eyes, tips his head and swallows the pill back.

Adam's arm moves slightly as if sensing my unrest, his hand sliding up under the covers until it finds my hand, and after a moment he releases it softly as he drifts back to sleep.

I smile idiotically as Kieran streaks easily across the beach to get more cigarettes and alcohol from his camper van that's parked a mile or so up the beach front. I don't need drugs and adrenalin highs to feel on top of the world and nor does Kieran.

'You're kidding yourself if you think he loves you, you know,' Elliot

into my ear.

step away from him, finding his closeness disconcerting. Feeling

confident in myself than usual, I turn around and smile at

you couldn't possibly understand what Kieran and I have.' I know I sound pious but I can't help it. I'm drunk on love and high on life. A heady combination.

Elliot steps closer to me and puts his hand on my shoulder. 'He'll break your heart, just like he does with every other girl he's had.'

I swallow. It's been three months and I can't imagine my life without Kieran any more. I need him. I don't know what I'd do if he left me – and that scares me. I have a momentary flashback to five years earlier. I'm in my bedroom, Cal is yelling down the phone and talking to me, there's the sound of the ambulance racing up our drive.

'You know what I think?' Elliot says. 'You're the type of girl that guys always leave . . .' He laughs suddenly, a wild triumphant hoot, and I feel another part of myself disappear.

I stare down the beachfront, hoping to see Kieran sprinting out of the darkness to save me but there is nothing.

'I know my brother,' Elliot continues. 'Blood's always gonna be thicker than water. He loves adventure, danger, he loves risk, and he'll soon get bored of playing happy ever after. I know all this because we're the same, me and him. We're twins.' He steps forward and catches my arm. 'We both want the same thing.' He takes my other arm and I inhale sharply and turn my face away from his. His breath smells pungent, of smoke and alcohol. I try to pull away as he leans in closer, his lips coming perilously close to mine. 'And believe me when I say that what we want isn't a good girl like you.' He pushes me away and I stagger over to the railings, where he'd stood just minutes before. I look at them and then down into the yawn-ing mouth of the wild, crashing waves and feel certain that I ca *prove once and for all that I'm enough for Kieran.*

'He doesn't love you,' Elliot taunts, 'he doesn't love you, he do love you . . .'

I clamber up quickly, my bare feet supple and hardene years of running across beaches, toes curled, arches gripping bars like a gymnast on a beam. I look back at Elliot who's staring up at me in disbelief and – yes – admiration. I smile at him, enjoying my moment in the spotlight, and turn back to face the sea. And then, I make the craziest, most reckless and rebellious decision of my life.

'You think I'm such a good girl, huh? So sensible, so averse to risk?' I yell. 'Well, I bet you can't do this!' I lean forward and with my eyes closed fall off the side, flatlining into the water like a corpse.

'You jumped first?' Adam had said in shock as I'd nodded, then with a muffled cry I had covered my face with my hands, wanting to hide again from the shame and sorrow and regret that has, over the years, made me question my whole existence, and constantly question *myself*.

One decision, one stupid, thoughtless decision had ended up costing a life. And not even mine. How could I live with myself – and how could I ever trust myself to make a decision again? I didn't physically push him, no. But I cajoled him. I dared him to do the same.

Adam had shaken his head. 'And you didn't tell anyone?'

'Only Kieran, after we tried to save Elliot. He said he'd tell everyone that he alone jumped. We were all soaked through from the rain anyway so no one knew the difference . . .'

'Oh Bea,' Adam said, pulling my head against his chest. I could feel his heartbeat against my head, like a ticking clock, indicating the passing seconds before he spoke again. I'd counted them, each and every one, and as they accumulated I knew that ᵉ was gearing up to tell me he couldn't ever love someone as ᵏless and thoughtless and stupid as me.

ʸou could have died,' he said at last, lifting my head off his and gazing into my eyes. His were filled with shimmering f tears. 'You could have died and I would never have met

I pull myself out of the water and onto the beach, coughing and spluttering as the rain pounds against my back. It feels like hands congratulating me. Then, I sprint across the beach and back up onto the pier, pounding down on the wooden slats, my bare feet thundering like hooves.

Elliot is waiting for me as I run to the end, laughing and whooping and jumping up and down manically. And for a brief moment as I yell, 'You didn't think I'd do it!' I feel that at last the battle is over and I've proved myself.

'That looked fucking AWESOME!' he cries, his eyes wild as he leans over the railing. The rain is lashing down even harder now and I'm starting to shiver. I wipe my face with my hand and shake my hair on the boardwalk, and by the time I look back, Elliot is climbing up on the rails. He turns, crouches like a monkey, and grins.

'You don't think I'd chicken out on a bet, do you? I'm INVIN-CIBLE!' he shouts.

'Don't, Elliot, it's not safe!' I scream. 'You've drunk too much. You're off your head. I was lucky, that's all!'

'Luck's my middle name!'

I turn and see Kieran at the other end of the pier. I wave at him desperately, but I'm not sure he can see me in the dark.

'KIERAN!' I see him start to run and I turn back to Elliot.

'Look at me, bro!' Elliot laughs and I can see Kieran is running down the pier lightning fast; he's shouting but his words are being carried away by the wind and rain.

Elliot stands up suddenly but then his face changes as he loses his footing and he slips over the side, cracking his head as he body fli awkwardly and bangs against the side of the pier.

I scream and run to the railing where I watch his body spin like a dandelion seed on the wind before it drops with a spla a stone into the water.

Kieran's screams join mine, he's panting and hoarse and we lean over into the darkness but Elliot's been swallowed into the blackness. I look at Kieran who is stripping off his clothes.

'I'm going in after him!'

'Then I'm coming in with you!'

And I climb back up onto the rails, I take Kieran's hand and we jump.

'You jumped in *again*?' Adam said.

'I had to try to save him. It was my fault he was up there in the first place . . .'

'So what happened?'

'Kieran found him. I'll never know how he managed to drag him to the surface, but he did. Then the two of us pulled him back to the shore together. He had a massive gash on his head, there was blood everywhere. He'd been knocked unconscious on impact. Kieran tried to resuscitate him while I called an ambulance. The paramedics pronounced him dead when they arrived five minutes later.'

I'd lowered my head, aware that Adam had been stunned into silence. 'So now you know the truth. My actions caused a young man to die. I've spent eight years trying to live with the guilt – unable to make any decision about my life because I couldn't trust myself and because I didn't think I deserved any happiness. And then Kieran showed up on our wedding day and I realised that I hadn't really dealt with it at all. I hated myself for what I'd done. And if I couldn't live with myself – how could I expect you to?'

Adam had taken my arms then, his face was stricken with sadness, his voice emphatic. 'No, Bea, Elliot died because he was
crazy and off his head on drink and drugs. He climbed up there
his own volition. You didn't force him and you didn't push
t was an accident, a tragic accident. His, Bea, not yours.
urs.' And then he held me as I cried again, grieving for the

young boy who had lost his life, and the girl who had never got over it.

'It wasn't your fault,' Adam whispered over and over again as he stroked my head. 'You weren't to know. You have to let it go.'

Adam wakes up and he takes me in his arms and I close my eyes, luxuriating in his embrace, so much more appreciative of this amazing man after having spent nearly a year apart. Adam has always known how to lift me. I think of all the 'Do you remember when . . .?' stories he told me, recreating the happiest moments of our relationship to lift me out of dark places.

'Hey you,' he says sleepily. 'Watcha thinking about?'

'Oh, you know.' I nuzzle into his neck and close my eyes. 'Just stuff.'

He lifts up his elbow and supports his head on his hand. 'OK, so do you remember when . . .'

I put my finger over his lips, surprising him. 'Can we not talk about the past right now?' I say apologetically. 'I just want to be here . . . in this moment with you, right now.'

He nods and holds me tightly and once again I am moored.

And then he begins to murmur softly, not memories of happy moments past, but all the ones we have to come. I weep quietly as he paints a picture of our future life, our home, our family. He describes our children in detail, giving them equal parts of him and me, merging the best of us so that two people become three, and then four. He talks about his parents as grandparents, about Loni and Cal, making sure we see enough of them all so our family always has a strong, unbreakable bond. Many lives within one life.

'Let's go out tonight,' Adam suggests contentedly when finished plotting our future together. 'I'll pick you up from flower shop after work and we'll go for dinner.'

*

It's an unseasonably warm night as Adam and I walk through the starlit streets of Canary Wharf. It's strange being back here. I've had to come this evening to deliver one extra-special bouquet for a local garden designer who came in in a blind panic this morning needing some big displays for a party that evening. They got sent this afternoon but he called again just as Adam came to pick me up, asking for something more personal for a friend of his, and for me to hand-deliver them. He sounded so stressed, part of me has wondered if it's worth seeing if he needs some sort of an assistant. He – James – had been amazed how much I knew when he was discussing the displays he needed for the roof terrace project he'd been working on this morning. I had told him about the one I'd designed at my old flat and spent a happy ten minutes discussing lighting options, dividers and design features. He told me that if it went well, he was looking to expand his business. Maybe even open an office out of London.

'I dream about living a slower-paced life,' he'd sighed, dabbing his forehead with a handkerchief.

'You should consider Norfolk,' I'd smiled. 'It's my favourite place in the world . . . and has so many incredible gardens and country houses.'

'How strange you should say that. I love it there too!' he'd said, and had given me his card before he left. I pat it just to make sure it's there. I couldn't believe it when I realised he was the same designer I'd seen at the Chelsea Flower Show and whose garden I'd loved so much. It's made me think about contacting him. I mean, it kind of feels like fate. In all the shops in all the cosmos had to come in to this one, right?

The Cosmo Flowers van isn't parked far and I'm hurrying the street, wanting to drop the bouquets off so we can get ere. There are too many memories for us in Canary Wharf ne thing Adam and I said when we got back together is that we wanted to go back to the beginning: have a fresh start. That's why living at Milly's is perfect. We're back where we were when we first met. We're just going to make different decisions this time.

'I don't recognise the address,' I say to Adam as we stare down the street. I walk over to a building that looks like it has some sort of glass ball on top of it and stare at it, and then at the piece of paper I'm holding. I'm about to go in when Adam catches my arm.

I follow his gaze up to the sign above the glass doors that says Hudson, Grey & Friedman.

'What a weird coincidence!' People are streaming in through the doors of the glass building and I watch Adam quietly for a moment. 'Do you want to go in?' I ask. 'I don't mind if you do – I mean, I'm sure your dad would appreciate the support . . . he did invite you, after all.'

Adam doesn't say anything for a moment. We just both stare up at the party that's happening on the roof terrace above us; a party that once upon a time we would have been at.

'Do you know what? I really don't,' he says with a smile. 'Dad knows there will be no more networking events or corporate dinners, no more socialising as anything other than father and son. This isn't my world any more.'

I kiss him then slip inside the building to deliver the bouquet. I'm nervous in case I bump into anyone, so I quickly give it to the security guard with a request to take it up to the top floor.

'All done,' I say as I run back to Adam's side.

With one last look up at the building, Adam slips his ar around my waist and we walk along laughing and talking ur a perfectly starlit sky.

Chapter 71

Bea Hudson is wondering if it's all over.

It's past midnight by the time the last guests have gone and only the caterers and a couple of stragglers are left. I walk back out onto the terrace. I know I should feel relaxed, relieved now that it is all over but I just feel empty. It was a great success – even George took a moment out of his hectic networking schedule to come and congratulate me. 'Bloody good job,' he'd said and kissed me with a red-wine-stained smile. Then it had faded. 'I hope we'll see Adam soon.' He'd looked sad for a moment as he glanced around the emptied terrace. 'I'd hoped he'd be here tonight but he's told me firmly he's not coming back to the company. He made the rules for our relationship clear when he called me from India.' India? I had no idea he'd gone there . . . wonder why? Suddenly I feel like I can see him standing on the beautiful beach like the ones Loni always talks about. I ask her more about it. Maybe I'll go there with her one day. a girls' holiday. Reconnect with her again.

is back on George. 'No talking about work, he told me.

He said he wants to be his own man – my son, not my successor.' He sighed. 'I suppose I've got to let him lead his own life. The trouble is, the one I've worked so hard for is such a good one, I wanted it for him too. I miss him, you know, Bea. Often I wonder if I've been a good enough father, made the right choices.' And then he shook his head and disappeared into the throng again.

I see him now, saying goodbye to the caterers, and he comes back out onto the roof terrace. 'You coming, Bea? I'll call a car to take you home if you like.'

'I think I'll just stay here a few minutes more if that's OK, George. I just want to soak up the moment and the view for a little bit longer.'

He nods and lifts his hand. 'I'll let security know. Well done again, you did the family proud today, love.'

I grab two last glasses of champagne from a half-empty tray and go and sit at the iPad bar. I glance at my watch as I take a sip. I know he's going to come, I just know it. I look up at the full moon that shines above me, a pale white clock-face against the bright, almost digital glow of the city below. Each light that flickers in a window, or on a passing car, seems to me to be numbered, a steadily growing number of lives in a vast city of people all desperate to make their mark, make the right decisions, live the best version of their lives.

'What a beautiful view,' I hear a voice say. I smile and pick up the flowers that I ordered when I went into Sal's shop to see her and baby Aaron and asked if someone could deliver them here tonight. I turn and there he is. Adam. The same, but different somehow. Gone is the smart suit and stressed-out expression. He's wearing jeans and a hoodie, his hands are pushed deep down into his pockets, the uplights from the terrace illuminating his tanned, relaxed face.

'I knew you'd come,' I say softly as I step towards him, the scent of the flowers filling the air.

'Just in time, by the look of things.' Adam smiles but there is a hint of concern in his eyes. 'Are they from an admirer?' He nods at the bouquet in my arms.

I glance down at them and shake my head with an enigmatic smile.

'They should be,' Adam says, gazing around at the roof terrace as he tentatively takes my hand. 'What you've done here, it's incredible. I'm so proud of you.'

I feel a flush of pleasure. Not just because he's proud, but because I am. 'I couldn't have done it without you, Ad.'

'Of course you could,' he laughs. 'You just did!'

I take his other hand and we turn to face each other. 'Even so, I couldn't have done it without your support. You've always made me feel like I can do anything I want; you gave me the confidence to do something I've never really believed I deserved to do.' I lean in to him and lift my lips to his. It's been two months since I saw my husband and I don't want to talk any more. I want to kiss him. I want us to start the next stage of our life together.

'You must believe it now though, right?' Adam says, stroking my hair that's blowing around my face. I'm thinking about getting it cut short; it'd be much easier with my job. I look up at him and nod.

'And I've decided what I want too,' I say determinedly. I weave my arms around his neck and clasp my hands so Adam can't tell they're shaking. I don't want him to feel sorry for me, or feel like he doesn't have a choice. Neither of us knows what decision the other person has come to. He's back, but are either of us willing to merge our worlds, cross the line that forced us apart last time?

He gazes at me as I stare out at the city, feeling my pulse race and my voice shake as I prepare to take the first step.

'Ad, I've decided that I don't want to live in London any more. I don't belong here, I don't think I ever have. I only came because of Milly, and then I stayed because of you. But if there's one thing I've learned this year, it is that I have to make decisions based on what I think will make me happy.' I take a deep breath. 'I want to move back home for a while. I want to go back to university and finish the degree I started all those years ago. I found out last week that I've got a place at UEA to do the third year of my garden design degree.'

'That's amazing news!' Adam says and I smile. I'm so happy, but I still don't know if choosing it will cost me my relationship. It's a chance I've decided I have to take.

'I want, no, I know that for my own happiness -- and health -- I need to be able to run along the beach, to tend to a garden, to see my mum whenever I want, find out more about my dad. Maybe I'll try and find him, maybe I won't, but the one thing I do know is I can't live here any more, in London.' He nods and looks up into the night sky. 'I know none of this may be compatible with your dreams, Adam,' I blurt out, 'or your vision for the future – and that thought petrifies me because I can't imagine doing any of it without you.' I feel sick as I stare at the face I love and that I'm not sure if I'm about to lose. He then steps forward and looks down into the street below, as if he is imagining himself elsewhere – wandering through the city streets perhaps, laughing with someone who is happy to follow him wherever he wants to go. 'What about you?' I ask, swallowing back the fear I feel. Whatever the outcome, I'm strong enough to deal with it. 'What have you decided?'

He pauses for a moment before he turns around. 'I think I'm still working it out to be honest,' Adam says, looking back at m his grey eyes fixed firmly on mine. It is a strange turnaround for me to be the one certain of my choices, while Adam is still floundering. 'I left you knowing that I had to have some time to myself. I wanted to work out where in my life I'd been happiest. I went to Paris first, back to all the places we visited on our honeymoon, I visited loads of galleries and museums, I even went back to our secret garden . . . none of it was the same without you. I went to New York next, just to get an idea of whether I'd want to live there. I love that city but, again, I couldn't imagine being there without you. I flew out to India as I thought I'd find the answers there. But I just felt lonely. All I could think about was watching the incredible sunsets with you, browsing the night market together or riding pillion on the back of a moped.' He grasps my hand and I can see he is as petrified of this moment as me. 'I know now that life isn't about winning pitches, or getting promoted, it's not about being seen in the right places, or having a career that my parents are proud of. It's about doing what makes *me* happy, with the people – the *person* who makes me happiest.' I look at him hopefully. 'The thing is, Bea, I don't know what I want from my future yet, I've had it mapped out for me for so long I need more time. But the one thing I do know is who I want to spend it with . . .'

I take a sharp breath as he cups my face. 'Just to clarify, it's you,' he says.

'Really?' I ask, feeling like my heart has burst into bloom.

He smiles and points at the sky. 'As certain as night follows day, the moon circles the earth, and the stars will always shine . . .'

'So what now?' I whisper as he leans his forehead against mine.

He shrugs. 'I don't know! God, it feels liberating to say that! or the first time in my life I don't have to look at a diary, or think about my career plan. I don't have to listen to Dad telling me what he was doing at my age. I'm just going to take my time and enjoy . . . not knowing. In the meantime I plan on supporting you in your career. I'm going to put the flat on the market, hopefully start looking for a place for us in Norfolk. Maybe I'll set up my own business, I might freelance for a while . . .'

'You're going to temp?' I raise my eyebrow and he laughs.

'Why not? You've inspired me. I think everyone could do with taking some time to work out what will make them truly happy . . .' He trails off. 'Maybe not seven years though,' he says with a wink. 'I'll try and work it out quicker than that.' I hit his chest playfully and he laughs and lowers his mouth to mine and as our lips meet, I close my eyes and feel myself being lifted high up off the terrace as if I'm soaring through the air. I'm flying, not falling, and I know I'm being carried to a place where I will land safely. Where I can be myself, make my own decisions but be kept afloat with the full support of all the people who love me.

This is being happy.

'Hey,' I murmur at last as I come up for air and remember what I'm holding. 'You're squashing the flowers.'

'I can see what order of priority I'm going to come in this relationship already,' Adam says, looking warily at the flowers, and I smack him lightly with them. 'I'm going to be a gardening widow, right?'

'They're for you, actually,' I say, pushing him away from me a little so I can show them to him properly. 'I chose them because I knew you'd come here tonight. I knew it as much as I know who I am and what I want. I knew it because I know you.' I give the bouquet of blue and white flowers to him and start talking him through each stem. 'Each one represents who you are and wha you mean to me.' He looks down at the flowers. They are r cohesive, as a bouquet, they would not win any prizes, and

they say everything I want to express about him. 'Bluebells for
your constancy, snowdrops for your positivity and for never giving
up on me, ranunculas for being rich in attractions.' I pause. 'In
other words, because you're really gorgeous.' He throws his head
back and laughs as I continue to talk him through the flowers.
'Violets for your modesty – because you don't realise just how gorgeous you are – and forget-me-nots because you have the key to
my heart.' I break off for a moment, suddenly recalling a long-lost
memory of the man I last gave forget-me-nots to. My dad. I close
my eyes and open them again. This seems to be the best way to
move on from that memory. To let go.

'And then,' I continue, 'surrounding them all is ivy because it
symbolises friendship, fidelity and marriage. And I want you to
know that being married to you is the best decision I have ever
made.'

15 October 1989

My dear, darling little Bea

It is October as I write this note to you, the day after your seventh birthday, and the leaves are falling from the trees, and spring is like a distant star in the cosmos. I'm leaving today, because I can't stand another dark winter. I'm leaving you this diary as a gift, a symbol of my deep-rooted love, in the hope that it will help you to keep growing, keep flowering, long after I've gone. I'm sorry it has come to this, but sometimes old plants like me need to find new soil in which to grow. But I need you to promise me you'll grow big and strong. That you'll trust in yourself and every decision you make, and always remember this: in the garden – and life – everything is cyclical. Each path we choose, every decision we make may one day take us back to the very same one we turned away from. And if sometimes you think you're going round in circles, remember, you will always know where you are if you keep looking up at the stars.

All my love, forever, Dad x

Chapter 72

30 April 2014

Bea Bishop is preparing for the biggest day of her life. And this time I'm one hundred per cent ready.

'So! Are you ready for your big day, *Julia*?' Milly says jokily as she pokes her head around the spare-room door. I sit up in bed and quickly shut Dad's diary and look at my reflection in the mirror and smile. When I woke up, I felt this urgent need to have a final read of the note Dad wrote at the beginning. I plan on putting the diary away again somewhere safe now because I know I don't need to be guided by anything except my heart any more. But I'm happy that I'll always know exactly where it – no – *he* is. And I want him here with me today, if not in body, then in spirit.

It's what I've always wanted.

Having found my dad and dealt with what happened to Elliot I'm ready for today in a way I wasn't a year ago. I'll never forget Kieran and Elliot, but nor do I have to carry the weight of the memory or the guilt any more. Kieran has gone too, I had a final message from him. He went back to Portsmouth but then decided to leave the Navy and join the Royal Lifeboat Crew down there. He says he wants to settle down, make roots somewhere but still feel close to Elliot. He thanked me for helping him over the last few months and I did the same, then I de-friended him on Facebook. I know I'll never hear from him again.

'Julia?' I say, raising an eyebrow inquisitively at my friend.

'Roberts. Julia Roberts,' she says. 'You know, *The Runaway Bride*.' Milly laughs, baby Holly bouncing on her chest with each guffaw.

'Ho ho, very funny,' I retort, flinging my legs out of bed so I can tickle Holly on her tummy. 'Your mummy thinks she's very funny.' I give her a kiss on her rose-tinted cheek. She gurgles at me and then pukes up milk on Milly's collarbone.

'Good girl!' I say, giving the baby a little high-five as Milly grabs a muslin and dabs the milk-sick off herself.

It's so much fun getting ready. It's just like the old days and the whole experience feels completely different from how it felt last year. More relaxed, more me. There's no champagne, no corset-fitting or hair and make-up artist, no formal photographs, just some strong G&T courtesy of Loni, some loud music and a lot of laughter as we all get ready together. I slip into the bedroom on my own to get into my dress. I want to have a minute alone – and also I want to see their reaction when I come out.

Loni looks up first and beams at me, hands clasped in a prayer position in front of her mouth.

'Oh my beautiful baby girl . . . you look just like your mam It's like looking in a mirror!'

'Thanks . . .' I say doubtfully. Loni is wearing another s creation – lime-green and purple – and her hair has bee her classic electric-shock look.

Milly is uncharacteristically quiet. She's wearing a

yellow day dress, bought off eBay, which she's teamed with simple white pumps. No designer labels, we decided. Milly is cutting back now she's not working and has vowed to live a different, more economical life to go with the company she's launching in September. 'You can't be strutting around in Prada whilst asking people to pledge their investments money to charitable causes!' she pointed out.

'You look beautiful, Bea,' she says now as she looks at me.

'Thanks . . . the dress is rather lovely.' I brush my hand over the floaty cream 1970s number of Loni's that she's given to me and is my something old.

'It's like it's been made for you, darling,' Loni cuts in. 'Of course, I used to be your shape, once upon a time . . .' She looks down despairingly at her generous curves – they're back in abundance since she and Roger officially became an item and she stopped trying to hide him. 'I'm out of the closet,' as she said, 'and back in my old fat clothes.'

My wedding dress is empire line with long chiffon peasant sleeves and a soft, layered skirt that cascades to my ankles. It feels like I'm wearing fresh air. Loni told me it was always my dad's favourite dress. I notice that she is crying and I wonder if it's because she's letting go of him too. Their divorce has finally gone through. She admitted she could have done it years ago – there are ways to divorce a missing person – but she just wasn't ready. 'But now I've seen him again, I feel like I've had closure and I can ·ay goodbye officially,' she said. I'm pretty sure Roger is the ,son behind her decision.

You look like the perfect bride,' Milly says.

Ion't think I've ever been described as that before,' I joke laugh. We can laugh about it all now. Enough time has he *past* has passed.

· down and see my something blue, Dad's small gilt-edged diary which I've tied to my bouquet of forget-me-nots. One last outing before I put the book away forever.

Bea Hudson: This time last year I was preparing for the biggest day of my life . . .

'I can't believe this time last year we were getting married.' Adam glances at me in his rear-view mirror and I smile and nod, fingering the folds of the floaty cream dress Loni gave me when she was clearing out her attic, as I press 'status update' and put away my phone. 'This was your dad's favourite,' she'd smiled. 'I'd like you to have it.' She'd given me the address too, of the place Len moved to after he left us. 'I don't know where he went from here, but if you really want to find him, darling, this might be the place to start? I could help you, if you like . . .'

I'd stared at it, before putting the address back in my pocket. But strangely, I feel that having Dad's diary, Adam, my job, my university course to look forward to and moving back here is enough. But who knows if I'll feel differently in the future?

We're making our way into Greenwich after another glorious weekend in Norfolk. We've been going there a lot now that Adam is in between work, looking for a cottage to rent there from September – and making the most of the opportunity to spend time with Loni, Cal, Lucy, Nico and Neve.

Adam and I are becoming pretty expert babysitters while Cal and Lucy go out, or just catch up on some sleep. I don't think I'd realised the kind of pressure they'd been under until Cal took me home after I left Adam. I didn't realise how much I'd missed b only communicating with them through my phone: texts, ca Facebook updates . . . none of those things scratch the surfac people's lives. Now I've spent so much more time with my f I don't understand how I could have stayed away for so l

We've spent the last couple of days going through loads of old boxes that had been hidden up in the loft, talking over old times with Cal and Loni, talking about Dad. Something seems to have happened to make Loni want to talk about it now. Maybe it was seeing Adam and me come so close to splitting up that made her want to be more open, maybe it was Adam talking about travelling around Goa in the two months we were apart that did it (it was one of the places he went to 'find himself') and it just seemed to ignite Loni's memories. Maybe it's the fact that she's finally met someone and is ready to let go of the past and move on. She's been researching how to divorce a missing person and has finally filed the necessary forms. Apparently you can give your local court details of the person's last known address and they will let you know if the divorce petition comes back unopened. Then, if you can prove you've tried all other means of contacting them – which she has over the years – you can fill in the statement to dispense with the service of divorce petition.

I'm ready to move on too. I don't feel the same urgent need to find Dad any more. Maybe it's because I've finally let go of past. Maybe it's because when I left Adam Loni finally told me the truth as to why Dad left. I found it upsetting learning about his depression. It reminded me of my own struggles but also made me realise how far I have come. I know I'm not on the same path as him any more. I'm making my own destiny, following my own set of stars.

There is another life out there for me. I look at Adam and mile.

And I know it will be a happy one.

' you got anything to drink?' I whisper to Loni as our little ion made up of me, Loni, Cal, Milly, Sal and Aaron walk through the park. I realise that half our guests are already with me and I smile. We're having a very different wedding this time.

'Of course I have, darling.' She pulls out a plastic bottle and winks at me.

I take a long swig from it and then splutter in surprise. 'It's water! I thought it was gin . . .'

Loni blinks at me. 'Darling, I swore to Adam I'd send you off in style this time – *sober* style. We don't want any more trip-ups, do we? Besides,' she adds and taps my hand, 'I get the feeling you don't need Dutch courage this time, am I right?'

I smile at her. Her hair looks like an electric current has been put through it and she is glinting with gigantic costume jewellery but the main sparkle comes from her smile. I'm not entirely sure what has changed about her – just that she seems more comfortable somehow. I realise she was trying so hard to appear happy before – to be 'Loni Bishop' all the time. Now she *is* happy and it radiates effortlessly from her. Roger is meeting us at the venue and I can see she's excited. She talked a lot about him after we left Dad in Goa. She told me how she had known him for months but that she had held back a lot from him, not allowed him to get properly close because after Dad, she felt unable to fall in love again. Sex was fine, sex was uncomplicated, but love was different. She couldn't trust anyone as she was sure they would leave her like Dad did, but Roger was the first person who has broken through that emotional barrier. He was the reason she was struggling to focus on work. He was why the place was a tip and she wasn't on top of things. Since seeing Dad she knows it wasn't her fault that he left; his fate – and in turn hers – had been sealed a long time before and she's finally stopped blaming herself. Roger has quickly become part of family and I don't think it's a coincidence that she's decided no longer has to be 'Loni Bishop: single self-help guru' any more. After months of writer's block she's written and self-published her own ebook, releasing it on Amazon under her maiden name Loni Hart. It shot straight into the bestseller list and in four weeks has already tripled the sales of her last book. It's called *The Art of Letting Go: How to Live a Brand-New Life Without Any Baggage.* It is brilliant. Not least because it's the first book of hers I've ever read that hasn't made me blush.

We walk through the gorgeous gilt-edged gates and up King William's Walk, passing the herb garden in Greenwich Park which seems to have suddenly sprung into life on this sunny April day. The ancient trees are rich with fresh green leaves and pale blossom, and lilac-pink magnolia petals are bursting with the secret promise of new beginnings. I think of my meeting with James Fischer, who was really interested in the fact that I was doing my final year of my Garden Design degree at UEA. 'I've been looking into opening an office there as my boyfriend and I have decided we want to divide our time between London and Norfolk. If you want some experience, I'd be very interested in employing a part-time assistant. I can be your mentor. I've lectured at UEA before so I'm sure they'll approve ...'

I smile as I stare up at the Royal Observatory that sits on the hill; a place where astronomers have long since measured time and navigation, the place where the Greenwich meridian line is marked and where the planetarium is now based. The earth, sea and stars are all measured from there. Today it feels like the centre of the universe. Or rather, the centre of *my* universe. Everything has aligned. Greenwich, after all, is where my life egan again. It was my second chance of happiness. It's why I nted us to get married here. I look up at the red time ball, ing to drop, and suddenly I feel this urge overtake me.

eed to go,' I gasp and I pull my arm from Milly's.

'What? Wait! STOP!' I hear her shout as I begin to run. But I ignore her. I don't have much time.

'Stop!' I command and Adam swerves alongside Greenwich Park. I open my window to stick my head out and get a better view. The sky is forget-me-not blue and the sparse clouds that are scattered across it are blushed pink like a teething baby. Daffodils line every small patch of grass in sight, yellow bells chiming in celebration of spring. Adam expertly pulls into a parking space and I immediately open the door. I can't see the Observatory on top of the hill, but I can feel it. It is like there is an invisible string pulling me towards it.

'Where are you going?'

'I won't be a minute!' I run around to the other side of the car, knock on his window and kiss him on the lips. He looks surprised, bemused, but not unduly concerned. 'There's something I have to do before we go back to Milly's. Somewhere I have to be . . .'

'Where are you going?' Milly puffs as she runs up to me, Holly bouncing up and down in the Baby Bjorn attached to her body. She grasps my arm and I skid to a halt. 'Bea, I can't let you do this, not again!'

'I won't be long, Milly, I promise,' I say, looking desperately up at the Observatory. I feel like it has been watching me all along, waiting for the right moment, the right time to bring me to it.

'I can't explain it but there's something I need to do, son where I have to be before I marry Adam.' I wriggle my arm and start backing up the hill like there is a magnetic force p me. 'I have to go but I promise I'll be back in time.'

'This is no time for sodding stargazing, Bea!' Milly

'Chill out, Milly!' I laugh. 'I'll meet you at the flower garden in a minute!' And then I start running again.

I dash through the gilt-edged gates on King William's Walk, Loni's dress billowing around my legs as I pass the herb garden and the little café. I have this incredible sense of certainty that I was meant to come here.

I can feel it.

The park is already busy on this sunny spring Saturday morning. I weave through the people streaming down the pathways, some walking dogs, some on varying forms of wheels – cycles, scooters, line skates. There are couples arm in arm and on the grass families throwing Frisbees and balls. The park is a sea of life and colour. Daffodils, tulips and crocuses are scattered over the ground.

I spot the Observatory on top of the hill and start running faster, listening to the squawks of the local parakeets and the laughs of a group of kids playing hide and seek.

'Found you!' one says as she pulls her friend out from behind a tree. I realise then that this is exactly how I feel. I've found what I've been looking for. I know exactly where I need to be and who I am. And it feels good. I stop briefly to pick a little bouquet of forget-me-nots that are clustered under a tree. I notice how the blue matches the diary that I carry everywhere with me since I found it at Milly's flat. I tie it to the flowers. It's my reminder 'o never lose sight of where my life is going again.

'oon as I see the Observatory I have an overwhelming urge to ere as quickly as I can. My long cream dress billows around s like waves as I weave through cyclists, kids on skateboards rskates, mums pushing prams, dog walkers. I don't stop the bottom of the steps that lead up the hill to the

Observatory. I don't listen to the busker like I normally would. Instead I hitch up my dress and cling on to my forget-me-not bouquet feeling the familiar burn in my calves and roar of adrenalin in my ears. I smile as I pass people on the steps, all of whom are stopping to stare at the crazy bride.

'Can I just get past, please? Oops, sorry!' I apologise as I accidentally nudge shoulders and bump into people in my haste. I feel exactly the same as when I used to sprint across beaches in my youth. I realise how much I've missed running and vow to start doing it again. The park sweeps out to the left of me, the paths criss-crossing in lines that lead towards the City that's just a grey spectre in the distance.

Finally, panting with exertion, I reach the top and stand in front of the Shepherd Gate twenty-four-hour clock that marks the entrance to the Royal Observatory. The hands stretch vertically in a straight line like the meridian line itself. It is 12.55. The ball will drop in five minutes.

I'm just in time.

If only I knew what for.

I pause at the bottom of the steps to catch my breath and to listen to the busker for a moment. Clutching my forget-me-nots in one hand, I put the other into my jacket and pull out a couple of pound coins. He nods at me and smiles as I throw them into his guitar case and I listen for a moment more before setting off up the steps. I start fast and have to immediately stop when I realise that the steps are steeper than they look and I'm not a fit as I'd like to be. Seven years of office work and having a l in our apartment building in Canary Wharf has put paid to t That'll soon change though. I think of the daily runs Adar I have vowed to take when we move to Norfolk, the ga can work on, all in the name of my degree. And also, ·

with James. Everything has come together so perfectly it almost feels ... predestined. I can't imagine my life ending up any other way.

I carry on climbing, slower this time. I reach the top as the hands of the Shepherd Gate clock point to 12.55. The place is so crowded I can't see anything other than a big foreign school group wearing identical red macs. I bob my head impatiently, trying to see more before giving up and going in.

I walk into Flamsteed House and up to the desk and thrust out some money for a ticket to enter the courtyard. The cashier raises her eyebrows at me as she takes in my outfit.

'Shouldn't you be at the Queen's House, dear? That's where we normally do weddings ...'

As I go back out into the courtyard a man appears and announces that it's time for the next tour. People flock around him and after a small introduction, they move away, leaving the courtyard empty. It is a magical moment. I feel like I'm standing on top of the world and right on time's doorstep. This is how a bride is meant to feel on her wedding day. I'm not thinking about my past or worrying about the future. I am in this moment completely – and yet for some reason I feel like there is a part of me missing. It's not Dad, or Kieran ... so what ... who?

For reasons I can't explain I find myself walking over to the meridian line that stretches down the right-hand side of the court-ard like metal to a magnet. I place my feet either side of it and ok up at the sky, imagining the stars that are waiting to come and I, too, wait.

hrough Flamsteed House and step out into the courtyard. cked with tourists five minutes ago but it has suddenly emptied, the last people trailing off around the Observatory with a jauntily dressed tour guide. There is someone standing with their back to me, feet either side of the meridian line, like thousands — no, millions of people have stood. The sun is beaming down, bouncing light off the red-brick walls of the Octagon Room and refracting back off the time ball above. I look out to the Royal Naval College and the sky diving into the Thames beyond it and I think of Kieran for a moment, of our brief affair. I know with all the certainty within me that even though I'll never forget him — or Elliot — our ship has long since sailed. Clinging tightly on to my forget-me-not bouquet I glance down at my watch, backing away a little as I see the time. I keep reversing slowly so I can get a better view of the City's panorama, holding my hand up in front of my face to shade the glare of sunlight that seems to be shining directly in my eyes.

A dark cloud passes over the courtyard suddenly, turning the bronze of the meridian line mulchy brown. I glance up just as the time ball drops to signal 1 p.m., and then, out of nowhere, I feel myself bang into someone with some force and I cry out.

I feel the weight of someone bang in to me and the force knocks me off my feet; I hear the other person cry out as I topple forwards. The last thing I see before I hit the ground is the bronze meridian line in front of my eyes. I feel like I'm falling into it and when I land face down on the line the last thing I see is stars.

And then, there's just black.

I find myself twisting and falling, and the last thing I see bef I hit the ground backwards is stars.

And then, there's just black.

Chapter 73

I come to and find the courtyard still empty. I blink and rub my head. The sun is still shining directly above me. There is a stillness in the air – a silence that feels almost other-worldly, like time has stopped and I am here in this little vacuum alone. The sky yawns above me like it has split. I feel confused, bruised but at the same time more together than I've felt for a long time.

I sit up suddenly and instantly regret it as I feel a wave of dizziness overcome me. I close my eyes, trying to force myself to focus. I know I'm meant to be somewhere but for the life of me I can't remember where. I hold up my hand in front of my face. Have I died? Am I a ghost? I hope not. That would be really annoying when I've finally sorted my life out.

Still feeling dizzy I pull my knees up in front of me and bury my face in them. It's then that I realise I'm wearing a long cream dress, a floaty cream dress that feels very bridal-like. And then it me. Not the ground, for once, but . . .

cramble to my feet. I'm meant to be getting *MARRIED*.

ering a little I close my eyes to try and recalibrate. Not to think any more, I begin to run, hesitantly at first, in oncussed. But my head has never been clearer. I pick up speed, skipping at first, my feet hitting the ground as if in time with the ticking of a clock. I look across the green park, see the blankets of spring flowers, the bright daffodils and crocuses, the forget-me-nots and tulips that have emerged, and think how *I* have bloomed too. I know my roots and now, now I can look up at the stars and to the future. I run faster, my feet pounding like hooves across the ground, the sound thudding in my ear as I run back through Flamsteed House and out of the gates, past the statue of James Wolfe that looks out across the park and the entire panaroma of the City. I stare across for a moment at the glimmering Thames, I see the Royal Naval College and the *Cutty Sark* to the left of it and briefly think of Kieran. The thought dissipates as quickly as it came. Now that I've seen him again that ship has finally sailed. I begin to run again, knowing exactly where I'm going because I'm finally on the right course. I charge past the Pavilion Tea House, taking a left and running down Great Cross Avenue, passing some kids playing football who point at me and laugh – the crazy lady in a wedding dress. A girl and boy skate down the cycle path, each of their legs straddling the path like it's the meridian line itself. I glance to the left and see some younger kids making a camp under the oak trees and as my feet drum against the ground I feel like they're stirring up my past. But as I run towards the flower garden, where I know Adam will be, I can feel myself leave it all behind. Suddenly my vision switches like a kaleidoscope and a new image forms of Adam and me sitting in a sprawling garden, watching two kids, a curly-haired boy and a girl playing on a climbing frame. The image floats in my mind like a bubble in front of my eyes, bef it pops. And this time I know it isn't a dream, or a life not l a path not taken. It is my future I'm heading for now.

I'm out of breath, sweaty and red-faced when I arrive a bemused set of about fifteen guests staring at me. Th and Cal, obviously, Adam's mum and dad, Sal and baby Aaron. She's standing next to Tim and they're the only ones who have barely noticed I've arrived as they're deep in conversation. There's Nick and Glenda, Milly, of course, and Holly. And that's it. No extended family. No old business colleagues or clients, no long-lost school chums, no spurious Facebook friends. Just a select handful of people whom we care about – and who really care about us.

'Thank God you're here!' Milly says, hurrying up to me.

'Is Adam here?' I ask, holding a finger up and panting to get my breath.

'He's waiting in there with Jay,' Milly says. 'You had us all really worried, you know.'

'I know,' I smile. 'But you needn't have been. I know what I'm doing.'

I wave everyone over to stand behind me, and taking hold of Loni and Cal's arms, I walk into the flower garden and towards my future husband. The sun has flooded the sky with lemony light, swathes of blossom appear to be lifting their petals like bridesmaids' skirts in the breeze as the rest of the flowers bob and sway.

And as Adam turns and looks at me I feel like I have experienced two different lives and right now I know, with every grain of certainty, that this is the moment they merge. This is what every decision, every mistake, every path, every star has been leading me to. Whatever choice I have made in my life, left or right, forward or back, right or wrong – I was always going to end up right here. On this day. With this man. Whatever choices I could have made that would have led to a different journey, I the destination was always going to be the same.

re meant to be.

ny hand into Adam's and our guests melt away as I get

ready to say the words that will determine my future. And this time, there is not a single doubt in my mind.

I do. This time, I definitely, completely and utterly with all my heart, do.

Epilogue

30 April 2014

'I didn't intend to be a runaway bride. Honestly, I didn't. I didn't wake up that morning thinking: What can I do to cause as much shock and distress as possible to the people I love most in the world? The person I love most in the world . . .' I trail off momentarily, unable to continue my well-practised speech. I look around at all the expectant faces shining as brightly as the tulips. Is it really worth dragging all this up again? Today of all days, when everyone just wants to celebrate this momentous occasion?

There are a couple of awkward coughs, a few whispers and I feel a rising panic in my chest, like I'm about to be sick, or worse, pass out. Oh God, please not that. Not again. Just then I feel a squeeze of encouragement to my left hand and I suddenly feel buoyed by warmth and support, anchored by familiarity and self-belief. I turn and look at him and he smiles and nods and I know that he's telling me to trust my instincts.

'The truth is, I'm not sure I was thinking much at all that d I continue. 'I knew I was nervous, but that was all. I wa focused on dealing with each "Got To" stage as it cam know, got to get up, got to get ready, got to get in the car, got to walk down the aisle. And well . . .' I pause and smile wryly. 'We all know how *that* turned out.'

Laughter floats like petals through the air.

'There were many times that I questioned myself,' I go on. 'Leaving my husband at the altar was the hardest decision I've ever made. Many people said it was the worst.' I smile at my best friend, Milly, who nods and holds her hand up in a gesture of agreement. 'But no matter how much I doubted myself, I knew that wasn't true.' I close my eyes momentarily, remembering a long-ago mistake. I will never forget, but now at last I *have* moved on. Even though it was heartbreakingly hard, I always *knew* it was the right choice.

I look around at everyone again and then back at the man standing next to me. It feels like he's always been there; like this was all meant to be. 'I hope you can now all see that I'm happier than I ever thought possible because of that decision . . .'

I look around again at our guests, gathered in Greenwich Park on this momentous, life-changing day and I feel a swell of happiness at the thought I have crossed over into a new life. The future. Our future.

Adam smiles and lifts his champagne glass. I know he feels the same.

'So now, please, will you raise your glasses because I want to make a toast. Not to our future but to the present; to every experience, both good and bad, and to every person who is here' – I grip Dad's diary – 'or who can't be here but nevertheless has helped lead Adam and me to this moment. I know we took a rather unusual route to get here, but I hope you'll agree that it truly feels like today was written in the stars . . .'

And when we kiss, that is what I see.

The End!

Acknowledgements

Writing a book is a lot like starting a new relationship: you always think it's going to be better this time. That's what I said to my husband after the emotional second book that was *The First Last Kiss*. 'I'm going to enjoy this one!' He raised an eyebrow in reply. 'I promise I won't cry!' And then to my agent: 'Don't worry,' I said airily and confidently. 'I know EXACTLY how to make this very confusing *Sliding Doors*-style concept book work, no problem at all . . .' HA! The truth is at times I found it impossible and it would NEVER have seen the light of day were it not for the following people.

My great friend and writing crusader, Nick Smithers, who once again swooped in superhero style when I was in what I would call a proper pickle, dragged me out of my writing hole, did character and plot brainstorms with me, forced me to do happy dances when I finished a chapter, allowed me to rant about how rubbish it was and that I'd never EVER get to the end – and then who stayed with me, doing all of the above, unt' I had done just that. Thank you, Nick. I love you, my kids lc you, my husband loves you. The annex is yours!

To my uber-agent Lizzy Kremer, who always goes abov

beyond the call of duty in her job: friend, mentor, editor, counsellor and work 'mum'. Thank you for all you do and for never failing to tell me when I have food on my face/in my hair/on my top when on business lunches (delete as appropriate!). What would I do without you? Also big thanks to the rest of the team at David Higham, especially Laura West and Harriet Moore and the incredible translation rights team for selling my books so brilliantly overseas.

To Clare Hey, my acting editor, who stepped into very big shoes when my editor Maxine Hitchcock left – and strutted with style. Thanks too to Jo Dickinson – you both helped transform this book into something, not just publishable, but something I'm incredibly proud of. I really *couldn't* have done it without you! Special thanks to Mel Four for the beautiful cover and – as always – to the rest of the incredible team at Simon & Schuster, particularly Sara-Jade Virtue, Rumana Haider, Alice Murphy-Pyle, Ally Grant, Dawn Burnett, Nico Poilblanc and Elinor Fewster who are all, always endlessly brilliant. I feel lucky to have you all!

Thanks (again!) to my great friend Paige Toon. Having someone so close who is in the same boat (Books! Kids! Deadlines!) has kept me sane. Although saying that, yours seems to be a much faster, more productive boat so not *quite* the same! Thanks too, to fellow writers Katy Regan & Lucy Robinson for always reassuring me that I'm not the only nutjob on Lizzy's list! I must also mention the rest of the brilliantly inspiring, funny, supportive, encouraging Kremer Krew – too many to mention here, but I feel very proud to be a part of such a great group of women writers. Here's to more champagne, cake and chats in future!

Enormous thanks to my great network of local friends – particularly (and in alphabetical order!) Helen Bord, Isabelle ndson, Emma Evans, Michelle Jones, Louisa Gordon, Nicola

Grantham, Sue Matthews, Dana Payne, Lindsay Thornton and Rachel Widdicombe who have all provided tea and sympathy and/or wine and drunken nights out when needed, who have looked after my kids when I'm on deadline (and looked after me when I've needed it, too!). Oh and a special mention to Caroline and all the staff at The Geographer, my lovely local café where I sometimes go to write and drink rocket-fuel lattes!

To my incredible family, especially the grandparents for the endless last-minute babysitting duties during the writing of this book. And of course, my gorgeous nephews and niece, Ethan Whiting, Zack and Amelie Anderson and my cousins Jess Southgate, Jordan, Libby and Finn March who tell EVERYONE about my books. You should be on the pay roll!

An extra special and rather enormous thanks to all my readers, facebook and twitter followers, not forgetting the brilliant book bloggers who support, encourage and inspire me every single day. Your tweets, reviews and messages keep me writing. I hope I've done you proud.

And last but never ever least, to my amazingly patient husband Ben for putting up with me through it all. Next time it'll be better, I promise … (!)

Ali Harris

Miracle on Regent Street

Dreams can come true – it could happen to you ...

For the past two years, Evie Taylor has lived an
invisible existence in London, a city she hoped would
bring sparkle to her life. But all that is about to
change. For winter has brought a flurry of snow and
unexpected possibilities

Hidden away in the basement of Hardy's – once
London's most elegant department store – Evie
manages the stockroom of a shop whose glory days
have long since passed. When Evie overhears that
Hardy's is at risk of being sold, she secretly hatches
a plan. If she can reverse the store's fortunes by
December 26th – three weeks away – and transform
it into a magical destination once again, she
might just be able to save it.

But she's going to need every ounce of talent
and determination she has. In fact, she's going
to need a miracle ...

ISBN 978-0-85720-290-1
Price £6.99

Ali Harris

The First Last Kiss

How do you hold on to a love that is slowly slipping
away from you?

Can you let go of the past when you know
what is in the future?

And how do you cope when you know that every
kiss is a countdown to goodbye?

This is the story of a love affair, of Ryan and Molly
and how they fell in love and were torn apart. The
first time Molly kissed Ryan, she knew they'd be
together forever. Six years and thousands of kisses
later she's married to the man she loves.

But today, when Ryan kisses her, Molly realises
how many of them she wasted because the future
holds something which neither of them could have
ever predicted...

ISBN 978-0-85720-293-2
Price £6.99

If they caught up with him, Zoey thought and bit her bottom lip. The Hummer was already several cars ahead and moving, whereas their part of the traffic jam was stopped dead. There was a good possibility that they'd lose the Hummer in the traffic. She kept her eyes firmly fixed on the massive lump of yellow steel. She wasn't letting it out of her sight. That truck contained a kidnapper with a gun and a very important little piece of humanity. 'Cause the kidnapper hadn't taken just any baby.

He'd taken Pete.